a memory that once was

Copyright © 2024 Lexi Bissen
All rights reserved. No part of this publication may be reproduced, distrusted, or transmitted in any form or by any means including photocopying, recording, or other electronic or mechanical methods, without the prior written permission of the publisher, except in the case of brief quotations embodied in the critical reviews and certain other noncommercial permitted by copyright law.
This novel is fiction. That means all its content inducing characters, names, places, and brands are products of the author's imagination or used in a fictional manner. Any similarities to actual people, living or dead, places, or events are purely accidental.
Editing: Rumi Khan, and My Brother's Editor
Cover Design: Wildheart Graphics
Formatting: Swoonworthy Designs
Cover Image: Cadwallader Photography

PROLOGUE

TRAZIA

THREE YEARS AGO

Moving my brother into his dorm for his first year of college is bittersweet. Part of me is happy for Camden to begin this journey and work toward something he has always wanted. He's put in countless hours of blood and sweat into his soccer career, and getting a full-ride scholarship to Braxton University has been a dream of his. The other part of me is sad he won't be around as much.

While Braxton is not far from the house we grew up in, I know Camden will be busy with school and practice. Plus, me only being fifteen means I don't have a set of wheels or a driver's license to get to him anytime I want.

"Are you sure you packed enough underwear?" my mom asks as she neatly transfers clothing from the stuffed suitcase to the dresser provided by the school.

Camden's dorm room isn't that small, but it's supposed to house two guys. Since he is in the athletic building, they have the luxury of having their own bathroom and small kitchenette area with a mini fridge, sink, and microwave. The non-athlete students are stuck sharing a community bathroom with every other person on their floor, and they have to shower behind a thin curtain and use the toilet while several other people come in and out of the room for various reasons.

"Knock, knock," someone calls out from the partially closed door leading to the hallway. It slowly opens and in walks a guy I can only describe as the best-looking boy I have ever seen. His dark blond hair is cut short and styled in a messy look, like he has been running his fingers through it. He's tall, probably around my brother's height, at over six feet, and has long legs and arms.

The stranger raises his hand and waves at the three of us. "Hey, I'm Maddox Stone. I'm guessing you're my roommate?" He walks farther into the room and holds a large hand out to my brother.

Camden smiles and they shake hands. "Nice to meet you. I'm Camden, and this is my mom, Claire, and sister, Trazia."

Maddox cocks a brow. "Trazia? That's different." His green eyes stare into mine as he studies me.

Smiling, I break our connection and look over to my mother. "She felt like after giving my brother a boring-ass name, something unique was needed for the next child."

"Trazia, language," my mother scolds under her breath.

Rolling my eyes, I wave a hand at the beautiful boy standing only a few feet from me. "He's starting college, Mom. I'm sure he's heard worse than *ass*."

Mom rubs her temples with both her pointer fingers. "*Oy vey*. You're going to give me early gray hairs, I swear."

Camden laughs and throws his arm over her shoulders. "We all know Traz is the one who is going to keep you on your toes, Ma." He laughs and grabs my mom's keys off the bed after removing his arm. "How about you and I get the last of the boxes from the car and talk shit about your second favorite while we're gone?"

Mom raises an eyebrow at me. "Start unpacking his clothes, please. And keep the language clean. I don't want this young man to think I raised unruly children."

"Fine, but I'm not touching his underwear."

The two make their way out of the room, leaving me alone with Maddox. He takes one of the large duffle bags into his hands and drops it on the extra-long twin bed. The muscles in his triceps flex as he grabs the other one and deposits it beside the first.

"You going to school here too?" he asks as he starts unloading clothes.

I begin to do the same with Camden's jeans and shorts, trying to keep my cool with an older, hot guy talking to me. It's not like I'm some shy girl who has never spoken to a boy before, but not one like Maddox. None who make my stomach flutter. That is new for me, and I'm not sure what to make of it.

Folding Camden's jeans so they aren't rolled into a ball like they were when he packed them, I answer him. "No. I'm still in high school, but hopefully I can get in here when it's my time."

Truthfully, three more years of high school sounds terrible. Next year I won't have my big brother there with me, and making friends has always been a struggle of mine. Most girls I go to school with wanted to be friends because they saw it as a way to get closer to Camden, but luckily I was able to see through the fake people. Having a popular brother, whom many find attractive, makes it hard to find true friends and not ones who want to use you.

"That's a shame. We could have had some fun this year." I look up at Maddox and he winks at me before going back to stuffing clothes in his drawers.

Before I can ask him what he means by that, Camden and my mom walk in with more stuff to unpack.

My brain is jumbled trying to figure out what Maddox meant as we all take on the tasks of unpacking, folding, and finding homes for random items. Camden and Maddox get to know each other a little more as Mom and I work in the bathroom.

By the time we're finished, the guys have freshman orientation, and Mom and I are ready to head back home.

Mom grabs Camden in a tight hug and buries her face in his chest, hiding what I assume are a few tears. Maddox and I stand off to the side, letting them have a mother-and-son moment.

"Maybe we'll see each other around? I mean, you should come visit the campus sometimes. Get to know the area before you become a student," Maddox whispers to me.

Smiling, I duck my head. "Yeah, maybe. Think you could show me around?"

"Seeing as how it took me three buildings to find this one, I'm sure I'll make an excellent tour guide."

Mom breaks away from Camden, and he wipes under her eyes before giving her a kiss on her forehead.

"Give me a hug, little sis." Camden holds his arms out and I fall into them. He squeezes me to his chest, and I fight to hold back tears. Even though he won't be far, it's going to be hard not having him around all the time. We've been close since we were little, and knowing he isn't going to be in his room right down the hall makes me sad.

"Don't miss me too much," he whispers into my hair.

"Like that could ever happen. Now I'll have my own bathroom."

His chest rumbles with a laugh, and we pull apart. "Stay out of trouble while I'm not home, okay? I don't need to be coming over all the time to knock you out for causing problems."

A mock gasp makes its way past my lips. "Me? Causing

problems? The audacity you have to insult me like that. I am a mature woman, Camden Collins."

He shoves my shoulder. "Sure you are. Just don't give Mom a heart attack or anything."

"Come on, sweetie. We have to get going if we want to beat traffic on the highway." Mom's tears have dried up, but her face is still etched in sadness.

"It was nice meeting you, Maddox. I'll make a care package for you both soon. Let Camden know what kind of sweets and baked goods you like, and I'll get working on it." Mom gives him a warm hug before going back to Camden for one last final goodbye.

"I'll see you around, I guess." I offer an awkward wave and Maddox smiles, biting down on his bottom lip in the process. That single look alone has those stomach flutters making an appearance again.

"See ya soon, Peach." The nickname falls easily from his mouth but has me confused. Before I can ask him what he's talking about, Mom is linking our arms and blowing Camden a kiss goodbye. We walk away, and just as we round the corner of the hallway, I hear my brother's voice.

"Dude, I know we don't know each other yet, but if you keep staring at my sister's ass, we're going to have a problem. She's fifteen."

"Oh fuck," Maddox groans.

We're too far for me to hear the rest of the conversation, but based on him coming to the realization that I'm not even able to drive yet, I'm going to assume Maddox won't be giving me that campus tour anytime soon.

The butterflies are replaced with a heavy weight. I'm just a young, immature girl to a guy like Maddox. Three years is not a big age difference when you're thirty and twenty-seven, but me only being a sophomore in high school makes it seem like we're decades apart.

Even though I only spent a few hours around him, Maddox left an impression on my heart. Maybe in a different life. At a different time. When I'm older and not reduced to my age. Maybe then something could happen between us.

Until then, I'll keep hoping that maybe he can see me as Trazia Collins, the woman, and not Trazia Collins, his roommate's little sister and the high school girl.

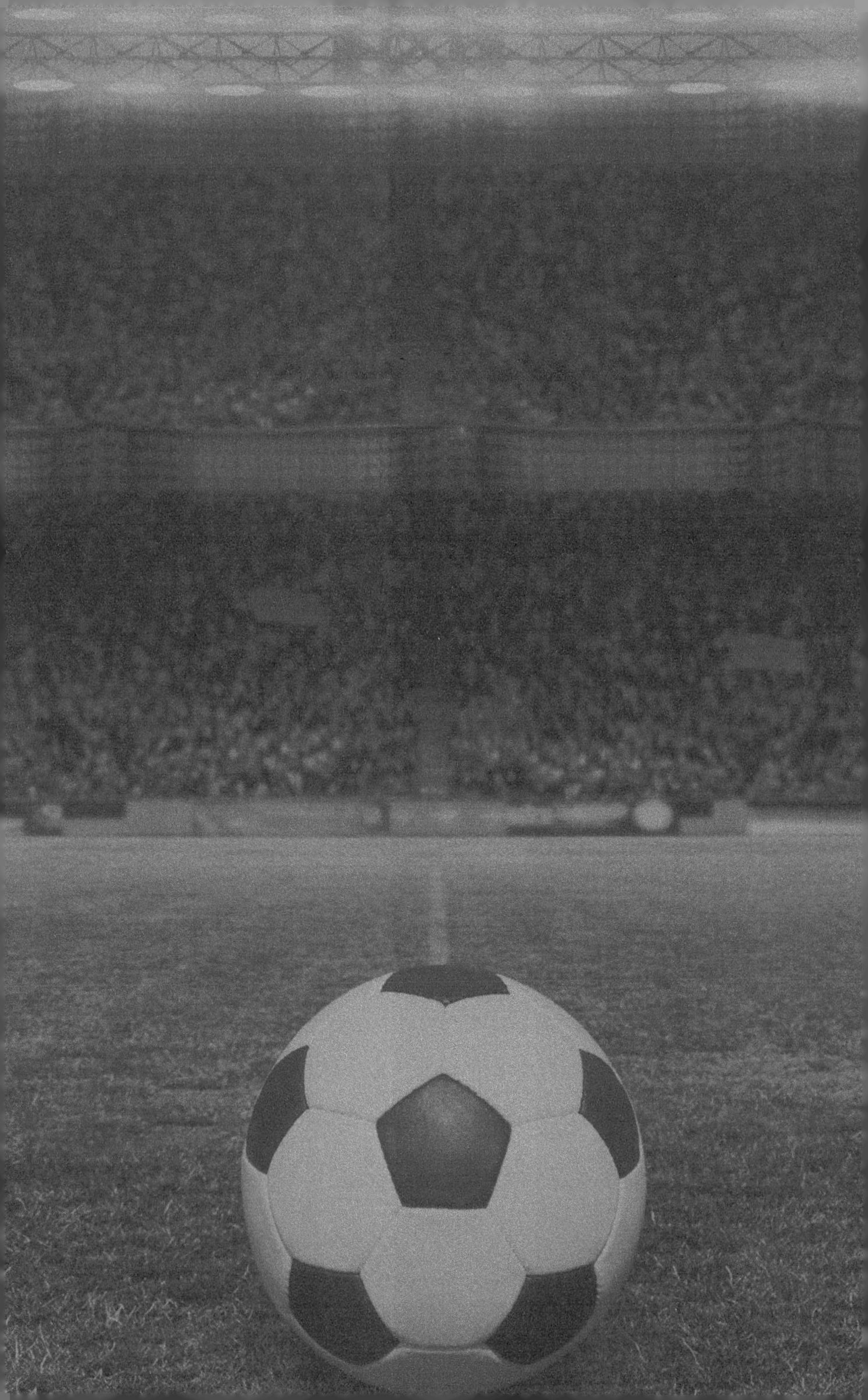

CHAPTER ONE

TRAZIA

Spring break is here, and I'm enjoying the freedom of no schoolwork and lazy days on the beach. There is nothing better than leaving your responsibilities behind for a week. What makes this the perfect vacation is seeing the man I've had a crush on for the last three years running around on the beach with his tanned skin glowing in the sunlight and his shaggy hair wet from the ocean. Maddox Stone looks like the guys I read about in my romance books and has only gotten more attractive as the years go on.

It's my senior year of high school, and Camden invited me to Maddox's parents' beach house for spring break. It was unexpected because Camden hasn't liked me being around his friends in the past, but since I'm starting at Braxton University in the fall, maybe he wants me to get to know some people. Going to the same college as my brother has helped relieve some of the stress about going away to school, but knowing that Maddox is going to be around has me worried.

I first met Maddox when my mom and I dropped Camden off at school his freshman year. Maddox was his dormmate, and I, being a fifteen-year-old filled with confusing hormones, fell into an instant crush. Even then, he was the most handsome man I had ever seen, and he only got better looking.

"Traz, you okay? You've been sitting there with your mouth hanging open for a while." My brother's voice is filled with concern.

I close my mouth and wipe, just in case of drool, and try to act cool that I just got caught staring at my brother's best friend. "Sorry, I was daydreaming."

Camden's eyebrow rises as he studies me. Luckily, Blaire walks over after grabbing a drink from the cooler the guys brought out and pulls his attention away from me. She sits down on his towel in front of him, and he wraps his arms around her as she rests her back to his chest.

Trying not to get caught again, I pull my sunglasses out of my bag and put them on. It shields my eyes in case they drift toward Maddox once again.

We have been at his family's beach house for three days now, and the more time I spend around him, the more my young teenage crush deepens. It was bad enough I had to ride in the front seat of his truck between him and Levi. In reality, they should have put Levi somewhere where there was more room because the guy is a giant, and with the limited space, I was almost plastered against Maddox's body during the long drive. The only time I felt like I could catch my breath was when we stopped for food or to use the bathroom. Unfortunately, that was only three times on the nine-hour drive.

Coming to the beach house for spring break was a mistake for a few reasons. Mainly being that I have to be around a half-naked Maddox almost all day because even if he is not at the beach or pool, Maddox refuses to put a shirt on. It was also a mistake because before now, I didn't know Maddox, the person. Sure, I heard about my brother's roommate during

A MEMORY THAT ONCE WAS

phone calls or visits from Camden, but they were mostly funny stories or about girls who Maddox left heartbroken after a hookup at one of their parties. I didn't know he was caring toward his friends or thoughtful. He always seemed like the jokester of the group and was never too serious.

While Maddox is those things and has shown us that side several times this trip, including pantsing a still pissed-off Mateo, getting to see this sweet side of him has done nothing to dissolve my crush on him. If anything, it has only grown over the last few days here.

It's our second-to-last night here at the beach house and I never want to leave. Growing up, our family struggled when it came to money. My father abandoned us when I was five, chasing after a younger woman, and left Camden and me with a single mother who struggled, working multiple jobs for most of my childhood.

My mom is the most incredible person out there, but I've never experienced the life of the rich like I have this week. Maddox's family's house is only something that could be described in magazines. It's large, with three spots for cars in the garage and a porch with a full outdoor grill, pool, and firepit. Maddox's mom had the house professionally designed and every room is perfect. I'm staying in the smallest room with a queen bed and a Jack-and-Jill bathroom shared with Maddox and Levi. Mateo and Jules are sharing a room down the hall with full-size bunk beds and a bathroom in the hall. The couples, Camden and Blaire and Conrad and Emree have the two largest rooms.

This vacation house is nothing compared to the small, three-bedroom home I have lived in with my mom and brother up until Camden went to college. If this is only a second house for Maddox's parents, I wonder what their everyday home is like.

"Do you all want to grill tonight or go out?" Emree asks

from her spot on one of the beach chairs. She wears a large floppy hat on her head and a pair of sunglasses while she reads a gossip magazine.

Camden looks up from where he was tucking his face into Blaire's neck. "Since we got all that stuff to grill for our final night here, why don't we head up to that seafood restaurant on the pier?"

At the mention of seafood, my stomach tightens. Fish and other foods from the ocean and I do not mix well together after an unfortunate food poisoning incident two years ago that resulted in me not leaving the bathroom for two days.

"Oh, I could really go for some crab cakes. Or maybe paella. That sounds good too." Blaire's mouth is practically watering as she talks about food for tonight.

Camden calls over to the guys and they begin jogging toward us. I try to avoid looking at Maddox, but it's hard when my eyes seem to gravitate toward him. His damp hair is whipping around him as he makes his way over to our group.

"What's up?" Conrad asks when he stops in front of Camden.

"You guys good with going to that seafood restaurant tonight?"

"Doesn't Trazia hate seafood?" Maddox asks, and my head snaps in his direction.

Camden looks to me. "Wait, I thought you loved shrimp Alfredo?"

Still surprised Maddox knew I didn't eat seafood, I shake my head and turn to my brother. "After getting food poisoning a couple years ago, I haven't been able to eat seafood."

"How did I not know about that?" Camden asks.

Maddox rolls his eyes. "Do you not remember last summer when Mateo made salmon, and she basically ran to the bathroom gagging at the smell?"

"Shit, I forgot about that. I'm sorry, Traz. We can go somewhere else."

Waving a hand, I smile at him. "Don't worry about me. There are always a few non-seafood options at these places."

In all honesty, I'm kind of nervous about my reaction to the smell inside the restaurant and hoping I won't get too nauseous. But I don't want to cause a scene and be the difficult one of the group.

Emree bounces out of her seat and pulls the oversized sunglasses off her face. "Well, now I'm hungry, so how about we all go get ready and head out in an hour?"

"Sounds good to me," Jules agrees as she collects her stuff.

After making sure we are not leaving anything behind on the beach, we head inside and take turns using the showers.

Once the seawater and sand are washed away, I head into my room with a white, fluffy towel wrapped around my body. Shutting the door, I make sure to lock it since Levi was using the shower next and I don't want to risk anyone coming into my room through the Jack-and-Jill bathroom door.

Making sure the main bedroom door is also locked, I remove the towel and lay it over one of the bedposts while I go to the closet to figure out something to wear while I air-dry.

Since I'm not one to pack light, even for a week-long trip, the closet and dresser provided in the room are filled with a variety of dresses, tops, and bottoms. I have also packed enough shoes for any occasion. Like when we went to a local club during the week, I was prepared with a cute pair of strappy heels. The restaurant at the pier is more casual, and I figure I'll go with some white sneakers in case we go exploring the shops after.

The weather here in Wrightsville Beach, North Carolina, has been perfect. During the day it is in the high seventies, and in the nighttime it only gets to the low sixties. Since the sun is already setting, I grab a pair of mid-rise straight jeans with a rip in one of the knees and a cropped tank top. I borrowed one of Blaire's cardigans our first night here since she packed a few. Blaire is constantly getting cold and usually layers up, so it's helpful that she packed where I was lacking.

Once the sweater is on, I check myself out in the mirror above the dresser and make sure everything looks good. The tank top is a little lower cut than I'm used to, but I haven't been shopping for new clothes in almost two years and things have...developed more since then. I hate asking my mom for money, and my part-time job cleaning at the daycare I work at doesn't pay much. Luckily the jeans were borrowed from a friend and fit perfectly.

After swiping on some mascara and applying a layer of ChapStick, I grab my small crossbody bag and head out of the room. Not paying attention, I collide with a hard body. We lose our balance, and I end up falling on top of them.

Looking down, I take in a freshly showered Maddox in nothing but a towel. "Wh-what are you doing *naked?*"

With his arms circled around my waist, Maddox smirks up at me. "Technically I'm not naked, but I do have a feeling this towel loosened a bit with you jumping me and all."

"I did not jump you," I tell him, my voice elevated. My hands are resting on his chest as I hold my top half up. One of my legs is tangled between his and the moment I look down, I realize what is resting against my thigh. His towel is slightly open, and my leg is beside his not-so-covered penis.

"Oh my gosh!" Jumping up, I scurry away from him as fast as possible.

"Fuck!" he shouts and rolls over, gripping between his legs. I may or may not have accidentally kneed him somewhere sensitive in my hurry to get away.

The towel is long forgotten as he groans in agony, and I now have a clear view of his pale butt. While Maddox may be tanned in most areas from the hours he spends outside because of soccer, his ass and upper thighs look like they have never seen the sun.

Maddox is moaning and groaning on the ground, not giving a shit that he is on full display for anyone to see. A door down the hall opens, and Jules comes out looking ready for our dinner.

"Well, what do we have here? Why is Little Maddox making an appearance this evening?" she asks as she smiles down at her friend, who is clearly not in the mood for jokes.

A hand comes out of nowhere and covers my eyes. "Dude, fucking cover yourself. My sister's young eyes don't need to see that."

"Seeing as how she's the one who inflicted pain in my balls, she isn't so innocent right now," Maddox replies to my brother. Based on the struggle in his voice, I can tell he is talking through clenched teeth.

With his hand still covering my eyes, Camden questions, "Why the hell was my sister that close to your dick?"

Sometimes I think my brother forgets I'm an adult now. He still treats me like a little girl and not the young woman I have become. What he fails to realize is that I've experienced what most teenagers have during my years of high school. I've had sex (twice, but that was enough for me), gotten drunk at parties, snuck out of my house to meet a boy, and smoked weed. He may still see me as the little, innocent girl, but sooner or later he is going to have to open his eyes to the fact that I'm a woman entering college. The last thing I want is a helicopter brother following me around while I'm there.

Grabbing Camden's wrist, I pull his hand off my face and step away from him. From the corner of my eye I can see that Maddox is still on the ground, but the towel is now lazily thrown over his nether regions.

"Your friend here needs to wear more clothes. His dick touched my leg—"

"Whoa," Camden says, holding his hands up. "His *what* touched you?"

"My dick. She was on top of me and the towel kind of... shifted."

Camden looks as if he is fighting a battle between going after his best friend for having his junk anywhere near his little sister and remaining calm. "Someone want to give me the whole story from start to finish?"

"Oh Lord, chill with the overprotective big brother act. I was coming out of my room as Maddox was passing by my door and we clumsily collided. You can calm down, nothing was going on."

Camden visibly relaxes after learning the truth and that his best friend was not corrupting his little sister. "Just keep your clothes on, Stone. And stop walking around in a towel."

Maddox clutches the towel at his waist. "Before we get to the hugging and making up part of this, I'm going to the dryer to grab my briefs. Which is where I was heading in the first place."

Once he is gone, we all go our separate ways. I escape back into my room rather than going downstairs and wait until everyone is ready.

Safe behind the confines of the bedroom door, I lean against it and take a deep breath. While I may have been keeping my cool in the hallway, having my hands against Maddox's bare chest and feeling every bit of him against my body was more than I could handle.

My crush on Maddox started years ago, but it has not fizzled out like I hoped it would. The two guys I dated in high school were great boyfriends, but my stupid brain kept comparing them to Maddox Stone. The two times I had sex with my last boyfriend, I was left unsatisfied, and when I got back home, I dreamed about how it would be if I ever got that opportunity with Maddox. How his body would feel against mine. How he would feel between my legs. How his large hands would feel touching my soft body.

My skin tingles with the thoughts and I shake my hands out beside me, trying to stop these feelings and thoughts. I should not be fantasizing about my brother's best friend. That is the biggest cliché there is and with how Camden reacted to the innocent interaction in the hallway, it will not end well.

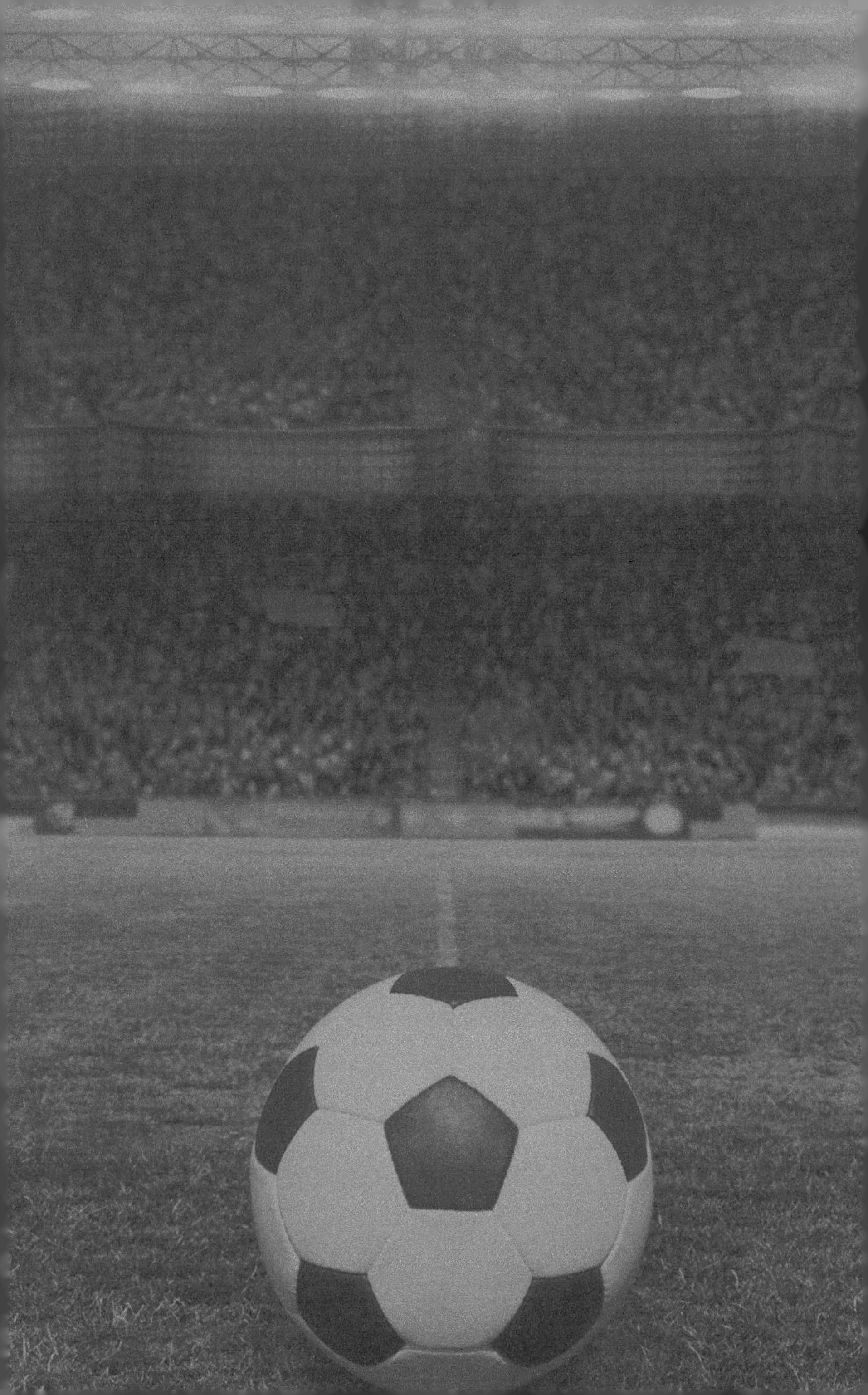

CHAPTER TWO

MADDOX

Even with the fresh ocean scent of the restaurant we're dining at, I can smell her fruity perfume. It's intoxicating and has me wanting to bury my face in her neck to take a deep breath.

Trazia and I somehow ended up seated beside each other tonight, and since I can't get the memory of her body pressed against mine earlier this evening, I know being near her is dangerous. She's too tempting when she is the one girl who is completely off-limits.

When I first met Traz, I knew there was something different about her. She's a girl who is always smiling and willing to do anything to make those around her happy. Even tonight, when she hates seafood as much as she does, she's here because everyone else wanted to be.

Looking at her from the corner of my eye, I can tell she is trying to breathe through her mouth as much as possible. Thankfully we were able to get a table for our large group out on the dock, but there is still a lingering fishy scent around us.

Trazia chugs her ginger ale until there is nothing but ice left and nibbles on some bread the waiter brought to our table.

He comes with the last tray of drinks that the bartender had to make. "Can I get anyone else something? Do we want to put in some appetizers?" he asks with an over-the-top smile.

"Yeah, but first could you bring her another ginger ale, please?" I ask him, pointing to Trazia's empty cup.

"Of course." He grabs it and scurries off again.

Emree pulls Blaire and Camden into a conversation about not wanting this trip to be over and having to go back to classes and work. Blaire and Emree are both waitresses at the local college bar, Whiskey Joe's, and while they love their jobs, serving customers too much alcohol is not everyone's dream.

"You didn't have to do that, but thank you." A soft voice comes from my right.

Trazia is looking down at some silverware covered with cloth that she is toying with as she speaks. Her long hair is creating a curtain around her face. When I first met Trazia, she had shoulder-length blonde hair. Since then it has changed each time I see her. From black to a light red, and now a faded pink.

Shrugging, I take a sip of my draft beer. "He should have noticed before asking if we wanted apps."

Trazia isn't usually shy, but all evening she's been quiet and not her bubbly self. I'm wondering if the hallway collision has her acting differently. She isn't the first one in that house to see me without clothes on. I'm not a fan of clothing and grew up in a house with no one around most of the time, so I was free to let everything breathe whenever I wanted.

The waiter comes back with a full glass of ginger ale and places it in front of Trazia. "Is everyone ready to order, or did we want some appetizers?" he asks again.

Jules lifts her pointer finger in the air while looking at the menu. "I'm going to speak for the table and order the fried calamari, buffalo shrimp, fried pickles, and mozzarella sticks. That work for everyone else?" she asks the table.

We all nod, as no one has any objections. Sometimes it's easier to have one person take control when you're in a larger group rather than spend half an hour going back and forth on what to order.

"Trazia, are you excited to be starting at Braxton next semester?" Jules asks from across the table. She is sitting in front of me, with Levi and Mateo beside her.

"I'm nervous. Mainly to leave the comfort of my school, but also having to share a room with a stranger. That is going to be hard for me."

I shift in my seat, and my thigh touches Trazia's. She adjusts and moves a few inches away. "Maybe it'll work out like your brother and me. Your roommate could be cool."

She looks over at me with a small smirk. "Or she could be a complete weirdo who snores and wears a fuzzy tail. Knowing my luck, I'll be sharing a small room with someone who watches me sleep."

Our half of the table laughs. "Whoever she is can't be worse than my freshman roommate. The guy had some type of lizard, and he tracked its shit cycle. Then he got a mate for it and basically had this lizard porn documentary going on. He said it was for research to track their mating, but I swear he had a lizard OnlyFans." Levi shivers at the reminder of his roommate.

"At least your roommate didn't try to get you to be the girlfriend in her relationship. Liz never stopped asking, and when her boyfriend was over, he kept giving me the creepiest look. Plus, I swear they would be having sex in our room at times she knew I was coming back from class and wanted me to catch them."

With a mouthful of beer, I choke on it and a few drops escape, but I manage to keep the rest down. "Jules, I'm not sure that's as big of a problem as you think it is. You could have made a killing if you all went online with that. Hell, I'd watch it."

She rolls her eyes. "You're such a pig, Mad. I'm not joining some threesome relationship. When I find someone worthy of being my boyfriend, it will be him and me in that relationship. Not another girl or people on the internet."

"Damn shame. I'd have paid a good amount to see you on screen," I tell her with a wink. Jules knows I'm messing with her, to a point. Would I pay to watch her getting it on with another girl and guy? Fuck yeah. Jules is hot as hell and has a body most women envy. If she didn't turn me down every time I came near her for the last three years, I would love to get her under me. Or on top. Basically, any way where she has no clothing on and I'm in the room.

"You're nasty, dude," Mateo chimes in.

I can't help but roll my eyes. "Oh, don't tell me if Jules made an OnlyFans, you wouldn't be on it right away."

Mateo's face scrunches up in disgust. "Fuck no. She's like my little sister."

"Like, but no blood relation. Wouldn't be the same as Camden peeking on Trazia's OnlyFans and seeing her tits."

"Excuse me?" Camden says from a few seats down.

Leaning back in my seat, I let out a breath. "Oh no, I woke the brother bear."

"You know he's eventually going to end up just laying into you one day if you talk about Traz like that or run into her in a towel again?" Levi informs me.

Sucking in a breath, I turn to my best friend. "We were talking hypotheticals. Settle down and let Blaire touch you under the table or something."

His girlfriend's mouth drops open in shock. "Do you have no filter?"

"Nope."

She appears surprised by my honesty before turning to continue her conversation with Emree.

Camden glares at me. "Keep it appropriate with Traz, or I'm making her switch seats with me."

My three friends across from me are trying to hide their laughs. Trazia looks frustrated as she stares at the side of her brother's face.

"I swear, he's never going to see me as an adult," she whispers so that only I can hear her.

Looking over, I take in Camden with his arm around Blaire, who is beside me. He's smiling as Conrad talks about our club adventure this week and how it was very much not our scene.

"He realizes you're eighteen, right? You can vote, buy weed or cigarettes, and go to war. I mean, you can't legally drink alcohol or rent a car, but those are stupid rules."

Trazia stares at me. "You know you talk really fast?"

"We're pretty sure it's undiagnosed ADHD," Mateo voices.

With my beer in hand, I point the neck at him. "Hey, I'll have you know it is diagnosed. It's just not treated. Those drugs kept me up all night, and the heartburn was unbearable."

"You know, that makes a lot of sense," Jules tells me. "You do seem to have difficulty focusing, and I can't keep track of the number of times you've forgotten something I've told you."

"Julesy, there are several tabs open in this beautiful head of mine. I can't handle having all your information in there also."

The waiter comes over to deliver our appetizers and take everyone's order. Since I'm beside Trazia and I'm sure having more seafood near her would be a struggle, I decide to order off their land menu and get the rib eye with a baked potato and broccoli.

"Moving on from Maddox's medical history. Trazia, tell me more about you starting college. Have you chosen a major yet? When do you get your dorm assignment?" Jules asks before shoving a few fried pickles in her mouth. Extremely unladylike.

Trazia nibbles on a mozzarella stick before answering. "I'm studying child and adolescent psychology. I was fascinated with it in high school and after taking the two different types of psychology classes they had, I was approved to take some offered by the local community college. It's actually helped me get ahead, and, if I stay on track, I'll be able to graduate at least a semester early. As for the dorm building, I haven't gotten that far. I'm still trying to decide if I want to start right after graduation or wait until spring. Starting earlier means I can graduate early and start my master's program if I wanted to."

"Damn girl, you're already planning a master's? I'm still not sure if sports therapy is what I want to do."

Mateo has been undecided about his degree since starting school. He's changed it twice now, and we all had bets on whether he would switch it again last semester, but he's held on strong to sports medicine thus far.

After swallowing the bite she had taken and sipping some of her ginger ale, Trazia replies, "Working with children has always been my goal. I've actually been working at a daycare close to my house after school and some weekends since I turned eighteen. It's hard work, but I love those little kiddos."

"Girl, that's awesome. Are you looking to work at a daycare closer to Braxton when you transfer? Or something else with kids?" Jules asks.

A warm smile graces Trazia's face. "I'd love nothing more than that. Hopefully there is an opening somewhere. I've even considered getting my certification for being a teacher's aide and taking night classes. That wouldn't be ideal, but it does give me more hands-on experience working with kids."

Jules and Trazia go on about potential jobs she could get and daycares in the area. I tune them out as I watch Trazia deep in conversation. She is passionate about this—working with kids—and I'm surprised someone so young already knows what they want to do as their career. She has a plan set and seems determined to stick with it.

The waiter appears with a tray of food, followed by another

guy dressed in the same uniform behind him, also carrying a large circular tray. They start passing out plates of food. A large dish of garlic shrimp skewers and snow crab legs are passed across the table toward Emree and Conrad.

"Oh shit." Trazia rushes out as she jumps up from her seat.

With a hand covering her mouth, she rushes toward a corner of the restaurant that has a large bathroom sign at the top. Before any of my friends can say anything, I'm out of my seat and chasing after her.

Dodging patrons with questioning looks on their faces, I speed walk toward the restrooms. Bypassing the men's, I walk into the women's with a hand covering my eyes.

"Sorry, ladies. If anyone here is less than decent, I'm announcing myself because a friend needs help."

"Maddox?" someone calls from one of the stalls.

Peeking one eye open, I check to make sure there are no other women in the bathroom. While everyone's bits would be covered behind the safety of the stalls, my intention is not to make anyone uncomfortable with me being in here. Luckily, it sounds like the only ones here are Traz and me.

"Yeah, it's me," I answer her as I walk down the row of stalls, ducking down to find her feet. When I finally see a pair of shoes under the stall, I push the door and it swings open with a slight creek.

Inside, Trazia is hunched over the toilet bowl. Her face is paler than it usually is, and she has her long hair clutched in her right hand with the other on her thigh, propping her up. Even after vomiting, she is too fucking gorgeous. Part of me wonders if it's some kind of sick joke that I'm still so attracted to her in this condition. She opens her eyes, and they are slightly glossy.

Looking up at me, Trazia offers a small smile. "You really don't want to be in here."

Without thinking, I enter the small stall and gather her soft hair in my hands. "A little puke isn't going to scare me away."

With her hand now free, Traz wipes around her mouth. "Not my finest moment. I thought I was handling the smells well enough, but that plate in front of me was too much."

A strand of hair didn't make it into the bunch in the back, and I reach forward and tuck it behind her ear. "I think you were pretty badass. Seafood smells like ass anyway. I can't imagine having food poisoning from it and sitting in a place like this."

Trazia studies me for a few seconds. "You continue to surprise me."

"What do you mean?"

"There's more to you than on the surface that you show people. You come across like everything is a joke to you, but there is something deeper there."

Her words leave me somewhat speechless. I've always been the person in the room with the witty comments and ready to lighten the mood. What I want to hide from people is how much I care about them. No one has ever seen past the mask I put on until now. Showing people—especially friends—my true self makes me feel vulnerable.

Blowing out a breath, I release her hair and rise to my feet. "Not sure what you're seeing, but it must be the seafood smell getting to you. You done or still have something brewing in there?"

Trazia begins to stand, and I step back out of the stall to give her some room. The door separating us from everyone outside opens, and an older woman enters. "Young man, it is not appropriate for you to be in the ladies' room."

"You're good. I'm not going to peek in your stall like some creep. My friend is puking up her appetizer, so it may be in your best interest to wait outside a minute."

She huffs and turns to leave, giving me a dirty look on her way out.

"I see you're back, and the sweet and caring Maddox is gone," Trazia tells me as she steps past me toward the row of sinks. After rinsing off her hands, she gathers a scoop of water and swishes it around in her mouth.

"You're delusional, Peach. The only thing deep about me are my daddy's pockets, so stop trying to see something that isn't there."

After drying her hands off with a paper towel, Traz turns to face me and leans against the counter. "Why do you call me Peach?"

Fuck. I keep forgetting that nickname is something that has been stuck in my head since the day I met Trazia my freshman year of college, and no one knows why I say it or what it means. It has only slipped out a few times, but I've been able to brush it off as just something stupid to call her.

Shrugging my shoulders, I try to play it off. "Dunno. Just kind of comes out."

With her arms crossed over her chest, Trazia stares at me through squinted eyes. "Keep lying, Maddox, but I see right through you. One day you're going to be tired of putting on this façade." Without another word, she goes toward the exit door and pulls it open.

The woman who entered the bathroom is standing in the hallway with the same glare gracing her face. Once I'm through the door, I hold it open for her and wave my hand inside. "Freshened it in there for you, so don't stink it up too much."

She stops at the threshold. "Young man, get some help."

The door closes in my face, and a muffled laugh comes from behind me. Trazia is there, covering her mouth with her hand.

"Not funny, Traz. She insulted me."

She points a finger at me. "Or did she give you some solid life advice?"

Rolling my eyes, I head toward the doors in the back of the restaurant that lead to the patio where our friends are. Everyone is eating their meals, and I'm sure mine and Trazia's are cold by now.

Camden sets his fork down and sits higher in his seat. "Hey, how are you? Blaire kept forcing me to stay here and stay out of the bathroom."

Trazia goes back to her seat and takes a sip of watered-down ginger ale. "I'm fine, and it was better you stayed. I feel good now. The smell from whatever that was they put in front of my face was just a little too much."

"I'm surprised you ran after her, Maddox," Emree states with clear suspicion in her eyes.

Taking my seat, I grab my fork and start stabbing at the broccoli on my plate. "Wouldn't be the first time I held a puking girl's hair back. I'm basically an expert at this point."

The table vibrates with collective laughter. Everyone except Trazia, that is. She has her head turned to me, once again studying me as if she can see something no one else can.

With a shake of her head, she turns back to her cold pasta dish without a word.

Everyone goes back to light conversation, but I refrain from joining in this time. Having my best friend's little sister, the girl I need to stop having these feelings for, around me for this long is turning out to be a mistake. She's a damn mind reader or something. I can't handle being under her microscope anymore.

Waving down the waiter, I order a beer. That's what I need. Alcohol will help me avoid Trazia and maybe get her to stop seeing so much of myself that I try to hide from others.

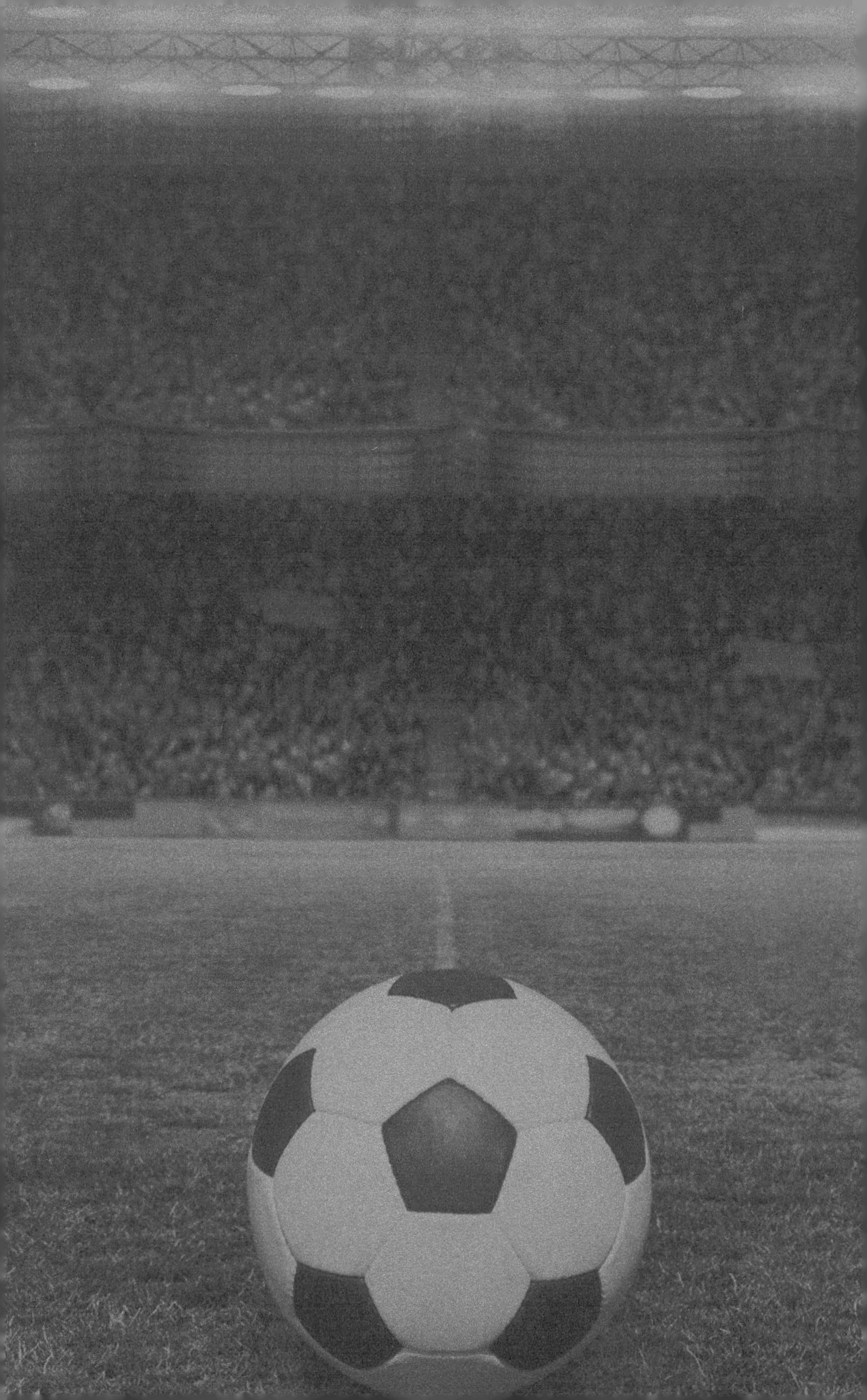

CHAPTER THREE

TRAZIA

The crashing of the waves has always been a sound that brings me peace. Maybe it's because of the noise machine my mom had in my room growing up or the fact that I have lived half an hour from the beach my whole life. Some may find the swish of waves an annoyance that keeps them awake, but to me it's a comforting sound.

Anytime I need to escape and think or want to get away and read a book, I find myself by the water. Even though I rarely get in because the unknowns of what could be below scare me, just the sound of the water, the fresh salty air, and seagulls preparing for their attack on innocent tourists bring me joy.

After a few drinks on the deck, everyone went to bed about an hour ago. Not being able to sleep, I snuck downstairs to take in the sound of waves in the dark with a cup of hot chocolate. It's eerie since the only light outside is from the glow by the back door and the moon.

A sliding noise mixes with a loud wave crashing, and I turn my head to see who has come out and joined me.

Blaire is wrapped in a blanket with her fuzzy slippers secured on her feet. "Girl, what are you doing out here?"

"Couldn't sleep," I tell her as she takes a seat in one of the wooden beach chairs beside me.

"Me too. Your brother doesn't usually snore, but he was complaining of a stuffy nose, and that combined with the sleeping medicine he took makes it hard for me to even think, let alone sleep in that room."

I can't help but laugh because I know that sound all too well. "Our rooms shared a wall growing up. He would always deny it, but that man snores horribly when he's sick."

"Maybe I should video him so he can stop being a baby and denying it."

Wrapping my hands around the warm mug, I take a sip of the hot chocolate I made before coming out here. "Knowing my brother, he wouldn't believe that was him on video."

Blaire laughs and wraps her arms around her legs as she pulls them up to her chest. "You're probably right. That man is stubborn."

A comfortable silence grows between us. The only sound once again was the waves crashing. I always hoped whoever my brother ended up falling for would be someone I got along with and even felt more like a friend or older sister. Blaire is perfect for him in every way. Not only does she support his dreams of playing soccer—even though she knows nothing about the sport—but she has also taught him a lot about being gentler and more caring. Their relationship was hard in the beginning because of Blaire's trust issues, but Camden broke through her hard exterior and now they are happier than ever —aside from the occasional snoring.

"I have a weird question to ask, and you can tell me this is none of my business, but it has been in my head for a few days now," Blaire says after a few minutes.

Turning away from looking into the darkness past the porch, I look at her. "What's up?"

She chews on her bottom lip. "Is there something going on with you and Maddox?"

The small hairs on the back of my neck stand. "Why would you ask that?"

There is no reason for me to be nervous about her inquiry. Truthfully, there is nothing going on between Maddox and me besides that incident in the hallway, but that was only an accident. Sometimes I wonder if there could ever be something there, but each time I've seen him, he keeps our conversations very platonic and friendly. It's probably the hopeless fifteen-year-old in me wishing for something more.

Blaire shrugs her shoulders. "I don't know. Something Emree said to me about the way Maddox looks at you got me thinking."

As if she heard her name, the back door creaks open, and the blonde bombshell herself walks out to us. "Are you two having a little sneak-away girls' time without me?" She takes a seat in the patio chair on the other side of me with a glass of water in hand.

"I was asking Trazia if anything was going on with her and Maddox." Blaire catches her up.

Emree leans over the arm of her chair. "Oh, I like this conversation. Please tell me something has developed there, because I swear that boy was going to crack on this trip when he found out you were coming."

"Wait, what are you talking about?" I ask her, confused.

She smiles wide, showing more of her teeth than usual. "Girl, have you not seen the way he looks at you? Or how he tries *not* to look at you?"

Thinking back, I try to remember any time Maddox has been staring or looking at me differently than any of the other guys. I do sometimes realize that he's around more than they are. Or that he'll notice I'm standing off alone, feeling sort of like an outsider in their tight-knit group, and he would come keep me company. Never did I think any of those incidents were anything other than him being a nice guy.

I wave her off. "He's just being sweet. I've known Maddox for three years, and he's treated me like nothing more than Camden's little sister."

Emree huffs. "You are as blind as Blaire. She had no clue Camden was into her at first, and look at them now. On their way to being a happily married couple with a white picket fence, two point five kids, and a golden retriever named Buddy."

"Hey, I'll have you know we have agreed on three kids, and there is no way Camden could handle the suburban lifestyle. Can you imagine him making small talk with other neighbors? He would hate that. Plus, we would have a cat."

"Oh, I am so sorry I got your hypothetical future wrong," Emree says with her hands up in a surrender move. "The fact that you two have discussed how many children you plan on bringing into this world is enough to make my point."

"It's what people in serious relationships do, I guess. At least Camden said it was normal. I felt it was a little fast, but the moment he said our kids were going to be playing soccer right away, we got into the discussion of how many and whatnot."

I can't help but smile. My brother played a big part in raising me. Even though we aren't too far apart in age, after my dad left, Camden grew up faster than any other kid. Our mom worked multiple jobs to make sure we were clothed, fed, and had a safe place to sleep at night, but she wasn't around as much as she would have liked. Camden was more than just a big brother to me. He has always been someone I looked up to as a father figure since that was missing from my life. Hearing that he is talking about his own kids with Blaire makes me happy because he will be one of the best dads out there. Much better than the one who abandoned us.

"We're getting off topic. Trazia and Maddox. Anything going on there, or potentially?" Emree probes.

Even though my answer is still no, my cheeks heat thinking about the two of us. "Nothing at all. Is Maddox attractive? Of course he is, but he's also Camden's best friend. Imagine my brother's reaction if he even overheard this conversation."

Blaire shudders at the thought. "You are right there. It's a good thing he's oblivious because, I'm not sure if you know this, but he is kind of protective of you."

A snort escapes me. "Kind of? I swear that guy would bubble wrap me and keep me locked away if he could. If he ever found out some of the things I've done, I'm sure he would have a heart attack or something."

"Oh boy, don't even mention to him if a guy has touched you," Emree says with a laugh. "Remember over winter break when you came to visit and one of their teammates hit on you at their party? I swear, he never looked Camden in the eyes after that."

"Do you remember what Maddox did after?" Blaire asks.

My ears buzz with interest. "Maddox? What do you mean?"

Blaire bites her lip as if she doesn't want to say any more. "You must not have seen, but Maddox forced him out of the party. Like, literally. He was pushing and shoving the guy until he fell in the front yard. Another teammate had to keep Maddox away from him. Camden thought it was because you're his sister and Maddox was defending you for his friend, but now that I'm thinking back to it, I don't think Maddox's intentions were all that innocent."

Hope flutters inside me. Maybe I haven't been imagining it, and Maddox feels the same way about me that I do about him. Or even a fraction of the same. I've always thought I was making it up in my head because of my crush on him, but why else would he treat his own teammate like that after they hit on me?

"This is an interesting new development," Emree states as she leans back in her chair, looking out to the ocean. "Seems pretty boy may have a craving for the forbidden fruit. Now, how do we control the overprotective brother to play matchmaker?"

"Matchmaker? No freaking way. You two are nuts. Nothing is happening or will ever happen between Maddox and me. For several reasons." Even as I say the words, I don't want to believe them.

Being a hopeless romantic who has grown up reading all and every type of romance novel does something to you. One of those things is holding out hope for something that won't happen, like getting my brother's best friend to fall in love with me. It's one of the biggest clichés in romance books, and I've read enough of them to know that it is extremely unrealistic.

"I'm telling you right now, young Collins, that boy has feelings for you. He is going to break eventually, especially with you coming to Braxton and being around more often," Emree predicts.

Taking a sip of my drink, I smile around the rim of the mug, thinking about the possibility of Maddox having feelings for me. It's every girl's dream for the guy they like to return their feelings. Maybe this upcoming year will be the one where I find love, and with the boy who has consumed my thoughts for years.

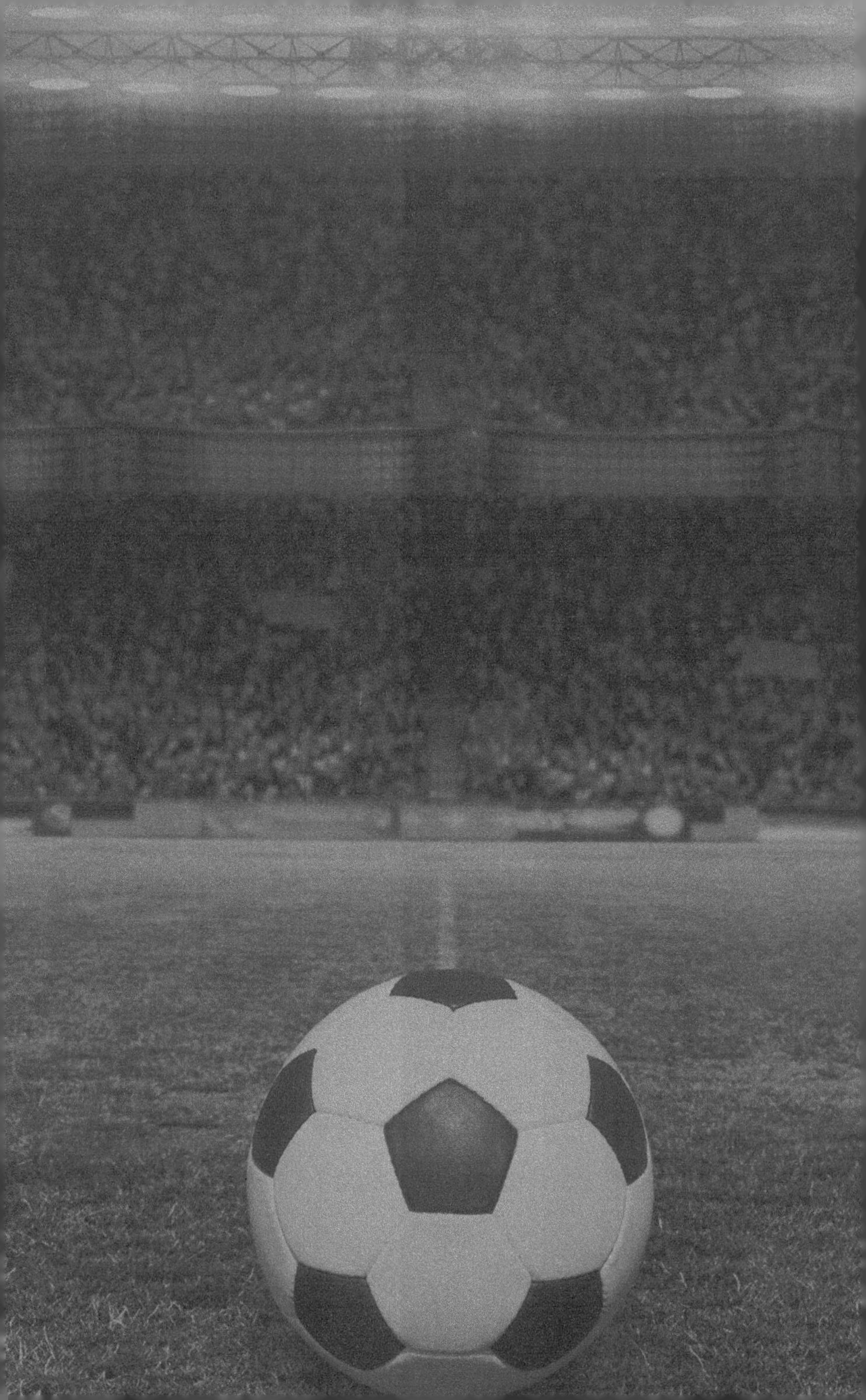

CHAPTER FOUR

TRAZIA

Our spring break is coming to an end, and on the last night at the house, we have all decided to have a big barbecue on the patio. Camden is manning the grill that is filled with steaks while Jules and I take care of the sides. Blaire, Maddox, and Emree went to the store earlier to get supplies for s'mores since we have the perfect fire set up and Blaire has never had them before.

"I don't understand why you won't just let me cook something," Maddox tells Camden. There is a slight slur in his voice, and if I've counted correctly, he has had five beers tonight already. Three more than the rest of the guys, and five more than my brother.

Camden rolls his eyes. "Not only are you already tipsy, but your track record with cooking means you do *not* get to touch anything with flames. Go sit by the fire and drink some water to sober up."

Maddox huffs. "Oh, fuck off, man. I'm perfectly fine." The word perfectly comes out more like *pefecy*.

Instead of continuing their argument, Maddox comes over to the firepit circle and falls into one of the chairs. His bottle of beer sloshes some, and he wipes the liquid off his hand. "Stupid bottle," he mumbles before bringing the neck up to his mouth and taking a long pull of the amber liquid.

Something is off with Maddox tonight. He's not only drinking more than usual, but he is being short with everyone. I don't know if it's because come tomorrow morning they are all headed back to the house and then practice and classes start back up, but either way, he is acting out of character.

Mateo comes out and takes in Maddox's slouched position and beer in hand. "Starting a little early, aren't we? I thought you were stepping back from the alcohol this semester."

"Can't a man have a few drinks without the entire fucking house up his ass? If I wanted you in my business, I'd ask."

Mateo holds his hands up in a surrender motion. "Whoa, man, no need to get feisty with me. I was only reminding you of what you told me. Drink until you pass out, but stay away from the water and know that none of us are hauling your ass to bed." He heads back into the house in the direction of the family room. Blaire has been perched on the couch reading a book while some sports game plays in the background.

During this vacation, she and I have bonded over our love of a good romantic story, and while I would normally be in there with her, I wanted to be closer to Maddox on our last night here. I keep trying to see if I can notice any sort of sign that there may be something between us that Emree was talking about, but with him drinking more and more, it's getting harder to see anything other than a man on his way to being drunk.

Maddox scoffs and pours the remaining liquid down his throat. With unsteady legs, he makes his way to the outdoor fridge and grabs another one. After a few tries, he gets the top popped off. Levi watches him the entire time from his seat across from me. Maddox collapses back into his chair and swallows a good amount of his sixth beer.

A MEMORY THAT ONCE WAS

Since it's our last night here, I've been nursing a couple cups of margaritas Emree and Jules made. I'm not a fan of alcohol, and definitely won't be touching beer ever again, but a good mixed drink like this is right up my alley. Not too sweet but hides the gross taste of tequila.

"Who's down for a game of beer pong while we wait for the food to cook?" Jules asks as she exits the back door. She has a stack of red cups in one hand and a couple of beer bottles in another.

"I'm in." Levi stands to his full, large frame and makes his way to the fold-up table the guys brought from their house that they deemed perfect for beer pong with its ability to bounce a ping-pong ball on.

"Lumberjack, you're on my team. Now find me two opponents to crush."

Levi's eyes roam across the outdoor area and land on me. "Come on, young Collins. Join in on the fun while Camden is distracted."

I smile and push myself out of the seat. "Fine, but I'm not drinking that nasty beer."

Levi laughs and looks over to the outdoor kitchen table where Emree has been sketching some designs. "Em, take a break and come play."

She pops her head up and smiles. "I'm not sure you want me to participate. I may not look athletic, but beer pong is my sport." She closes her notebook and joins us.

Camden looks away from the grill, where Conrad has come to help him. "You better not be getting my sister drunk," he warns.

Jules rolls her eyes. "Lighten up. She's safe here with us, and no one is driving anywhere tonight. It will all be okay."

Camden looks conflicted, but his shoulders relax. "Traz, just stay away from the pool and make sure to eat food to absorb the alcohol."

Smiling, I nod.

While most may see his objection to me drinking as a bit overboard on the protective side, after what happened to him last year, I understand where he is coming from. During a party, Camden's beer was spiked by a horrible woman they went to school with. She was trying to tear Blaire and my brother apart, and in the worst way. Luckily the drugs she used knocked him out so that he was too far gone to get it up, but he was violated nonetheless. With the encouragement of his friends, Camden pressed charges, and the girl got a hefty sentence, as she should.

Emree fills up our cups with her margarita mix, while Levi does the same to theirs but with beer instead. The hairs on the back of my neck rise, and I feel a pair of eyes on me. Camden is focused on the grill while chatting with Conrad. Turning to the side, I catch pale green eyes boring into me. Maddox is perched on his seat with a bottle in hand and his full attention solely on me.

Focusing back on the table, I smile at Levi when he announces they're ready to play. We each grab a ball, and Levi and I keep eye contact as we throw the balls toward the cups. Levi's sinks in while mine goes far over, winning his team the first go.

"Don't worry, young Collins, you'll have a lot of time to learn when you start at Braxton next semester." Levi laughs as he throws the first shot. He misses this time as it bounces off the rim of a cup at the back.

"Better not let Camden hear you, or I'll be banned from college parties before I even get there."

Emree laughs after sinking a shot for our team. "You're brave for going to the same school as him. I don't know how you handle the overprotective brother situation."

I smile at her and offer a small laugh. The truth is, I'm not entirely going to Braxton to be near my brother. While yes, it is a wonderful school, I was offered scholarships at other universities too. The fact that Maddox attends Braxton should not have been a factor in my decision, but I would be lying if I said it wasn't. My heart overpowered my brain, and I ended up choosing to go to the same school as a boy who may not even like me back. If I told the truth to anyone, they would look at me like I was the dumbest lovesick puppy.

Grabbing the ping-pong ball, I toss it and it sinks into the center cup. "Maybe I'll get better than Camden."

"Keep dreaming, little sis," my brother calls from the grill. "Food is ready. Levi, dunk the last few shots and end this game."

Emree turns toward him, one of the small balls in hand. "Hey, how about a little support for the all-girls team?"

Camden piles the last of the food from the grill onto a platter and brings it to the long patio table we have been having meals at all week. "I fully support your all-girls team, but I also know that Levi is most likely holding back because he's missed more shots than he has made."

"Had to give the kid a chance," Levi says as he sinks the final cup. "Turns out she's not too bad. Next time, I won't be going easy on you," he tells me.

Grabbing the cup, I down the margarita and try not to make a face at the sour and tequila taste. After drinking a few cups worth of the stuff, I'm starting to taste the alcohol more than I was before.

As we clear the beer pong table, I can still feel those same eyes on me. Knowing that Maddox is watching my movements, I am more cautious of how I look and try to make sure my bloated stomach—thanks to the copious amounts of alcohol—isn't on full display.

With more food than any of us could eat covering the table, we all sit around and start piling our plates. Maddox grabs another beer on his way over and takes a seat at the table. We pass around platters of steak, corn, and mashed potatoes.

"Hmm, tastes better than that burned steak Maddox cooked for family night," Mateo states while chewing on a bite of food. He smirks over at Maddox.

"We don't discuss that anymore," Maddox states while cutting into his piece.

Something I've noticed this week is that the guys were not joking about Maddox's lack of cooking skills. There are people who can't cook, and then there is Maddox. Just the other morning, he tried cooking scrambled eggs in the microwave, and they ended up exploding. Jules and I were poking fun at him and said we should sign him up for that *Worst Cooks in America* show.

The table falls into easy conversation while we all enjoy the food that was prepared. My brother outdid himself with the steak, and one of the benefits of going to Braxton is having more meals with him. Camden learned to cook at a young age and can whip up some of the best meals, but his talents lie behind the grill.

Looking around, I can't help but smile. Not only has my brother found a group of friends that are more like family, but they easily accepted me as their own. Going to college and having these as my guides into this new step in life is going to be an experience I cannot wait for.

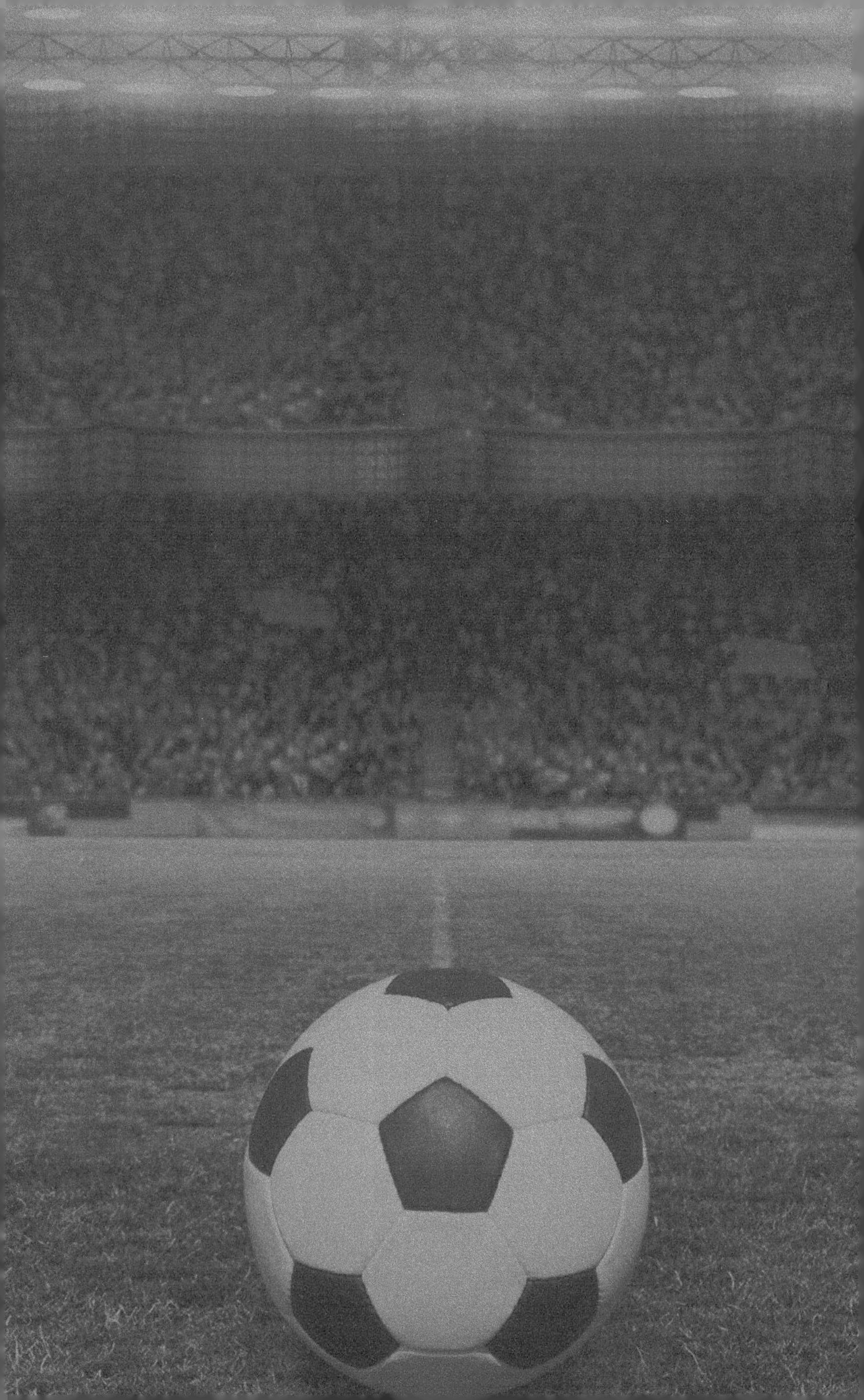

CHAPTER FIVE

TRAZIA

Everyone has gone to bed, and I have been nursing my last margarita for the night. I should have stopped a few cups ago, but the buzz provided by the liquor has felt nice. The later it got, the stronger Emree was making the batches.

Draining the last of the liquid, I stand from the patio chair and toss the plastic cup into the trash. We have to be up early tomorrow, and I've stayed out here later than I should have. Instead of curling back up in my seat like I want to, I make my way inside and make sure to lock the door behind me.

On slightly unsteady feet, I climb the twenty-three steps to the second floor and into my bedroom. I was lucky enough to get a room to myself while living in this professionally designed house, with its thousand-count sheets and a deep soaker tub in the Jack-and-Jill guest bathroom I have been sharing with Levi and Maddox.

I start pulling my clothes off while walking toward my towel hanging from the hooks on the back of the bathroom door. Since we have an early morning, I would rather get a shower out of the way tonight than fight for a turn in the morning.

With my towel tightly secured around my chest, I open the bathroom door and almost fall back when I see a shirtless Maddox standing in front of the sink, brushing his teeth. He's sporting a pair of gray sweatpants that hang low on his narrow hips, and I swear those things should be banned for men with bodies like his to wear.

With his toothbrush still in his mouth, Maddox turns to look at me, and his eyes start on my face and slowly make their way down my towel-covered body. While everything that needs to be covered is covered, I have never felt more exposed than I do right now.

"Oh, sorry. I thought everyone was asleep," I explain to him as I keep a grip on the bathroom door.

Maddox goes back to the sink and spits out a mouthful of toothpaste. After taking a swig of water from the faucet, he turns his entire body to face me. With his full torso on display, I run my eyes down his body and take in every smooth divot. Even though I've seen him without a shirt more times this week than I can count, it feels different when we're in a small bathroom together. More intimate. His tanned chest is on full display, and I try not to bite my lip as my eyes skate over the ridges of his abs and those lines near his hips that disappear into the waistband of his pants that I read about in my romance books.

"If you keep looking at me like that, I'm going to forget who you're related to and who else is in this house and fuck you against this counter right now." His voice is gruff but strained. When I look back up at his face, Maddox's nostrils are flared and his hands are balled at his sides.

My breaths are more ragged as I digest his words. Maddox may be a flirt with almost everyone he encounters, but I have never seen this serious side of him. His usually bright eyes are dark and a little hazy as he stares at me.

"Wh-what?" I stutter.

"You're standing there in nothing but a tiny fucking towel, looking more stunning than every other woman I have ever seen, and now you're biting your lip. This isn't fair, Traz. I've tried being good all week, but you're killing me."

Not realizing I was biting it, I release my lip. "Then stop being good," I breathe out.

Not a second passes before Maddox crosses the small distance between us and pulls me into his arms. With his hand resting against my neck under my jaw, he tilts my head up. "I've had a little too much to drink tonight, so I need you to be completely clear with me, Peach. Do you want this?"

"I'm drunk enough to have the courage to say yes, but sober enough to know I want this," I tell him honestly.

Without another word, Maddox's mouth comes down on mine and the moment our lips touch, my body goes limp in his arms. His strong arm comes around my waist, and he pulls me so our bodies are flush against each other's.

My senses have been invaded by Maddox Stone. I can smell the powerful scent of his woodsy body wash and feel his smooth chest beneath my hands. Taste the mint from his toothpaste. Maddox groans and grips the hair at the base of my head before forcing me to walk backward until my lower back hits the vanity counter. His hands tightly grip my waist and lift me up.

"God, you're sweeter than I imagined," Maddox groans against my lips. His hands leave my waist and move up to cup my face, bringing our lips together again in a rough kiss.

Feeling exposed with nothing under my towel and him standing between my legs, I try to adjust the cloth while my head is swimming from sitting here and kissing my crush. I want to pinch myself and make sure I didn't fall asleep on the patio from the margaritas I had.

While trying to push the extra material from the towel between my legs, it somehow gets loose on top and falls, pooling around my waist and leaving my top half completely exposed.

Maddox ends our kiss and squeezes his eyes shut as he rests his forehead against mine. "Tell me that didn't just happen." He opens his eyes and takes in my nakedness. "Holy hell, Peach."

The way he is staring has me wanting to bring my hands up to cover myself. I've been naked in front of exactly one guy in my life, and he never looked at me like this. The two times we had sex lasted about five minutes each, and the first time he didn't even get my bra off.

The man before me is staring as if he can't look away. Like I would disappear if he did. I feel more exposed as his hands leave my face and slide down my arms to my waist. He unfolds the rest of the towel so that I am now completely bare to him.

Looking up, he cups my jaw. "You're incredible."

"Madd—"

He cuts me off with a gentle kiss before eagerly trailing his mouth down my neck and to my chest. His hand cups my breast while he kisses and sucks the other, leaving me panting.

Not wanting to wait any longer, I slide my hands from his shoulders to the waistband of his pants and shove them down. His hard-on springs free since he's going commando, and I gulp because this is really happening. I'm naked in front of Maddox—my brother's best friend—and we are about to have sex.

"You sure about this?" he asks me again.

Reaching down, I grip him and stroke. "I want you, Maddox. I've wanted this for a long time now."

Maddox grips my waist and pulls me to the edge of the counter, lining himself up with my entrance. With his hand at the back of my neck, he looks into my eyes as he enters me, and I gasp at the new feeling.

"Ah," I squeak out as he thrusts his hips. I grip his shoulders, trying to be mindful of my nails, but it's hard to hold on.

"Fuck, fuck, fuck," he grunts with every movement of his hips. Each thrust has me sliding on the counter.

He keeps a hand on the side of my neck while holding on to my hip with the other. His mouth comes down on mine, lightly biting my bottom lip.

A familiar sensation starts to build inside me and I wrap my arms around Maddox's shoulders as I fall over the edge, relishing in the bliss while trying to control my breathing.

With his hand gripping my hip hard enough to leave a bruise, Maddox thrusts hard a few more times before completely stilling and groaning in my ear. While he comes down from his own high, I run my fingers through his hair, threading my fingers in the long strands.

"That was—"

"Unbelievable," he finishes, out of breath.

I can't help but smile against Maddox's neck because he's right. That was unbelievable. Incredible. Sensational. Everything I could have dreamed about.

The man I've fantasized about is holding me in his arms while I wrap myself around him, and I couldn't be happier than I am right now.

LIFTING my arms above my head, I release a much-needed morning stretch. My body is sore, and remembering why and what happened last night, my eyes pop open. Taking in the room, I realize I'm alone and wrapped in one of the guest robes left for us in our rooms. My hair is tangled, and I realize I never brushed or dried it last night after taking a shower.

A shower I finally got to after having sex with Maddox

Stone. My teenage crush. My brother's best friend. The last guy on this planet I should be having sex with.

Thinking about what we did last night, I can't help but smile because even though this is going to create unnecessary drama within this friend group, I don't have a single ounce of regret in me. Being with Maddox was more than I could have hoped for.

After we both came down from the high, he gave me a gentle kiss and told me he didn't want Levi to catch us before he slipped back into his room. The entire rest of the night I couldn't wipe the smile off my face. He wanted me. Maddox wanted *me* and acted on it. This was all I could have hoped for going into my first year of college.

My door rattles as someone pounds their fist against it. "Traz, you up? Levi wants to leave in half an hour."

Jumping from the bed, I make my way to the door and swing it open. "Hey. Morning, big brother. I'll be down in fifteen."

Camden eyes me suspiciously. "What the hell happened to your hair?"

Patting the knotted mess, I try to somehow make it look less like a disaster. "Accidentally went to bed with my hair wet. I need to get another shower and I'll be ready to go."

"Okay, sounds good. Hopefully we can leave on time, but Levi said he was having a hard time waking Mad up."

At the mention of his best friend, my ears perk up. "Oh, what's wrong with him?"

"Drank too much last night," Camden tells me with an eye roll. "Levi had to pour ice water on him this morning just to get him to open his eyes. Dude was knocked out cold. Jules and Blaire are making a small breakfast for everyone, so hopefully that and some coffee will sober him up." He shakes his head and begins walking down the hallway toward the stairs.

Closing the door, I lean against it as I think back to last

night. Maddox wasn't that drunk, was he? We had both been a little tipsy, but how could he go from that to a coma hangover the next morning? I didn't even smell or taste alcohol on his breath when he kissed me. Although he had just brushed his teeth.

Shaking off the weird feeling that sits at the bottom of my stomach, I shower and pack up the rest of my belongings. With my hair brushed and dried and my bag packed, I head downstairs and am met with most of our group.

Camden and Maddox are sitting on the barstools, enjoying their breakfast on the island. Grabbing a plate, I pile on a small amount of eggs and bacon and take the empty seat beside Maddox. He doesn't look at me, but instead pushes his food around like a disgruntled child.

"You going to be good to drive, man?" Camden asks as he watches Maddox.

"You filled me with almost a full pot of coffee, so I should be good. Just give me a few more minutes to let it kick fully in." A cup—that is more like the size of a bowl—of coffee sits beside Maddox's plate, and it is almost empty.

Knowing I can't say anything to raise suspicion, especially with Camden, I focus on my breakfast, but with the ongoing odd feeling I'm having, the eggs taste bitter as they go down.

Emree comes in and greets everyone.

"Hey, girl," Blaire says from her spot on the other side of Camden. "Jules and I made some eggs and bacon if you want any. I left the bread and butter out too." She smiles as she takes a bite of her toast.

"Thanks," Emree replies as she grabs a paper plate and begins filling it with food. She sets it on the counter and opens the fridge, which has been emptied.

"You're damn right I made sure to pack that shit up. I couldn't handle another morning of you putting ketchup on your eggs like a serial killer," Maddox announces.

Emree shuts the fridge and glares at him. "A serial killer? Really, Maddox? Putting ketchup on your eggs is very normal and common and does not make me a serial killer." Rolling her eyes, she walks over to where she left her plate on the island. "I have no idea where you come up with the thoughts that go through your brain."

He points his fork at her, not realizing there is some egg hanging off the end. "You notice any of these *normal* people around us putting ketchup on their eggs? No, you don't. That makes you a freak and probably a serial killer. It's just a good thing we're leaving when we are before you kill one of us." He points his fork at all of us and ends up flinging bits of egg through the air.

"What the hell, Maddy? I lecture him with a raised voice. The egg pieces flew through the air and ended up smacking me in the chest and falling down my shirt.

"Maddy?" Camden questions, but everyone ignores him.

"Shit. Sorry, Peach. Here, let me get that out for you." He reaches toward the top of my tank top, but before he can get close enough to touch me, Camden pulls him back by his shirt.

"Touch my sister and I'll break your arm, Stone." Camden's eyes are narrowed at his best friend.

Maddox looks to his right and then to his left, back at me. "Apologies, my lady. Big brother over here has some issues with me helping clean up the mess I made in your cleavage."

I gawk at him. "Do you not have a filter?"

He shrugs his shoulders and begins shoveling his food into his mouth. "Why filter our most honest thoughts?"

Camden rolls his eyes. "Maybe because you make people uncomfortable."

I study Maddox as he finishes his plate of food and try to gauge if he is acting indifferent toward me because my brother is in the room or…no. I can't even think that right now.

We finish off the rest of the food, and as everyone is loading their things into the cars, I hang back with Maddox. He is doing a last check of the downstairs area to make sure nothing is left behind. He assured us we didn't need to give the house a deep clean because he had a cleaning service coming in this afternoon that his mom regularly used.

Walking over to his side, I grip Maddox's upper arm. "Hey, can we talk?"

He looks down at where I'm gripping him, and I release my hold. "Sure. What's up?"

"About last night…"

Maddox's eyebrows pinch together and he studies me for several seconds. "Last night? Fuck, don't tell me I did something stupid."

My chest tightens, and I try to control my breathing. "Yo-you don't remember?"

His hands come up and he rubs his eyes with his palms. "Oh god, please tell me what happened. I swear I didn't drink that much, but fuck, I have the biggest hangover."

Maddox doesn't remember. He doesn't know about our time together. A moment that meant everything is nothing but a lost memory to him.

Taking a deep breath, I plaster the largest fake smile I can muster up. "Nothing. I just wanted to make sure you were okay with that hangover."

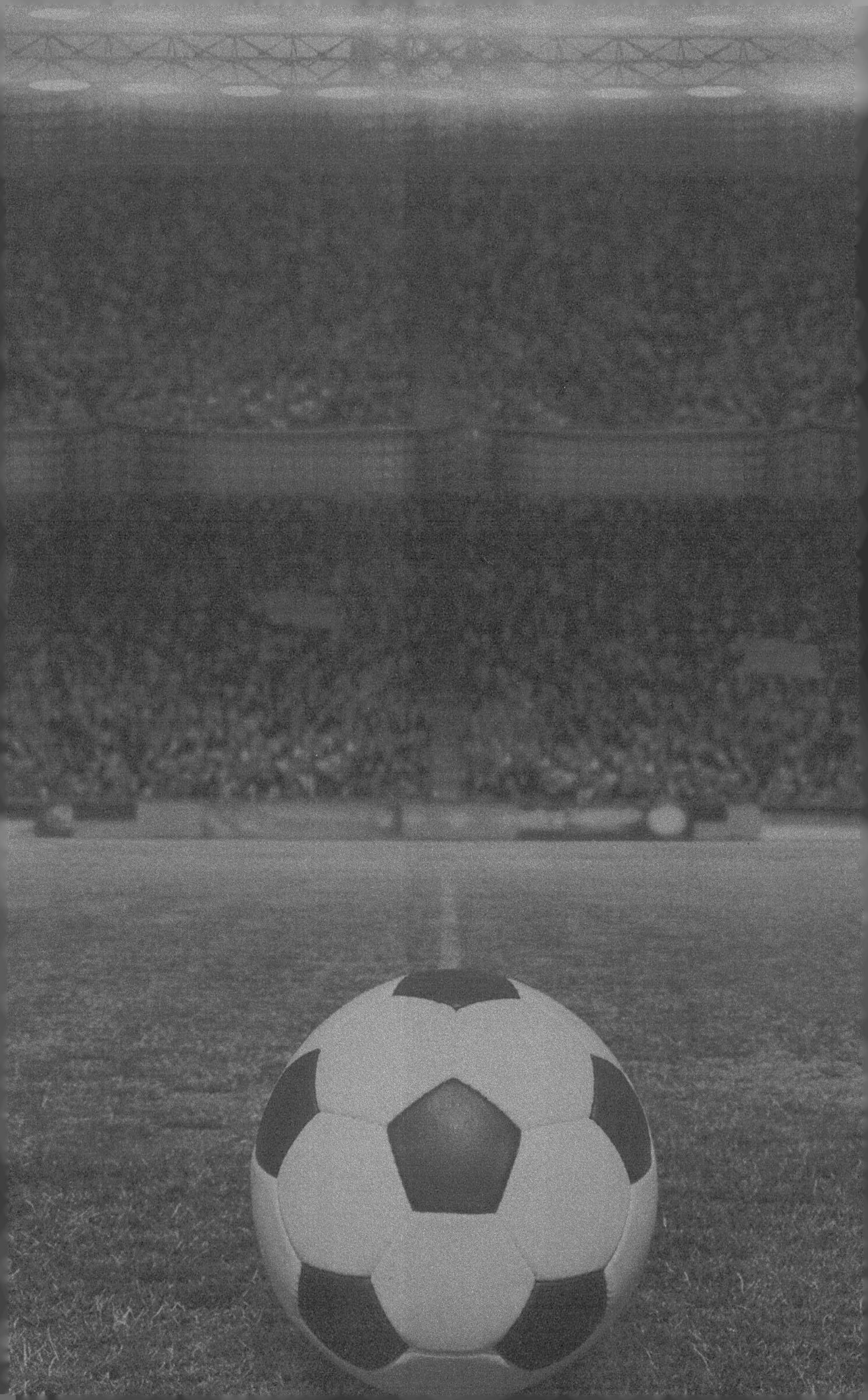

CHAPTER SIX

MADDOX

TWO MONTHS LATER

With her in my arms, I run my hands up and down her back. "I can't believe that just happened," she whispers in my ear.

Me neither, I want to tell her, but I'm still trying to catch my breath after the best fucking sex of my life. My Peach is more beautiful than I could ever imagine. She's damn near perfect. She has a lean but fit body, and I'm sure her years of playing volleyball in high school helped with that. She has the most grabbable ass I've ever seen, and her tits are what women pay thousands of dollars for. There is also this splattering of freckles across them that is fucking adorable.

Holding her naked body like this, I can't believe it's real. Like someone is playing a sick joke on me, and the woman with her arms and legs wrapped around my body is a figment of my imagination. The alcohol must have gone to my head, and I'm imagining something that I've wanted for so long.

My eyes snap open, and I groan at the dream that has been haunting me for two months since we got back from spring break. It's not my first dirty dream when it comes to Traz, but it is the hottest and feels almost…real. I've never dreamed of something that intimate with her, but I can't shake this dream.

For the past two months, I've woken up with a raging hard-on and thoughts of my best friend's little sister.

Trying to forget about Trazia Collins, I get out of bed and make my way to the private bathroom. One of the benefits of not giving a fuck about being nude around anyone is that my friends decided to forgo drawing straws and gave me the owner's bedroom in the house. It's large, which is an added benefit, but I also don't have to worry about sharing a shower or toilet with anyone. There have been a few instances when people walked in because the other bathroom was occupied, but some of them have been scarred by my bare ass too early in the morning to enter without knocking anymore. Those someones being Emree and Blaire.

Taking a piss with my dick like this is difficult, but I manage. After a quick shower, I change into a loose pair of shorts and a T-shirt.

Entering the kitchen, I inhale the smell of eggs and bacon. Camden is at the stove, scrambling some eggs. Mateo and Levi are seated on the barstools behind the sink with eager faces as they practically salivate over the food being prepared.

"Morning," Levi greets.

"Good to see you, Lumberjack."

Levi rolls his eyes. "The beard is trimmed for the summer. Are you ever going to stop with the lumberjack jokes?"

"Are you ever going to stop looking like a lumberjack?"

"He has stock in plaid, so I'm going to say no," Mateo chimes in.

"I hate you guys," Levi grumbles.

Taking the seat beside him, I sling my arm over the giant's shoulders. "Ah, don't be like that. You know you love us, and we love you and your variety of plaid shirts."

Camden serves up some eggs and bacon to all of us and

stands at the counter, eating his own breakfast. "Any of you interested in helping me move an incredibly stressed little sister into her dorm today?"

At the mention of Trazia, my ears perk.

"She's already moving in? Don't classes not start until August?" Mateo asks.

Camden chews his mouthful of food before answering. "She wants to do summer classes. The sooner she gets her degree, the sooner she can start finding a school that is hiring. Traz figures if she graduates at least a semester before everyone, she will avoid all the competition of fall graduates fighting for a job."

"Sorry, man. I have the morning shift at the bookstore today," Levi states as he gets up from his seat and drops his dishes in the sink. On his way to the door, he offers us a goodbye wave.

"Well, I'm free today, but you owe me if we're moving heavy shit," Mateo tells him, pointing his fork.

Camden rolls his eyes. "I'll make sure to do the heavy lifting."

"You have me too. Hey, why don't we do a family dinner since she's here now?" I offer.

"I'm down for that," Mateo agrees with his mouth full of eggs.

Turning, I give him a pointed look. "Chew your food before speaking. What are you, a Neanderthal?"

Mateo rolls his eyes. "Oh, shut up."

"This is a house of gentlemen. Act like one."

"Gentlemen?" Camden laughs. "We've all seen your naked ass more times than I can count. There is nothing gentlemanly about that."

"Nudity is a way of life, Cammy," I scoff. "Don't go being a prude."

"It's not being a prude if I want the only dick I see to be my own."

Arching a brow, I level him with a stare. "Scared of a little… competition with Blaire around?"

His nostrils flare just a tad. "My girl is extremely satisfied, thank you very much."

"Ah, but does she know the other possibilities in the house? I mean, size does matter, and fuck anyone who says differently," I tease.

"I'm getting a little weirded out by this conversation, so can we drop it and talk about moving Trazia into her new place?" Mateo suggests.

"Fine. Now that I've planted that thought in Cammy's head, let's get to moving young Collins into her dorm."

Camden tosses his plate and the pan he used to cook the food into the dishwasher. "Let's go. Oh, and she needs us to head to my mom's house to load up my Jeep. Apparently, she has more boxes of clothes than she anticipated, and most of her shit doesn't fit in the tiny car she just bought. May need someone to drive back with her to make more room in my car."

"Damn, Traz went and got herself a car? What'd she end up choosing?" Mateo asks as he loads his own plate into the dishwasher.

"Get this, she got one of those Bugs. A bright red one. About ten years old. It was driven by a senior woman, so the miles are low."

Mateo stops as he walks toward the kitchen exit and turns around. "Wait, like that Herbie car from the movie? That kind of Bug?"

Rolling my eyes, I press the start button after loading the last of the dishes to begin a new cycle. "Not sure there's any other kind of car called a Bug, dumbass."

"Fuck, man, that's a girly car. I'm not riding in that shit with her."

A sinister smirk creeps up on Camden's face. "We'll have Mad here take a ride in the lady car, since he's the man with the biggest dick in this house. He'll have no problem toughing it in there."

Straightening my shoulders, I walk toward them. "Your misogyny is showing. Tuck that away, will you."

Camden rolls his eyes and grabs the keys to his Jeep on the way out the door. Mateo takes the front—without calling shotgun, might I add—and I hop in the back seat.

The house Camden grew up in isn't far from campus. Unlike the rest of our roommates, he has lived in this area his entire life. While it made sense for Camden to move to campus because of the constant early morning practices and being at Coach's beck and call, I'm a bit more surprised Trazia is moving here. Sure, it would be more of a hassle to drive the hour to and from her house to campus, but I'd prefer that over sharing a dorm the size of a bedroom with a stranger.

Traffic is light and, we make it to Camden's childhood home in no time. The moment I open the door and leave the comfort of the air conditioning, I'm regretting my kind act of helping Camden's little sister move into her new place. There were some ulterior motives to me agreeing to this, and that is seeing Trazia is never a bad thing. Especially when she is wearing a pair of tiny jean shorts and a tank top like she is now, but this goddamn May heat is blurring my vision at the moment. Her hair has changed since the last time I saw her; she has darkened it and gotten rid of the pale pink look. Her tank top is riding up a little at the bottom, exposing a strip of tan skin.

"Did you have to pack every item you own?" Camden asks as we approach the front porch that is covered in moving boxes.

With her hands on her hips, Trazia gives him a pointed

look. "Do not judge me, Camden Collins. I'm packing only what I will need."

"These two boxes are labeled shoes. Do you really need that many pairs at school?"

"Yes, I do," she tells him matter-of-factly.

Camden rolls his eyes. "You have one pair of feet, Traz."

"And you have a pair of legs and how many pants? I rest my case. Now, help me with these boxes so I can go reassure our mom that I'm not leaving her forever so she will quit being sad about her favorite child moving out."

Before she walks away, Traz's eyes flash to me and she freezes for a moment, as if she is just realizing I'm standing behind her brother.

"Hey, Peach," I greet her with a smile.

She doesn't return my hello but rather ducks her head and goes into the house. For some reason I feel as though I just got the cold shoulder, but I'm not sure why. Maybe she's nervous about moving out and starting college.

"You think we should load as much as we can into her car and then stuff the rest in mine?" Camden asks us.

I look at the boxes and shrug my shoulders. "Might as well try and see if we can get this all done in one trip."

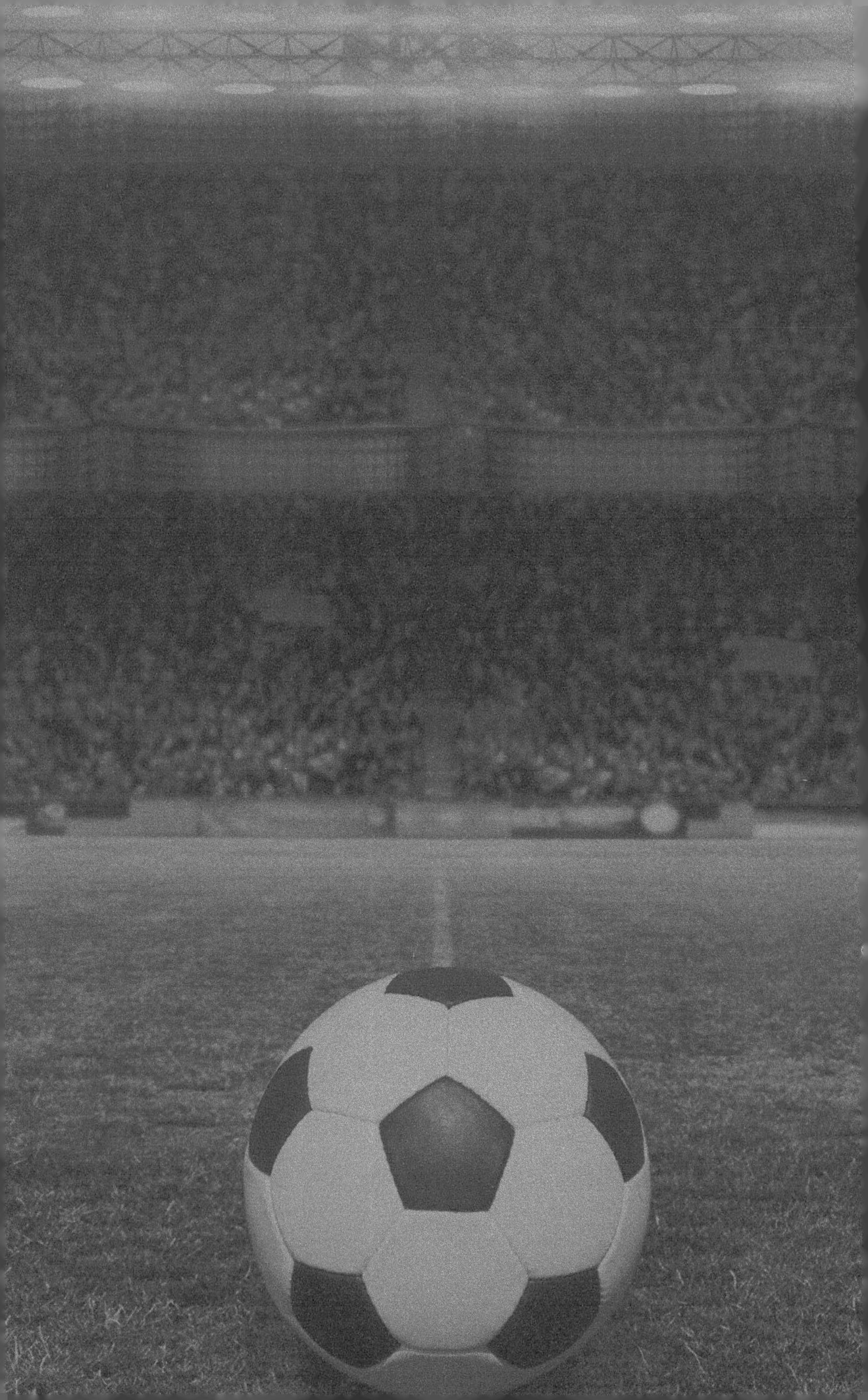

CHAPTER SEVEN

TRAZIA

Once inside the safety of my house, I take a deep breath to calm my nerves. Camden had told me he was going to try and bring a couple of the guys with him to help me move, but I was hoping Maddox wouldn't be one of them.

After our drunken hookup that he has no memory of, I find it hard to look at him. Finally being with the guy that has consumed my thoughts for so long should have excited me, but when he acted like nothing happened the next morning, I felt dirty and sad. Our moment together was special to me and I thought everything would be different after, but I'm still the little sister secretly pining after her brother's best friend.

"What are you doing leaning against the door, honey?" Mom asks as she comes into the living room from the kitchen.

Our house isn't large and has an open floor plan. When you enter the living room—that is big enough to fit two couches and a TV stand—the kitchen is straight through on the other side. Mom's bedroom is off from the kitchen, and mine and Camden's are down the hallway from the living room.

After our dad left when I was five, my mom did everything she could to provide for us. While I was too young to remember much, Camden tells me that we lived in a small one-bedroom apartment at first, and Mom slept on a pull-out couch and gave us the bedroom. She would sometimes work up to three jobs to make sure we never went without. We have been doing better the last few years and Mom doesn't have to work as much as she used to, but I can see her nervousness at times when something breaks or the electric bill is higher than usual. I'm glad to reduce her stress by getting an academic scholarship to Braxton so she doesn't have to worry about paying for my classes or dorm.

Plastering on a smile, I push myself off the door and walk toward my mom. "Oh, just resting after being in the heat for all of five minutes. Camden and some of the guys are here to help, so we can avoid the heavy lifting."

"Oh good, gives me more time with my girl," she replies with a smile as her arms wrap around my waist, pulling me in for a hug.

"Once again, Mom, I'm not going to be far. I'll probably be here as often as possible since I don't have a kitchen or anything." Unfortunately, the dorm that was part of my scholarship doesn't include a kitchenette like some of the others do, but I'm on the meal program, so as long as I can stretch that and make it home once in a while for dinner, I should be able to handle not having a kitchen.

Pulling back, she strokes the side of my head. "I know that, but my baby is leaving home. I'm going to miss having you around all the time." Her eyes begin to glisten, and I have to hold back my own tears. The last couple of weeks have been emotional for me because losing the familiarity and comfort of my home is scary.

The front door opens, and Maddox walks in, looking unfairly hot. "Morning, Ms. Collins," he greets as he lifts his shirt and wipes the sweat from his face. "We've fit all the boxes in the two cars, Traz. We can head toward the dorms whenever you're ready."

My mom grips my hand in hers. "That was too fast. I'm not ready to let my baby girl go."

Maddox presents her with his ever-charming smile. "Don't worry, we'll make sure to take good care of her."

I know he doesn't mean anything sexual by what he tells her, but my body tingles thinking about how he *took care of me* our last night at the beach house.

"Trazia, let's go. We have to unload all this shit!" Camden calls from the porch.

Mom holds on to my shoulders and squeezes tight. "I'll come visit you this weekend and bring a casserole or something easy for you to heat up."

"I'll miss you, Mama. And your cooking, so make sure to bring a good variety. Oh, and your homemade snickerdoodle cookies."

She smiles and pulls me in for another tight hug. "Of course, baby girl. I love you."

Blinking away the tears, I squeeze her back extra tight. "I love you, Mama."

After holding each other for several more seconds, we pull apart, and she walks me out to a now-loaded car. Camden says goodbye to Mom, making sure to wipe the sweat from his forehead on her arm.

My new car is filled to the top with boxes and random items from my room. The passenger seat is open, and I'm surprised they didn't load that spot up.

"I'll meet you guys back at the dorm building," I tell Camden before getting into my car.

Just as I start the engine, the passenger door opens, and a large frame lowers itself into the seat.

"What do you think you're doing?"

Maddox tucks his long legs as best he can with the little

room he's working with. "Well, I was catching a ride back to Braxton, but I'm not sure this toy car can accommodate me."

Gripping the steering wheel, I blow out a frustrated breath. "Why don't you just ride with Camden?"

"And miss out on your sweet hospitality? Why would I go and do that?"

He's right. I am being unfairly cold to him, but it's hard when I feel this pain in my chest every time I think about the morning after we had sex and how he had forgotten the entire night.

"I'm sorry. You're right. I'm just nervous about moving out on my own and being away from home," I tell him honestly.

Maddox reaches across the center console and places his hand on my bare knee. I try not to let my reaction show from the contact, but my breath hitches just slightly. "It's not like you'll be alone. You have all of us there for you."

"True," I tell him with a smile. "Levi already said he'd show me the bookstore he works at and offered an employee discount, as long as I promise not to tell anyone...although I kind of just broke that rule already."

With an eye roll, Maddox removes his hand from my leg. "Don't let the lumberjack suck you into his weird *Harry Potter* fanfiction. I swear that guy is the coolest-looking nerd I've ever seen."

I put the car in reverse and drive toward campus. "A hot nerd is like finding a prom dress your size at the thrift store. Damn near impossible."

"You got the hots for Levi, Peach?" Maddox asks. There is a joking tone to his voice, but I hear something else underneath. Jealousy, maybe?

I hop on the interstate and pick up speed. "Not sure there's a single straight woman out there who wouldn't find Levi hot."

"Pff, not like he would date any of them. I swear the guy is a monk. Not once in the three years I've known him have I seen him hook up with someone."

"Maybe some guys are waiting for the right girl."

A moment of silence falls between us, and I think that is the end of the conversation. "You waiting for the right guy, Peach?"

My stomach does flips as I think over my answer. "I thought I was. But it turns out reality is much more heartbreaking than your fantasies."

The sound of traffic and the radio on low fills the lull in conversation, and the energy turns awkward. "Hey, Mad, why do you call me Peach?"

"Oh, um," he stumbles over his words. "It's just a nickname."

Looking over, I catch Maddox avoiding my direction. "Come on, tell me. You don't just come up with a nickname for someone without there being any meaning to it."

"Maybe you just smell like peaches."

I wish I wasn't driving so that I could see him because Maddox is acting unusually shy. "I use cherry blossom lotion, so good try. Tell me or I'll pull over and kick you out of my car."

A deep laugh escapes him. "I would like to see you try because I'm pretty sure it's going to take some effort to get me out of this fishbowl on wheels."

"You would be surprised what I'm capable of. Now, give me an answer, Stone."

He blows out a defeated breath. "Fine, I'll tell you. You have a peach-shaped ass."

Not expecting that response, I bust out laughing and focus on keeping my eyes open so we don't end up colliding with another vehicle. "Please, that is not the reason."

"What can I say, I'm an ass man. And you have a nice one. Worthy enough of a nickname."

"You started calling me Peach three years ago, Mad. I know my ass was not what it was back then." The short time I played volleyball in high school helped shape my body, including giving me a nicely sculpted butt.

"That's my truth and I'm sticking to it," he proclaims as he crosses his arms over his chest.

"I'll get the truth out of you one way or another."

Reaching forward, Maddox turns up the radio. "Oh look, I love this song."

Listening to the music as it filters through the speakers, I can't help but laugh. "You're a Miley fan?"

"Of course," he says with confidence. "When she dropped 'Flowers' even I began to hate all men until I realized I have a dick and all. But I'm totally Team Miley, and Liam can get fucked."

Maddox begins to poorly sing along as Miley Cyrus goes on about how she can buy herself flowers and write her name in the sand. Basically being a badass and announcing she doesn't need a man to make her feel special.

Taking this drive with Maddox has helped calm me in a way. I'm still hurt by him not remembering our time together, but in this car, everything feels normal. We can go back to joking and laughing together. I just hope my heart can handle the friend zone with Maddox, especially after experiencing being with him in the most intimate of ways.

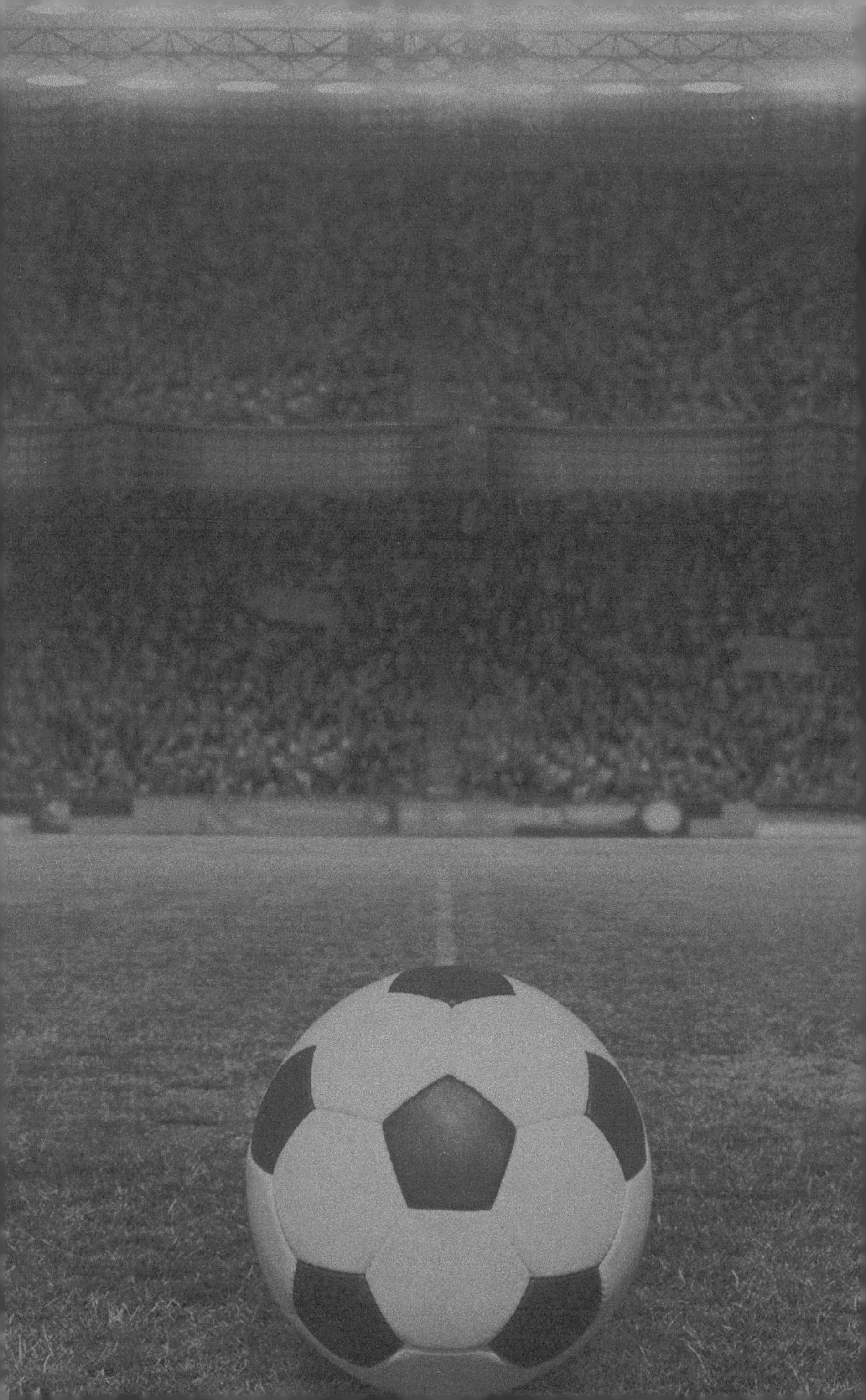

CHAPTER EIGHT

TRAZIA

Camden's Jeep is already in the parking lot when I pull in. His car is still loaded, but he and Mateo are leaning against the trunk. I whip the steering wheel and pull into the spot beside theirs.

Starting classes during the summer instead of fall means there are far less students moving into the dorms this week. The parking lot is littered with fellow college students hauling their items, but nowhere near how packed it was when Camden started at Braxton.

"You're going to need to get the guys to help me out. Pretty sure my knees are now part of your dashboard," Maddox whines from the passenger seat.

"I'll make sure to bring you water and snacks to your new home," I tell him as I exit the car.

Standing to my full frame, I stretch out my arms and legs. Braxton isn't far from my hometown, but the over-an-hour-long drive on the highway can do you in. Luckily the tension I was harboring because of Maddox's presence fizzled out, and we enjoyed each other's company while listening to music.

"You know what dorm you are?" Camden asks as he and Mateo make their way over.

Mateo peeks his head around my car to the passenger side. "Why isn't he getting out?"

Covering my mouth with my hand, I try to hide my smile from them. "He was, um…having difficulty getting in and out. He says my car is too small."

"It's a fishbowl!" he yells from the open door. "My fucking knees won't budge, and this seat is all the way back."

Mateo shakes his head. "I'll go help him."

Camden comes over to me and throws his arm over my shoulders. "How're you doing?"

Smiling, I look up at my big brother. "Good. I'm sad for Mom more than anything. I don't want her to feel lonely now that we're both out of the house."

"You kidding me? Carrie already said now that we're out of the house she's taking Mom out every weekend. She's going to have more of a social life than we do." Carrie is Mom's best friend who is opposed to marriage, has no kids of her own, and still thinks she's in her twenties. She used to be a middle school teacher but couldn't handle the stress of budget cuts and parents thinking they know what's best when it comes to teaching, so now she owns a medical marijuana dispensary and has never been happier.

Carrie is the one who inspired me to become a teacher, and even though she took a different route later in life, she doesn't regret the years she taught and the students who changed her life. It hasn't deterred me from wanting to teach elementary school children after I graduate.

"That makes me feel better. Honestly, I could see Mom and Carrie just buying a place and living out their lives together. I've heard Carrie joke about it, but how great would that be? To live and grow old with your best friend."

Camden laughs and removes his arm from my shoulder. "Mom has no plans to remarry, or even date, so I think she should go for that. A nurse and legal weed dealer living together. Imagine the trouble they'd get in."

Mateo and Maddox come around my trunk to stand with us. "That car is a joke," Maddox complains. "Good thing Lumberjack isn't here with us because there was no way his legs would be fitting. Plus, I feel like your car would spit him out because of the plaid. Too manly for such a...dainty vehicle."

"Enough with the car hate. Let's go see this room and make sure my roommate isn't a serial killer or something."

The three guys follow me as we enter the three-story building. There is a woman behind a desk in the common room with a sign that reads *Check-In*. She has lightly grayed hair that is held up by a clip, and she is wearing a black dress with paintbrushes on it. If I had to guess, I would assume she is some kind of art teacher here. I approach her while the guys stay back, and she offers a welcoming smile.

"Good morning. What's your name and what building were you assigned to?" she asks me.

"Trazia Collins and I'm supposed to be in the Williamson building."

As she flips through a short stack of papers, I begin to get nervous that she hasn't found my name yet. Collins should be at the beginning if they have a normal organizing system.

"Could you spell the last name for me, dear?" she asks after going through the list twice.

I wet my suddenly dry lips. "C-O-L-L-I-N-S."

She riffles through the papers again, and my heartbeat picks up when she looks at me with sorrow. "I'm sorry, sweetie, but your name isn't in here. Are you sure you were assigned a dorm this semester?"

"I-I'm almost positive. There was an email sent to me with a confirmation and everything." I pull out my cell phone and go to my email folder labeled *School*. "See, here." I hand the phone to her.

The woman pulls the phone close to her face and squints as she tries reading the small letters. "Oh, honey, this is for a dorm in the fall semester. Summer deadlines closed a while ago."

Sweat starts to drip down my back, and my breathing becomes labored. "That...that can't be possible. I have classes starting next week. There has to be some way I can move into a dorm by then."

She offers a sympathetic smile. "I'm afraid we're completely filled until August."

"But I'm small!" I practically shout at the woman. "Stick me anywhere. Please. I can't be homeless for the next three months."

"Traz," Camden calls from behind, just before his hands rest on my shoulders. "What's going on?"

"I'm homeless, that's what's going on." A little dramatic, sure, but I'm annoyed.

"Whoa, what?" Camden comes around to face me. "What happened?"

"This lovely woman here just told me I have housing for fall semester, *not* summer. Which means I'm shit out of luck for the next three months."

The maybe art teacher offers a tight smile. "I really am sorry, sweetie, but I have other students to check in. You can take this up with administration, but there isn't much that can be done."

With a huff, I storm away and back out to my car. Or my new home, as I now see it.

"Well, I guess I live here now," I announce to no one in particular as I wave my hands at my car.

"Don't be so dramatic," Camden tells me as the three of them approach the car. "We'll work something out."

Resting my head on the doorframe, I try to relax my shoulders. "I'm sorry. It's just, I'm hungry and skipped breakfast this morning and this is the last thing I need right now. Being homeless will not look good on me."

My brother laughs at my life struggles. "You won't ever be homeless. If you have to, living with Mom and commuting to classes from there wouldn't be the worst-case scenario."

Whipping around, I glare at him. "Are you kidding me? I have an 8 a.m. class, Camden Collins."

"How about we chill for a moment? Cammy, why don't you and Toe head to the house? I'll stop by Dunkin' and pick up some food for everyone, including the cranky homeless lady here." Leave it to Maddox to try and lighten the mood with his natural humor.

"And what the hell is up with the nickname *Toe*? What goes through your mind on a daily basis?" I'm practically yelling at Maddox, and he doesn't deserve it. It's not like he's the reason I don't have housing this semester.

"Sounds like a plan," Camden answers Maddox, completely ignoring my outburst. "You okay to drive, Traz? Or do you need Mad to?"

"I'm fine," I assure him with an eye roll. "Plus, daddy longlegs over there won't be able to handle driving the Bug."

Maddox and I load back into my car, and he keeps the complaining to a minimum. We drive through a Dunkin' close to campus and he orders a dozen donuts and half a dozen bagels. I add my favorite iced chai tea latte to the order and offer Maddox a five-dollar bill.

"I'm not taking that," he states while pushing my hand away.

Rolling my eyes, I thrust the money back at him. "Please. I can buy my own drink."

"And sometimes it makes others feel good to take care of their friends. Now, pull forward so we can get our shit and figure out your living situation."

Trying to hide my smile, I tuck the money back into my

center console and drive up to the window. Maddox hands me a heavy metal credit card, and I pass it to the worker.

With the food now secured, we head to the house that the guys share off-campus. The whole time I try not to stress about where I will be sleeping tonight.

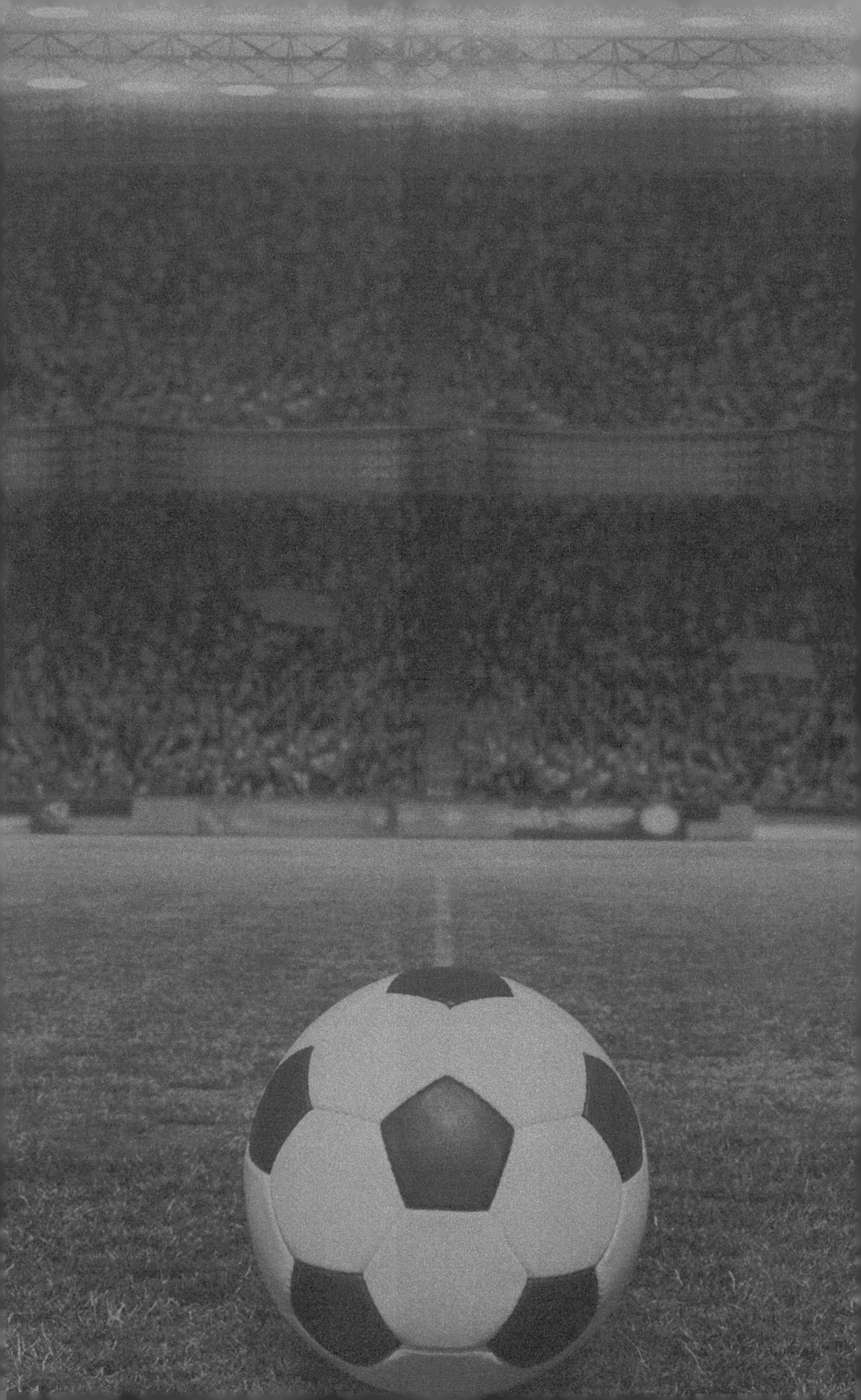

CHAPTER NINE

MADDOX

The entire drive back to the house, all I want to do is tell Trazia that there is an easy solution to her living situation: move in with us. We have a small spare room downstairs we use for our junk and soccer equipment, but even if that doesn't work, Conrad is practically living with Emree now after they broke up and got back together last month. I'm sure he would be more than happy to give his room up for three months and live with his girlfriend.

I don't voice this because the thought of Trazia Collins living under the same roof as me is like an alcoholic moving into a brewery. When you have something tempting you find hard to resist, don't stick it right under your nose.

Even though I know it will be damn near impossible for her to find housing this close to the summer semester, I can't have the first option be her moving in with us. Especially with her brother there also. My dick can't handle her walking around in some skimpy sleepwear.

Traz pulls the tiny vehicle into our driveway. Levi's shift must be over because his car is parked beside Camden's. We don't have the largest of driveways, and with all four of us owning cars, I find it easier to park my truck on the road so that no one blocks me in.

Once in park, Trazia removes the keys and is out of the vehicle with her iced drink in hand before I even have a chance to say anything. "No, no, don't mind me with a lap full of baked goods and legs losing circulation. I got it," I say loud enough through my open door for her to hear.

She stops in front of the car and then comes around to my side, grabbing the boxes of food from my lap. "You're such a baby."

Without the added struggle of not dropping the food, I'm able to maneuver out of Trazia's car, having to lift one leg at a time through the door. I've never thought that there were cars specifically meant for men or women, but after driving in this thing, I can't imagine the average-sized guy being comfortable behind the wheel.

Seeing that Camden's Jeep is still packed with Traz's stuff, I leave her car filled until we figure out what the next step is.

The living room is filled with all of our friends. Camden is sitting on the single-seater sofa with Blaire in his lap. Levi, Mateo, and Jules are on the largest sofa, and Conrad and Emree are snuggled on the two-seater.

"There you are," Camden greets his sister as she walks through the door. Trazia heads into the living room and sets the boxes on the coffee table. Opening the largest one, she pulls out a chocolate-covered donut before sitting on the floor in front of the TV console.

"Mmm, this was worth the detour." Trazia's moan sends a zap straight to my dick, and I have to look away from her to not sport a giant bulge in a room full of my friends. Her closed eyes, small smile, and head tilted back is a vision worthy of saving for the spank bank later.

Not wanting to get too close to the woman who is my own personal temptress, I join the loving couple on the couch not meant for three people. "Move over, you horndogs. Make some room for the best-looking one in the friend group."

Emree shifts closer to Conrad, as if she wasn't already practically in his lap. "You did rank high on the best butt competition we had, but Conrad is by far the best-looking."

Her boyfriend groans. "Enough with that stupid fucking competition."

"Someone is still salty his own girlfriend said he doesn't have the best ass," I mutter loud enough for everyone to hear.

Trazia finishes off her donut and looks between the three of us on the couch. "Wait, what happened? You all had a best ass competition?"

Emree leans forward. "Oh, hell yeah. Jules, Blaire, and I spent one of their scrimmage games purely looking at all the teammates' butts to see who has the best."

Traz lets out a laugh. "And who came out on top?"

Jules wraps her arms around Levi. "Our very handsome goalie here won by a landslide. There wasn't even a competition because the moment we saw his bubble butt in those tight shorts as he did some squats, it was over."

The lumberjack's face turns a few shades red. "Can we be done with this and discuss what's going on with Trazia?" Levi leans forward and snags a bagel before slouching down onto the couch.

"Ah, yes." Em slaps her thigh and turns her attention to Trazia on the floor. "So we talked a little and came up with a couple options. I'll be honest, they aren't so great, but it's only three months."

"I'm open to anything that isn't me living in my car or having to leave the house at six in the morning for class," Traz replies with desperation in her voice.

"You may change your mind when you hear them." Emree laughs. "The first is staying with Blaire and me. It's only a two-bedroom and one-bath apartment, but our couch isn't the worst. Jules and her roommate, Piper, said they would be willing to offer their couch too, and they have two bathrooms."

Trazia smiles at the girls' generosity, but I can tell this isn't how she would want to live her first semester in college. She shouldn't have to bum it on someone's couch for over three months. She already has the stress of starting classes and taking on a much larger course load than in high school.

"There is a third option," I announce to the room.

Camden arches a brow. "What's that, man?"

Looking to Trazia, I offer a small smile. "Move in here."

Her eyes widen. "Wh-what? I can't move in here. It's athletic student housing, and you guys are pretty full here." She's right about the house being for athletic—specifically soccer—students. It's paid for by boosters.

"We have a small room downstairs that's barely a bedroom, but it's better than living in your car or someone's couch," I tell her with a shrug.

Traz looks at Camden with wide eyes. "This is crazy. I can't move in with you."

Camden runs a hand over his stubbled chin. "He's got a point, Traz. It's not permanent, and we have that room no one is officially using."

"Hell, I'm barely here as is. If Emree is okay with it, you can just take my room. It's already furnished," Conrad offers. *Bingo!* I smile to myself because that is the offer I was hoping he'd give. Trazia would be much more inclined to stay in an empty bedroom rather than having us fuss over creating one for her.

"Of course, baby," Emree coos.

Standing, I clap my hands together. "It's settled then. Lumberjack, put those strong arms and that nice ass to work and help unload the cars since you got off on packing duty this morning. Conny, clean those sheets for our new roomie. Who knows when the last time that area had a good sanitizing."

Conrad huffs, but he and Emree head upstairs to clean the

room and pack his shit. Levi, Mateo, Camden, and I go outside to get the boxes from the two cars.

"Shit, man, how much stuff does one girl need for school while she's barely an hour and a half away from home?" Levi asks when we open the trunks and he takes inventory.

"Apparently my sister needs a pair of shoes for each day of the month," Camden answers as he lifts a box from Trazia's car.

"Would you stop bitching about my shoes and just be grateful I didn't pack all my books?" Traz lectures from the front porch.

The four of us start removing boxes and bringing them up to Conrad's—now Trazia's—room and insist the girls focus on unpacking while we handle the lifting. Blaire says she has no issue with that as she snacks on another donut.

In no time, we have both vehicles unloaded. Conrad has his stuff packed in a few suitcases and moved everything he won't need at Emree and Blaire's to the small room downstairs so it's out of Trazia's way and she can set up the room however she wants it.

In a matter of hours, we lost a roommate and gained a new one. I can already tell this is going to be a hard three months for me.

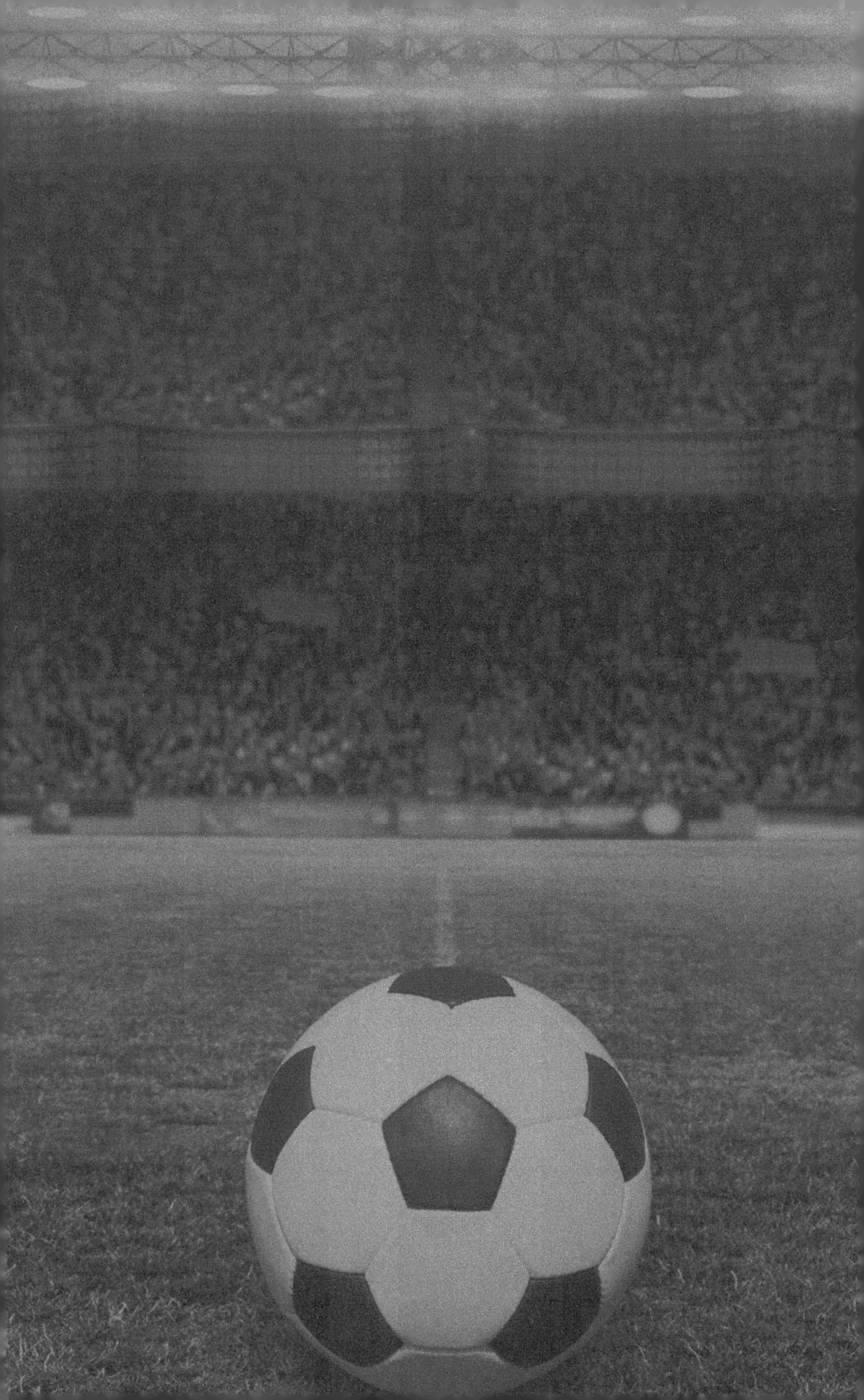

CHAPTER TEN

TRAZIA

Officially one day down of living with all boys. So far I have only had to put the toilet seat down twice and cleaned toothpaste splatter off the mirror once. I don't know what they're doing in there when they brush their teeth, but someone is going at it way too aggressively for there to be that much splatter.

Tonight we're having a family dinner, which is basically a night where everyone makes sure they aren't busy and the gang gets together for drinks and a meal at the house. From what Blaire tells me, it's hard to get everyone together with the guys' soccer practice, classes, and a variety of work schedules. Blaire and Emree are usually working nights at Whiskey Joe's, which is the college bar hangout I have yet to go to.

Trying on my third outfit, I let out a huff because these jean shorts don't fit either. I've always fluctuated with my weight, so I try to keep a few items in different size ranges. Right now, my normally loose pants are fighting to clasp in the front, just barely, but enough for me to be uncomfortable.

Pulling off the crop top and shorts, I stand in front of the long mirror Conrad has hanging on the back of his bedroom door. With the stress of graduation and starting college, I have put on a few pounds, and it is starting to show. My stomach is a bit bloated right now, and part of me wonders if that's because I'm sharing a bathroom with guys I've barely known—aside from Camden—and taking a number two makes me extremely nervous.

With none of the clothes working out, I decide on a flowy white lace dress that hits above my knee. It's stretchy and one of my favorite summer outfits. My long hair is in natural waves, and I decided to go with the makeup-free look with just a small bit of concealer and mascara.

Leaving the room, I bounce down the stairs on the balls of my bare feet and wander into the kitchen to find my brother and fellow roommates littered around. "Evening, boys," I greet them as I make my way to the kitchen table and join Mateo.

Usually Maddox is restricted from the kitchen, but he is currently seasoning what looks like chicken breasts. Beside him, Camden is draining some spaghetti in the sink, and Levi is chopping lettuce and other vegetables for a salad.

"Hope you are in the mood for some of Mom's famous fettuccine Alfredo because she sent over the recipe this morning and I'm pretty sure I perfected it," my brother tells me with a proud smile on his face.

"I'll be the judge of that."

Someone clears their throat rather loudly.

Camden rolls his eyes and points to Maddox. "Oh, and Mad here convinced us to let him back in the kitchen. He saw a video online on how to make Cajun chicken and would like for us to trust him and his cooking skills."

"Why, thank you, Cammy. I can hear the sincerity coming off your voice." Maddox is flipping the chicken strips just as the front door opens.

"Hello," Emree announces before coming into the kitchen.

"Oh, smells good in here. We come bearing alcohol." She holds up a case of hard seltzers, and the guys groan.

"Really? Chick drinks?" Mateo complains.

Emree glares at him. "I am in fact a chick, so yes. If you wanted something specific, you should have texted the group chat like Levi did. He got his weird stout."

"That's worse. I'll just stick with the Buds we have."

Conrad and Blaire come in behind Emree, and the moment Blaire spots Maddox in the kitchen, she stops in her tracks. "Oh no. Who let you cook?"

"I find that genuinely offensive, Blaire baby. You haven't even tried my cooking yet."

Blaire approaches the stove and looks at what Maddox is working on. "I don't mean to be harsh, but I've heard enough horror stories from the guys to know you shouldn't be in here."

Maddox puts his hand to his chest. "I have grown since then and watched videos on how to use the appropriate spice and not overcook food. Just look at this juicy chicken. Don't tell me your mouth isn't watering."

"It looks okay, though I'm still skeptical." She moves away and goes into the arms of my brother.

Emree and Conrad join Mateo and me at the kitchen table. "Is anyone else extremely nervous about eating whatever Mad cooks?"

I look at Emree and laugh. "He can't be that bad, can he?"

Conrad leans around her. "He can. Our first semester living together, he didn't know how to keep his area clean when prepping food and ended up giving Mateo and I salmonella because he didn't wash the cutting board after dicing the chicken to chop a salad."

"Let. It. Go," Maddox tells him.

Camden starts mixing the homemade sauce in with the pasta just as Jules shows up. Blaire and Levi work on setting up the table on the patio and each time I try to offer help, I'm shut down and told to enjoy a drink until dinner is ready.

Even though I haven't known most of these people that long, it's strange how much they feel like family. They are a tight group of friends but welcoming to newcomers almost automatically. None of them have ever made me feel like an outsider or left out of the group.

With the food ready, we all head outside to the large table set up. Camden said with their friend group growing, they've had to get another folded white table and set them up together. Now instead of six chairs fitting, they can comfortably seat twelve.

Everyone chooses their seat, and I end up in the corner with Blaire beside me and Mateo on the end. The food is in serving dishes in the center of the table. Camden fills his plate with pasta, and the dish gets passed around until everyone has a hearty helping of fettuccine Alfredo.

"Don't forget about the Cajun chicken, ladies and gents," Maddox announces as he puts a piece on his own plate.

No one voices their excitement to try his food. "Um, I'll give it a try."

He passes the plate down, and I look at the dark, spice-covered chicken. "I made sure not to over spice it since that was a complaint in the past from some who have bland taste."

Placing one small piece on my plate, I pass it to Mateo, who hands it right off to Emree. "Ugh, fine, I'll be brave and take one for the team."

She tries passing the plate off to Conrad, and he shakes his head. "I'm not touching that shit."

Everyone digs into their food, and I intentionally avoid the piece of meat that Maddox cooked. It doesn't look bad, but I'm nervous after hearing what happened in the past and how all the guys were quick to decline a piece. Deciding to suck it up, I cut the chicken and take my first bite.

"Well?" Maddox questions before I've had a chance to swallow.

"It's good," I tell him honestly. The seasoning isn't too much, and the chicken is cooked through.

Maddox looks around at the table. "Bite me, bitches. Your boy can cook now."

"Let's give it twenty-four hours to make sure the food actually stays down," my brother states just as I swallow my fourth bite.

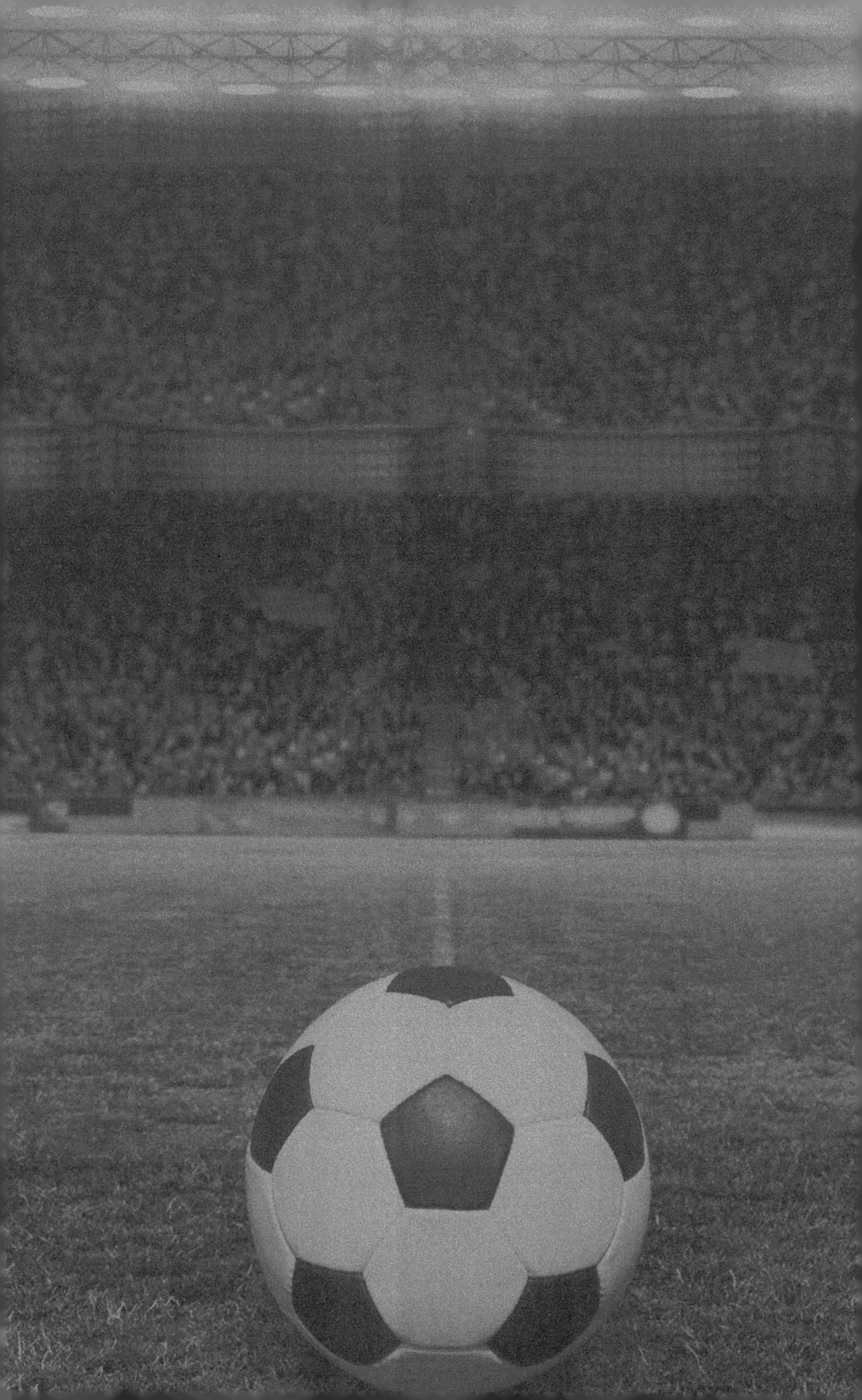

CHAPTER ELEVEN

TRAZIA

I should not have been a guinea pig for Maddox's kitchen comeback last night. With my head in the toilet, I groan after another wave of nausea hits me. Over the last few hours I have emptied everything that could possibly be in my stomach into the porcelain bowl. Judging by the fact that none of my other roommates have been in the bathroom tonight and they didn't consume Maddox's rancid chicken, I would say I'm the lucky one who caught a case of food poisoning.

"Trazia?" someone calls out as they knock on the closed door. "You in there?"

"Ugh, leave me be," I moan.

The door opens slowly, and Levi walks in wearing a pair of low-hanging sleep pants. "What the hell happened?" he asks after taking in my slumped-over position and pale face that has a layer of sweat on it.

"Maddox's—" I'm cut off by another round of stomach pain and gag into the toilet.

Levi leans against the doorframe and crosses his arms over his chest. "I feel like getting sick by Mad's cooking is some kind of initiation to becoming a roommate here."

Another moan comes out of me. "If that's the case, I want a do-over. Let me take up residency on Blaire and Emree's couch."

The large man chuckles. "Little too late. I'll be right back." He turns on his heel and heads down the hall.

Based on the sun coming out of the small bathroom window, I'm assuming it's morning and Levi probably has to get ready for work. With classes being over for them, Mateo is working his usual summer job as a lifeguard and will probably be up soon and need the bathroom to get ready.

A door closes, and I hear footsteps approaching. "Oh fuck."

Looking up, a shirtless Maddox is standing just inside the bathroom in nothing but a pair of boxer briefs. His grown-out hair has that *just woke up* look, and there is a red mark from his pillow on the side of his face.

Levi comes up behind him. "Mateo and I need to get ready for work, so since you created this, you're on sick girl duty." He looks at me and offers a small smile. "Sorry, Traz. I'll send Camden a text and let him know what's going on. Why don't we get you to Mad's bed since it's close to the bathroom?"

Both guys come forward, but Maddox puts his hand on Levi's chest. "I got her."

Bending at the knees, Maddox slides one arm under the back of my knees and the other around my torso. "Wrap your arms around my neck, Peach."

I do as he says, not having the energy to put up a fight right now.

Maddox walks the short distance down the hall to his bedroom. It's spacious, with a large window facing the front of the house. His walls are a medium gray, and there is an oversized TV mounted to the wall with a dresser beneath it. Across from that is an unmade king-size bed that looks plush and welcoming.

He places me on the side of the bed closest to the door

leading to the connected bathroom. Small waves of nausea are still passing through me, but I don't see how there is anything left to come up after the hours I spent in the bathroom.

Shutting my eyes, I sink into the memory foam pillow and mattress. A hand comes down on my clammy forehead.

"You're burning up," Maddox informs me as he pulls his hand away. "I'll go get some Tylenol and a drink. Anything in particular you want?"

Without opening my eyes, I answer him. "Ginger ale, maybe? Or a Gatorade?"

"I'll grab both." Before leaving, I feel the backs of his fingers run down the side of my face.

With the help of Maddox's blackout curtains and the comfort of his bed, I start to drift off to sleep for the first time since I got sick hours ago.

"Trazia, baby, you need to sit up and drink this," someone tells me as they nudge my hip. Squinting, I take in a now-clothed Maddox sitting on the edge of the bed beside me.

I groan and wrap my arms around my stomach. "No. Go away."

He lets out a soft chuckle. "No can do, sickie. I need you to take this because you're burning up. Got to get that fever down before anything else."

Reluctantly, I sit up. Each movement is like a stab to my gut. "Fine. Gimme, so I can go back to bed."

Maddox hands me the white pills and an orange Gatorade, and I down them as fast as possible. When I go to hand him the bottle back, he pushes my hand toward me. "Nope. Drink at least half of that. You're pale and dehydrated."

"Ugh, that's just going to make me vomit it up soon after."

He smiles and tucks a piece of damp hair behind my ear. "You'll be fine. I even put a trash can right here in case it happens, but I think the worst of it is over."

"If you say so," I mutter as I bring the bottle to my lips.

MADDOX COULD NOT HAVE BEEN MORE wrong. Two hours later, I'm struggling to keep my fever down, have constant chills, and have released whatever is left in my stomach into the trash and toilet twice.

"Man, I don't know what to do. She still has a fever of 101.5, and the pain in her stomach hasn't gone away. She isn't keeping down the meds I've given her," Maddox tells someone on the phone.

He pauses to listen to their reply. "Yes, you have already yelled at me for buying chicken on sale from a street vendor. I get that I fucked up, but what do I do about Traz?"

The person goes on for over a minute. "Okay, I'll take her. How are Blaire and Emree?"

He waits for a response. "Good, good. At least they're holding food down now. I'll get her to the hospital and let you know when she's got a room."

My eyes drift closed once again as Mad hangs up the phone. He comes to my side and pushes my hair back in the most tender way.

"Baby, I need to get you to the hospital. Do you want to change or wear your pajamas?" His voice is unlike anything I've heard from Maddox's mouth before. He's sweet and caring and sounds worried.

With a groan, I roll to my side. "I can't wear this. I'm covered in sweat."

He looks down at my sleep shorts and long-sleeve shirt. "Okay. Let's get you to your room and into something else."

With little effort on my end, we manage to make the walk down to my bedroom. Maddox sets me down on the bed and asks me to direct him to where the clothes are that I want to wear. Since it's the hospital, I want to be comfortable and warm. I settle on a pair of black leggings, a T-shirt, and a zip-up jacket.

With the clothing in hand, he comes over to me. "Um, do you think you can handle the rest?" He's so cute when he's nervous. I hate that he doesn't remember he's already seen me completely naked, but this moment is one that will stay with me.

Grabbing the pile from his hands, I smile up at him. "Thank you. I can take care of that part."

He nods and steps backward. "Okay, good. I'll be right outside the door if you feel dizzy or need anything."

The process is slow, but I manage to get the clothes on without falling over or calling him for help. I forgo a bra because I can't think of anything worse to wear when you're sick, and the one I've been wearing felt tight yesterday, leaving imprints in my skin where the band goes around me.

Slipping on my Crocs, I take the few steps from the bed to the bedroom door and open it. "I did it," I announce to him, slightly out of breath.

Maddox smiles at me and wraps his arm around my waist to provide support. Getting dressed drained me of the little amount of energy I had and I'm starting to feel dizzy again, but I'm afraid to tell him that.

"I grabbed the trash can from my room for the ride there in case you need it." He's holding the black, plastic bucket in the hand that's not supporting me.

We make our way downstairs, and Maddox slips his shoes on and grabs his keys while I get my purse off the hook by the front door. He helps me outside and into his lifted truck where I melt into the cushion right away.

Once Maddox is in the driver's seat, I speak up. "I think the hospital is a little excessive. We can just go to the student health center."

"That shithole? No way. The only reason anyone goes there is for free condoms and STD tests. You need fluids and other shit. Hospital is the best option."

Not having the energy to put up a fight, I switch the seat heater on and close my eyes as we drive through town.

The hospital isn't too far from the house, and within twenty minutes we are pulling into a spot in the emergency department. Without any need to use the trash can, might I add. I do think that Mad was driving a little more cautiously because of my queasiness.

"Wait there and I'll come around to the side to help you," he tells me after shutting the truck off.

Maddox keeps me secured in his arms as we walk through the parking lot. He sets me up in a chair in the waiting area while he heads to the front desk to talk to the woman there. After a few minutes, he comes back with some papers attached to a clipboard.

"She said it's a slow day, so they'll have a room available for you soon, but this paperwork needs to be filled out. I would like to mention that she also told me she's glad we came here instead of the student health center because with how sick you've been, you'll need fluids." He has a cocky *I told you so* look on his face that is too cute to be annoyed with.

"Shut up and give me the papers." I reach for the clipboard, but the movement causes a sharp pain in my abdomen, making me hiss out a breath.

"Fuck, what happened?" He sets the papers down on the empty seat beside him and puts one of his arms around my shoulders and the other on my thigh.

"My stomach," I wheeze out.

He begins rubbing my back. "Okay, just take deep breaths."

"I'm good. I think it's just in so much pain from, you know, all the throwing up," I try to joke.

Maddox's movements on my back become less soothing

and more…intimate as he starts rubbing my side also. "Shit, Peach, I'm really fucking sorry about this. I swear I'll never cook another thing in that kitchen. Not even toast."

Looking over at him, I take in the genuine worry etched on his face and the small bags under his eyes. "I don't think it was the cooking that was the problem. Maybe we avoid buying foods—especially meat—from street vendors from now on?"

He rubs his forehead. "He kept telling me how great locally sourced meat is and how much better it is for us because it's not full of all the shit they put in the large corporation chickens. I thought it would be a better choice, but looking back, he was keeping it in a cooler. That probably wasn't proper storage."

Oh, poor, sweet Maddox. He may have a heart of gold, but common sense is not always there. He grew up having someone cook all his meals and take care of him on a regular basis, so it's hard to blame him for having zero home skills.

"Let's get these papers filled out so we can get out of here," I tell him with a smile.

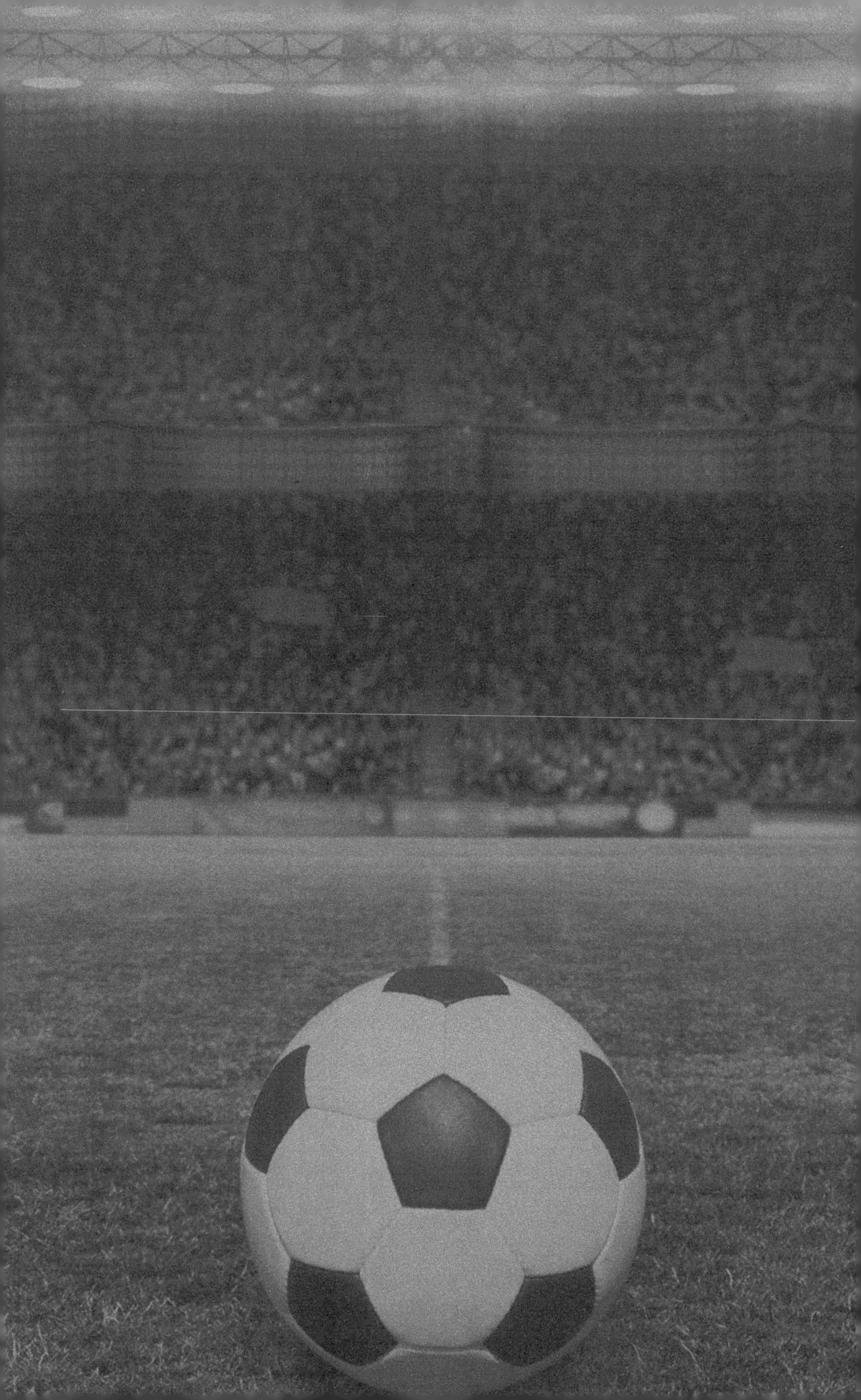

CHAPTER TWELVE

TRAZIA

Finally in a hospital room and hooked up to an IV that is filling me with the fluids my body so desperately needs, I start to feel better already. The doctor came in to run some vitals and take tests, which included a urine sample that was more difficult given how dehydrated I was.

She confirmed it's a bad case of food poisoning but assured me I was on the mend. Her biggest worry was the dehydration, which the fluids are going to be helping with.

Maddox hasn't left my side since we got here. He even helped me into the bathroom after I assured him I was feeling more balanced than I was when we were at home. He is currently in the uncomfortable wooden chair with his elbows propped up on his thighs and his head resting in the palms of his hands.

A knock comes from the door, followed by someone calling my name. Camden peeks his head in just as Maddox lifts his. "Hey, little sister." He greets me with a bright smile as he comes to my side and kisses the top of my head.

"What are you doing here? How's Blaire?" I ask.

He sits at the end of my hospital bed and faces me. "She's a lot better than you, that's for sure. She and Em are cozied up on the couch watching *Love Is Blind*. Conrad got them homemade soup from Mom and some crackers and drinks from the store. Blaire assured me she's good and told me to come here. Maybe relieve Mad of his duties."

My stomach clenches, but for a different reason this time. I've liked having Maddox here with me. Taking care of me and being there when I need him. I love my brother, but I don't want to lose that.

"Nah, man, I'm good here," Maddox voices. I can tell he is tired, but selfishly I don't want him to go.

Camden nods at his best friend and turns his attention back to me. "How're you feeling? Did they give you any good drugs?"

A small laugh escapes me, but I try not to move too much. "No drugs yet, but these fluids are helping a lot already. The doc was worried about how sick I was and the dehydration. She said even when I get home to drink a lot of Gatorade."

"Knock, knock," someone announces rather than knocking on the door. Dr. Patel walks in with a bright smile and a clipboard in her hands. "Oh, I see we have another visitor."

"Hi, yes, this is my brother, Camden," I inform her.

She looks between the two guys. "You sure do have a good support system. I love seeing that, especially with students who are away from home."

"I'm pretty grateful."

Dr. Patel looks down at my records and back up with a more serious face. "I do have something I need to discuss with you. If you would be more comfortable, we can talk about it alone."

"Oh, um. I mean, they're going to find out anyway. I'm okay discussing it with them in the room." I can't think of anything she would have to tell me that would be serious enough for my brother and Maddox to have to leave the room. Maybe I have a tapeworm or something from the vendor chicken.

Her eyebrows pinch together. "Miss Collins, I had to run a pregnancy test before I could prescribe you any kind of antibiotics. It came back positive. You're pregnant, honey."

All the air leaves my lungs. "Excuse me?" The room starts to spin as I try to catch my breath. Then everything turns black.

MADDOX

"I'll fucking kill him. I'm going to strangle whatever limp dick touched my little sister." Camden is on a rampage in the hospital emergency room hallway. Dr. Patel asked us to leave after Trazia passed out from the news. Since then, I have been trying to calm my best friend down while also attempting to process the fact that the girl who lives rent-free in my mind is having another man's baby.

"Dude, you need to chill out. Going in there all hot and ready to knock someone out isn't going to help her."

Camden tugs at the ends of his hair and turns to me. "She's barely graduated from high school, Mad. Now she's going to be a mother. How the hell is she going to handle that? This is going to ruin her future. She'll have to drop out of school, move back in with my mom, and get some basic-ass job just to pay the bills. That isn't the life she's meant to have."

He might be right, but this doesn't have to be the end of Trazia's dreams. "Let's just focus on one thing at a time. First, we need her to process the fact that she is carrying a baby now. I'm sure she is freaking the fuck out. Then we can move on to the other shit."

One of the nurses who went in to assist Dr. Patel comes out. "She's awake now. She's asking for you."

Camden begins to walk toward the door, but she holds her hand up. "Oh sorry, I meant him." She points to me. "She is going to need some rest and to stick with a bland diet and make sure she gets enough fluids in. Maybe try some Pedialyte as well as Gatorade."

Nodding, I take mental notes for later. "Got it. I'll make a grocery store run when we're back home."

"I will send a prescription for prenatal vitamins as well. She gave me the information for your pharmacy." Dr. Patel drops the clipboard with Trazia's records into a box outside her door and heads down the hall to the nurses' station.

Camden is looking at me dumbfounded. "Why the hell would she not want me in there and ask for you?"

Honestly, I can't answer that for him. I'm surprised she wouldn't want her big brother. "Maybe she's worried about disappointing you."

His face softens, and he sinks down against the wall and onto the floor. "Man, I don't want her thinking that. I'm just... I'm worried about her, Mad. She has this incredible future ahead of her."

"She can still have that, but if you go in there telling her that her future is basically over, she's going to believe she can't do it. You need to support her, not be the one who is going to drag her down. Society will do that enough seeing she's a young mom."

He nods. "You're right. Hey, and thanks for being here. I know you didn't have to stay and take care of her, but I really appreciate it."

"I did kind of cause the food poisoning," I say with a shrug.

"True," he laughs. "It's nice knowing she has someone like a brother around when I can't be. Thanks for taking care of her."

"Brother. Right." I'm not sure what else to say to him because the thoughts and fantasies I have about Trazia Collins are anything but *brotherly*.

Camden stands and brushes off his jeans. "Go on in and see how she is. I'm going to walk to the cafeteria and get a coffee to cool off. You want anything?"

I think about how Traz can't eat or drink much right now and don't want to do so in front of her. "I'm good. Thanks."

He wanders off down the hall and around the corner.

Taking a deep breath, I push open her room door and take in the scene in front of me. Traz has her shirt lifted up and is rubbing her flat stomach while she stares at it.

The moment she hears the door squeak, she looks up. "Oh, hi." Gripping the bottom of her shirt, she pulls it down.

"Hey, Peach." I go around her bed and sink down into the chair I was occupying earlier. "How're you doing?"

She offers a weak smile. "Oh, you know, recovering from puking my guts out and discovering I've been carrying a baby for over two months now and how dumb I am to not even notice I haven't had a period in that time."

"I heard something about that." She continues to stare at me as if she is waiting for me to say more. "Do you, um, know what you're going to end up doing?"

Ducking her head, she shakes it. "Not exactly. Dr. Patel gave me some information for places that can help. She said with the new laws, I still have time if I want to…end it, or there are adoption options. If I wanted to keep the baby, she said she would recommend a few doctors in the area I would like."

My head starts to spin with all the information, and I'm not even the one having to make a final decision. "That's great she's given you the information you need. And you know you have a support system at home. I mean, if you want to keep the baby. We would all be there for you."

"Is Camden angry?" she whispers.

"He's worried more than anything. You're young and are just starting college. He doesn't want this to mess that up." I debate mentioning the father, but better me than Camden. "He also wants to murder whoever the father is. Do you…know who it is?"

Trazia slowly turns her head in my direction. Her eyes begin filling with tears as she stares at me with an almost pleading, desperate look. "I can't believe you're asking me that," she tells me, barely above a whisper.

Sitting up straighter, I hold up both hands. "Whoa, I'm not slut-shaming or anything. Really, I'm not one to talk in that department. Just a question with no meaning behind it."

She wipes away the tears that escaped. "I know who it is." Her voice cracks at the end.

"Are you going to tell him?" The question is out of my mouth before I think better of it.

Traz drops her head back to rest on the pillow behind her. "I really need you to stop asking me questions about the father. I don't even know if I'm keeping the baby."

For some reason that statement has my chest clenching. Being a single, young mom has got to be really fucking hard, but I don't see Trazia easily making the decision not to keep her child. She loves kids and wants to dedicate herself to working with them.

Reaching forward, I clasp her hand in mine. "I'm sorry. I won't bring it up again. Just know we're all going to be there for you. Especially Camden. Can you imagine him as an uncle?"

Her smile is small, but at least the tears have stopped.

The cracked door begins to widen, and Camden appears in the doorway with a hot coffee cup in hand. "Hey, Trazzy."

She sniffles. "Hey, Cammy."

He comes to her side, and the moment his arms are wrapped around her shoulders, the floodgates let loose. Deciding to give them some privacy, I step out of the room and lean against the wall in the hallway.

Being away from her helps me to digest the news. Trazia is

having a baby. With some other man. Fuck, I can't stand the thought of some needle dick touching her. She deserves someone who cares about what an amazing person she is rather than a chick to get into bed. Clearly she hasn't been dating this guy because he wasn't there to move all her shit the other day.

Whoever he is, I hope he steps up and realizes a kid needs both parents and doesn't leave her to sacrifice herself for their child.

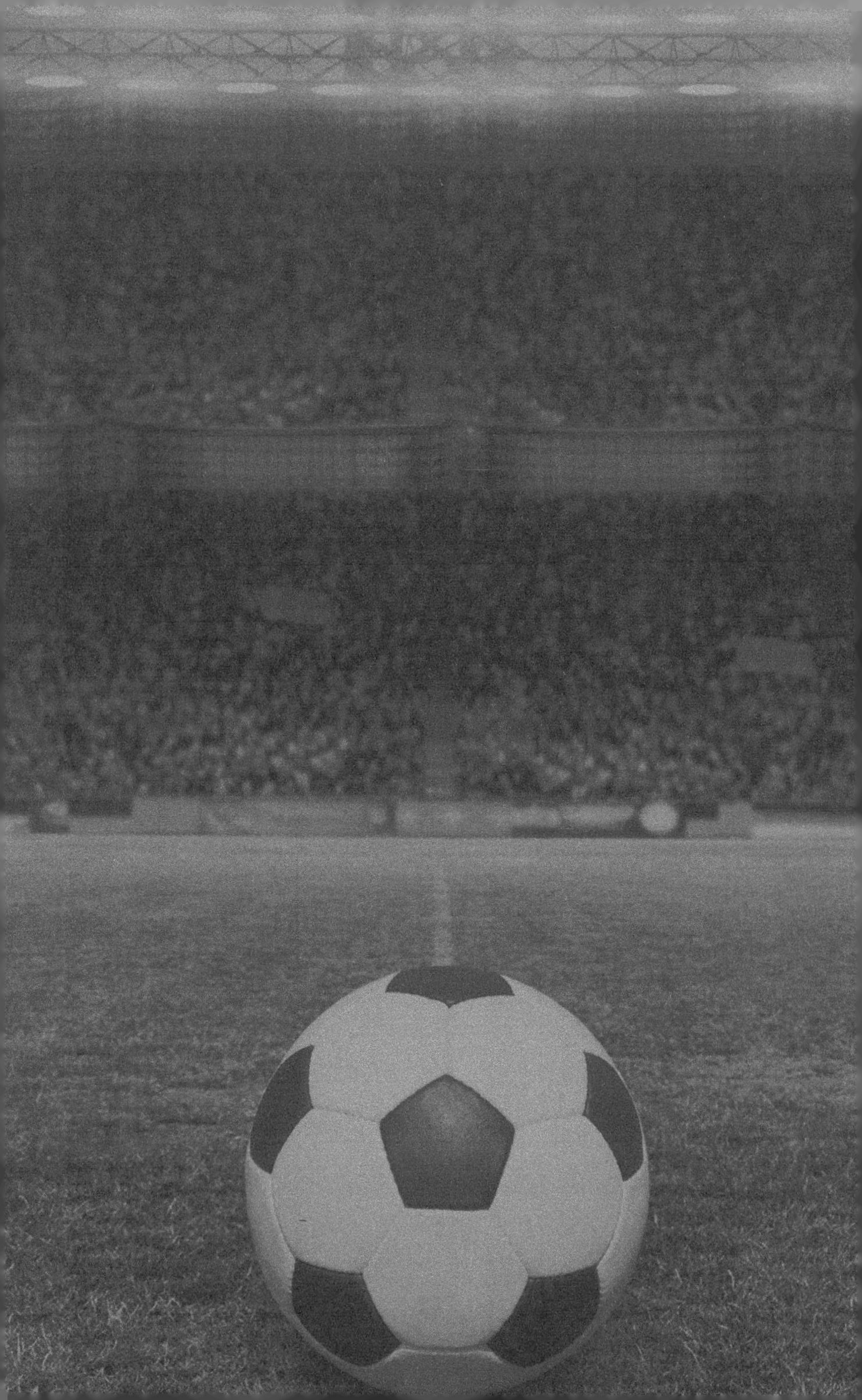

CHAPTER THIRTEEN

TRAZIA

I've worried my lip raw. Since coming home from the hospital, I have felt sick, but for a different reason. I have a tiny human growing inside me. One that was created out of a drunken bathroom hookup where the dad doesn't even remember. And I'm living under the same roof as that man.

I feel like I can't even write this shit up.

The moment Maddox asked me if I knew who the father was, I wanted to scream at him to remember our time together two months ago. I wanted to beg and plead with him to rattle that brain and come up with even just the slightest bit of memory from that night. But I didn't, and he hasn't.

All day, I have been weighing out my options. Camden had Maddox drive me home since his Jeep is a little jerkier than the truck. My caring brother went to the store and bought the standard sick person's essentials. Since getting back, I have kept down a can of chicken noodle soup and some saltine crackers. I've stuck with Gatorade for now.

Sitting alone in my room has given me the time to think about my future and the best decision for myself. I'm not opposed to abortion or adoption but know that those are not the routes my life is meant to go. I can raise this baby, alone or not. It may not be how the start of my freshman year of college was supposed to go, but what is life without a few detours? If I have to drop a class or two and not take a full course load once the baby is here, that is always an option. My mom raised two kids on her own. I can handle one.

With that decision made, I have two more hard things to do. One is telling my mom, and the other is figuring out how to tell Maddox. I almost blurted it out several times on the drive home. That would have probably caused an accident, though.

Telling my mom will be difficult, but nowhere near how hard it is going to be for me to drop this bomb on Mad. Not only am I telling him that he is about to become a father, but that we had drunken sex and he doesn't remember. I'm not sure what he—and everyone else—will think of me after that. The fact that I have kept this from him for over two months makes me feel like a horrible person.

The IV fluids from the hospital have been flowing through me, and I get up—once again—to use the bathroom. On my way, I hear voices from Mateo's room.

"Fuck, man, could you imagine? A kid while in college. How does anyone handle that?" Maddox asks.

Stopping before the doorframe, I lean in a little to listen. "Not sure. It's got to be hard, but there are several students who do it."

"There's no way I could. Shit, just thinking about it has me stressed. I'd bail. Having a kid that young is too much."

A noise escapes me, and I throw a hand over my mouth to stop any more from coming out. Before they can catch me, I turn and head back into my room.

Once under the safety of my covers, I let out the sob that has been trying to get free. The tears follow as I cry into my pillow, trying to muffle my sounds.

Hearing the man whose baby I am carrying say that he

would bail has my heart hurting. How could he abandon his own child? How could any parent create life and then leave it? A child doesn't choose to be born. That is the choice of the ones who created them.

My father chose a woman over his kids and wife. He chose a new life and abandoned us. Abandoned me.

Sliding my hands down to my stomach, I hold my midsection in a defensive way. I could never do that to my little bean. No matter how they were created, I will love and protect them no matter what. They will never live a day wondering if their mom loves them or not.

Maddox's words have me second-guessing telling him. What if he wants nothing to do with this baby and I have to explain to my child for the rest of their life that their dad didn't want them? What if he decides to be there for them and then up and leaves like my dad did?

The confession he made to Mateo shows me that Maddox Stone is not ready for this, and I will be damned if my child's heart gets broken like mine did as a kid.

A soft knock sounds from my door. "Trazia, are you awake?" Blaire's sweet voice comes through the thick wood.

My tears have dried, but I am sure my eyes are puffy and red. Flipping my pillow so she doesn't see the tearstains, I call her in.

Blaire looks exhausted and is wearing her pajamas. With the night she, Emree, and I have had, I completely understand. The moment we got home, I changed out of the leggings and T-shirt and into sleep shorts and one of Camden's old high school soccer shirts.

She comes into the room and shuts the door. "Hey, girl. How are you feeling?" The bed dips as she sits beside me and leans against the headboard.

"I've been better," I tell her honestly. I'm assuming Camden told her the news, and that saves me from having another person to share it with.

Blaire and I have gotten close over the last eight months she and my brother have been dating. It feels longer, if I'm being honest. She and I clicked from the beginning and it's been amazing having her as a friend. Blaire is shy and quiet, and I can somewhat relate to that. I prefer a night in with my favorite book or a nice campfire with friends rather than a large crowd. I didn't have a lot of friends in high school, and Blaire has quickly become the closest thing to a best friend I have had.

She reaches over and grabs my hand. "Whatever you decide, I just want you to know that Camden and I are going to be there for you no matter what. If we need to come up with a schedule during classes, we will do that. Or if you need someone to be beside you if you decide not to go through with this, I'm here for you then too. No matter what, Tra."

My eyes begin to fill with unshed tears. "I'm keeping it," I whisper to her.

She squeezes my hand. "Then a schedule it is."

No other words are needed. Blaire scoots down on the bed so that we are side by side and continues holding my hand. Knowing I have people around me who are going to be supportive means more than anything. No matter what, I know Little Bean and I will be cared for by my friends and family.

"Whatever you do, don't let Camden convince you to name the baby something soccer-related. I could see him trying to make Beckham or Lionel a name. My future niece or nephew can't go through life getting picked on for having a weird name."

I'm grateful to Blaire for making me laugh for the first time today. "Trust me, as someone who grew up with a unique name, I would never do that to my child."

"It is kind of funny how Camden got a semi-common name and your mom just went off the charts with yours. At least you didn't have three girls with the same name as you in all your classes growing up," she laughs.

Rolling onto my side, I smile at Blaire. "That's true. I can't imagine how strange that must have felt. I'll make sure not to give Little Bean a basic name like John or Samantha but will stay away from creating a new one."

A knock comes from the other side of the room. Camden appears with a smile and ginger ale in hand. "Brought you a drink. How're you feeling?" He enters the room and places the can on the nightstand before taking a seat on the desk chair.

Sitting up, I lean against the headboard to face him. "I haven't thrown up since getting home, so that's a good sign. Other than the baby thing, everything is gravy."

Camden tries to hide it, but his smile pops out. "Already cracking jokes about it. You sound like Maddox."

My ears tingle at the mention of him. "Mad? How is he? Kind of a crazy day for him too."

"He's sort of in shock about you being pregnant like I am. Come on, Tra, how did this happen? And who the fuck with?" Serious big brother Camden was bound to come out sooner or later. I figured I would have had a few days to digest the news before more questions were thrown at me.

Taking a deep breath, I lift my shoulders. "It was a drunken, sloppy hookup that I may not be proud of but do not regret. I will never regret this baby, Camden. I am going to love them unconditionally and be the best mom, just like ours was." His face softens. "I know I'm young, and I know this was irresponsible. What I don't want is for this baby to ever think they were a mistake or feel unloved."

My brother stares at me for several seconds before dropping his head. "I get it, Trazia. We had a shit dad growing up, and I don't ever want my niece or nephew to feel like that." He lifts his head to look into my eyes. "Tell me what I can do to help and I'm there."

Nibbling on my bottom lip, I try to think of the best way to bring this up. "Well, would you mind coming with me to tell Mom this weekend?"

He smiles and nods. "You got it, baby sis."

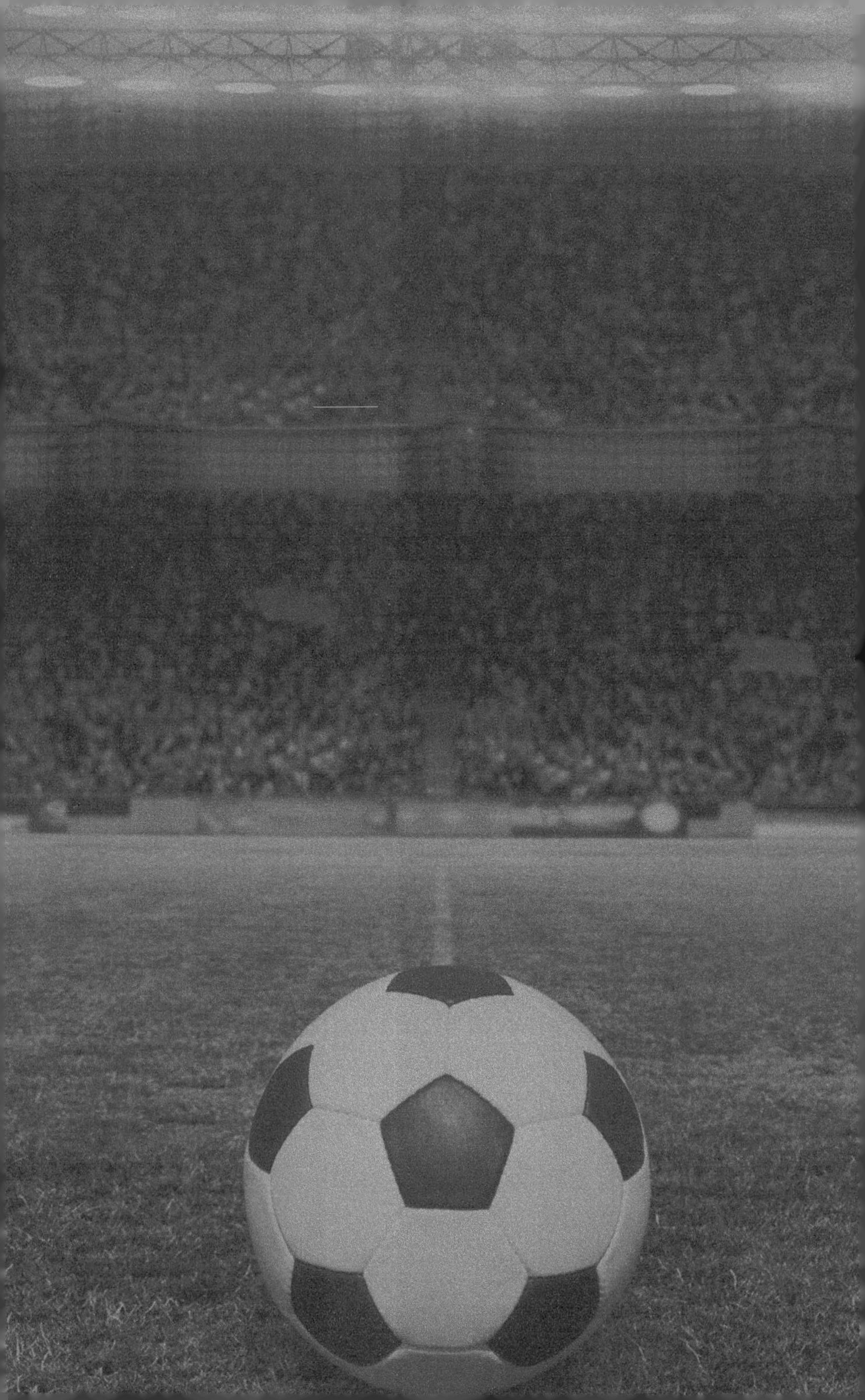

CHAPTER FOURTEEN

MADDOX

With Trazia living at the house and being pregnant now, I had to do a few Google searches about pregnancies. It's not like we smoke in the house or are putting fresh paint in her room, but I've never been around a pregnant chick long enough to know what they can and can't do or eat.

One of the biggest things I read online is that her temperature is going to fluctuate more now. I made sure we had throw blankets in the living room in case she got cold. We usually keep the thermostat low seeing as it's constantly sweltering in Florida, and personally, I run hot.

Another thing I read was that pregnant women love to snack. Makes sense since they're growing a human and all. Trazia hasn't lived here long, so the kitchen isn't stocked with the things she likes yet. I know money is also something she is going to worry about. While at the hospital, Traz did tell me she applied for jobs at two daycares in the area and has enough money from her high school job for a month or two, but she wanted to get to working as soon as she could.

She slept in late this morning. Probably still recovering from everything yesterday. I ran out to the store and got everything I would want to eat after smoking our stash of joints during the off-season.

The kitchen counters are covered in whole grain cereals, Pop-Tarts, a variety of candies, yogurts—because I read online that's good for pregnant women also—more eggs to make sure she gets enough protein, and chocolate milk. I also grabbed a large jar of peanut butter because I saw in some movie that women crave weird things when they're pregnant, and it's common to mix stuff with peanut butter.

Just as I unload the last grocery bag, our resident mama comes walking in. Her eyes are still filled with sleep, and her hair has seen better days. She pauses at the threshold as she takes in all the new items.

"What's all this?" she asks, her voice groggy.

Waving my hand in front of the cornucopia I've put together, I smile. "Well, little mama, I did some internet searching last night, and it seems pregnant women need to stick with certain foods and will go through moments of cravings and snacking. I have provided you with enough substance for now. If you are having a sweet tooth, there are some candies over here," I tell her as I point to a bowl with different chocolate bars and sweets. "I also got some whole grain cereals and yogurt because, I guess those are things you're supposed to eat. Oh, and Pop-Tarts, because who doesn't love those?"

As I'm rambling off all the items I bought, Trazia stares at me in disbelief. Her eyes begin to glisten. "Hey now, what's wrong?"

She shakes her head and holds a hand out as I come closer to her. "Nothing. Just…it's just hormones. Thank you for all of this, Maddox. I can't believe you researched pregnancy."

I offer a shrug. "It wasn't much. I looked up porn after if you want to thank me for that too." I wink at her, and she throws her head back, laughing.

"Of course you did."

"Hey, sex creates life. Why is it okay for me to look up the baking process and not the preparation?"

She moves around me and straight for the Pop-Tarts. "You know, I should be shocked when things like that come out of someone's mouth, but why is it I'm already immune to the ridiculousness you say?"

I watch as she unwraps the pastries and puts them into the toaster. "It's because you're one of the few people who seem to get me."

She turns and stares into my eyes. Something flashes through my mind. A memory? A dream? Her wearing nothing but a towel and those clear green eyes looking back at me with lust and need. I shake my head, trying not to get a boner in the middle of the kitchen.

"You're right, Mad." Trazia's voice is soft yet husky. "I do get you."

There is something more to what she is saying, but before I can ask her, the toaster pops out her breakfast.

She places them on a paper towel and makes her way to the kitchen table. I follow her with the coffee I picked up on the way home. Another thing she is limited to now that she is with child. The list is long and includes things I would have never thought of. We have the obvious like alcohol and cigarettes, but then there is soft cheese and raw bean sprouts. When the fuck did those two become dangerous?

Traz takes a seat and I follow suit, sitting at the end of the long table near her. "I know it's early and you've only had a day to digest this, but do you know what you're going to do?"

She breaks apart her breakfast. "I'm keeping it. Beyond that, I don't know what I'm doing."

"Do you think you'll stay in school?" The question comes out of my mouth before I can think better of asking it.

After finishing the piece of food in her mouth, Trazia looks up at me. "Honestly? I have no idea. I desperately want to get my degree, but doing it with a baby? Is that even possible?"

"Out of everyone in our friend group, I'd put my money on you being able to do it. Mateo and I are clearly out because there is no way anyone would trust us with a baby. Your brother and Blaire, maybe. Same goes for Conny and Blondie. Jules is too much of a prude to do the nasty to create a kid. But you? You have more determination than any of us. Plus, you like kids and want to make that your career. You'd rock this whole mom thing."

With a soft smile on her face, she stares at me. "You have no idea how much that means to me, Mad. I've always wanted to be a mom, though I thought it would be later in life and with my husband."

"Who knows. Maybe baby daddy could be the guy." Even as I say the words, I hate the thought. It's already hard enough thinking about Trazia having a baby with some guy. Thinking of him seeing her naked and being inside her. It shouldn't fuck with my head like it does because she isn't mine, but sometimes I feel like she is.

Her smile turns down. "Maddox, there's actually—"

"Morning, roomies." Mateo cuts her off as he walks into the kitchen. He's wearing nothing but a pair of boxer shorts.

"Put on some clothes, you animal. There is a lady present."

He turns to me after grabbing the orange juice from the fridge. "You're one to talk. Haven't all the girls in our group seen you buck naked?"

Not this again. "It's not my fault if someone sees my ass when I am in the comfort of my own room and they walk in. Blaire should've waited for the other bathroom."

Mateo crosses his arms over his chest. "What about when you went down early in the morning for water and Jules got a full-frontal view?"

Trazia's eyes widen. "You just walk around here naked like that?"

"Well, obviously not anymore."

Mateo tips his glass in my direction. "Don't call me out when you're much worse. Hell, even Tra has seen that pale ass."

She snaps her head in his direction. "What? I haven't seen Maddox naked."

"Um, yeah. Remember the collision in the hallway at the beach house?" he asks with an eyebrow raised.

She lets out a deep breath. "Oh yeah, that. I did see your butt then."

Just then, Camden walks in and looks at the three of us with suspicion. "Why're you all talking about butts?"

Mateo, Trazia, and I all look at each other and bust out laughing. It feels good to have a moment like this with all the seriousness going on in our world.

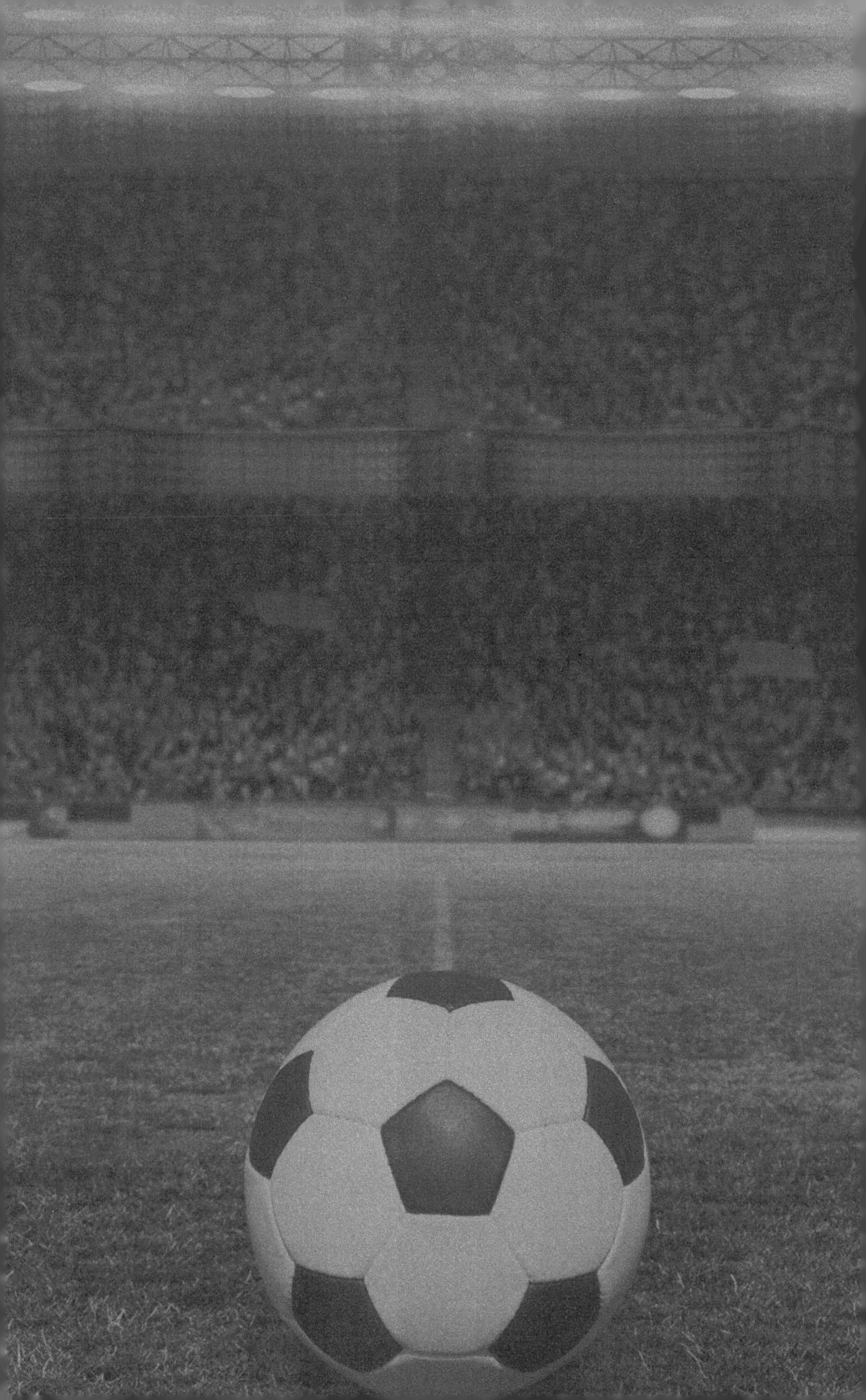

CHAPTER FIFTEEN

TRAZIA

The house I grew up in has always felt like the warmest home to me. There was never a time in my life that I would rather be out with my friends or stay the night at someone's house over being home. It took my mom a lot of work to create a place where we were safe, loved, and cared for in the way she wanted us to be.

After my dad left, my mom had no money to put into a new home like she would have wanted to. My dad spent all the money he had on his new girlfriend. Anything she wanted, he bought for her. She got a new, expensive car, plastic surgery, the fanciest of clothes, and pricey jewelry. My mom didn't want anything after he left because by taking child support from him, she would have to share custody. She would rather work several jobs to take care of us than take a cent from him and force us to spend any amount of time with him.

At this moment, as I sit in the front seat of Camden's Jeep, staring at the front of the house, I have a belly full of nerves. It's Saturday and Mom has the day off, so we decided to do a family dinner. I asked Blaire to come with us since she is basically family now, but it may also help Mom keep her cool if we have a special guest.

"You know we're going to have to get out of the car eventually?" my brother asks. We've been sitting here for more than five minutes already.

Blaire softly smacks his upper arm. "Leave her be. She's building up courage."

Courage. That is the opposite of what I have. The reality is, I'm a young girl afraid of failing and disappointing those around her. I can't even tell the father of my baby that we had sex and he's going to be a dad now.

I almost broke down and told him everything at breakfast a couple days ago, but was saved when Mateo walked into the kitchen. The longer I go without telling Maddox, the more in my head I get. Now I can't stop thinking about how this could ruin his life. He's only twenty-one, and clearly a baby was not in the cards for him this early on.

Telling my mom is next on the list of things I need to do, and today is the day. I'm ten weeks pregnant now. I don't know when women start showing, but I'd rather not have my mom find out by seeing a belly versus her only daughter telling her.

Taking a deep breath, I hold it in before releasing it slowly through my nose. "Okay. Let's do this."

Camden mumbles under his breath, something that sounds like *finally*, but I ignore him and focus on the task at hand.

The three of us make it up the walkway. I stay behind the couple, needing the extra coverage before seeing Mom.

Camden opens the front door without knocking. "Mama, where you at?"

Our beautiful mother pops her head around the corner in the kitchen. "My babies are here," she says as she comes over to hug each of us. At the mention of babies, I stumble in my tracks, but right myself before anyone can notice.

She holds Camden and Blaire for uncomfortably long hugs

before coming to me. Arms out as she walks in my direction, Mom has a wide smile on her face as she pulls me in. Once in the embrace of the woman who gave up everything to raise my brother and me, a sense of relief washes over me. I've been terrified to tell her about the baby, but I know deep down my mom would never judge or lecture me about this. She's always been supportive and loving, and this wouldn't be any different.

"It's been quiet around here without you, baby girl," she whispers in my ear.

I squeeze her just a little tighter. "I've missed you too, Mama."

She pulls back, and her eyes are glossy. "Enough of that. I made stuffed chicken and rice pilaf. Come eat." She wraps her arm around my waist and guides us into the kitchen.

Camden helps her carry the heavy dish over while Blaire and I take a seat at the table. My mom's stuffed chicken is a favorite of mine. She creates a mixture of goat cheese, spinach, and a little bit of feta mixed with spices and jams it all into the chicken breasts. It comes out flavorful and gooey.

Once everyone is at the table, we dig into the chicken, rice, and salad Mom made.

"This all looks and smells delicious, Claire," Blaire tells my mom as she scoops some more rice onto her plate.

Mom smiles around a mouthful of salad. "Thank you, sweetie. I'm glad you three are getting a nice, home-cooked meal. After the food poisoning incident earlier this week, I'm concerned for my babies over at that house." Camden ended up calling Mom to get advice on how to take care of Blaire and me. She told him the same thing the doctor at the hospital said, but he felt better hearing it from our mom.

"Trust me, we're going to keep Maddox away from anything kitchen-related." My brother laughs.

I smile, thinking about the groceries Maddox went out and bought for me. I didn't end up seeing him yesterday, but I enjoyed a nice bowl of cereal he got me before heading to the two daycares I applied at to introduce myself. Maddox and my brother started their summer jobs as lifeguards at a beach nearby. They got the jobs after a glowing reference from Mateo, who has been doing it since he was a freshman, and works a few days a week.

We scarf down our meals while we talk here and there. Blaire tells Mom about the paid internship she was offered for spring semester at a youth program where she would be providing after-school tutoring to kids struggling with math. Teaching math has been what Blaire has wanted to do for a while now, and this gives her firsthand experience to prepare her. She's been a great help with guiding me through starting classes since she took similar ones for her education degree, although mine are more specific to elementary rather than mathematics.

"That was one of your best dishes yet, Ma," Camden tells her as he leans back in his chair and links his fingers behind his head. "I'm going to need to add another training session after that one."

We all laugh because a large meal isn't going to do much to Camden's physique.

"It was delicious." After finishing the last bite, I grab my plate and Camden's empty one. "I'll do the dishes since you cooked and Camden helped serve."

Blaire jumps up to grab the other empty plates. "We'll do them together."

As we wash and dry the plates, Mom puts on a pot of coffee before she and Camden retreat to the living room.

After looking behind us to check where they are, Blaire leans over and whispers in my ear. "You plan on doing it during coffee?"

I nod. "I feel like after a full stomach, maybe she'll take the news better."

"We should have brought a dessert or something. Sweets make everyone happy."

I laugh and get back to my cleaning duties.

Once the leftovers are put away, the dishes are cleaned and dried, and four cups of coffee are prepared, Blaire and I carry the hot mugs into the living room and place them on the table in front of the sofa.

I take a seat in the single sofa chair while Blaire joins Mom and Camden on the larger one.

Taking a much-needed breath to prepare myself, I release it and try to steady my shaking hands. "Ma, there was actually something I wanted to tell you. Something I found out recently."

She looks at me with caution in her eyes as she brings the mug down from her lips. "I have to say, sweetie, you've hit me with a few curveballs this last week. First, not moving into a dorm like you were supposed to, and then moving in with your brother and his friends. What more could there be?"

I turn to my brother for help. He sets his mug down and faces our mom. "Actually, Mom, when we were at the hospital, they gave us some other news. I mean, more than Tra being hella dehydrated."

Mom looks worried. "What do you mean? Did they find something? Are you okay, honey?"

"Mama," I whisper. "I'm pregnant."

She stares at me with wide eyes, and I'm worried she is going to drop her cup of coffee. I wait for her to say something as her mouth opens and closes several times, but no words come out.

"Ma, I'm getting nervous. Please say something." Camden's voice is filled with worry.

My mom sacrificed everything for me, and I don't know if I can handle disappointing her. The years of hard work and scary times were to see her children succeed. My brother and I were meant for bigger things, but I ended up in a much similar situation that my mom was in when she was just a couple years older than me.

Mom stands and comes to me, holding my face between her two hands. "I love you, sweetheart." She kisses me on the cheek before squatting down and taking my hands in hers. "This is a scary time and you are very young, but I know that no matter what, you will make the most wonderful mother."

The dam breaks, and tears are streaming down my face faster than I can blink them away. Wrapping her arms around my shoulders, Mom pulls me into a hug that has me struggling for breath.

"I'm so-sorry," I manage to stutter out, my voice clogged because of all the emotions.

She pulls back and looks into my eyes. "Sorry? For what?"

"For making such a big mistake. I swear, Mom, I never meant for this to happen."

"Oh, sweetie." She caresses the side of my face and wipes away the tears. "I had your brother young, so you know I have firsthand experience of how hard it was, but that doesn't mean he was a mistake, and neither is your baby."

I sniffle. "You're not mad?"

She smiles and shakes her head, looking to my brother and Blaire and then back to me. "Is that what you all thought? I wouldn't say I'm jumping up for joy, seeing as how you're just starting college and—as far as I know—you're not in a relationship, but I could never be mad at you for something like this."

Camden shrugs. "I mean, most parents wouldn't be too happy and would go on to lecturing their kid about how this will ruin their life. Not really sure what I was prepared for here."

Mom stands and goes back to her seat beside my brother while I get rid of the last few tears. "You two know me better than that. There is no use in pointing out someone's life choices. All we can do is prepare for what is to come and create a plan. First things first, I'm assuming since you've made this announcement that you're keeping the baby?"

"Yes," I tell her while nodding.

She smiles. "All right. And have you thought much about school? Do you plan to continue, or do you want to move back here? Get a job instead?"

Looking down, I focus on picking at my fingernails. "I want to stay in school." I lift my head. "There are a couple of daycares near campus that are hiring, and I applied to them and went to introduce myself yesterday. They're going to review my résumé and contact me."

"Good, good. And where would you live? I don't imagine the dorms would allow a baby in there."

Crap. I hadn't thought about that yet. The single dorms aren't part of my budget, and living in an off-campus apartment is out of the question.

"Actually, I have an answer for that one," my brother chimes in. "I talked with the guys, and as long as you're okay with it, you can stay with us until we graduate. We'll still list Conrad as a resident, but he would continue living with Emree and Blaire. Maddox even said he would give up the large bedroom with the private bathroom."

The tears show up once again. "I couldn't ask you all to do that."

He waves me off. "It's already been decided. The guys are cool with it, so there is no worry there. We're busy with classes and soccer anyway. You'll have the house to yourself a lot of the time."

My heart warms. Never did I think some college friends my brother met would welcome me in this warmly. "I don't know what to say."

"You don't need to say anything," he replies. "We all love you, Tra. And this is my niece or nephew. I love them already."

After discussing it more with my mom, brother, and Blaire, I feel confident and comfortable with my decisions. I'm still scared shitless, but knowing I have a strong support system means more to me than anything.

Now I need to figure out what I'm going to do about Maddox and his views on becoming a young parent. I'm a mom now. My baby comes first, and I will not let their father hurt them like mine hurt me.

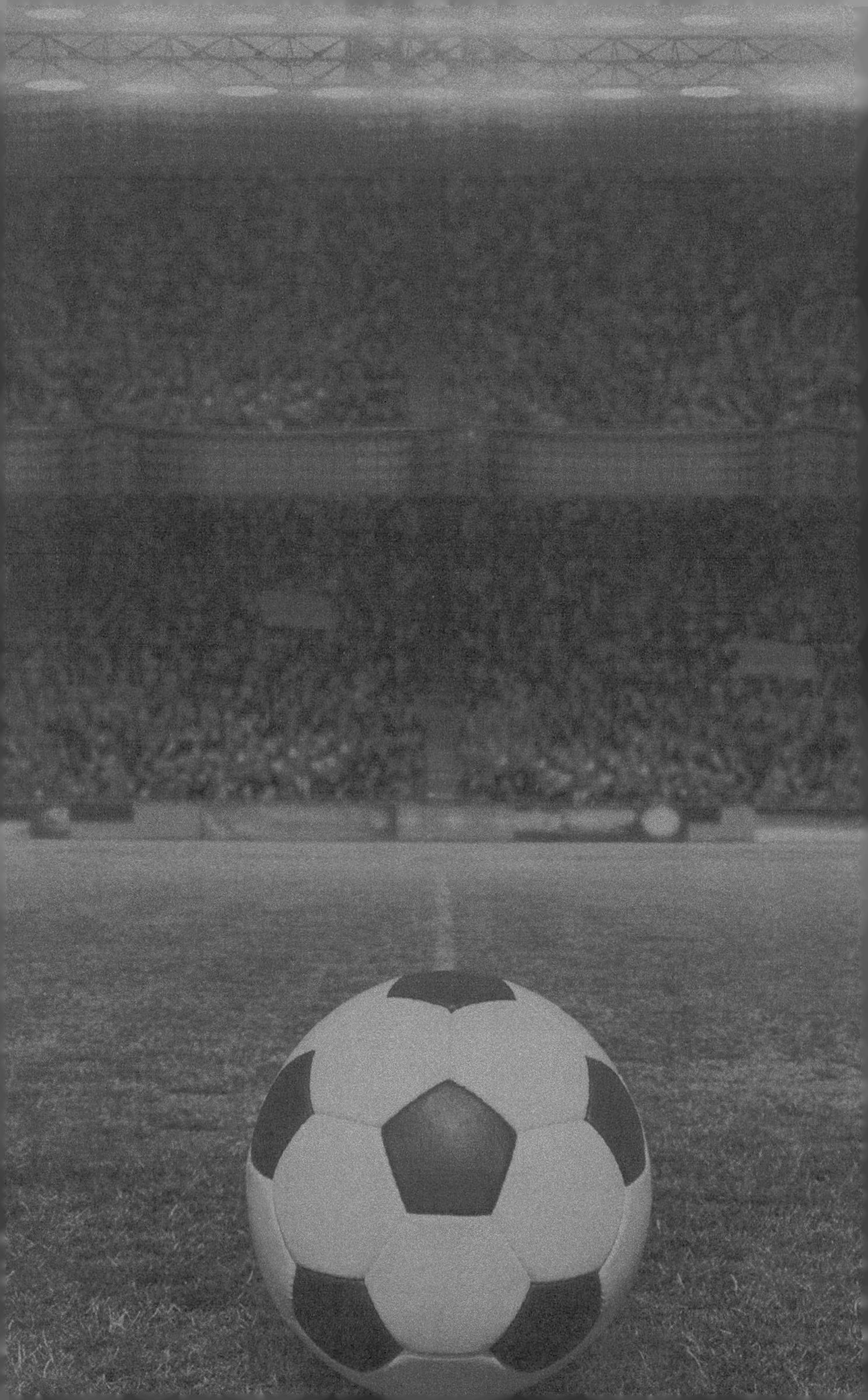

CHAPTER SIXTEEN

MADDOX

It's been three weeks since Trazia moved in with us, and I'm almost at my breaking point. She's a great roommate and we love having her around, but being in her presence this much is doing nothing to stop me from wanting her. Especially seeing her early in the morning in a tight pair of shorts and tank top with her hair tied up in a messy bun. Her face is always freshly cleaned, and she greets each of us with a bright smile.

Trazia has somehow avoided the morning sickness that many mothers experience. She had her first doctor's appointment last week and asked why she hadn't had that yet. The doctor said not every mother has the same symptoms during pregnancy, and she's one of the lucky ones.

Claire went with Traz to that appointment, and I got this strange urge to want to be there beside her during it. I'm not sure why because babies and birth freak me out. Especially babies. I grew up with several little cousins and wasn't a fan. Somehow they're always sticky, even if they haven't been around anything to get them that way. Their noses are constantly running, and they cry for no reason. I'm sure one day when I'm older, I'll have a kid or two and love them, but now at twenty-one, I don't want any part of that.

Given that Trazia is going to be living with us until graduation next year, I guess I have to get used to babies. Their crying and stinkiness will be difficult to overcome. When Camden asked us about Traz moving in here longer than just the summer, I was fully on board with that plan. I mean, at the time, I didn't think about the fact that a baby was going to be living here also. We still have a few months to deal with that, though. For now, the hottest girl who can simply smile and get me hard is living under the same roof as me, and I'm stressed.

To avoid Traz, I decided to attend one of the frat parties tonight. It's much chiller than their normal gatherings since a lot of people go home for the summer, but there's enough of a crowd to distract me from the woman who invades my constant thoughts.

"Mad, I'm glad you came. Been a while since I've seen you," Alex greets me as he grabs my free hand and pulls me in for that manly one-arm hug that ends with a slap on the back.

"Needed to get out tonight. You have a good turnout for summer." I take a sip of my beer as we both look around the crowd. Alex's fraternity is notorious for throwing complete ragers. One they threw a few months ago had kid pools filled with whipped cream, and there were girls in bikinis—and a few topless—fighting in them. When they throw larger parties, they also bring out the stripper poles in hopes that some of the more…talented…ladies hop on and give us a free show. I have yet to attend a party where there aren't a few confident coeds swinging around on those babies with little to no clothing.

Morally, I'm sure frat parties aren't everyone's cup of tea, but everything is consensual. They make sure the freshmen stay sober to keep everyone under control. Last thing anyone wants is for someone to get seriously hurt on their watch.

Alex tips his cup in the direction of a group of girls playing flip cup. "Izzy is here. You still hitting that?"

Izzy and I were in a casual friends-with-benefits agreement last summer. She's hot as fuck and wasn't looking for anything serious. That was until she met a transfer from Alabama on the football team. Said she was a sucker for a southern accent.

"Nah. That ended a while ago. She started dating the new QB."

Alex turns to me with a knowing smile. "Shit, dude, did you not hear? She walked in on him having a three-way with her roommate and another chick. They've been over for a while. Iz trashed his room too. Threw all his shit out the window and everything."

"Fuck," I laugh out. "This is why people in college should avoid relationships. There's too much temptation to commit to one person."

As if she can hear us, Izzy turns and gives me a sultry smile. She's wearing a tight, short, bright pink dress that is low enough to expose her small amount of cleavage. I'm not one to criticize a woman's appearance, but we all have a preference. Doesn't mean I will turn a beautiful woman down because she is lacking in that department. I'm not an asshole.

At the thought of nice boobs, my mind automatically goes to Trazia. She has the perfect size. Not too big that you can't handle them, but large enough for more than a handful. They've grown noticeably since she got pregnant, and I've had to put effort into not staring when she talks to me. It's a struggle I face every day.

I shake my head to clear it of Trazia and her fantastic tits. She shouldn't be on my mind right now. She is having a movie night with Emree, Blaire, and Jules, and I am trying to do something—anything—to get her off my mind. Maybe a good, hard fuck will do the job.

"Excuse me. I'm going to go visit an old flame," I tell Alex as I make my way to Izzy.

She watches my every move as I cross the room. With her game now over, her friends disappear from the table, leaving her and me alone at it.

"Well, if it isn't Maddox Stone. Haven't seen you around the last few months." Izzy is a beautiful woman and she knows it. She is the type of girl who oozes sexiness. In the way she walks, talks, and even stares at you. Her hair is pin-straight and a little longer than shoulder-length. She always has a full face of makeup with false eyelashes that make her bright blue eyes stand out more. She's tall—especially in heels—with legs for days. Basically, Izzy is most men's dream woman, and I'm trying to figure out why my body is not reacting to her in the way it normally would.

"You been missing me, Iz?" I ask her as I rest my hand on the table behind her and lean in. She smells spicy, like cinnamon, with a mix of beer.

Izzy's hand runs up my chest and wraps around the back of my neck. "You know I have. I've been thinking about you lately. How good we were together. How much I miss your hard body against mine and that thing you do with your tongue." She leans in close and runs her tongue against my neck, landing on my ear and biting my lobe between her teeth.

This is about the time Little Maddox would make an appearance and greet a beautiful woman. But he's apparently in hibernation right now because the fucker doesn't even twitch.

"All you have to do is ask, and you can have all of that again," I tell her as she drags her hand down my chest and to the front of my pants.

Pulling back, Iz looks into my eyes. "You sure about that? Because it doesn't feel like that's the case."

I curse under my breath. Fuck, I need this. I need to do something to try to get my mind and body off Trazia.

A MEMORY THAT ONCE WAS

"Just give him a moment. It's been a while. He's shy." With my hand under her jaw, I bring my head down to Izzy's and touch her lips softly. They're full, but in an unnatural way. Not like Trazia's plush ones, where the top is bigger than the bottom.

Fuck. I have a beautiful woman in my arms and my mouth on hers, yet my mind still drifts off to the smoke show who is living with me. The *pregnant* smoke show. That alone should cut off my attraction to her, but weirdly, I think she has gotten hotter in the last few weeks.

Izzy's tongue escapes and tries to gain access into my mouth. I pull back before she can. "How about we head back to my house?"

Her eyes light up. "Let me just tell my friends. We all walked over from the sorority house together." She joins the group of girls who have taken up the space in the living room and whispers in one of their ears before coming back over to me.

"Let's go, babe." I smile at her as she reaches for my hand.

Greek Row isn't far from the house we're living in, but the area is much quieter. I'm not opposed to parties and enjoy attending them, but my social meter has a limit and once that is hit, I want nothing more than to go the fuck to bed without drunken college students yelling outside my window. Maybe my freshman and sophomore years I would have been more open to living on the party block, but I'm a senior now. Daddy needs his beauty sleep.

Parking in my usual spot, I take notice that the only cars in the driveway are Mateo's and Camden's. Luckily, Trazia is still having a movie night with the other girls. I have this weird feeling with her knowing I'm hooking up with a girl and I'm not sure why that is crossing my mind. Trazia is nothing but an ongoing crush that I'm not supposed to have.

On the walk up to the front door, Izzy doesn't take her hands off me. From rubbing my forearm to kissing my shoulder, she remains attached. As I fumble with the keys to unlock the door, she runs one hand through my shaggy hair and pushes her other down the front of my pants while her lips suck at my neck.

"God, I want you so bad. It's been too long since I've had a good fucking, and no one compares to you," she says against my neck.

Just as I open the door, she removes her hand from my soft dick and jumps into my arms, wrapping her legs around my waist. "Take me right here against the wall." Izzy starts unbuttoning my jeans until she gets to what she wants and wraps her hand around me.

"Shit, Iz, I have roommates," I try to say around her mouth that is trying to dominate mine.

"Don't care," she breathes. "Just take me, Maddox. Right here."

Trying to move past the unsettling feeling I have deep in my gut, I push Izzy against the wall and slam my lips to hers, earning a moan out of her. She kisses me in a frenzy, and I try to keep up. Her hands are in my hair, and she's moving her hips and rubbing against the front of my jeans.

The dark entryway suddenly brightens. I look around to see who turned the light on and come face-to-face with a shocked Trazia. She's wearing a pair of sweatpants and a T-shirt. Her hair is in her signature messy bun and the look on her face deepens that ill feeling in my gut I've been having.

"I-I'm so-rry. I th-thought someone was trying to get in." Her eyes go from me to Izzy, who is catching her breath. I still have her against the wall, and at that thought, I drop her, not paying attention if she caught herself of not.

"Shit, Traz, I thought you were at the girls' place having a movie night." I look past her and see the glow from the TV in the living room and three heads turned in my direction. The movie they're watching must be hella dark because I didn't even notice it was on when I got in. Although I did have a woman's face against mine at the time.

Trazia looks down at her feet and begins kicking around nothing on the ground. "Their internet went out and we weren't able to stream the movie, so we came here. I, um, didn't realize you would have a guest over. I'm sorry. Just—just go back to what you're doing."

"Traz—"

She turns to the girls on the couch. "I'm really tired tonight. I'm just going to head to bed. You guys finish the movie."

As Traz turns back to me, I can see the tears start to flow over and drop down her face. She tries to blink them away as she goes to the stairs, and I hear the door to her room—my old one—close.

Why do I feel like I just royally fucked something up?

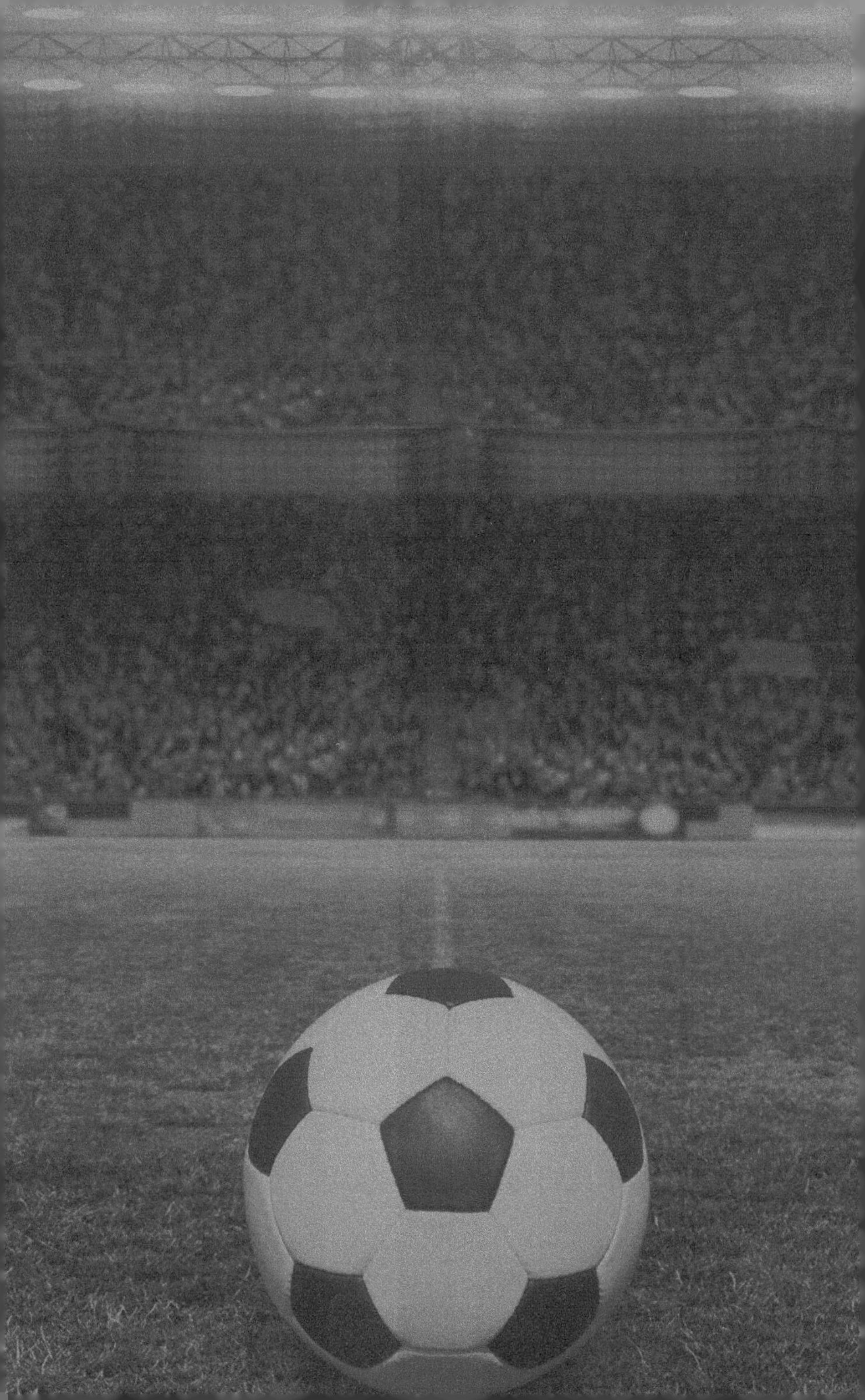

CHAPTER SEVENTEEN

TRAZIA

"What should we watch tonight?" Jules asks as she enters the living room with a bowl of freshly popped popcorn.

Movie night was supposed to be at Blaire and Emree's place, but a mishap with their internet meant we moved it to the house. I'm happier with that option because it means I won't have to crash on their couch or drive home late.

The last week I've been more tired than usual. I read online that it is normal as I'm growing a person, and that takes a lot of energy out of you. Add in my course load and the new job I started two weeks ago at Dandelion Daycare, and I'm ready for bed by eight most nights.

Blaire convinced me to join in on movie night by guilt-tripping me and saying that I haven't come out for their girls' nights the last two weekends. The truth is, I'm struggling with more than they know right now. Not only do I have my little bean, school, and work, but I have a constant reminder that I have not told my child's father of their existence or conception. The weight of that secret has been sitting heavy on me, and I don't know how to handle it.

"Do we want to see something new or a classic?" Blaire asks as she scrolls through different streaming services.

Emree is nestled into the single-seater couch with a blanket wrapped around her and a Slurpee from the gas station in her hands. "You know I'm always down for a classic. Oh, what about *Magic Mike*, or maybe a comedy? You can't go wrong with *White Chicks*."

Jules bounces in her seat beside me. "Oh yes. My vote is for *White Chicks*. I haven't watched that in years."

"Any objections?" Blaire asks, and I shake my head.

A comedy is better than a romance right now. I'm not sure I would be able to handle some cute, in-love couple and not want to stab the TV as they stare at each other all lovey-dovey.

As the movie starts, I can't help but zone out thinking about Maddox. He didn't go out with the guys tonight to Topgolf, and I wonder where he ended up going. I heard the tail end of a conversation between Levi and Mateo about a frat party happening tonight, but neither of them wanted to go.

My stomach has been in small knots thinking he is at a party and what he's doing. I have no claim on Maddox, but that doesn't change the fact that thinking about him hooking up with a girl makes me sick.

The girls laugh as one of the Wayans brothers makes a joke on the TV, and I shake my head to try and pay attention to what is happening on the screen and not think about Maddox.

With the room completely dark—Emree says that's the only way to watch any movie—I don't notice the front door open until I hear noise behind me. Even over the sound of the TV, it is hard to see.

Getting up, I point to the front of the house when Jules gives me a questioning look. Rounding the corner to the front door, I flip the light on, and the image before me is enough to steal my breath.

Maddox has a girl pinned up against the wall. Her legs are

wrapped around his waist, and she is grinding her hips against him while letting out a string of breathy moans that sound faker than any porn I've watched.

With the darkness now gone, they break apart and Maddox turns to face me. He drops the beautiful woman, and she stumbles while trying to catch herself. I mumble out an apology to him before retreating to my room. Truth is, seeing him with another woman is harder than I thought it would be.

Once in the safety of my room, I dive onto the bed and bury my head in the soft pillow. The tears are streaming and soaking my pillowcase in the process. I shouldn't even be crying or acting like some jealous girlfriend right now. I should be able to control myself and handle this like an adult. Everyone downstairs, including the Victoria Secret model Maddox brought home, probably thinks I've lost my damn mind.

A soft knock comes from the other side of the room, and I wipe the tears and snot onto my sheets as the door opens. "Traz, can I come in?" Blaire's sweet voice makes me smile even as my eyes are fighting back releasing more tears.

"Yeah," I tell her, my throat somewhat scratchy from crying.

She enters my room and shuts the door behind her before walking over and joining me on the bed. As she takes in my tearstained face and red eyes, she offers up a small, sympathetic smile. I can only imagine what she thinks of me after what she witnessed.

"You want to talk to me about it?" she asks. Blaire has no idea how badly I want to talk to her or anybody about it. About drunken sex with Maddox over spring break. About him not remembering. About me being pregnant with his baby. About how I'm terrified to tell him because, what if he leaves me and Little Bean like my dad left us?

The number of secrets I'm keeping is weighing heavy on my chest, and sooner or later, they're going to have me combusting.

Instead of blurting out what I really want to say, I plaster on a fake smile. "Nothing. I think it's just the hormones and being tired. Having a job now on top of school and growing a human has been a lot."

She eyes me as I speak, and I can tell the moment she doesn't believe what I told her. "You can trust me, Trazia. Something has been bugging you for a while now, and I've noticed. I don't want to pressure you or overstep, but I'm here if you need someone to talk to about anything."

The words fight their way to come out. "It...it's the baby's father."

Her eyes widen, clearly surprised. I don't talk about Little Bean's dad to anyone, and our friends, my brother, and my mom have respected that. "Is he giving you trouble? Have you told him about the baby yet? We've been trying to give you space about this, but I will say, Camden is itching to know who it is and have some kind of weird man discussion with him. Camden's words, not mine."

Blaire makes it so easy to talk to her. She is a trustworthy person, and I know if I confide in her about Maddox, she will keep that secret until I'm ready for anyone else to know.

Taking a deep breath, I square my shoulders and prepare to tell the first person a secret that has kept me up most nights. "Blaire...I haven't exactly told the father because it's more complicated than you could ever imagine."

Her eyebrows pinch together, and she reaches across the bed to grasp my hand. "Hey, you can trust me, okay? I'm here for you no matter what."

Staring into her eyes, I can see the truth behind her words. "Maddox. Maddox is Little Bean's father."

Even though I warned her it was complicated, I don't think she was expecting this. I'm not sure anyone would be prepared for a situation as screwed up as this one. Even I wasn't.

"Come again?" she whispers.

"Maddox is the father of my baby."

Blaire stands from the bed and begins pacing the open area. "How did this even happen? You and Maddox? Just...when? And why is he down there with some other girl against the wall while you're carrying his child?" Her voice grows during her last sentence.

"First, I really don't want anyone to find out through the walls, so could we whisper please? And second, he doesn't know about Bean because we were both drunk when it happened, and I didn't realize until the next morning that he was drunk enough not to remember."

She gasps, and her hands come up to cover her mouth. "A drunken hookup? Oh no, did this happen over spring break? Wow, and the worst Camden was worried about was you falling in the pool after drinking. I doubt he thought it would have you sleeping with his best friend."

Blaire's frantic rant has me laughing because she's right. I'm sure if Camden knew this was what happened after I got drunk at the beach house, he wouldn't be too worried about me and a pool after some drinks.

"See how this whole situation has been much more complicated?"

She shakes her head and sits back on the bed. "I don't even know what to say. Why not tell him, though?"

This is the more difficult part, but each time I think about telling Maddox, my mind goes straight to him abandoning Bean, like we are nothing to him. "Something I overheard Maddox say to Mateo after the hospital visit. He said he would bail if this happened to him, and all I could think about was my dad leaving and how hurt Camden and I were. We felt like we weren't good enough for him, and I can't have anyone do that to Little Bean." I cradle my stomach that looks more bloated than pregnant.

Blaire's eyes soften. "Traz, I'm sure his mind would change

if you told him that. Not only does Maddox have a thing for you, but he would never do what your dad did."

"How can I take that risk?"

"It's not fair for you or him to keep this a secret. I promise not to tell anyone, but I do strongly encourage you to tell him the truth. Maddox may surprise you. I would be more worried about your brother finding out than anything else."

I already know when I reveal the truth to Camden that there is going to be a lot of backlash, and he will not be taking it well.

"But what if he doesn't want anything to do with Bean? What if he leaves them years later like my dad? I don't want my baby to go through what I had to and wonder if their father loves them or not."

Blaire tilts her head and casts those gray eyes deep into mine. "But what if he's nothing like your dad?"

Maybe I'm not giving Maddox enough credit. He hasn't even had the chance to fail, and I'm already prepared for it. What if he surprises me and wants to be the dad this baby will need? He deserves to at least make that decision with the entire truth laid out in front of him.

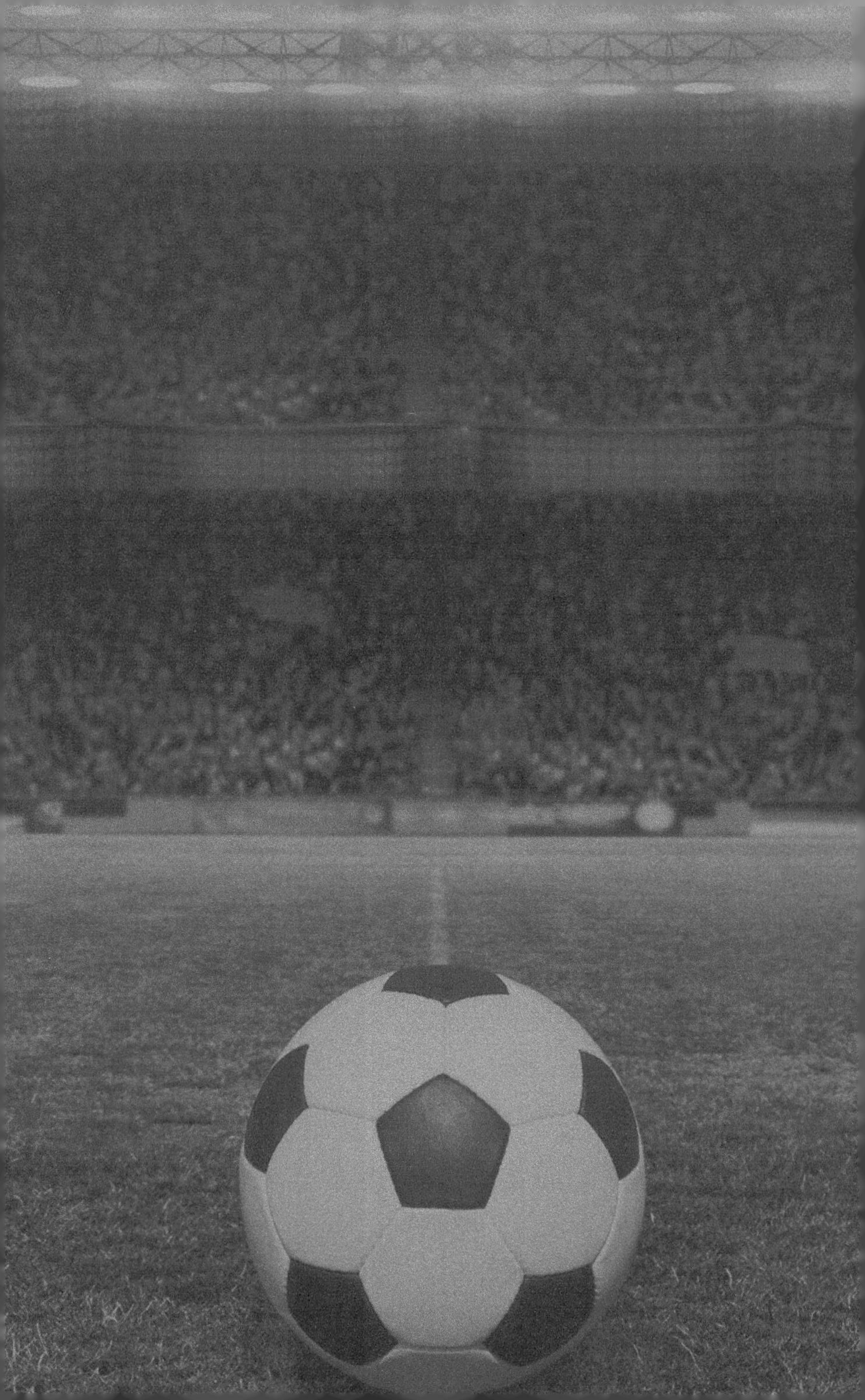

CHAPTER EIGHTEEN

MADDOX

The burning fireball in the sky beats down on my exposed skin as if it has something personal against me. I know that isn't the case, but by the way it feels right about now, the sunburn it's creating on me feels like I owe the sun money or something.

Working during the summer was not something I wanted or needed to do, but when the majority of your friends have jobs, it leaves you a bit bored during the day. A couple summers ago, Mateo was telling us about this gig he got as a lifeguard, and Camden was interested. He grew up in Florida and is a pretty good swimmer. Feeling left out, I decided to join in, and the two of us took the required classes and have been doing this each summer ever since.

I've grown to enjoy being a lifeguard. Who wouldn't like chilling on the beach and scoping out hot girls in swimsuits?

The only issue I'm having today—other than the excruciating heat—is I have no desire to ogle these women. None of them do anything for me. Even the ones with their asses on full display.

Ever since the mishap in the house last weekend when

Trazia caught me with Izzy, I've come to a new realization: Trazia Collins has broken my dick. Little Maddox finds no one obtainable anymore because the woman he wants is living under the same roof and he can't have her.

It's only been four days since that incident, and I have chatted up and eyeballed several girls at this beach since then and I feel nothing. Not even a little jump in my pants. He has basically gone into hibernation because the little—I mean big—guy wants nothing to do with a person of the opposite sex unless it's Trazia.

As if my thoughts summoned her, the woman struts across the sand with Blaire, Emree, Jules, Mateo, Conrad, and Levi. While the other six walk like they are newborn babies through the sand, Traz practically glides. Her long hair is blowing behind her in the wind as she makes her way toward an empty spot in the sand. She has a pair of oversized sunglasses resting on her nose and is wearing a white, long-sleeve cover-up that buttons in the front.

Blaire looks over to where I'm perched at my stand, and the moment we make eye contact, I wave and she turns away as if to pretend she doesn't see me. She has been acting weird the last few days, and I want to ask Camden about it, but he has had enough stress going on with Trazia and the baby.

Camden has been holding back on asking Trazia about the baby's father, but I know it is eating at him. She brushes it off anytime the sperm donor comes up, claiming that she is going to tell him soon and to let her handle it. Honestly, I'm starting to wonder if that's true. It's been over a month since she found out, and Traz is starting to show. If they have mutual friends or he goes to Braxton, the guy is going to find out.

While I try to stay out of that drama, part of me is worried about her telling him. I've been an eighteen-year-old guy before, and I would bet money that this one is going to do what the majority of us would in this situation and not stick around.

It's shitty to think of, but it's also an all-too-common reality. Guys have it easy and can become deadbeats with little consequences. A perfect example is Camden and Trazia's father. He left them at a young age and put Claire and her kids through hell, but he got off scot-free with no more responsibilities.

I've always struggled with my relationship with my parents. While they aren't like Camden's dad, they also weren't very present during my childhood. I was raised by a nanny who was more like a parent than the ones I had. They traveled together a lot and preferred to do that child-free. My dad is also the CEO and chairman of a large bank in the States, and that had him away on business trips several times a month.

My parents missed more milestones during my childhood than I can count. The big ones were my graduation, almost all my soccer games, and me moving into my dorm the first year of college. Our relationship is strained, but I'm used to that. I've come to the realization that it's not because they don't care about or love me, but because there are some people on this planet that don't have a parental bone in their body. Mine are that way, which is why I think they didn't have any more kids after me. At least they realized it and didn't bring more babies into this world.

My mind drifts away from my fucked-up family as Trazia slowly removes the cover-up she had on, revealing her body in a bikini that has me needing to readjust my pants. Her bottoms are high-waisted and navy blue with white buttons on the sides. The top ties around her neck and the small triangle pieces in the front are doing nothing to hold in her large breasts. She adjusts them, as if that is going to do anything.

As I take Trazia in, I can't help but notice the small bump she is sporting under the fabric of her bottoms. If no one knew, they would assume she is either bloated or ate a large lunch, but I know that the woman on the other side of the beach is growing a human inside there. Crazy to think about it.

Sometimes I forget Trazia is pregnant because she doesn't look it, but then there are other times when I can't help but be in awe of her. She is working several hours a week, going to school full-time, and creating life. Being a parent as young as she is may be bananas to me, but she seems to be handling the adjustment well.

"Hey, man, shift's over. Eddie and Trent just got here." Camden climbs halfway up the ladder to my lifeguard stand. "Everyone is here, and they want to stay until sunset if you're in?"

"You think after spending all day on the beach protecting people, I'd want to continue being here?"

Camden rolls his eyes. "I'll take that as a no." He begins climbing down the ladder.

"No, no. I'll come hang out." I stand from my perch and gather my bag that is holding a towel, water bottle, and change of clothes. Trent is walking over toward us to take my place, and I offer him a wave.

"You don't make anything easy, do you?" Camden asks as we make our way over to our friends.

"Of course not."

We walk in silence the remaining distance to our group. They have set up a large beach blanket that can fit a few bodies. Emree, Trazia, and Blaire put up low beach chairs, and Blaire has her trusty beach umbrella above her.

"You two are looking extra tan today," Jules tells Camden and me from where she is lying on the oversized blanket.

"Camden, are you wearing that sunscreen I got you?" Blaire asks, concern evident in her voice.

He leans down and kisses her softly on the lips. "No, because no one here but you needs SPF 100. I'm good with what I have."

She rolls her eyes. "Don't come crying to me when you have skin cancer when you're older."

"Thank you for being concerned about my skin, babe."

She scoffs at him as she opens one of her romance books and begins reading.

Trazia pulls out her own and leans back in the chair. Her long, dark hair is now pulled back and held together in a loose braid that falls over her shoulder. She is resting the book on her small bump, and I can't help but smile. I don't think she realizes she does that often. I catch her here and there rubbing her stomach or cradling it when she's studying in the living room or watching TV.

Conrad is making an obnoxious amount of noise digging through the cooler until he finds his bougie beers at the bottom. "Anyone want anything? Traz, we got water and ginger ale for you since…you know. You can't drink with the baby and everything."

"Oh, you're good. I won't be drinking for a while anyway. Kind of how I got into this situation," she says around a laugh as she gestures to her bump with the book in hand.

Camden's head whips around so fast, I'm not even sure his brain had enough time to process. "What are you talking about? Were you drunk when you got pregnant? Did he take advantage of you? Is that why you won't tell me who it is?"

She groans, clearly regretting her statement. "No, there was no taking advantage of anyone. We both had too much to drink and were loose with our decision-making, but I can assure you that everything was consensual."

"I don't like this." Camden sulks from his spot on the blanket. "Just tell me who the fucker is. Better yet, have you told him? Are you ever going to tell him he's going to be a father?"

"Of course I am," she replies to him in a soft tone.

Camden crosses his arms over his chest. "Yeah? Well, when?"

Trazia looks around at our friend group, clearly uncomfortable having this conversation with everyone around. "When

I'm ready. It's more difficult than just going up to him and saying, 'hey, you're going to be a father in a few months.'"

"Doesn't seem that difficult," he argues. "Why not just do that?"

"Because I'm scared, all right?" she practically shouts.

Mateo, Levi, and Conrad wander off toward the water with a soccer ball as Trazia and Camden have a staring contest in front of us.

"Scared?" His tone has changed to something softer. "Why would you be scared?"

Trazia sets her book down on her lap and settles her hands on the small bump. "What if he's like Dad? I don't want Bean here to go through life feeling unloved by their dad. What if I tell him and he wants nothing to do with them? Or feels some sort of obligation to stick around but abandons them later on, like Dad did. I'm terrified for Bean to go through the kind of heartbreak I went through." She readjusts her sunglasses, but I catch her wiping a tear from under her eye during the process.

"Ah, come on, Traz. I'm sure this guy won't be like that," Camden lies to her.

Not wanting him to get her hopes up, I feel the need to step in. "Sorry, man, but she has a point. What barely-out-of-high-school guys do you know that have made the right decision and stepped up to fatherhood?"

Camden thinks for a moment. "I mean, I don't know any personally, but I'm sure there are some."

Walking over to the cooler, I pull out a can of beer and pop it open. "Traz is justified here, especially after the shit your dad pulled. I wouldn't fault her for embracing single motherhood and not telling needle dick."

Blaire chokes and leans forward, trying to catch her breath. "Whoa, Blaire baby. Settle down there or you'll have to make me test out my CPR skills on you."

Camden jumps up and pats his girlfriend on the back. "Keep your mouth-to-mouth to yourself, Stone."

After Blaire composes herself, Camden goes back to his spot on the blanket. "Even if the guy takes the easy way out, he deserves a chance to step up. I don't want to give him the benefit of the doubt, but I couldn't imagine a girl I slept with in the past keeping something like that from me."

Trazia chews on her bottom lip as she absorbs his words. "I know," she admits to him. "I'll tell him soon, I promise. I just... it's hard."

Camden's face softens. "Let's say he does pull a move like Dad. The important thing to think about is your kid is going to have you as a mom. No matter how shitty their dad is, that kid won the jackpot in the mom department."

Though it is a compliment, Trazia's face drops and she stares at her growing stomach. Whoever the guy is, I hope he makes the right choice and beats the odds that are against him.

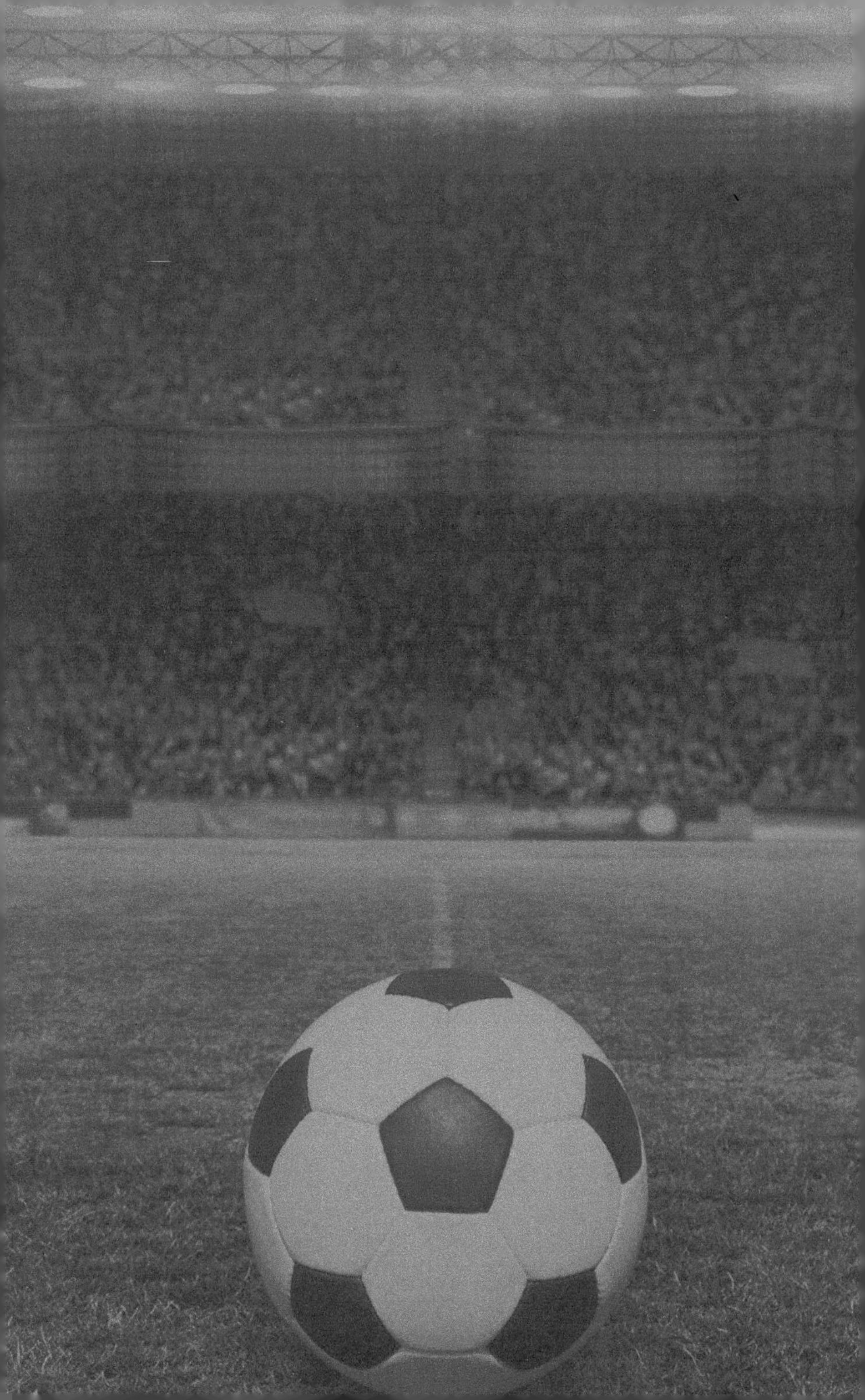

CHAPTER NINETEEN

TRAZIA

"During summer, we get a lot more kids daily, so it's good to have every employee familiar with each room. The toddlers and middle school-age kids love you already. Now it's time for you to meet the babies," my manager, Jannette, tells me as we walk toward the classroom that is designated for infants and babies.

Since starting at Dandelion Daycare, I have worked in every room besides this one. The toddlers have been the most fun, especially when helping them with arts and crafts. The middle schoolers are cool but would much rather be on their phones or play the video games we provide. They have more freedom since they are older and too cool for crafts, as they have told me. A few of them have tried teaching me how to play, but I've accepted video games are not for me.

The infant and baby room has a keypad on the door to gain entrance. It's an added protection measure Dandelion included not long ago. Something I've learned about this daycare is that they take the safety of their kids seriously. Every parent is given a unique number to access the building, and there are cameras everywhere inside the daycare and in the playground.

Jannette opens the door, and I am immediately hit with the smell of baby—a mixture of baby powder and their shampoo. Inside is spacious, with a wall of cribs, some rocking chairs in the corner, and a reading area with baby swings.

"We are selective on who works with the infants and babies, but I've seen how you are with the other kids and think you would be a great fit here also. It's a bit more work, but you are rewarded with baby snuggles." Jannette smiles as she talks, and you can tell she is someone who loves her job.

"That's one of the best benefits of working with babies. Who doesn't love those snuggles and giggles?"

Jannette laughs. "See, you get it. Not everyone wants to work in this room, and we have some employees who prefer the older kids because they get to play basketball or video games with them."

"I'm not very athletic, and they all laugh at me trying to learn their video games. I can't get the hang of that Minecraft one. But I am good for showing them how to spike a volleyball."

"I know exactly what you're talking about. They like to think we're old because we aren't into their games. In reality, I didn't like video games when I was a kid myself."

"Girl, I know exactly what you're talking about," I echo.

Jannette shows me the room and the different areas where the babies and toddlers are taken care of. This room of the daycare has its own door that leads outside and to a small playground that is shared with the toddlers. The toddlers go out there while the babies nap, and playing outside tires them enough that they crash when they come inside.

"We try to have two to three childcare workers here at a time, depending on how many little ones are in that day. It will always vary. Having more help when it comes to the babies is better," Jannette informs me as we walk around. "We do story time at least twice a day with the babies, and they are allowed at least half an hour of TV time, but we stick with Ms. Rachel. One of the biggest benefits of Dandelion is that we don't plop someone's child in front of a cartoon all day and leave them. We are much more interactive."

"I've noticed that compared to the last daycare I worked at. They weren't bad by any means, but with limited help, it was easier to put on a movie to keep more of the kids under control while trying to handle the babies and children who weren't entertained by something on a screen." While I was only there a few months before starting college, my previous job was much less staffed and didn't have the resources that Dandelion has.

Jannette stops at the long craft table and takes a seat, motioning for me to sit as well. The toddlers are currently outside on the playground since it is later in the day, and there is another employee with a few of the babies in the splash area while the two infants we have are napping.

"Our facility may be more expensive than others in the area, but I feel as though we bring much more to the table. We only employ the best and be sure to pay everyone a fair wage, which ensures we always have enough staff and no one is overworked. Our employees also get free childcare here, which is a great benefit. A few of the kids you see around are your coworkers' little ones. My own is in the older kids' room."

When I was hired, the employee benefits were made clear in my handbook, but having Jannette bring them up opens the door to something I have wanted to mention to her since I started. With classes, it will be hard to take care of Little Bean during those hours, and I can't rely on my mom or friends when my baby is my responsibility.

"Actually, Jannette, I wanted to bring something up to you."

She smiles. "Of course."

This would be the first person I tell about Little Bean outside of my family and friends. I'm afraid of the judgment that comes from others for being a young mother. "I'm fourteen weeks pregnant. I love working here and the great group of employees you've put together. While I'm only here part-time and just started, I was wondering once my little bean is here, is that a benefit of mine?"

Jannette reaches forward and pats my hand. "First of all, congratulations. Becoming a mother is a wonderful time in your life. Of course you will be able to leave your baby here, and we also give paid maternity and paternity leave for all employees. We want new parents to take at least eight weeks to adjust to parenthood. You would have all the same benefits."

My hormones have been all over the place lately, and I have to blink multiple times to control the tears trying to break free. "You have no idea how grateful I am for you and this job, Jannette. I've been terrified since I found out I'm pregnant, and knowing this means more to me than you could understand."

"Oh, sweetie," she says softly as she grasps my hand. "No need to thank me. When I started this daycare, part of my goal was to create an environment that employees feel appreciated and cared for. Working with kids is hard enough, and your employer should never make it more difficult."

Before I can respond, a quiet cry comes from one of the cribs.

Jannette stands and points in the direction of the little one. "Why don't you get some practice in, Mama?"

At the crib, I pick up the small baby. She can't be more than three months old and is a little thing. The moment I cradle her to my chest, something inside me flutters, and I think of my own baby that will be here in a few months. How I'm going to be the one to soothe them when they're crying. I'll be their protector, educator, and nurturer.

The baby in my arms begins sucking her fist, and I look to Jannette. "I think this little one is hungry."

Jannette goes to the kitchen area and grabs a bottle out of a plastic bag with a last name on it. "We have everything labeled in here to know whose milk and food belongs to whom. I'll get this one heated up in the warmer for you."

While she takes care of getting the bottle ready, I bounce and sway with the sweet baby in my arms. Her eyes shut as she suckles on her hand and I lean my cheek on the top of her head, getting a whiff of her baby scent.

Once ready, Jannette brings the bottle over to me. "I think you're going to be a wonderful mother, Trazia."

My heart warms at her honest words. I hope to be half the mother mine was, but I know without a doubt that Little Bean is going to be loved and cared for.

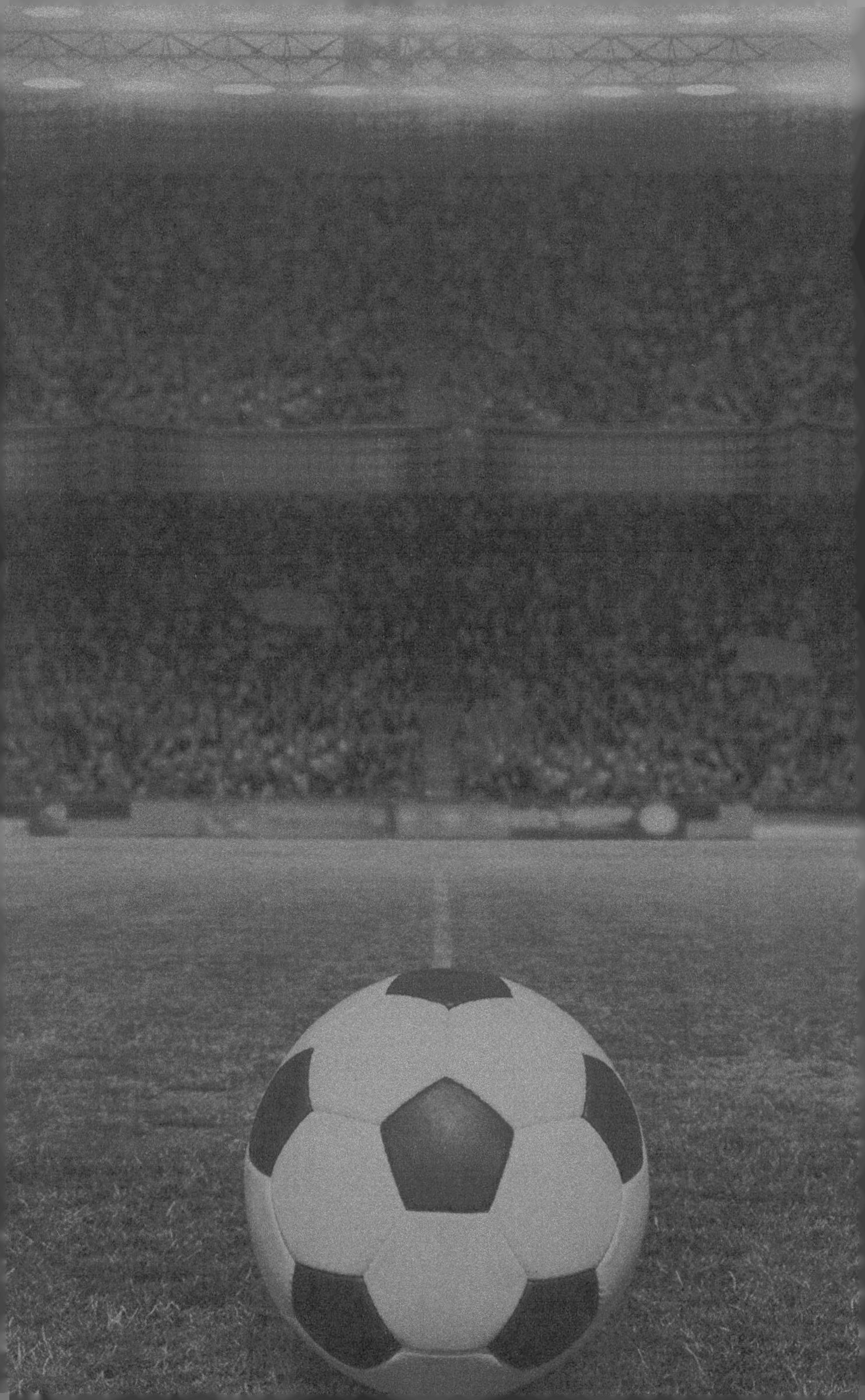

CHAPTER TWENTY

MADDOX

"Coach, I swear I wasn't the one who started that fight," Mateo explains. More like lies because he was totally the one who started the fight. Mateo was only blocking the guy from making a goal, but it was a dirty block, and the guy was pissed the ref didn't call it.

Even though most of our teammates aren't here, Coach asked anyone who wanted to partake in the scrimmage games over the summer to reach out to him. Since the five of us stayed in Braxton, we were down to join the fun. Camden, as our team captain, encouraged as many players as possible to come out. Some drove in from other cities around Florida, and we were able to get a full team plus two subs on the sides.

Coach looks at Mateo with disbelief. "McKay, given your track record, I'm finding that hard to believe."

Camden comes over, guzzling a Gatorade. He slaps Mateo on the shoulder, leaving his hand there. "We'll be sure to keep our resident hothead under control," Camden—always the golden boy—promises.

Coach gives them both a stern look before turning to the rest of the team. "For having some time off from practice, you boys are doing well for yourselves. Keep the momentum up the rest of this game and for our summer scrimmages coming up, and we'll have a top-notch team for next season. Got to keep that championship title we earned last season."

Everyone cheers at the mention of last year when we dominated our season. Our best year yet. Braxton's best year ever.

After a pep talk, the team marches outside to finish the second half of the game.

Our team is currently up by one, and the college we're playing is good competition. The game could be anyone's at this point. Camden and I are both starting forwards, and we work in sync more than I have with anyone else on the field. Conrad and Mateo are defenders who are ruthless when it comes to protecting the goal, and Levi is our goalie. The guy has a wingspan almost long enough to block half the goal, making it harder for other teams to score on him.

We take our places on the field, and while waiting for the ref to whistle off the start of the second half, I look out into the crowd where the girls are. Trazia joined the trio that is our fan club. Blaire and Emree are sporting their boyfriends' jerseys while Jules is wearing Mateo's this game. She usually wears either mine, Levi's, or Mateo's to show support for us equally.

Trazia is wearing Lumberjack's number 16, and the moment I saw that number on her back, jealousy flared inside me. She looks fucking adorable with her tiny bump and long hair sectioned into two braids falling over the number. She paired the outfit with short jean shorts and a pair of Converse, which I noticed she seems to wear often, but these ones are maroon to match our school colors.

While I know there is nothing going on between Traz and Levi, after hearing her say she thinks he's a hot nerd and now seeing her in his jersey, I'm wanting to go rip that off her and replace it with my name and number on her back.

The whistle blows, and I'm snapped back to the task at

A MEMORY THAT ONCE WAS

hand. The other team's forward captures the ball and dribbles past me easily.

"Fuck, Mad, get your head in the game!" Camden shouts as he chases after the player.

As I watch my best friend run down the field toward our goal, someone shoulder-checks me. Looking to my left, the fucker who got pissy with Mateo smirks at me. "Come on, pretty boy. Gonna let your team do all the work?"

Annoyance courses through me as I watch him run to where Camden gets the ball back and kicks it down the field with every bit of strength he has in his left leg. Since everyone and their fucking mother were down by our goal, I'm the closest to the ball and only have two defenders and a goalie to get past.

Getting the ball, I dribble it down the field and weigh my options while I have no one on me at the moment. One defender is a starter and the other a freshman, so my best option is to fake it to the better one and psych out freshy over here to make him think he's in the clear. Their goalie looks like he is out for blood, and I'm hoping I'll be fast enough with the fake out to confuse him for a few seconds and be able to kick the ball into the top left corner with ease.

Needing to take my chance now, I dribble a few steps toward the senior player, and he braces for a fight. Just before I'm close enough to see the sweat dripping from his forehead, I shuffle my feet and fake him out and dribble in the direction of the freshman. Knowing I can maneuver this ball around him easily, I gauge which direction he thinks I'm going to take—all while keeping an eye on the ball—and sneak past his right when he goes left.

The only thing standing in my way of scoring is the seasoned goalie who looks ready for blood. With the rest of the players coming in hot toward me, I decide on my next move, and with the top of my boot, I make contact with the ball to my laces and send it flying through the air. It's almost like everything around me stops as I hold my breath and wait for the ball to sink into the goal. In a matter of seconds, the ball has curved enough to slip into the top left corner of the net, grazing the goalie's fingertips in the process.

"Hell yeah, motherfuckers!" I cheer as my teammates tackle me to the ground. We become a pile of sweaty, grown men on the field, and in the distance I can hear Coach's deep voice yelling at us to get it together and get back to the game.

As we get back into position, I look out to the crowd and my eyes connect with Trazia's. Her smile is wide; face filled with pure joy. She may be wearing Lumberjack's jersey, but as we finish off the rest of the second half, I can feel her eyes on me the entire time.

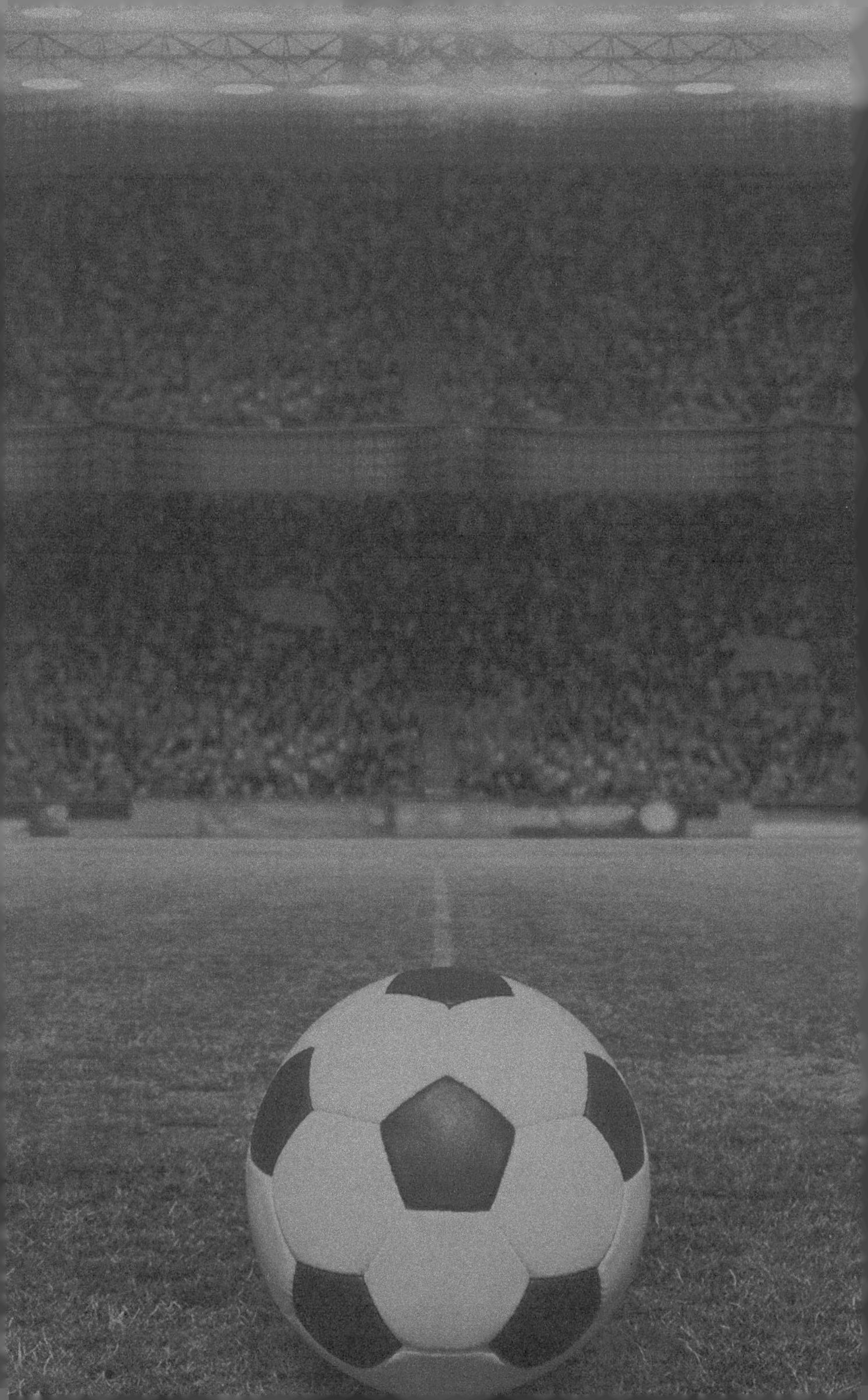

CHAPTER TWENTY-ONE

TRAZIA

I'm a coward. A chicken. A weakling. A scaredy-cat. Basically any word you could use to describe me backing out of telling Maddox at every opportunity I've had would work.

I'm fifteen weeks pregnant and haven't told the father of my baby that he's, well, the father. Or that we had sex about three and a half months ago. There have been several opportunities for me to drop the truth bomb on Maddox. Like when we're alone at the house and watching TV or when we are on grocery shopping duty. Each chance, I choke up, and the words don't come out.

Talking to Maddox isn't the problem. We've gotten back to our normal selves after the hallway incident with the supermodel whose face he was sucking. Maddox stopped avoiding me, and I've noticed he's here every night and alone in his room. Not that he shouldn't be hooking up like most college guys around here, but it makes me feel better that he is making that choice.

Blaire has been pushing me to tell him more and more, and

I know she is right. If too much time goes by, it is going to be hard to explain why I haven't told him.

Today is the appointment I have been a nervous wreck about. My doctor said that my little bean is growing faster than normal and I may be able to find out the gender today. The last time I saw my doctor, she told me usually it's around seventeen to twenty weeks when they can get a clear view for determining the gender, but I'm keeping my fingers crossed that Little Bean will be a good baby and give us the best view to tell whether they are a boy or girl.

Since I don't know what I'm having yet, I've tried my hardest to not go overboard with buying baby clothes, but anytime I enter a Target, my body is pulled toward the baby section. Yesterday, I ended up spending half my last paycheck on baby clothes and toys. They were too tiny and cute to resist.

My appointment isn't for another couple hours, and I've been going through the baby clothes I've bought so far. Most of it is in gender-neutral colors, and I'm loving the earthy tones of what I have so far.

"Knock, knock." Looking up, Blaire is standing in the doorway of my bedroom.

Folding the teeny overalls, I add them to the growing pile on my bed. "Hey, girl, what are you doing here?"

She comes into the room and plops onto the bed beside the clean baby clothes I haven't folded yet. "You really think I was going to let you go to this appointment on your own? I want to know if I'm going to have a niece or nephew."

A smile grows on my face. My family and friends know this could be the day I find out the gender, but Mom wasn't able to find anyone to take her shift at the hospital. I also felt weird having Camden in there with my stomach on display and didn't know if they would need to do any kind of vaginal examination. The guys have a summer practice today anyway, and he feels the need to be present at each of them even though they are voluntary.

"I'm glad you're here," I tell her as I rub my baby bump. "Little Bean better make an appearance now that there will be an audience in the room."

Blaire picks up a hunter-green linen onesie that I fell in love with the moment I saw it and knew Bean would look adorable in it. "No way could I miss this. I mean, it would be the best if the baby's dad was there, but seeing as he doesn't know about them..." She lets the rest of her sentence drift off.

"Blaire, I'm used to Emree and her sassiness. Not sure I can handle both of you now."

She lets out a huff. "This is not sassiness. It's honesty, and really, Trazia, I would have thought you'd told Maddox by now."

I take a seat on the bed. "I can't help that I'm scared, Blaire. You know him. Do you really think Maddox wants to be a dad at twenty-one? That he will stick around for late-night feedings, poopy diapers, screaming, and spit-up. He's the fun-time, don't-take-life-seriously kind of guy. Little Bean needs consistency in their life, and I don't see Maddox providing that."

"Traz, I think you keep trying to convince yourself that Maddox is going to be a deadbeat dad when he hasn't even been given the chance to prove you wrong. He isn't like your dad, and comparing the two is unfair."

Before I can lie and tell her that isn't what I'm doing, a figure appears in the doorway, and all the air leaves my lungs. "Maddox," I whisper.

His nostrils are flared, and his hands clench at his sides. "What the fuck did you just say?"

Blaire fumbles off the bed and stands there, looking between me and him. "I...um."

Getting to my feet, I approach Maddox cautiously. I've

never seen him angry, and I am a little petrified. "Maddox, what did you hear?"

He looks down at me, and the anger on his face shifts to something different. Like he's...scared, maybe? "Am I? What Blaire said, is the baby..." He doesn't finish a single sentence.

"Maddox, I-I wanted to tell you so many times, but...I was scared."

His body relaxes as devastation hits him. "How?"

Tears are threatening to escape as I look at Maddox. His shoulders are slumped, eyes sad, and his breath is coming out ragged. "At the beach house. We were, um, drunk and...and you didn't remember it the next morning."

Maddox turns and punches the wall, making me jump and leaving a fist-shaped hole. "Fuck!" He paces the hallway while tugging at his blond strands. "I thought that was a fucking dream."

Not able to hold them back anymore, the tears are freely rolling down my face. Seeing the pain on Maddox's face hurts me more than anything else. I messed up and did this to him. Keeping this secret was wrong, and I should have told him what happened the day after we conceived Little Bean. He should have never found out this way.

"Maddox, I'm so sorr—"

He turns to me, the look on his face silencing the rest of my sentence. "Don't you fucking *dare*. You lied to me, Trazia. You lied to all of us. I should have known months ago about this." His voice cracks. "Why? Why didn't you tell me that's my fucking kid inside you?"

Wrapping my arms around my waist, I clutch onto my bean as I try to control my breathing and blink away the tears, but they keep flowing. "I was scared. You have no idea how sorry I am, Maddox. I never wanted you to find out this way."

He marches toward me, and I shrink back. "Scared? Of

what? That I'd be a *deadbeat*? That I wouldn't be there for *my child*? You think I would abandon my own kid?"

"Maddox, no." I reach for him, but he jerks back as if the idea of my touch disgusts him.

"Don't, Traz. That's exactly what you thought, and how you could think so little of me isn't fair. You *know* me. You *see* me. More than anyone else, I never would have thought you'd think the worst of me."

His eyes fill with moisture as he stares down at me as if I am a stranger. My heart cracks knowing I hurt him. Causing pain to someone I care about so much hurts more than anything.

"This wasn't fair, Trazia. I didn't deserve to be lied to."

Without another word, Maddox turns and storms down the stairs. The front door opens, and I jump when it slams shut.

A sob tears through me as I sink to the floor and pull my knees to my chest. A pair of arms wrap around my shoulders and pull me in close.

"It's going to be okay, Traz. He just needs to cool off alone for a little bit and then you two will be able to talk this out."

I don't believe a single word she says, but I let her try to soothe me. Truth is, I don't know if I would be able to forgive me if I were in his shoes.

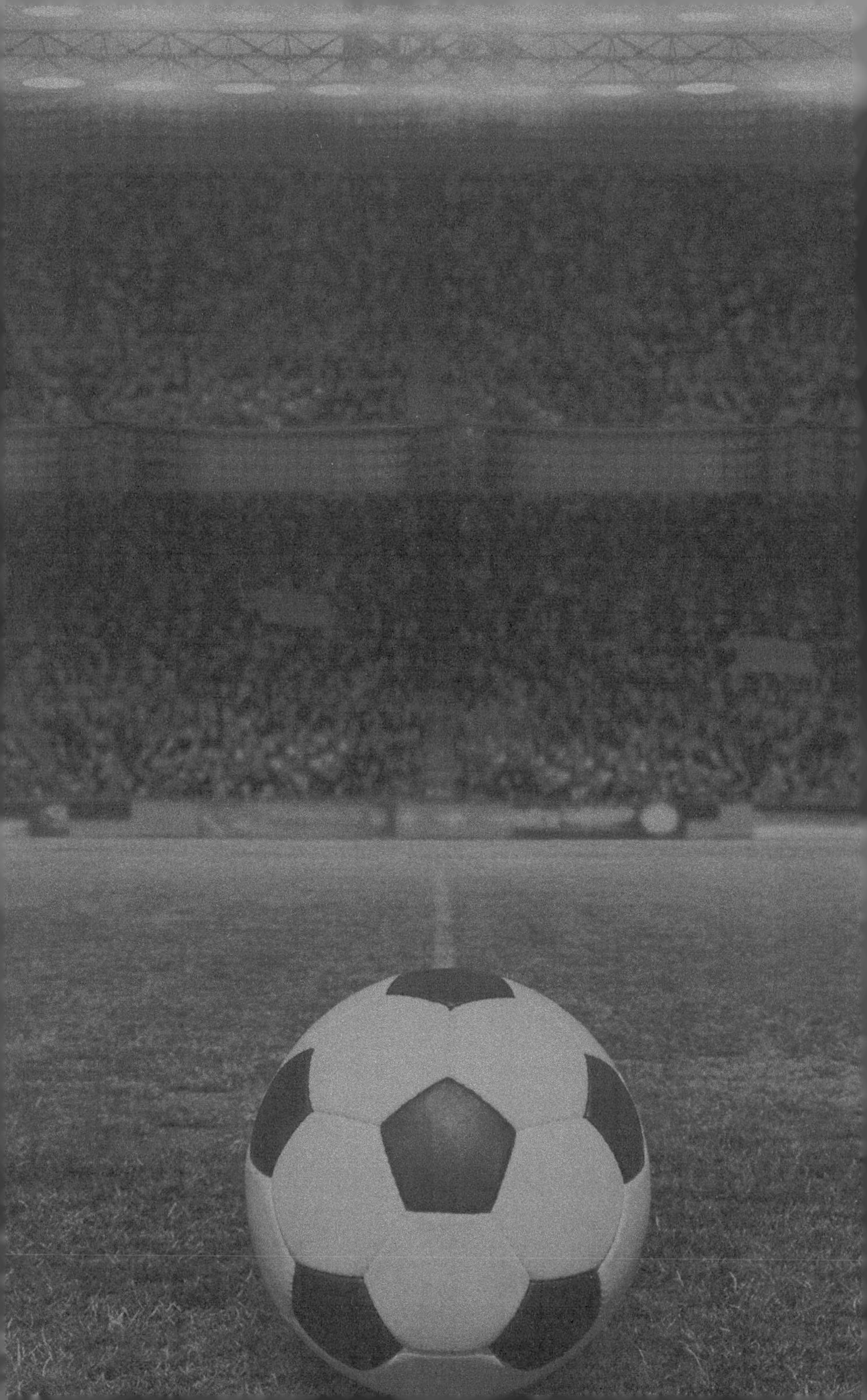

CHAPTER TWENTY-TWO

MADDOX

My fists grip the steering wheel so hard my knuckles are white. The speedometer hits ninety miles per hour as I blow past car after car in the direction of nowhere in particular. The moment I jumped into my truck, all I could think about was getting as far away from Trazia as possible. I've been driving on the highway for all of thirty minutes and have no idea where I am.

My mind still can't grasp that I'm the father of Trazia's baby.

My baby. *Our* baby.

She's been lying to me since March. Not telling me that we had a drunken hookup at the beach house, and then when she found out she was pregnant with *my baby,* she kept on with the lies. My stomach tightens at the thought of her keeping this from me for so long. Would she have ever told me I'm the father, or would her lies continue until after she had the baby? Would Traz have lived in the house with *our baby* and be content with me never knowing that was my son or daughter?

Shit. I'm going to have a son or daughter. My mind has been spinning trying to understand how Trazia could lie to me like this that I haven't stopped to think that I'm about to have a kid. I'll be someone's father.

The truck swerves to the right, and a car horn blares. I get back in my lane and try to pay attention to driving and not end up in an accident. An exit is coming up in half a mile, and I shift to the left lane to get off there instead of driving on a busy highway in this state.

Once I turn off the ramp, I pull into a large strip mall parking lot and put the car in park. Sitting back, I take a deep breath and try to calm my nerves.

Beside me, my phone buzzes on the passenger seat. I threw it there when Trazia was calling nonstop. Not wanting to talk to her, I grab my cell and go to turn it off, but another name is on the screen.

"What?" I answer with an annoyed tone.

"Hey, man, you coming to practice? Coach was asking because he wanted you to run some drills with the few freshmen we have here," Camden asks on the other line.

"Nope."

He pauses for a second. "You okay, Mad? Did something happen?"

Not wanting to be a liar like Trazia, I decide to respond with a grain of truth. "Ask your sister," I tell him before hanging up and turning my phone off.

While I was on my way to practice an hour ago, something felt wrong about being there and Traz going to her appointment alone. Her mom has been able to go with her to each one before now, but her coworker has two kids at home sick and they were already short-staffed at the hospital. I knew this appointment could be an important one and didn't want her to be by herself if she found out the gender.

Now I'm wondering if that feeling is because there has been some gravitational pull toward Traz lately. I haven't been freaked out by her growing a human like I thought I would and enjoy getting her favorite snacks from the grocery store or making McFlurry runs when she's having a craving. I thought wanting to take care of her was because of this crush I've had for years, but maybe it was because that's *my* baby I've been caring for.

There have been many days and nights where Traz and I were lounging on the couch watching mindless TV and she had every opportunity to tell me the truth. Instead, she kept something major from me because, what? She thinks I'm going to be a bad dad. How could she think that I would ever be a deadbeat or walk out on my kid like her dad did to her and Camden? The fact that she thinks so little of me shows me enough.

"Fuck!" I shout inside my car.

The girl of my goddamn dreams thinks I'm a fuckup and not good enough to be a father to our kid. The truth is, if it were with anyone else, I probably wouldn't be handling this as well as I am. This is Trazia, though. The girl who has been forbidden to me for three years and now I'm having a baby with.

Closing my eyes, I try to think back to the beach house over three months ago. Our last night there was the heaviest I drank, and that has to be the night of our hookup. I was shitfaced the next morning, and it took everything for Camden to get me to wake up. I guzzled more coffee than I ever had just to wake up enough to drive home because there was no way I was letting anyone else touch my truck.

Squeezing my eyes shut tighter, I replay the night in my head. We were having a big dinner out on the patio. Trazia was playing beer pong with Levi, Jules, and Emree. I remember I couldn't keep my eyes off her as she stretched up on her tiptoes each time she threw the small ball. Being near her all week and seeing her in a tiny bathing suit most days made it harder for me to not want her, and drinking was a solution of mine. The drunker I got, the easier it was not to get hard looking at her.

Apparently that idea backfired because we fucked in the bathroom. I've been getting these small visions here and there when I'm dreaming and I thought it was my imagination, not a memory. Trazia in nothing but a plush, white towel. Little words said between us, my lips coming down on hers. Traz on the counter with me between her legs as the towel falls, revealing the most beautiful body I have ever seen.

All my visions stop there, but now knowing they're actually memories, I'm pissed at myself for not realizing it before. I've never had dreams as vivid as those, and that should have been the biggest clue to tell me they were real.

Someone taps on my window and looking to my left, a mall security guard is standing there with a flashlight in his hand. In broad daylight.

I roll my window down. "Yes?"

With the lift on my truck and how short he is, the man's eyes barely see over the window. "Care to explain what you're doing out here?"

I look around the empty parking lot and back to him. "Um, being parked? Is that against the law?"

He looks caught off guard from my question to his question. "No, but from my experience, the only people who are sitting in the back of a parking lot with dark-tinted windows like these are teenagers hooking up or creeps jerking off after spying on women in the dressing rooms. Since I don't see anyone else in your car, I can assume you're the latter?"

"Ew, hell no, dude. I'm not jerking it in here. I have better manners than that. I'll rub one out in the comfort of my own home, thank you very much."

"Then what are you doing in the back of a parking lot alone in your car?" he asks again.

This guy takes his mall cop job seriously, and I don't see him leaving me alone until he gets a satisfied answer. "My girlfriend and I got in a fight. Instead of driving while angry, I decided to pull up in here until I'm ready to go home."

The Paul Blart wannabe nods his head as if we're in some kind of club and he understands what I'm talking about. "Women can be a handful," he tells me as he holsters his flashlight and hooks his fingers into the waistband of his belt. "If you want some advice from someone who has held on to the same woman for over two decades now, let it go and take responsibility for whatever she's mad at. Much easier than fighting, and we all know women don't like to admit when they're wrong. Plus, there may be some bonus nooky in it for you for being the 'bigger person.'"

I stare at this middle-aged man as if I'm waiting for him to say "psych" and tell me everything he just said was a joke. "You can't be serious? That is the dumbest fucking advice I have ever been given, and I hope you realize how shitty that is to say about the woman you supposedly love."

Not wanting to hear another word from him, I put my truck in drive and get away from that pathetic excuse of a man. Admitting to a stranger that you would rather say whatever your fight with your wife was about is your fault because women don't admit when they're wrong is disgusting. Adding in he looks forward to apology sex makes my skin crawl. Not sure how men like that find women to put up with them.

The mall parking lot holds little desire for me now, so I leave and jump back on the highway toward Braxton. I've cooled off somewhat now and am in a better headspace than I was earlier. Partly because I was able to calm down and also because of the weird interaction I had with the mall cop.

My phone is still off, and I wonder if Trazia stopped calling. Camden probably ditched practice after I hung up on him and raced home to talk to his sister. I haven't even thought about what he's going to do to me when he finds out I screwed his sister and knocked her up. That his niece or nephew is my kid.

At the thought of the baby, I wonder if Traz made it to her appointment. Is she finding out the gender of our baby right now and I'm missing that moment? Is Blaire at least with her?

I step on the gas a little more to try and get home faster without drawing too much attention to my truck and getting a ticket.

Now that I've had some time to process the news of me becoming a father, I can't help but think that storming off like that probably wasn't the best idea. I was angry and reacted. Leaving seemed like the best thing to do rather than one of us —mainly me—say something we don't mean in the heat of the moment.

Trazia still has a lot of questions to answer, and I don't know how I'll feel after hearing them, but now that I know that baby is mine, I'm not going anywhere.

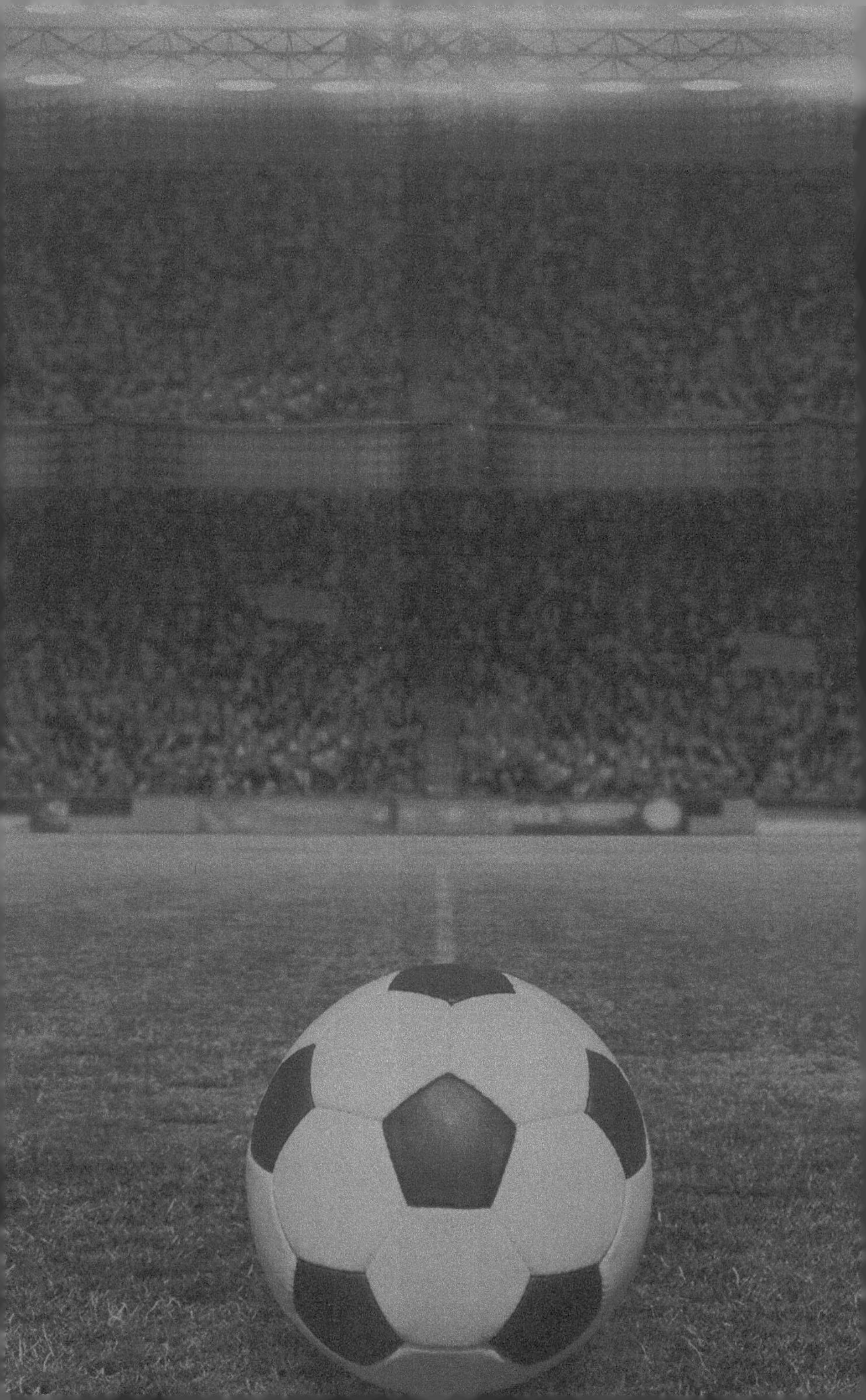

CHAPTER TWENTY-THREE

TRAZIA

"Trazia!" someone yells from downstairs. Angry footsteps grow louder as the person makes their way upstairs. In a matter of seconds, Camden is slamming my bedroom door open. He's still wearing his kit from practice, even down to his boots.

Blaire's hand tightens in mine when she sees the look on Camden's face. My usually fun-loving brother looks as if he ran here from the soccer field in a fit of fury. His breathing is labored, face red.

"Camden, now isn't a good time," Blaire tells him. She and I have been tucked under the covers since Maddox stormed off. After my calls went directly to voicemail, I gave up trying to reach him. He needs time to process the secrets I've been keeping from him, and I'm not sure how long that will take, but I'm willing to give him as much time as he needs.

My brother ignores her. "Want to explain to me why Maddox bailed on practice, and when I asked him what's going on, he told me to talk to you? Have something to tell me? And why aren't you at your appointment?"

Shit. With everything going on, I completely forgot that my appointment was soon. There is no way I can be there in this state, especially not without talking to Maddox first.

"Honey, I really think this conversation needs to happen later. Trazia is going through something right now—"

"It's okay." I cut her off. "He needs to know."

Camden takes a cautious step forward. "Know what?"

Sitting up against the headboard, I release Blaire's hand and pull the comforter closer to my body. It covers Bean, and part of me hopes that if he can't see my baby bump, maybe breaking this news to him will be easier.

"The father found out today. About the baby."

Camden's jaw slacks, and he rubs his stubble with the palm of his hand. "Well, that's good. How did he take it?"

Holding the covers tighter against me, I try to protect Bean as best I can from the wrath of their uncle that is about to be unleashed. "It's Maddox."

Blaire goes completely still beside me as Camden's eyebrows pull together, and he looks at me as if I just asked him to do long division. "Come again?"

"Maddox. He's Bean's father and he found out today."

Camden takes a ragged breath through his nose and releases it slowly. "Really don't give a shit if he found out right now. How in the hell is Maddox Stone the father of your baby?"

My chest grows heavy as I try to focus on my breathing. "Spring break. It was stupid, Camden. We…we had a drunken hookup, and Maddox doesn't even remember—"

"Did he take advantage of you?" Camden's hands are balled into fists at his sides. His eyes are dark, almost black, as he asks his question.

"God, no. He would never do anything like that."

Camden throws his hands up in the air. "Not sure I know

anymore, Traz. Apparently, I don't know my best friend at all, seeing as he is the father of my niece or nephew. Fuck, how could you let this happen?"

"Let this happen?" Throwing off the covers, I stand and approach my brother. Our height difference gives him an advantage, but I'm not going to let him intimidate me. "You think I *wanted* to get pregnant at eighteen? You think I wanted to wake up the next morning and find out the guy I've had a crush on for years didn't remember the night we spent together? You really think raising a baby as a teen mom is something I'm excited about? I didn't want any of this, but it's my reality and I'm dealing with it the best I can."

My brother's face drops as he takes in my evident anger and the frustration in my voice. "Traz, I didn't mean you did this on purpose. I'm just trying to understand how this happened."

"Well, Camden, when a penis enters a vagina—"

He holds his hands up. "Not needing the visual right now." The look on his face is pure disgust. "I meant that you're a smart girl. You know random hookups and not using protection can lead to shit getting complicated. Why weren't you thinking?"

"Clearly I wasn't," I tell him honestly. Looking at Blaire, I smile, knowing how much my brother loves her and how hard he fell the moment he saw her at a party. "Imagine you had a crush on Blaire for the longest time and you finally get your shot with her. All rational thinking goes out the window in that moment because you are *finally* with the person you have longed for. That was me the last night at the beach house. It was the first time Maddox looked at me as more than his best friend's little sister, and I wasn't going to let that moment pass."

Camden studies me. His nostrils are no longer flared, and he seems to have calmed down based on the tension leaving his shoulders. "You've liked him for years? What about that guy you dated?"

I can't help but laugh because Camden didn't like Pete from the moment he heard about him. "He was sweet, but I never felt what I feel for Maddox with Pete. Not even close."

He runs his fingers through his hair and tugs at the strands. "This is fucked up, Traz. And where is the baby daddy, huh? Don't see him here with you."

"Oh, um. H-he left after finding out. Maddox just needs to cool down and then we'll talk." *I hope*, but I leave that part of my thought in my head only.

"Sounds like this is going to be the perfect co-parenting situation," he snaps in a harsh tone.

"Camden Collins," Blaire lectures.

I hold my hand up toward her. "No, he's right." I turn to face my brother. "This isn't ideal for anyone, but it's happening either way. Whether Maddox decides he wants nothing to do with this baby or that he wants to be their dad, you're going to have a niece or nephew in a few months."

Camden steps forward and looks down at me with pity in his eyes. "Good luck trying to get him to step up because for the three years I've known Maddox, he doesn't handle difficult situations well."

He shifts on his feet and goes out the open bedroom door. Loud footsteps fill the silence before the front door opens and slams shut, vibrating the walls.

Blaire comes over and wraps me in her arms, but it does nothing to comfort me like it did before. I just disappointed one of the most important people in my life, and that hurts more than anything I've ever experienced.

"It's going to be okay. I promise." Her words are meant to comfort, but all I'm doing is having a hard time believing them.

A MEMORY THAT ONCE WAS

THE WARM BATHWATER does wonders to soothe my aching muscles as I soak in the oversized tub. Switching rooms with Maddox had many benefits, and one of them is the deep soaker spa bathtub with jets that mold a person's body perfectly.

I've been pruning it up in here for over half an hour. The bubbles cover my entire body, and the Epsom salt is helping to relieve the lower back pain I've been having the last week. When I called my doctor's office earlier to reschedule the appointment I was going to miss, I asked the nurse practitioner if there was anything besides pain relief medicine I could take for the stiffness in my back. She suggested a long soak in a warm bath with some Epsom, and boy was she right.

After Camden left, it took every bit of convincing to get Blaire to leave and go after him. I was fine, but someone needed to be with my brother right now, and she is the best person for the job. Plus, I didn't like the idea of him driving in his angry state. Same with how I've been chewing my lip raw worrying where Maddox was and if he was okay. No one has been able to get ahold of him and it's dark outside now.

When Mateo, Levi, and Conrad got home from practice, they wouldn't stop asking me what was wrong with Camden and why he left without a word. Their pestering finally got me to break and I told them about me, Maddox, and the baby. Mateo and Conrad were stunned, and I could tell Conrad seemed a little angry at my lies, but Levi didn't seem at all surprised. He remained quiet with a small smile on his face while I told them what happened.

The cracked bathroom door begins to open, and I groan. "Blaire, I swear I'm fine. Please focus on your boyfriend right now."

"Not Blaire, Peach," a deep voice says.

Peach. I've never been so happy to hear that nickname before, and knowing he came back has me close to another crying episode. Damn hormones.

"Maddox," I choke out. "Um, I'm not really decent."

He enters the large bathroom, and even though the soapy bubbles cover everything indecent, I put a hand over certain areas in case anything shifts.

In a few short strides, he's beside the tub, crouching down. His hair is disheveled, and there are dark circles under his eyes. My hand itches to reach out and touch his beautiful face and soothe those worry lines in his forehead.

"Based on the bomb you dropped on me today, pretty sure I've seen you in more than one indecent position." His playful smirk appears, and I can't help the smile that grows on my face.

Maddox sits on the bathroom floor, making us eye level. "And if I remember correctly, you don't have any memory of my indecent positions."

He winces. "I'm still having a hard time imagining not remembering a night with you. Trust me, if I could have one wish, it would be to never forget that night."

"I would wish for the same," I painfully tell him, my voice but a whisper.

Leaning forward, Maddox rests his arm on the edge of the tub. "Why didn't you tell me, Peach?"

That's the million-dollar question everyone has asked, and I haven't given anyone a truthful answer. Until now. "Picture having the night of your dreams with a guy you've been crushing on for years, all for him to forget it the next morning."

He regretfully drops his head. "Shit, Traz. I can't imagine how you felt. I'm so sorry."

Lifting my hand from the soapy water, I rest it on top of his and rub my thumb back and forth. "You were drunk. We both consumed too much that night. I should have realized how inebriated you were and stopped it."

"Not sure how drunk I was that I could still get it up," he mumbles.

"Drunk enough not to remember the next morning, but sober enough to be in control of your body," I laugh.

Maddox smiles and flips his hand, linking our fingers together. "We really doing this, Peach?"

"This, as in?"

He points to my belly beneath the water. "Having a baby. Being parents."

I look down and rub Bean. "I mean, if you want to. Never would I force you to do anything you didn't want, Maddox. I know this isn't something you planned, and I'm giving you an out."

His eyes narrow as he stares at me. "Do you really think I would leave my kid that easily?"

I debate telling him about what I overheard after we came home from the hospital but think better of it. That was a private conversation and wasn't meant for my ears. "No, I don't think you would. What I do know is that you're a twenty-one-year-old guy who is going to graduate from college in a year and plan his future. A baby hinders the path you're on."

"I'm going to stop you right there." Maddox removes his hand from mine and runs them both down his tired face. "My future is just that. *Mine*. I get to decide what choices I make and how I want to live my life. If that means being a parent to my son or daughter, then that's what I'm doing."

"But—"

"No, Traz. You don't get to try and talk me out of sticking around. Really, you should want me to be there. Raising a kid isn't easy for two people who are married, let alone a young single mom. I have no doubt you would do anything for our child, but you won't have to. Lean on me. I'm here to support you."

My eyes sting with the start of tears, and I'm really disliking these hormones turning me into a crier. "I don't want to do this alone."

He smiles and engulfs my small hand in both of his large ones. "Then don't." Maddox leans forward and kisses my palm.

"How are we even going to do this?" I laugh around my tears. "Co-parent while living together? But we're not together? And what about when you graduate, and I have to move out of here?"

"How about we focus on getting through the next few months of him growing in there?"

"Him?" I ask, rubbing Bean with my free hand.

Maddox shrugs his shoulders. "Just a feeling. Did you make it to your appointment today?"

I shake my head. "No. I rescheduled it to their next availability in a few weeks."

His face looks conflicted as he bites his bottom lip. "Do you, um, mind if I come with you?"

My heart flutters. He wants to be there to see our baby. "Of course."

"Cool, cool." He nods his head. "And about the not-together thing…why don't you let me take you out tomorrow night?"

The fluttering is gone, and I'm pretty sure my heart full-on stops. "Out? Like a date?"

That smooth smirk I love so much appears. "Yeah, Peach. Like a date. Seeing as how I got you pregnant and all, I'm not so worried anymore about your brother kicking my ass for wanting to date you."

Water splashes as I let out a full belly laugh. "He knows, so I would be careful entering rooms for a little bit."

Maddox stands and leans down, kissing me on the cheek. "Worth it," he whispers.

Standing to his full height, he heads toward the bathroom door but stops and turns to me before leaving. "Full disclosure, I totally saw your nip when you took your arm out of the water. See you tomorrow night." His laughter fills the bathroom as he leaves and I sink under the water, letting out a groan.

In a matter of a day, my life has changed even more. My roommates, brother, baby daddy, and friends all know who the father of Bean is. And I now have a date with said baby daddy.

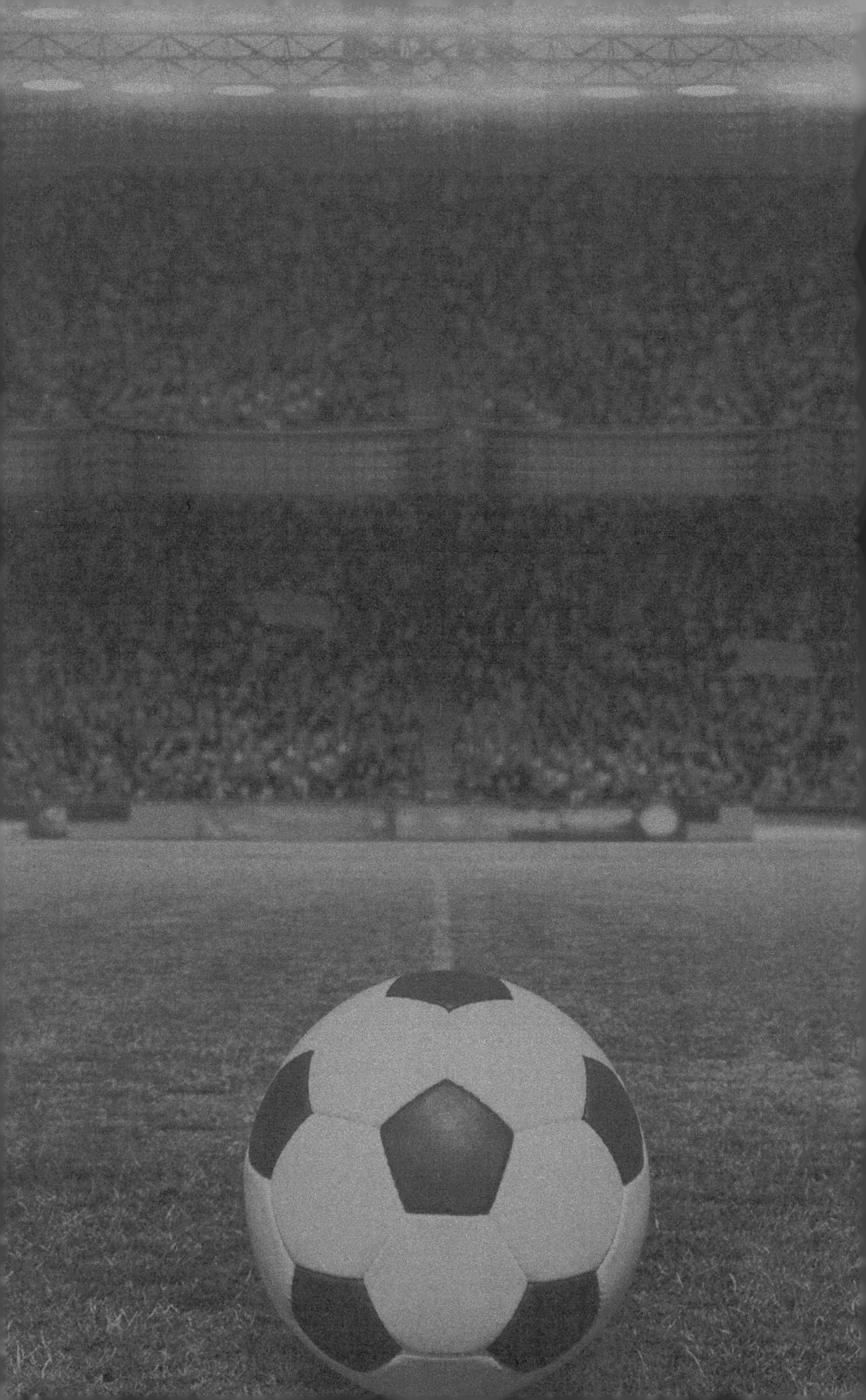

CHAPTER TWENTY-FOUR

MADDOX

"What does one wear on a first date with the woman carrying their child?" I ask Levi as I stare at my full closet.

He's spinning on my desk chair and lets out a laugh. "The fact that this is a legit question is fucked up, man."

Lumberjack is right, but I'm in uncharted territory and unsure of what to do. Am I looking forward to taking Trazia out on a date? Hell yeah. I feel like I don't have to hide my feelings for her from Camden anymore now that she's having my baby. Weird way to date my best friend's sister, but what is life if it's not interesting?

"Where are you taking her anyway?" Levi asks.

I pull a navy blue button-up dress shirt off the hanger and hold it up with a pair of dark jeans and my brown Oxfords. With the jeans, it's a casual enough outfit but well put together.

"Going to have dinner at *Sapori* on the water and watch the sunset. Reserved a table outside and everything." After doing some research of the best first-date restaurants in the area, I settled on an Italian place since most of the ones that came up were by the water and featured seafood. Last thing I want is for Trazia to get sick on our first date.

Levi's eyebrows rise. "Damn, dude. That's some fancy shit you have planned."

"Gotta win over my baby mama's heart," I tell him as I pull on a pair of boxer briefs under my towel. Our date isn't for another hour and Trazia has been locked in her room with Emree and Jules.

"You talk to Camden at all since yesterday?"

Dropping the towel, I turn away from Levi as I pull on the jeans. Having my best friend mad at me hurts more than I want anyone to know, but I understand his reasoning. "Haven't really had a chance to. He either blocked me or turned his phone off. I did text Blaire and got confirmation from her that he is doing okay and needs more time. He's staying at her place for now."

Camden is one of the most important people in Trazia's life, and knowing that he isn't speaking to her because of this makes me feel like the biggest asshole. The last thing I want is to come between two people I care so much about.

"You think he's going to forgive me?"

Levi gives me a pointed look. "For fucking and knocking up his sister? Doubt it."

A groan escapes my lips. "I was hoping for some motivational speech from our resident dad."

"Once again, stop calling me Dad. Really, that title goes to you now. And a motivational speech isn't what will help you. What you need is to man up and talk to your best friend. Avoiding a conversation with him isn't going to help your situation."

Lumberjack is right, but I'm not known for confrontational conversations. Working through this problem with Trazia is one thing, but I don't know how to get Camden to forgive me.

"How would I even begin to talk to him about this? 'Hey,

man, I've liked your sister for years now and was afraid of acting on those feelings because of our friendship, but over spring break we both got drunk and gave in to our feelings for each other and now we're going to be parents.'"

He blinks for several seconds before laughing, leaning back in the desk chair. "You're fucked if that's how you want to talk to Camden about this."

Grabbing the shirt from the bed, I push my arms through the sleeves and begin aggressively fastening the buttons. Levi is right, and I don't want to admit it to him. Having a conversation with Camden about this is going to be harder than I thought.

"I don't want to deal with this right now," I tell him as I loop the last button through its hole. "Tonight I'm taking Trazia out for a nice evening. We're going to have dinner, watch the sunset on the water, and maybe make out in my truck where she'll let me cop a feel. We'll see."

He rolls his eyes as he stands to his full, tall height. "Good luck with that, man. But sooner or later you're going to have to sit down with Camden and talk about this."

Alone in my room, I finish getting ready and slip my shoes on and apply some cologne. Having an adult conversation about this with Camden shouldn't be that hard. We're best friends, and who wouldn't want their closest friend being with their sister? What better man to trust her with? Camden knows me better than most people, and I'm a good guy. I treat women with respect and can confidently say I'd love for my daughter to end up with a guy like me.

Oh fuck. What if I have a daughter and she ends up with a guy like me?

Sure, I'm sweet and lovable, but I've fucked around with some ladies and broken a few hearts. It wasn't my fault they seemed to want more than I was willing to give. It's not like I cheated on a woman, because I've never put myself in a relationship to cheat on someone.

Are Trazia and I in a relationship? Does this date mean we're exclusive? Fuck, she's having my baby, so I sure hope she's not out banging other guys. But does that mean I'm shackled to one woman for the rest of my life? Do I even want another woman if I can have Peach?

Trazia and I have more to talk about than baby names and diaper creams. The status of our relationship being at the top of the list.

TRAZIA

"Wear the green dress." Jules points to the hunter-green strapless dress with small wildflowers embroidered into the fabric.

I pick it up and hold it against my body while looking in the mirror. The straps are thin and leave little support. The bust is tight and turns flowy the farther down it goes. It hits just above my knees and would look perfect with the strappy brown sandals I wanted to wear tonight.

"Oh yes, that would look beautiful with how we styled your hair," Emree agrees.

Jules and Emree came over the moment I texted the girls' group chat earlier that I had my first date with Maddox. Blaire sent her love but didn't want to leave my brother alone right now, especially if he found out she was over here helping me go on a date with his best friend.

After showering, I blew my hair dry to give it some extra volume, and Emree insisted on curling it to give my long locks that perfect beach wave look. Jules brought over her collection of makeup and went to work on contouring and highlighting my face. All of this is more than I have ever done, and I feel like a new person.

Standing in only my bra and underwear, I slip the dress up my body, thankful that it is a loose fit since many of my clothes are becoming too tight with Bean growing. The zipper on the side secures the top, and when I look in the mirror, I can't help but smile at how sexy I look. The girls' work on my hair and makeup makes me look older than I really am, and the dress hides my bump and shows off my tanned legs from our day at the beach.

"Damn, girl, if you weren't already pregnant, Maddox may have ended up putting a baby in you tonight," Emree states after a whistle as she takes in my appearance.

Jules laughs and lays across my bed on her stomach. "You kidding me? If she wasn't knocked up, there'd be no date and he'd drag her off to his room the moment he saw how damn hot she looks right now."

My stomach twists. "No date? What do you mean by that?"

Emree narrows her eyes at Jules. "She means nothing. Just that Maddox hasn't dated much in the past, but that has all changed with you."

I sit on the bed to slip my sandals on. "He's never dated? How can that be? Camden has told me some embarrassing stories about Maddox having women here before."

The two exchange a concerned look, and it takes me a moment to understand what they mean. "Oh. He's only done hookups in the past."

Jules bites her lip. "Let's just say this is the first date I've ever seen him go on. Plus, I can't think of a time I've seen him with the same girl twice."

I'm going on a date with a serial hookupper—a new term to describe my baby daddy.

"What if dating isn't what he wants? How can I expect a guy

who has never dated or been in a relationship before to forgo all he's done to be with me?"

Emree comes to stand in front of me and grips my shoulders. "You don't expect anything from him. If Maddox can't commit and wants to continue swinging his dick around town, it's a decision that is up to him. If you try to force him to choose something he doesn't truly want, it will end with you heartbroken down the road."

"She speaks from experience. Em had to let Conrad decide if their relationship was worth it, and look where they are now."

Jules is right. Emree didn't push Conrad to be with her, but he came to the conclusion that he was in love with Emree and wanted to commit to her. While I would love nothing more than a relationship with Maddox, I know he needs to be the one to decide if this is what he wants. A baby is enough of a change in his life, and I'm sure being in a relationship isn't going to be easy.

"Thank you both. I know it will be difficult, but ideally I would love to make something work between Maddox and me."

Jules grabs my small, dark brown crossbody purse from my closet and hands it to me. "It will all work out in the end, and in the meantime, you're going to knock Maddox away with how smokin' you look."

Laughing, I accept my bag and set it on the end of the bed. "Oh, shut up. He's already seen me naked. There isn't much left to show him."

"Yeah, but he barely remembers that night," Emree reminds me. "Plus, your boobs are huge now. Like, they are seriously fighting to stay in your dress."

I look down and groan because she's right. My bra is too tight since they've gotten bigger and it smooshes the girls together and creates ample amounts of cleavage.

"None of my bras fit me anymore, and this is the last one I've been able to suffer through wearing. By the end of the night, I'll have marks all along my skin. I swear, no one talks about little struggles like these when they're pregnant."

They both laugh. "Not sure many would call that a struggle. Women would kill for boobs like these," Jules says as she reaches forward and pushes my boobs even higher up.

I swat her away while giggling. "Yeah, except having to buy new bras and we all know those do not come cheap. I'd rather not waste my money on those right now."

"True. The last bra I bought was fifty dollars and it was from Target. When did underwear become this pricey? I vote we free the nip. Men can have their nipples poking through their shirts, I want to be able to do the same without judgment," Jules declares while pulling her black bra through the sleeve of her T-shirt.

Emree stares at her before letting out an awkward laugh and pointing to her boobs. "Free your nip and all, but these babies are too big to be swinging around like that. Plus, if Conrad caught some horny guy staring at my tits he'd flip."

Jules stuffs her bra into the large makeup bag she brought over. "Men can fuck right off. I'm starting a movement on campus to ban bras. Imagine how freeing it would feel to not be strapped in all day."

"All right, Susan B. Anthony, let's get going and leave Traz to her date."

They both collect the stuff they brought over to help beautify me and head out the door. Without them here it's too quiet, and I still have about five minutes until the time Maddox said he would be picking me up, by walking down the hall to my bedroom door.

Grabbing my newest book off the nightstand, I lay on my bed and open to the latest page. I got sucked into this series by Ana Huang, thanks to Instagram, and now that I'm on the fourth book, I have been savoring it because I get sad when a series ends. I'm invested in these characters' lives and feel connected to them.

I'm reading the part where one of the main characters, a morally gray man named Christian, just moved a girl he likes, who has a stalker, into his apartment to help her, when a body comes down on the bed beside me. Startled, I drop my book and look over to see who came in here uninvited.

Maddox is lounging with his arms behind his head and his legs crossed at the ankles. "What are you doing in here?"

He reveals that beautifully frustrating half-smile. "Knocked a few times and you didn't answer. Had to assume you fell in the shower or something, so I came in to rescue you like the good Boy Scout I am."

Closing my book, I smack him in the arm with it. "Oh, shut up, you were not a Boy Scout."

"I went to orientation," he laughs out while rubbing the spot I hit him, acting like it hurt. "But for real, I was knocking on the door for a while and got a little worried."

Turning on my side, I face him and smile. "Must have been sucked into my book a little too much."

Maddox mirrors my position. "Get to a sexy scene?"

"As a matter of fact, no. This one's a sweet one where the rich guy is trying to hide how much he cares for the girl, but we all know he's obsessed with her."

"You into some billionaire men, Peach?"

"Having some rich, hot man be head over heels in love with me? What woman wouldn't want that?"

He laughs and leans forward, bringing himself up close enough that I can smell the mint on his breath. "Guess I'll have to be on the lookout for some hot rich men trying to steal you."

"I'd have to be yours first in order to be stolen," I whisper back to him.

Maddox's breathing becomes heavier as he leans in. His soft

lips touch mine, and I melt into the mattress. A palm cups my cheek as Maddox tilts my head up to deepen the kiss.

"Hey, are you all, whoa—"

I jerk away from Maddox's mouth to find Levi standing at the entrance of my door. "Um, I'm sorry. What?"

He waves his other hand at me, still covering his eyes. "No, no. I'm the one that's sorry. I should have knocked. Wasn't sure if you two were leaving soon because Maddox's truck is blocking me in."

"Motherfucking cockblocker," Maddox mutters under his breath while getting up from the bed. He turns away and adjusts his pants, trying to do it in a casual way, but I caught it. I try to cover the smile that it brings to my face. A simple kiss from me turns him on that much.

I hop off the bed and grab my bag, joining the guys at the door. "I'm ready to go."

Maddox smiles down at me and leans in, kissing me on the cheek. "Let's get our date started."

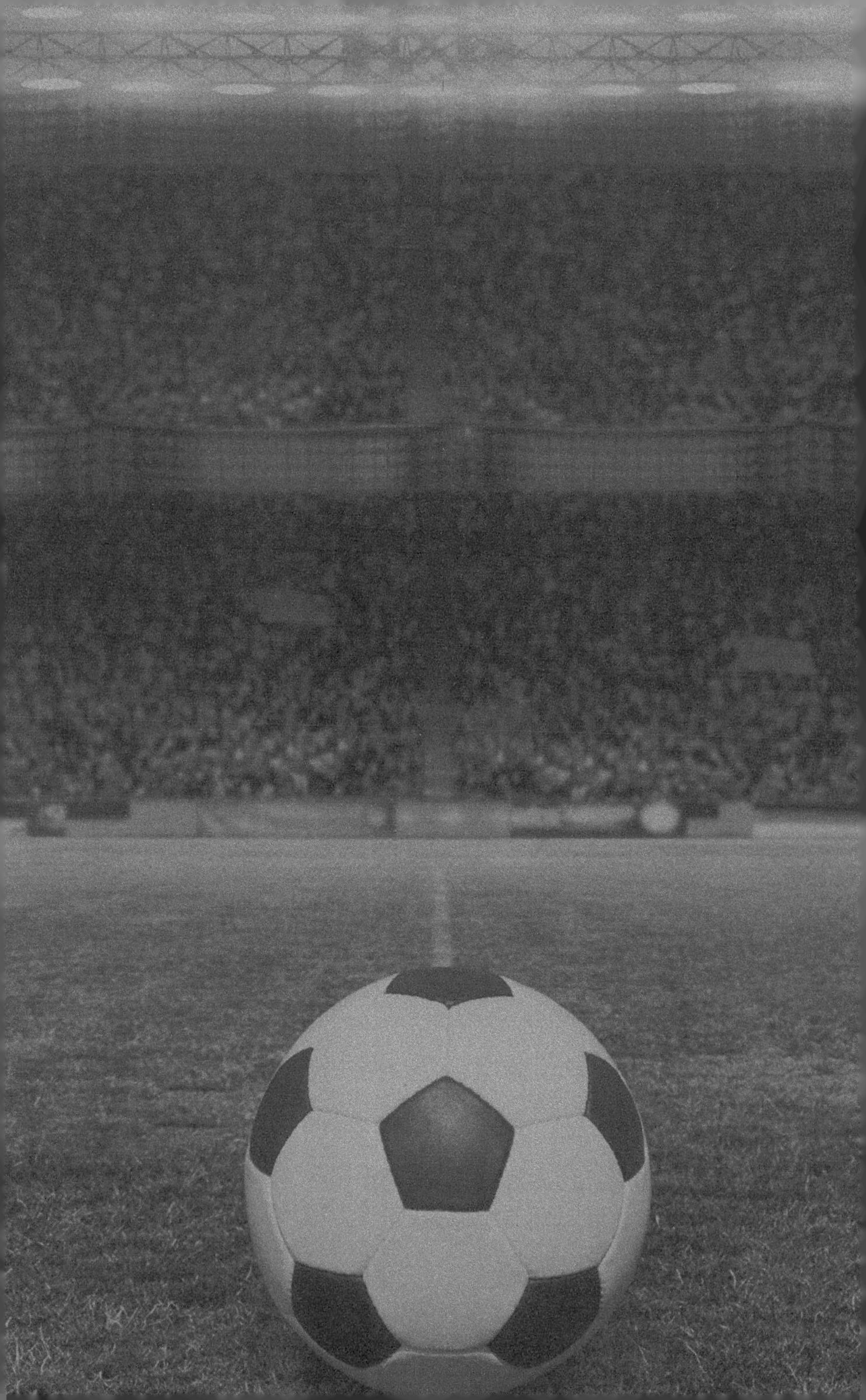

CHAPTER TWENTY-FIVE

MADDOX

My first date ever is going off well. After Levi broke up what I was hoping would be us skipping dinner and getting right to the naked skin-on-skin part of the date, I escorted Trazia to my truck and opened the door and helped her inside, like a gentleman does.

Since seeing her, I've had to keep my hands clenched at my sides because, goddamn, she is a vision. Trazia's legs are long and tan, with the short skirt of her dress showing enough skin to have me drooling. The top of her dress is hugging her breasts and giving them the perfect outline, all while showing enough cleavage to not be indecent. She's wearing more makeup tonight than she usually does, and it makes her eyes pop. Her showing up like this is doing nothing to help keep my dirty thoughts at bay.

"This place is beautiful, Maddox," she tells me as she looks over the wooden railing that our table is against. The water below us is a deep blue, and there are a few seagulls and pelicans floating around, waiting for someone to throw scraps their way.

At this angle, the sun is hitting Trazia's profile and making her glow. She's smiling while looking out on the water, and the breeze has her hair wisping around her face. She looks happy and carefree and more beautiful than ever. Being out with her like this allows me to carelessly ogle her and if I could forgo blinking, I would if it meant I could stare at her longer.

"This view is stunning," she says, closing her eyes and taking in a deep breath of the saltwater air.

Without looking away, I agree with her. "It is."

Trazia looks at me and raises a perfectly sculpted eyebrow. "You're not even looking at it."

I smile and reach for the glass of water the waiter filled earlier. "My view is much better. Trust me. I'll get you a mirror to admire it with me."

The softest shade of orange-pink tints her cheekbones, and I think back to the nickname I gave Traz the first time I met her. She would get this sweet shade to her cheeks that reminded me of peaches, and the name slipped out when I was talking to her. She still thinks it's because of her ass—which is perfectly shaped—and I'd feel like too much of a pussy telling her the truth.

"You're putting on a lot of charm tonight, Stone."

"Why wouldn't I try charming the mother of my child? Of all the people in this world, I feel like that title means you get the best of me."

She rolls her eyes. "That feels more like an obligation. Which is the last thing a woman wants to be."

"Trust me, Peach. If we could have done this without me knocking you up, I would have been all over that. I'm still probably going to be facing bodily harm like I would if we were on a date sans baby, but I'll take what I can get."

The waiter comes and asks us if we're ready to order. Truthfully, I hadn't looked at the menu, but Trazia was eager to let him know what she wanted, so I told the guy I'll take the first thing I saw on the menu, which ended up being a Cajun chicken pasta dish.

Once our waiter is gone, Trazia looks at me through her long lashes while breaking pieces of the bread he brought us. "Do you think Camden is going to be able to move past this?"

Her body is noticeably tense, and I already know that Camden's love means more to her than anything. Him being angry must be sitting heavy on Trazia right now. I didn't see Camden after he found out I'm the baby's father, but I can only imagine what his reaction was.

"Your brother loves you unconditionally and nothing will ever change that. He needs to blow off some steam and distance himself from the situation for a bit, but he'll come back and be the best uncle to our kid."

Trazia nibbles her bottom lip nervously. "What about you? Do you think he could move past this and get back to how your friendship was before?"

Lying to Trazia isn't an option, but the truth is difficult for me to accept. My friendship with Camden means more to me than anyone would think. He's my first true friend who didn't see me as Jack Stone's son but as just Maddox. My life has been me living in the shadows of a successful businessman for a dad who became a millionaire at the age of thirty when he took the few hundred thousands of dollars his father left him in his inheritance and invested it into multiple companies that took off. One of them being Amazon, which he now sits on the board of.

"I'm not sure. You're one of the most important people in Camden's life and I know this hurt him. He should have been able to trust me, and I broke that. You being pregnant at such a young age was already a hit to him, and now me being the dad most likely sent him over the edge. It's understandable that he'd be angry with me for a while."

The bread starts to become crumbs on her small plate as

she picks the hell out of it. "How do I get him to look at me like an adult and not his little sister? I love him and that will never change, but treating me like a disappointment now isn't fair." She looks up and our eyes connect. "I've liked you for far too long and those feelings got stronger over time. I don't regret a thing about that night—besides you forgetting. Do I wish I was starting a family later in life? Of course, but that doesn't mean I'm going to be angry or feel guilt for the life we created." Her hands automatically go to her stomach to comfort our baby while she talks about them.

I offer her a reassuring smile. "Trust me, Camden is going to forgive you and the moment he meets them, he will forget all about how he stormed off like a child throwing a temper tantrum. There's no point in living with regrets of the past when we can't go back and change it. All we have to do is make the best of the situation for our future. And this baby is our future, Trazia."

Her eyes begin to water. "Shit, I'm sorry," she says while wiping under her eyes. "These damn hormones, I swear. Last week I was reading a rom-com and cried when the couple broke up. Nothing about a comical romance should have me in tears, but there I was in my room, reaching for the tissues."

Her efforts to try and hide the tears are cute. "All parts of the joy of pregnancy. Try to avoid romantic movies for the next few months. Maybe we can watch some horrors."

"Maddox." She gapes at me. "You know how much I hate scary movies."

It's true. She practically peed herself a few weeks ago when she decided to hang out in the living room when Mateo and I were watching *The Conjuring*, which I wouldn't even say is a top-ten scary movie.

"Yeah, but watching horror movies with girls is the best for a guy. You get all cuddly and hide your face in a guy's chest, and they get to hold you close. We can do it in bed. Clothes off, of course, to make us more comfortable."

Gone are the hormonal tears, and replacing them is a genuine smile. "You really know how to put anyone at ease, don't you?"

"No use in being sad when happiness is an option."

We're interrupted by our waiter arriving with arms full of entrées that smell like heaven. Trazia ordered the chicken Parmesan with a side of pasta and red sauce. Her eyes widen as the large plate is placed in front of her and I swear if her mouth was open, drool would be slipping out.

After our drinks are refilled and fresh cheese is grated onto our food, we're left alone once again.

"If I eat this entire thing, you better not judge me or say a word about it because I'm starving," Trazia demands as she cuts into the chicken.

My chicken is spicier than I anticipated, and I guzzle some water to wash away the flames. "Peach, you're eating for two. I would expect nothing less from my baby mama."

She smiles around a mouthful of food.

We enter a comfortable conversation as we devour our delicious meals. Trazia tells me about her classes and which ones she enjoys the most. She officially chose the degree she is working toward after speaking with an adviser and will be getting a Bachelor of Science in Elementary Education. She wants to work with younger children because that way she can teach a variety of subjects, and she enjoys that age the most.

"Do you think you'll want to work at a school after graduating and having a toddler?" I ask her when she tells me about how she would like to get an internship her senior year and make connections to work at a private school.

After washing her food down with ginger ale, she answers, "Teaching is what I've wanted to do for so long and I know it will be hard with a little one, but I don't want to be part of the statistic for young mothers. Too many stop pursuing their dreams because they have kids, and I don't want that to happen to me." She offers a small smile. "It will be hard, especially being in school, but this is what I want."

She's determined, and it's admirable to see. Most eighteen-year-olds wouldn't stay committed to school after finding out they're pregnant. Trazia has a support system unlike any other. Between her mom, our friends, and the two of us, this baby is going to be well taken care of and have more than enough love.

Something I worry about bringing up, because one thing Trazia hasn't mentioned when she talks about her future…is me. How do I begin to show her that I want to be there for not only the baby but her too? That I finally feel free to express my feelings for her without worrying about losing my best friend. And when she talks about her plans for life after college, I want to be included because my thoughts are running wild with our future.

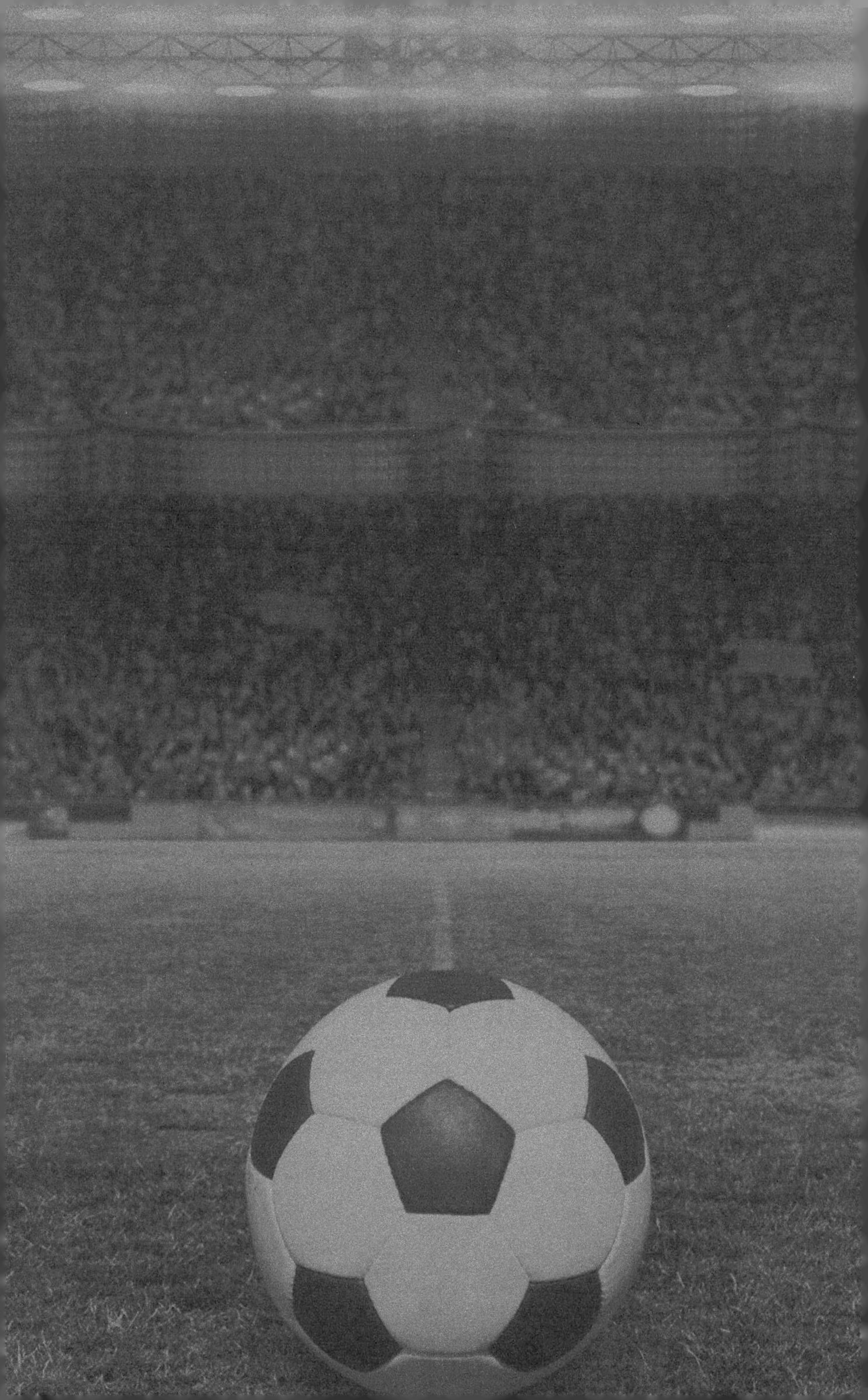

CHAPTER TWENTY-SIX

TRAZIA

Never in a million years did I think this is where I would be in my life. On a first date with the man I have longed for the last three years and pregnant with his baby. Life seems to put you on the most random and surprising of journeys, and this is where mine has landed.

Dinner has me stuffed, and after a short walk along the water we head back to the house, but Maddox misses the turn to take us in that direction.

"Wait, where are we going?"

He smirks and takes a right into a shopping center. "Dessert at the restaurant was boring and you've been throwing back milkshakes from Twistee Treat multiple times a week."

The hand not on the steering wheel is resting on my bare thigh, and I lay my hand on top of his. "You really surprised me tonight."

"Surprised you how?" he asks as he pulls into the back of the line.

"By how good you are at dating for someone who hasn't really done this before," I tell him honestly. "Jules told me she's never seen you with the same girl twice."

Maddox groans and rolls his eyes. "Jules needs to keep her mouth shut and stop obsessing over me."

Before I can answer, it's our turn to order. "Hi, can I get a chocolate milkshake with extra chocolate and a root beer float, please?" She gives him the total and asks him to pull around to the window.

Once we have our ice cream goodness, Maddox heads in the direction of the house.

"So it's true then?" I ask him after enough silence has passed.

Maddox inhales a deep breath and releases it slowly. "I'm not sure what will upset you more, the truth or the lie."

The shake sits heavy in my stomach. "I'd prefer the truth. Always."

He pulls into the driveway of our house, and I notice that Camden's Jeep still isn't here.

"I've never dated until tonight. Not once was there a woman that I felt like putting the time and effort into forming a relationship with, because there was always someone else in the back of my mind."

My breath catches. "Someone else?"

Maddox rolls his head to face me and rests it against the seat. "Don't play stupid, Peach. It's not an attractive look."

The milkshake continues to melt and leave my hands wet. "I need clear answers here, Maddox. Assuming anything will only end up with my heart broken."

He lifts his hand and rubs my cheek with his thumb. "Trazia, three years ago you left your mark on me. And since then, I haven't been able to stop comparing every girl I meet to you."

I lean into his gentle touch. "No one else caught your eye?"

He laughs. "Plenty of girls caught my eye, and I won't lie to you, Peach, I was a bit of a slut. But I couldn't commit to them. Not when I was crushing on my best friend's sister."

Leaning closer, I place a small kiss on his lips. "I hate how much time was wasted."

Maddox cups my face and tilts my head, allowing him to angle me just right to offer a deep kiss. His lips press firmly against mine, and the tip of his tongue peeks out to run along the seam of my lips. I eagerly open and am instantly invaded with the taste of spice and vanilla. Maddox's tongue tangles with mine, and his hand slides down from my face to the side of my neck where he holds a firm grip.

Getting lost in Maddox is easy, and I find myself almost in his lap over the center console. His lips leave mine and move to my neck as I catch my breath. I grip the long strands of his hair as Maddox bites, sucks, and kisses my neck and shoulder.

"M-Maddox, maybe we should—" A bang on my window cuts me off, and I jump away from Maddox and turn to the person who is responsible for my almost heart attack. The windows are too fogged for me to see who it is.

The window begins to roll down, and I snap my head to glare at Maddox. "What the hell are you doing? This could be a serial killer."

He raises a brow and looks behind me to the intruder. "Of all the people I know, I think Mateo is the least likely to be a killer."

"It's true, Traz. Blood makes me squeamish." My other roommate is leaning against my open window. "And what are you two doing late at night with the car all foggy?"

I can feel my face heat thinking about what we got caught doing. "We were saying good night after our date and trying to make it as normal as possible with both of us going home to the same place."

Mateo laughs and slaps the hood of the truck. "Funny, that sounds like the perfect setup. Just head on inside and work on baby number two."

Maddox leans forward and kisses my shoulder. "Oh yeah, I like his suggestion."

Shoving him away, I grab my bag and melted milkshake and open the door. "There will be no baby number two, and this is technically our first date and I don't put out then," I tell him with a stern look before exiting the car.

Maddox's laugh echoes in the dark, quiet night as he gets out of the car and rounds the front. He approaches Mateo and me and wraps his arms around my waist, resting his head on my shoulder.

Mateo crosses his arms and observes us. "You two do make a pretty adorable couple."

I try to hide my sigh as I melt into Maddox's touch. Thinking of us as a couple fills my stomach with butterflies because after our night together during spring break, I had given up hope of anything happening between us.

Maddox kisses my cheek before responding to Mateo. "Thanks, man. Where're you heading tonight?"

"Unlike you two, I have a date where I plan on being *very* satisfied at the end." He winks before walking off to his car.

A yawn sneaks up on me, and I'm unable to hide it from Maddox. He laughs and links our hands together. "All right, little mama, let's get you and that baby to bed."

We make our way into the house, and I get nervous that Maddox will expect more from me because we've already slept together. Truth is, I'm scared of us being intimate again. Finding out the morning after that he completely forgot about our time together hurt me more than I could explain to him, and I'm worried a second time would lead to another disaster like his memory being wiped with one of those *Men in Black* devices.

Once upstairs, Maddox stops at my bedroom door and cups my face with both hands. His lips brush against mine in a soft kiss. "I don't want this night to end," he whispers against my mouth.

Neither do I, I want to tell him. By saying that response aloud, I'm worried he will think that sex is on the table even though I said outside that was not happening tonight.

Do I want to sleep with Maddox? Yes. Is my heart ready? No.

Pulling back, I look up at him. "Do you, um, want to watch a movie?"

He smiles and kisses my cheek. "As long as it's not some cheesy romantic chick flick."

Rolling my eyes, I shove him away and open my bedroom door. "Such a guy."

Once inside my bedroom, I take a few deep breaths and tell Maddox I am going to change into lounge clothes in the bathroom while he picks a movie. When I'm alone, my thoughts run wild, and I try to calm my nerves. After changing into a simple tank top and sleep shorts set, I brush my teeth, wash my face, and detangle my hair.

Looking in the mirror, I grip the edge of the counter while building the courage to go out there and have a movie night in bed with the guy I have crushed on for far too long.

"Calm down. It's just a movie," I whisper to myself.

Straightening my shoulders, I go to the door and leave the safety of the bathroom. My bedroom is now lit only by the colors from the TV. My bed is turned down, and inside of it is a shirtless Maddox looking too handsome for his own good.

"When did watching a movie together mean you need to remove your shirt?" I ask him as I approach the bed.

His signature smirk appears. "Since I'm a man who detests clothes and wanted to be comfortable watching a movie with my girl."

"You better have bottoms on, mister," I tell him as I pull back the covers on my side of the bed.

Maddox grabs my arm and tugs me to his side. "Shorts, but all the good stuff is covered."

"You're ridiculous. What movie did you pick?"

Grabbing the remote, he clicks a few buttons on Netflix, and *The Hangover* begins playing. "A classic."

We get comfortable as the movie begins. Maddox's hand is lazily rubbing my back, and he inches up my tank top with every stroke. The tips of his fingers tickle my skin as they trail from the top of my shorts to my shoulder.

"Hey, what's this mark on your back?" Maddox asks when his hand stops just under my shoulder blade. He rolls me over and lifts my tank high enough to expose my entire back. "Traz, what the hell happened to your back?"

Jumping out of bed, I go to turn the lights on and inspect my back in the full-length mirror in my room. Lifting my shirt, I inspect the spot he was talking about and let out a laugh when I realize what it is he was feeling.

"It's just marks from my bra," I tell Maddox as I hit the lights off and get back in the bed.

He sits up, and the covers fall to his waist. "Why is your bra leaving those red indents on your skin?"

"It's gotten kind of small since I got pregnant. I'm fine, though. I have one that isn't too tight, and I wear that most of the time. If it was socially acceptable to go braless, I would be all over that, but until then I'll just tough it out."

Maddox's nostrils flare, and he grips my waist, pulling me against him. "Why haven't you just gotten a new bra?"

Sweet, clueless Maddox Stone knows little to nothing about the hardships of money. While his parents are distant, they provide him with more than enough money for anything he wants. Maddox has never gone without.

"Bras are over fifty dollars for a decent one, and with my breasts growing, I don't really want to waste money when my size will just change again."

His eyes widen. "They're going to get bigger?" he asks while looking at my boobs.

I cover myself, feeling exposed while talking about them. "Can we stop talking about my breasts?"

"Peach, you came out here in a white tank top with no bra. Your tits have been on my mind since the moment you stepped foot in this room, but I've been a gentleman." I roll my eyes. "How about I rub your back and help with the bra indents?"

I almost moan thinking about a relaxing back rub because truthfully, everything is sore. My body hasn't changed much, but I have put on a few pounds and feel like I'm holding on to more water than usual.

"You would do that?"

"Rub my hands all over your body? Yeah, what a hardship, Peach. Now, flop over and lift that top up."

I do as he says and pull my top up to my shoulders, being sure to not accidentally flash him. Maddox's warm hand glides over my skin, and I melt to the touch. His strong fingers work wonders for the soreness in my back that is not just from my bra.

"Do you have some lotion?" Maddox quietly asks.

I lift my heavy eyes and look toward the nightstand on his side. "Yeah, in the top drawer over there."

Maddox glances at the table. "I'm not going to find anything weird in there like a giant dildo?"

"Shut up." I shove him, and he laughs while leaning over and getting the lotion.

Not long after Maddox's talented fingers are back to rubbing the knots out, my eyes grow heavy, and I drift off feeling more relaxed than ever.

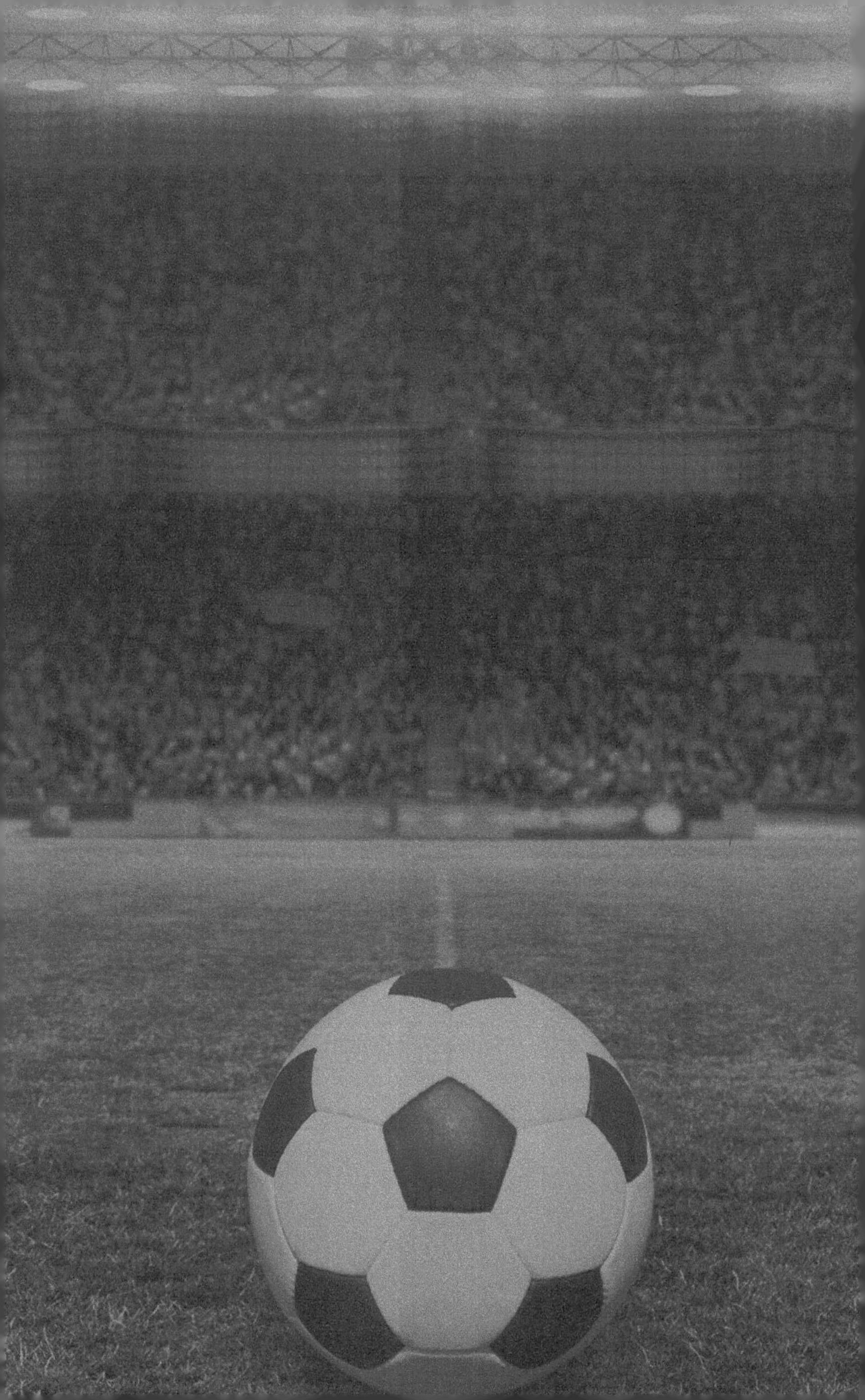

CHAPTER TWENTY-SEVEN

MADDOX

I'm adding waking up to a warm body snuggled against yours with an ass pressed to your dick as one of the top five best feelings in the world. I moan, tugging Trazia closer to me as I try to fight off waking up. My hand slides from her hip around the front to her stomach.

The scent of her shampoo overwhelms me as I nuzzle my face into her neck. After a thorough rubdown, Trazia crashed before the movie ended, and I drifted off shortly after her while lazily running my fingers through her hair. Sleeping next to a woman is a first for me. I've never been the kind of guy who wants to stick around for post-sex cuddles, but I have a feeling after today, I may be addicted to waking up beside Trazia.

"So this is real then?"

I jump at the intruder's voice and jostle Trazia awake in the process. Leaning against the doorframe is Camden, with his arms crossed and looking as if he hasn't slept in days. His hair is disheveled, beard grown out more than the usual scruff he has, and there are dark circles under his eyes.

"Jesus fuck, man. What the hell are you doing standing there like some stalker?"

Camden shakes his head and looks down. "Came to talk to my sister and was taken aback by you in her bed."

"Nothing happened, Cammy. I swear," Trazia reassures him, and she clutches the sheet to her chest as she sits up.

He rolls his eyes at her. "Come on, Traz. I know Maddox better than anyone."

"It's true, man. Look, I still have my shorts on," I tell him as I pull the comforter off to reveal my partial clothing.

"Trazia, can you give Maddox and I a few minutes, please?"

She looks between the two of us, biting her lip while deciding. "You're not going to hit him, are you?"

I flinch thinking of Camden's fist making contact with my face, but it would be deserved. If I were in his position, I don't think I'd be able to keep my cool like he is right now.

Camden's nostrils flare as he stares at me and answers her question. "I promise. Pretty boy's face will stay intact."

Trazia leans over and kisses me on the cheek before getting out of bed. Thankfully after she fell asleep, I had pulled her tank down to cover her. If her brother had walked in on me and a topless Trazia snuggling, I don't think he would have had the same reaction he is having now.

"Please stick to your promise. And hear Maddox out," she tells her brother as she walks out of the room.

Feeling a bit vulnerable with my limited clothing, I get out of bed and grab my shirt and jeans.

With the door closed, it's just Camden and me in the quiet room. Based on the lack of noise coming from the rest of the house, I'm guessing our roommates are either asleep or have stayed somewhere else last night.

"All right, lay it on me," I tell him as I sit on the edge of the bed, preparing for him to go off on me.

Camden blows out a breath. "What the fuck happened, Mad? I mean, my sister. You could fuck any girl out there and it had to be Trazia."

I've never confided in anyone about my feelings for Trazia because I knew the moment Camden found out I would have been knocked the hell out. Camden is the typical overprotective big brother, and Trazia means more to him than anything in the world. No one would ever be good enough for her, and I agree there, but I'd like the chance to make her happy.

"Pretty sure I fell for Trazia the moment I saw her the day we moved into the dorms." Admitting the truth to him feels freeing.

He stares at me for several seconds. "Why her, man? And why haven't you told me this before? She's pregnant, and it's your kid, Maddox. Nothing is adding up here, and I'm trying to keep my cool, but that's my baby sister."

"Could you imagine if I told you three years ago I found your sister attractive, and over time, the more I got to know Trazia, the more I had feelings for her? Pretty sure that wouldn't have gone over well, but it's the truth. I've tried ignoring how I feel about her out of respect for you, but getting drunk that night and finally giving in to my feelings isn't something I will ever regret."

Camden pushes off the door and begins pacing the area by the end of the bed. "You're a serial one-night stand kind of guy. What is this going to mean for my sister? You going to casually just sleep with her and all the other women you bang on the regular?"

Standing, I try to control the anger that is running through my veins. "Do you really fucking think that low of me? That I'm some scumbag womanizer who would treat your sister like shit?"

"If the shoe fits." His face is painted with disgust as he stares eye-to-eye with me.

I come face-to-face with him. "Nice to know what my supposed friend thinks of me. I get that this isn't an ideal situation, and this is not how I would have wanted to get with Trazia, but it's where we are. I'm going to do the best by her and the baby, and it would be nice to have the most important person in her life on our side."

Without another word, I swing open the door. It smacks against the wall, vibrating the room. In the hallway, Mateo pops out from the bathroom with a toothbrush hanging out of his mouth. He stares at me as I storm down the hall toward my bedroom.

"What the hell is going on?" he asks, the words mumbled by the object in his mouth.

Stopping, I look back at Trazia's door. "Apparently, I'm the biggest dickhead to women and am going to fuck around with Traz while also banging other girls on the side. But Camden can tell you all about that."

Once in my room, I slam the door and rip off my shirt, tossing it near the hamper in the corner. I'm not known for blowing up and getting into fights like this. Usually I'm the one to try and cool down arguments between teammates, but right now, I want nothing more than to throw all the shit around in my room.

Kicking off the rest of my clothes, I find a pair of workout shorts and a T-shirt and get dressed. After lacing up my tennis shoes, I grab my wallet and keys out of my pants pockets from last night and descend the stairs.

"Maddox?"

Trazia is sitting on the sofa with a coffee cup in hand and a blanket wrapped around her shoulders. I walk over to her and grab her face between my hands.

"I'm pretty angry right now, and I don't want you to see me like this. A few hours in the gym will help me cool down. I'll text you and maybe I can pick something up for us for lunch."

She places her hand over mine. "Please don't drive angry."
"I'm good. Promise."

Softly, I touch my lips to hers. No matter what battles we're going to face, I'll be there for Trazia and the baby. Even if the ones we're going against are family.

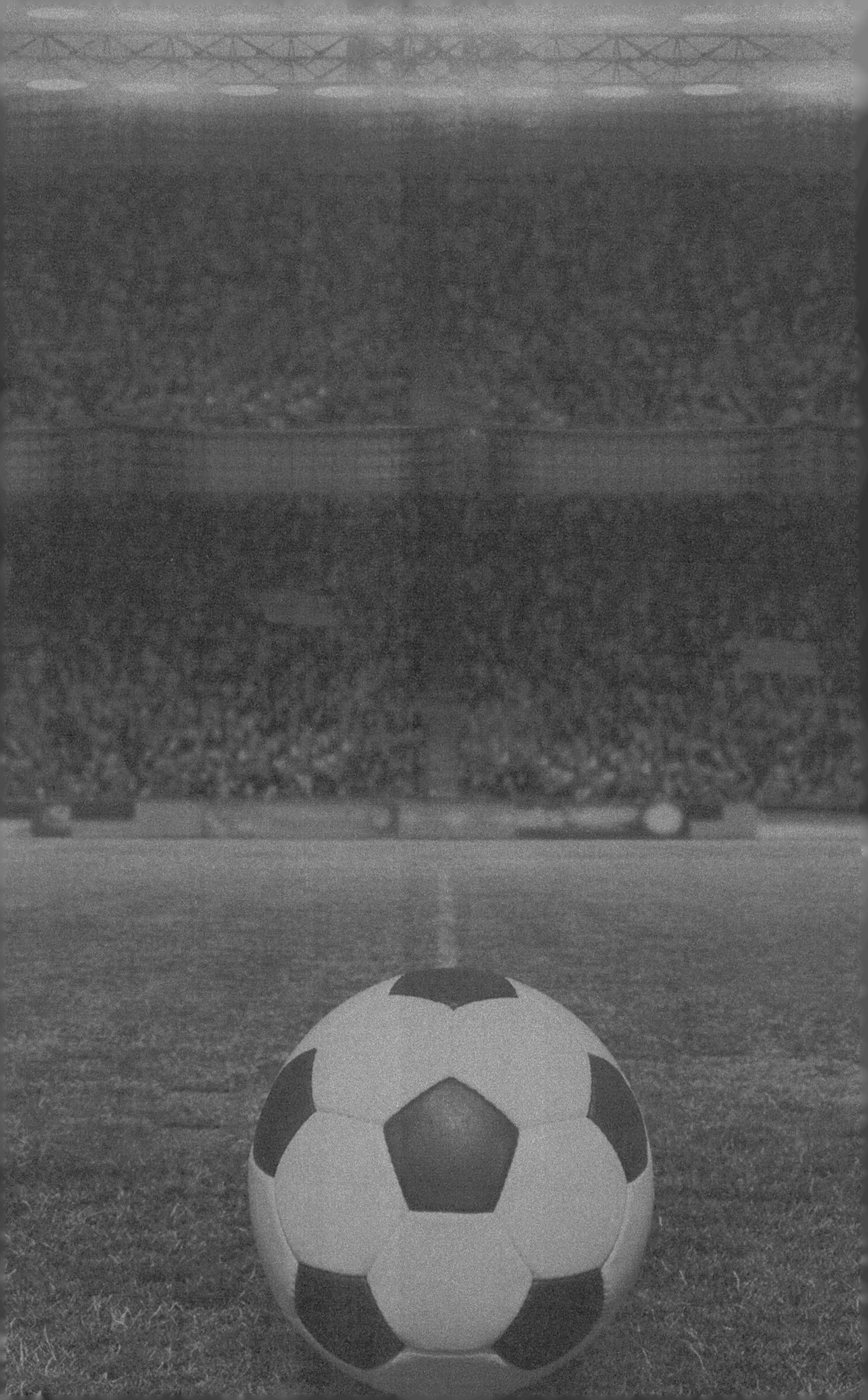

CHAPTER TWENTY-EIGHT

TRAZIA

"He didn't hit him? Like, not even just once?" Emree asks for the second time.

After finishing my sip of water, I answer her. "Once again, no. I could hear them arguing from downstairs, but it was all mumbled. Maddox came downstairs and went to the gym. Camden left shortly after and said he would talk to me later."

"Weird that no one threw any punches." Jules sits back in her chair, cocktail in hand.

"My money would be on Camden. He has a couple inches and about twenty pounds on Mad. Plus his rage would take over and he'd just go off."

Snapping my head to the side, I glare at Emree. "Could we not talk about anyone fighting, please? My stomach was in knots the entire time I was waiting on the couch for them."

Once Maddox had left, Camden barreled down the stairs, looking just as angry as his friend. While I wanted to talk to him and explain how we got to where we are, he said he couldn't deal with this right now and would text me when he was calmer. I cried for almost an hour right there on the couch until Emree and Conrad came in and found me. She called the girls and issued an emergency outing for tacos.

"Just focus on your tacos and not the disaster that is your life," Jules tells me before ripping off a bite of her burrito.

When I imagined my first year of college, I never thought it would be this big of a mess. I saw myself making friends with my roommate and other girls in the dorm, acing my classes, and graduating early. Maybe making a move on Maddox like I've dreamed of. Now I've caused a rift between two good friends, disappointed my brother, and changed my future.

As I rest my hand on the small bump that is now my stomach, I can't imagine regretting the decisions I've made. Having Bean means everything to me. I love this tiny human more than anything in this world already. They're a part of Maddox and me.

"Has Maddox reached out since leaving earlier?" Blaire asks as she mixes her taco salad.

I nod my head. "He let me know he was going to be later than usual. The fields are empty, so he's letting his frustration out with some soccer balls out there."

"This will all blow over. Trust me. Maddox and Camden are forever best friends. I mean, if you think about it, Camden should be happy his friend is the father of his niece or nephew. Now they're basically family." Emree's logic makes me laugh.

"I'm sure they'll be toasting with beers in no time," I tell her. "All of this is stressing me out, and I don't want this to be the memories I have from my pregnancy. The drama behind it all. Why can't everything be rainbows and sunshine?"

"Because you got pregnant at eighteen by your brother's best friend during a drunken hookup," Jules laughs. "Your life could basically be a soap opera at this point. Or one of those telenovelas. They always have way more drama."

Maybe I could make money from a movie about my life. What a shitshow that would be.

"Let's move past the baby daddy and brother drama and talk about the bomb-ass shower we're going to throw. When do you find out the baby's sex?" Emree asks, excitement evident in her voice.

"I had to reschedule the appointment I missed, and they said I could get in three weeks from now. I'll be eighteen weeks, so they should be able to tell the gender by then." Just talking about it has me nervous and excited. "Honestly, though, I'm not sure I want to know."

"Why the hell not? Knowing is essential for shopping."

I shrug and look down at my food. "I don't know. Imagine the excitement after having them when the doctor tells you if it's a boy or girl. I kind of want that moment."

"Oh, now that does sound nice." The smile on Blaire's face has me mirroring her.

Emree pulls out her phone and starts typing. "Does this mean we're planning a gender-neutral baby shower? That would be cute with some greens and earthy colors."

"I think I'd like that."

Jules looks over Emree's shoulder. "Oh, look at how cute that cake is. The bear and balloons would be perfect."

Emree turns her phone to me. "This is too cute not to have."

On top of the small cake is a teddy bear with little baby shoes beside it and balloons behind them. Written on the side of the cake is "Oh Baby" in some kind of gold lettering.

Tears well up, and I try to blink them away. "It's all becoming so real," I admit to them.

Emree puts her phone down, and all three of them stare at me. "Well, I mean, there really is a baby in there. We can all see that."

I laugh at Emree. "No, I know that. It's just...I'm scared. What if I can't do this?"

Blaire wraps her arm around my shoulders. "I feel like every mom has those thoughts, especially new and young ones. The truth is, you'll fail sometimes, and then other times you are going to nail this. Your support system is through the roof, and you know this baby is going to have several aunties and uncles there to help you along the way."

"It's true," Jules agrees. "I already bought a 'Coolest Aunt' T-shirt."

"You think a lame T-shirt is going to win you that title? Pretty sure the kick-ass toys I have saved in my Amazon cart are going to have me winning coolest aunt," Emree argues.

"I'm sure he or she is going to love you all equally. I'm more worried about the boys and how they'll handle a baby around."

Emree laughs. "You ever see that show *Baby Daddy*? That's how I imagine these guys in a few months. Have any of them even changed a diaper?"

"I can vouch for Mateo because he helped me babysit my little siblings growing up, but he would try to push the poop ones off on me often." Jules and Mateo have known each other since they were younger and are more like brother and sister than friends. From what I've heard, he practically lived at her house along with her six other siblings and parents.

"I don't even think Camden has ever held a baby before." I laugh and look at Blaire. "At least he'll get the practice now before you two start popping them out."

She smiles. "That will be a long time from now. He has plenty of years to practice."

"How great is this? Just think, a year from now, we'll be brunching it up with a cute-ass baby with us," Emree states as she grabs her margarita glass, sucking it dry.

As I rub my thumb back and forth against Bean, I can't help but smile, thinking about them sitting in my arms while enjoying the summer breeze. Or pushing their stroller down the boardwalk near the beach and listening to the waves and sea life.

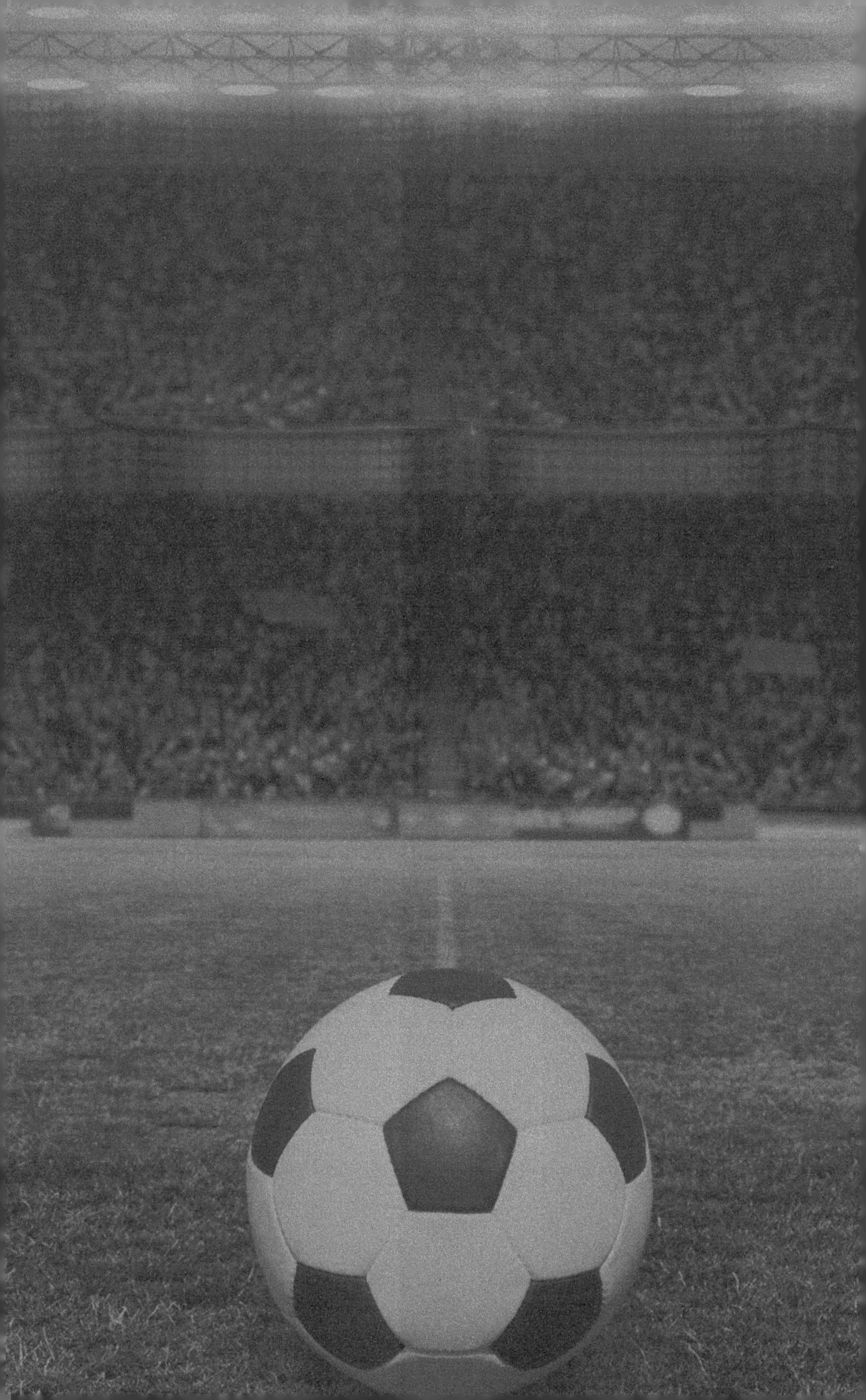

CHAPTER TWENTY-NINE

MADDOX

Knocking on Trazia's bedroom door, I wait and listen for any signs of life on the other end. When I'm met with nothing, I knock again. A few seconds later, a wild-haired and sleepy Traz comes into view. Her face has an imprint from her hand, and her hair is sticking up on one side. The sleep shorts and tank top—that I've come to realize is her staple sleep outfit—are tighter than normal and have shifted out of place.

"Can I help you?" she asks, clearly frustrated.

"Well, good morning to you too, baby mama. How did you sleep?"

She turns away from the door and plops back into bed. "Like shit. Apparently insomnia is another wonderful pregnancy symptom, and I tossed and turned all night."

Without invitation, I join her on the bed. "Would it make you feel better if I told you I have a surprise for today?"

Her head tilts in interest. "What kind of surprise?"

"The secret kind."

That gets me an eye roll. "How about you tell me what it is, and I'll decide if it's worth getting out of bed for."

"That defeats the purpose of it being a surprise."

With a groan, Trazia shoves her face into the pillow. "Your child is keeping me awake at night. The least you can do is tell me what you want to do today." Her words come out muffled, but I'm able to understand them.

"I'll throw in a Starbucks drink and cake pop."

She turns her head toward me. "A mocha frapp? The big one?"

"The biggest they have."

"Let me get dressed." As Traz gets out of bed, I lightly smack her on the ass, causing her to jump in surprise.

"Chop, chop, woman. And dress comfortably."

She closes the bathroom door while glaring at me. Not wanting to waste more of the day away, I head downstairs to fill up the water bottle Trazia has been taking to work with her every day and grab a few of the snacks she likes. Her prenatal vitamin and a glass of orange juice are part of her morning routine, so I make sure those are out and ready for her.

In less than ten minutes, she is downstairs with her long hair pulled back in a braid. She's wearing workout leggings and a loose T-shirt, along with a white pair of sneakers.

"I hope you're planning a casual outing because this is as good as it's going to get," she tells me as she walks over to the cabinet to get her vitamin, pausing when she sees it's not there.

I come up behind her and wrap my arms around her waist. "You look perfect, and I have all your shit out already."

"You're kinda sweet sometimes."

"You mean all the time, Peach."

As she downs the large glass and pills, I grab a protein bar and shove it in my pocket. Who knows how long today is going to be, and I don't want to end up hangry at some point.

Once all her snacks and the water are stored in the giant tote bag she carries around, we head out to my truck and toward our first stop.

"You're really going to continue with the mystery?" Trazia asks after we collect our Starbucks.

"You really going to keep asking me?"

"Fair," she tells me as she sucks down on her sugar-filled drink. "I feel better this morning now that I have my Starbies, so everything is right in the world."

I look over to her once we're at a stoplight. "Honestly, how do you drink those things? It's basically a milkshake."

"Exactly. And you're one to judge. Look at you with your bright pink drink."

While I would like to defend myself, when I look down at the drink in question I can't come up with a good response. "Whatever. It's delicious."

The light turns green, and our destination comes into view.

"Why are we at the mall? And who goes to the mall anymore?" Trazia asks as I pull into a parking spot.

"We're at the mall because you need new clothes and especially a new bra."

She drops her drink to her lap and turns to stare at me. "Are you serious? I told you it's not in my budget right now. I'm making do just fine."

"You're not making do. You showed me just the other night that your bra is causing you pain and you're running out of clothes that fit comfortably. They're only going to get smaller as you get bigger, Traz."

With a loud sigh, she slumps back into her seat. "I don't want to admit you're right, but I can't deny it. Especially since I couldn't even do that hair tie trick with my jeans this morning."

"What's the hair tie trick?"

"It's this cool way I found on TikTok of getting longer use out of your pants when they're too small. You loop the tie through the buttonhole and then wrap it around the button. Gave me a few more inches."

"Huh. That's pretty clever." I grab my drink and turn the engine off. "Now let's get you some sexy maternity clothes."

"If you think I feel sexy while growing a human, you have another thing coming."

"Peach, you could wear a potato sack and look sexy as hell."

A light shade of red creeps up on her cheeks as she exits the truck.

"You know I could come back there and help you pick one out? Make sure it's cute enough," I tell Trazia through the fitting room door.

"While that offer is very sweet, I think I can handle picking out a bra myself."

We've gone to three stores so far, including a small maternity boutique. Trazia has picked out just enough clothes to get by even after I kept encouraging her to grab more. She also tried to shove me out of the way each time I went to pay and insisted she could buy her own clothes. I won each time.

Trazia can be frustrated all she wants about me paying for the clothes, but I feel helpless while she's growing and taking care of our baby every minute of the day. She's doing the hard work and it's interfering with so much of her life, the least I could do is get her clothing that's comfortable.

"You never know. Maybe the colors wash you out. I'll just be here to let you know."

Her deep laugh echoes through the fitting room, and the sound makes me smile. Besides her trying to fight me to pay, today has been fun. I mean, as fun as shopping could be. It's still a pain in the ass and exhausting. Traz isn't one of those girls who could spend hours picking out the perfect outfits, though. She finds what she likes, tries them on, then returns what she doesn't want and leaves. No going back and grabbing more. Most of the items she's picked are the basics too. Mainly jeans, shirts, shorts, and a couple dresses. After the last store, she insisted getting some maternity bras would be our last stop because she was getting too hot and hungry.

The fitting room door opens, and Traz comes out. Her face is red and hair disheveled. "I'm officially done and never want to try on another article of clothing ever again." She comes over and collapses beside me on the bench.

"I would offer to get you a milkshake at the food court, but seeing as you didn't take pity on me wanting a peep show, I don't think you deserve one."

She shoves my shoulder. "Oh my gosh, stop acting like a pervert."

With a laugh, I stand, grabbing her other bags in one hand and holding out my other for her to hold. "Let's feed you."

She smiles and gathers the bras in her hand, linking her fingers with mine.

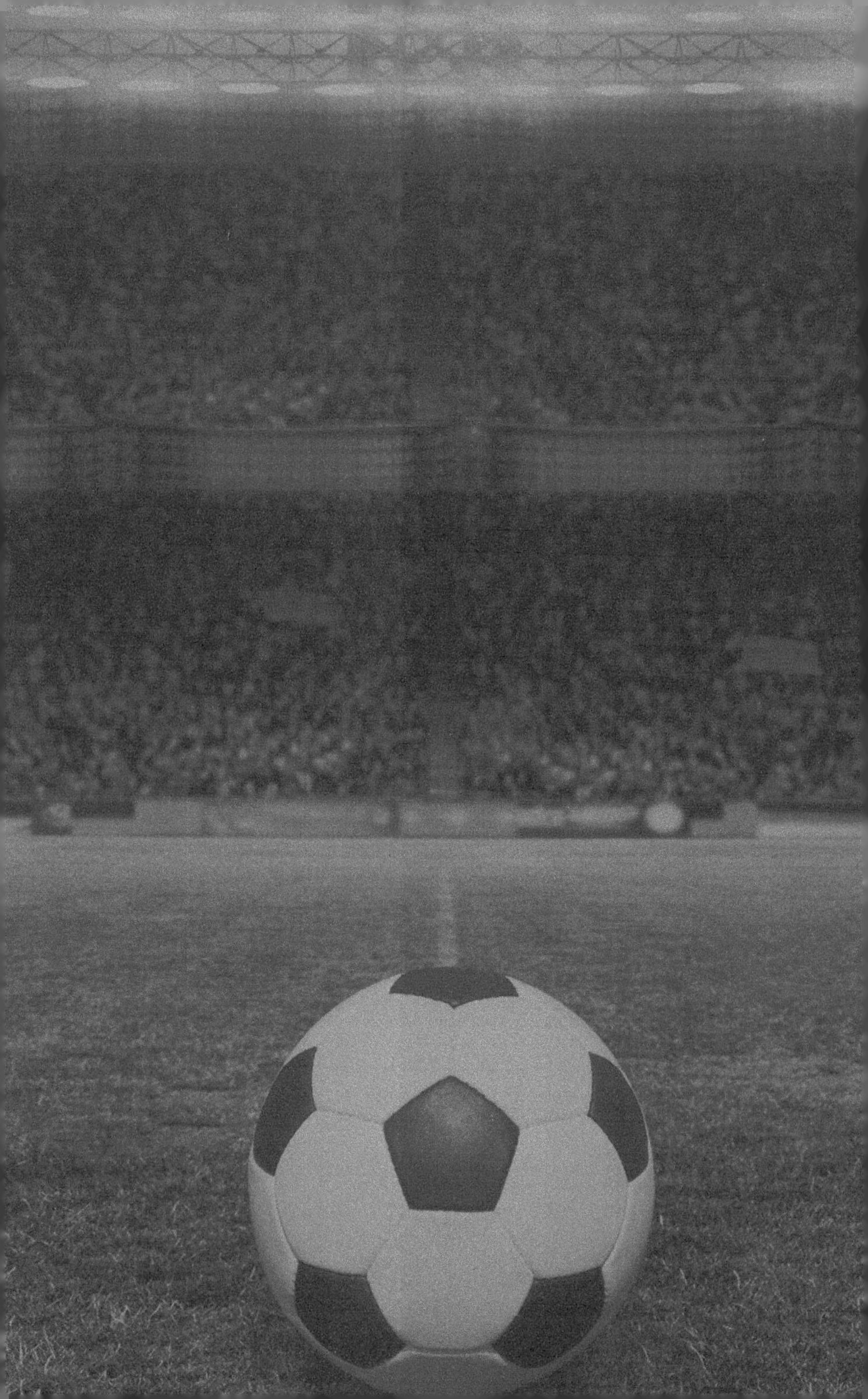

CHAPTER THIRTY

TRAZIA

"Do you mind changing baby Adam while I help bring the toddlers in for their nap?" Monica, my coworker, asks.

"Of course," I tell her while walking toward the cribs.

I've been working at Dandelion for a few weeks now and have never thought I would look forward to going into work each day, but coming here and spending time with the sweet kids has been constant fun. I get baby snuggles and enjoy funny moments with the toddlers. The older kids like to laugh at my continued failed attempts to learn their video games, but I accept that I will never be good.

"Hey, Trazia. How are you doing?" Jannette asks as she enters the room.

I pick up Adam and cuddle him to my chest. "Great, actually. I can't get enough of these cuties."

She smiles as he coos when being set down on the changing table. "You're such a natural with them. Shows you'll be a great mother already."

My stomach flutters. I will never get tired of people believing in me, especially when I am constantly doubting myself.

"Thank you. Babies like him make it easy." Adam laughs as I pick him up, his bum now fresh and clean.

"He is a special one." Jannette strolls over to my side and takes him out of my arms. "Why don't you head out? Your appointment is today, right?"

I nod. "Yeah. At three."

She looks over at the clock and then back to me. "Go on and get some rest before it. We have it covered here. And make sure you bring pictures in tomorrow. You know we all want to see that little bugger."

"Thank you, Jannette."

After gathering my stuff, I head home and am welcomed to an empty house. Maddox mentioned the guys have a small scrimmage match today, but he promised he would be ready to leave for our appointment in time.

While my bed looks inviting, with the extra time, I would like to shower before the appointment. Once I've exfoliated, shaved, washed, and lotioned my body, I put on one of the new flowy shirts and jeans from my shopping trip with Maddox and braid my hair, then hop into bed to get a little nap before he comes home.

I'm jostled awake when my bed shifts. The empty spot to my right is now occupied by a freshly clean Maddox. His arms are linked behind his head while he smiles at me.

"Have a nice nap, Peach?"

I roll over to my side. "I did until some big, hot soccer player jumped into my bed."

"Big?" he echoes while patting his flat stomach. "No need to bring up the baby weight I've gained. I'm sensitive about these things."

"Pretty sure I'm the one with the baby weight," I inform him while pointing to my bump.

"It's sympathy weight. Read in a baby book that it's a very common occurrence."

I pop up, holding my top half up with my elbow. "You read a baby book?"

Maddox sits up against my headboard. "Eh, read would be a stretch. I've skimmed the first few chapters. It's long and some of the stuff is a little TMI. I need to find a dad baby book version that doesn't talk about your breast tenderness."

"Yeah, I don't want you to know about that stuff."

"You and me both, sister."

My phone goes off with my Taylor Swift ringtone. I reach over to the nightstand and turn it off.

"Is it baby time?" Maddox asks.

Smiling, I turn to him. "Ready to see our bean?"

WHY ARE DOCTORS' offices always cold? Someone will probably say it's because of germs, but I think it's to make patients feel miserable. Especially the ones who have to strip down and wear that poor excuse of fabric to cover themselves.

Luckily, I'm far enough along that they can do the baby's checkup through a normal ultrasound and not the one that goes inside you. That traumatized me at the last appointment, and I never want to do it again.

Maddox is looking around at the posters and displays in the small room. He stops in front of one that is a diagram of a vagina. "You know, I've been up close and personal with a few of these but never knew how complex they were."

I groan. "Please don't remind me of the amount of women you've slept with."

He turns to give me his full attention. "Oh, Peach, don't think about them. I only have eyes for you." On the counter beside him is a 3D diagram of a full-term baby in the womb with its head down.

"Do not touch that," I warn him after noticing it catches his eye.

"Why would they put it here if it wasn't meant to be touched?"

His hand inches closer. "Maddox, it's a display. They're meant for you to look at."

He props the hand not near the display on his hip. "Posters are to look at. This is interactive."

Before I can respond, he touches the baby and—since the entire display is not held together well—it falls out. Maddox catches it, fumbling in the process.

Just when I think things can't get worse, my doctor walks in with one of the technicians and they stop and stare at the father of my child holding a plastic baby upside down in one hand.

He looks between them and the baby and holds up his other hand. "I swear it's not what it looks like. She wanted me to hold it and see if it was life-size. I told her these displays are not to be touched and are for observing only. Can't argue with a pregnant woman, am I right?"

Not sure my jaw could be any lower. Dr. Wilson tries to hide her laugh, but the shaking of her shoulders gives it away. She comes into the room and closes the door.

The technician approaches Maddox and takes the baby from him. "You'd be surprised how often this happens."

Dr. Wilson comes over and pats my shoulder. "I take it this is the father?"

I groan and give Maddox my attention. "I'm not sure if I should answer that confidently."

He scoffs. "Don't mind her. Yes, I am the father. Maddox Stone." He holds his hand out. "Excited to meet the doctor who will be pulling my baby out of this beautiful woman."

"Maddox," I hiss while Dr. Wilson lets out a full laugh, not bothering to hide it at this point.

My doctor waves me off as she shakes his hand. "No worries. Yes, Maddox, I will be the doctor helping to bring your baby into the world. It's nice to meet you." She turns to the other woman in the room. "This is Patty, our ultrasound technician. Throughout your pregnancy you won't always see me, so I would like you to get comfortable with other doctors in the practice in case they end up delivering your baby, but Patty will be a regular for you."

After going through the normal checkup procedures and questions, Dr. Wilson asks how I've been feeling and if there are any questions or concerns I have. The only issue I wanted to bring up was the sleep struggles, and she assures me that is normal, and something that helps many of her patients is a pregnancy pillow. Maddox makes note of it in his phone.

"Are you ready to see your baby?" she asks after putting my paperwork away.

My stomach flutters in anticipation of seeing them. "So ready."

Maddox stands at my side as Dr. Wilson lifts my shirt to expose my swollen stomach and applies some cold gel. She moves the wand around my lower abdomen while looking at the sonogram screen.

"Looks like they're playing hide-and-seek. Wait one second." She pushes on the side of my stomach with her free hand. "There they are."

In the center of the grainy gray screen is the outline of a head. It's small, but you can clearly tell what it is. My baby. Our baby. My first appointment, it looked like a small blob in there and when the doctor asked if I saw the baby, I agreed with her because I felt like it made me a terrible mother for not seeing them, but there they are.

The technician flicks a switch, and the most beautiful sound fills the room. Their heartbeat.

"Damn. There's really a baby in there," Maddox states from beside me. I look away from the screen and to the father of my baby. He's staring at them in awe. He doesn't look away but reaches out for my hand. "This is happening."

"Yeah, Mad. It's happening."

"They have a strong heartbeat." Dr. Wilson moves the wand around some more, getting a better view and capturing some pictures. "And are we wanting to know the sex of the baby?"

The ultimate question. I have been going back and forth on this for weeks. On one hand, it would be nice to shop specifically for a baby boy or girl, but on the other, I would love to have that exciting moment when they are welcomed into the world, and my anticipation is high right before finding out who they are and what their official name will be.

I look up at Maddox. "How do you feel about finding out at the birth?"

He nods. "I kind of like that. It's the old-school way. As long as you don't make me wait outside. I'd like to be there for you, if that's okay?"

"Of course I will want you there," I tell him honestly. When I think of who the people in the delivery room with me should be, the father and my mom are the only two that matter.

"Then it's settled," Dr. Wilson announces as she pulls the wand away from my stomach and hooks it back up to the machine. "We're going to have a gender reveal in the delivery room. How exciting. I haven't had one of those in a long time." The technician hands me a wad of paper towels to clean my stomach of the goo.

After I've cleaned myself and righted my shirt, she hands me the sonogram pictures. "Here you go. They were posing great."

I split them in half and handed part of the stack to Maddox.

He studies them closely. Watching him mesmerized by our baby has me feeling terrible that I doubted him in the beginning and didn't tell him right away about the pregnancy. He's shown me nothing but love and care since the moment he found out, even before he knew the baby was his.

"We'll give you two some time to look at those. No rush. Come on out to the front desk whenever you're ready, and I'll schedule your next appointment," the technician tells us as she and Dr. Wilson leave the room.

"You mind if I keep one of these, Peach? I want to carry it around. Show the guys what we got cooking in there," he asks as he points to my stomach.

I roll my eyes. "As long as you don't refer to me growing our baby as 'cooking,' then yes."

Maddox helps me down from the exam table and wraps his arms around my waist. "Fine. I promise. No comparing you to an oven."

"That's all I ask." With both hands, I hold his face and bring it closer to mine. Our lips softly brush together before Maddox applies more pressure, forcing my mouth open. As his grip on my hips gets tighter, I have to remind myself where we are and that my pregnant hormones should not be controlling me.

"You know, seeing our baby today shouldn't turn me on, but I am finding you incredibly sexy right now."

I shove his shoulders back. "Oh stop. Keep it in your pants, Stone." He laughs as we head to the door, hand in hand.

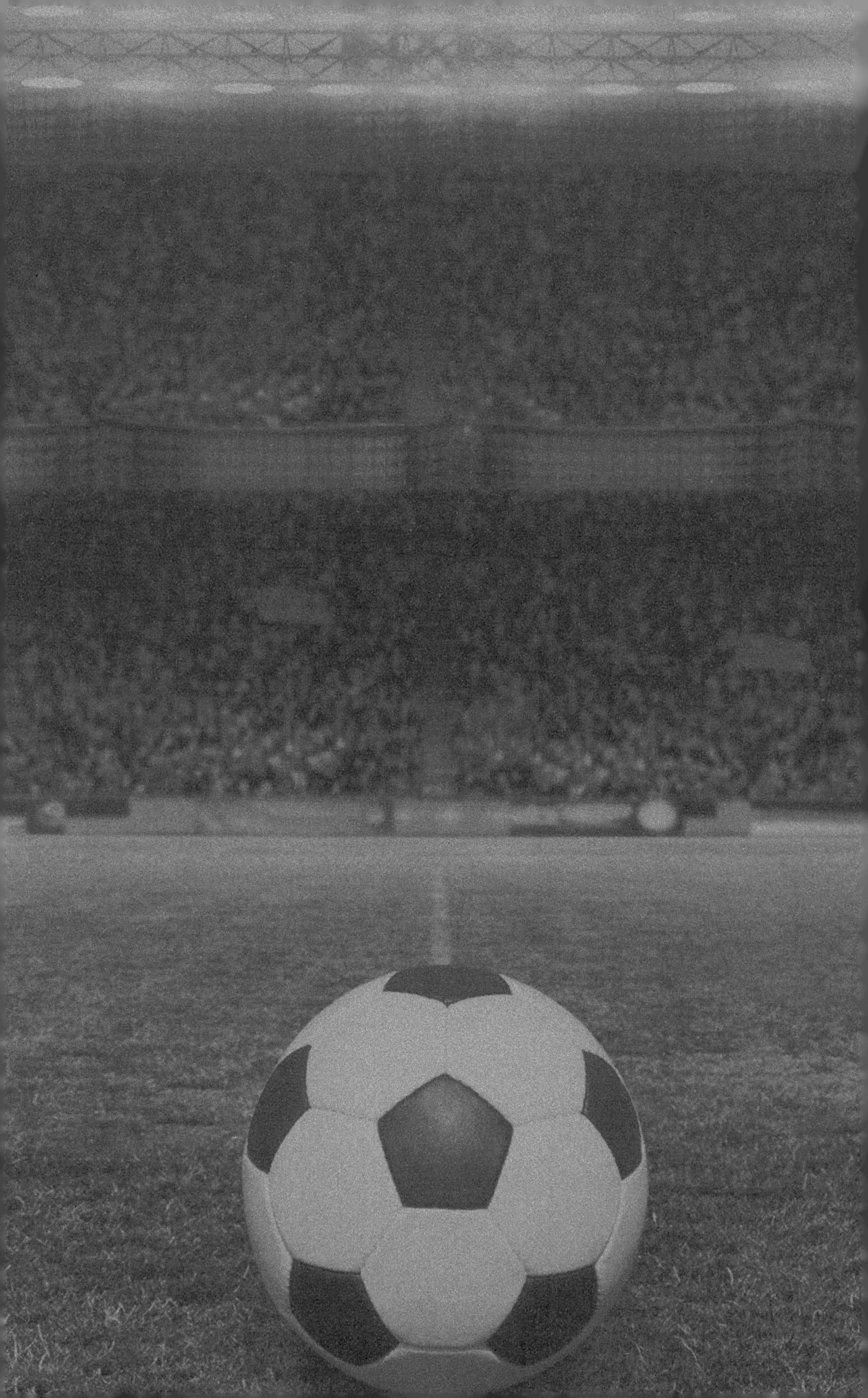

CHAPTER THIRTY-ONE

MADDOX

Rubbing the sleep from my eyes, I head downstairs to start the coffee and get Trazia's morning rituals ready. She had another sleepless night, and the pregnancy pillow Dr. Wilson suggested won't be here until tomorrow.

How do I know she had a sleepless night? I've basically moved into her room—my old bedroom.

Since our first date, I have been mainly sleeping in her room. Most of the time it's not on purpose because we both crash while watching a movie, but there are nights she falls asleep in my arms and I don't have it in me to leave.

With her cup of juice filled, I grab her vitamin bottles and begin getting the correct portions out. With her disgust for milk, Trazia has added in a calcium vitamin because she's read online somewhere that it was important to get even more calcium than normal.

"You really care about her, don't you?" a deep voice asks from somewhere in the room.

I jump, surprised because I thought no one else was up. At the kitchen table sits Camden with a cup of coffee in front of him. I haven't talked to him since our argument days ago, and with how we left things, I haven't felt up to chatting.

"Tried telling you that, but all my best friend had to say was how shitty of a person I am," I tell him as I focus on her pills.

He sighs, and the legs of the chair scrape against the floor.

For the last three years, Camden has become the closest person I've gotten to, and right now he feels like a complete stranger. I don't know if our friendship will ever be what it was before, but my priority will always be Trazia and our baby from now on.

"I think I owe you an apology," Camden tells me as he approaches the bar countertop.

I lift my head, arching an eyebrow. "You think?"

"Shit, man, I'm trying to apologize here."

Setting the bottle of Trazia's prenatal pills down, I stare at my friend through squinted eyes. "Are you now? Not a great start."

"I was wrong, okay? Blaire and Emree sat me down and talked some sense into me. I guess I never saw the way the two of you felt about each other. Blaire explained it to me, but I'm still oblivious."

I nod in understanding. "Dude, I get it. I do. Traz is your little sister, and I broke the guy code. The thing is, I know I fucked up with how we got together and her getting pregnant, but I won't apologize or regret anything. I'm not going to ever have her thinking I regret her or our baby."

Camden lowers himself into one of the bar chairs. "It took me some time, but I appreciate that." He sighs. "You know our messed-up childhood with our dad. I think part of me was afraid Trazia would end up like my mom."

My hands ball into fists at my sides. "I would *never* leave my child. Even if Trazia and I don't work out, that is my kid, and I will be in their life no matter what."

"I believe you. Trust me, after what I've seen and heard

since finding out, especially with you coming down here and getting this all prepared for my sister like you do every day, I can see that you're beside her in this." He waves a hand at Trazia's morning rituals.

"He is," a soft voice announces from the entryway.

Trazia comes in wearing one of my T-shirts—that is three sizes too big for her—and a pair of sweatpants. She looks tired with the dark circles and heaviness evident in her eyes, but I would never tell her that. The only thing she hears from me are daily affirmations. The baby blog for dads I follow said that's important.

Her arm wraps around my waist as she comes to my side. "And thank you for sitting down and listening to Blaire and Emree. That means a lot to me."

"I just want what's best for you, Traz. Your happiness is what's most important to me."

She leaves my side and goes to him. "Well, duh. You've been the best big brother there is, and this doesn't change that. I just need you to trust me with certain aspects of my life. Like whom I get to love."

My breath all but stops as I digest her words. Neither of them notices the panic her words have set in me, and I try to keep a neutral face. But that word...it's not something I've ever used with a girl before. Honestly, I can't remember the last time I told anyone I loved them.

"So, Blaire said you two had an appointment this week?"

Trazia's eyes light up as a smile grows on her face. "We did. Do you want to see your niece or nephew?"

He nods. "She also said you aren't finding out what they are, but I need to tell you that it is for sure a boy. He'll have a house full of soccer players, and we'll have to train him young if we want a future Messi in the family."

"Don't let Mateo hear you say that. You know he has that big old crush on Neymar and will fight with you over who's the better player." This is an ongoing debate among our roommates.

Camden scoffs. "He can believe all he wants. Messi was named the best player of 2022. That says it all right there."

I point my finger at him. "Yeah, but Neymar has more goals and assists. That should go on record too. Just because Messi is more popular with the public doesn't mean he's the best."

Trazia holds both of her hands up to us. "Can you two table this discussion while I show my brother the baby?"

"Oh, sure, Peach." I look to Camden. "But this isn't over."

She goes to the fridge and removes the magnet holding the sonogram picture up. Camden grabs the photo from her and looks at his niece or nephew. This picture is still grainy, but much better than the one from her first appointment since the baby is larger now.

"Damn, there's really a baby in there," he announces, not looking away from the photo.

Trazia laughs. "I think seeing this and hearing the heartbeat made it all real for Maddox too." She rubs her small bump. "For me, on the other hand, it's the fact that I've got a baby the size of a pomegranate living in here."

"Did you check your baby tracker this morning?" I ask her as she grabs her cup of vitamins and juice, downing them both.

"Yes, I did. And if you're curious, our baby is developing their hearing and feelings right now, and hopefully I will be able to feel them move soon."

The thought of him or her moving around inside of there would have freaked me out, but I am strangely fascinated with everything involving her growing our child. I may joke with her about the apps she has and how she checks those in the morning before anything else, but I'm right there along with her. Maybe not as knowledgeable since I only have one app, but I still knew everything she had just told me.

Reaching down, I spread my hand over her small stomach

and move it back and forth, rubbing where our baby is. "Maybe if we keep touching them, they'll try and kick us away and you'll feel it." With my other hand, I pull her to my chest by her hip and spread both my hands over our baby. "Here, I'll take the first shift. Just stay against me all day like this." I pull her as close as possible to me and try to ignore the fact that her ass is nestled against my dick in the most delicious way.

Camden groans. "Uh, yeah. I may be coming around to the fact that you two are together and having a baby, but I don't need to be around for this shit. Just keep it PG when I'm in the room. Thanks."

Not letting go of his sister, I respond, "When was the last time you watched a PG movie? Our pants are on and everything. This is more PG than *The Little Mermaid*. At least Trazia isn't wearing a bra around."

Trazia rolls her eyes. "You two are ridiculous. I'm going to get ready for work." She turns and kisses me on the cheek. "Now that we're all friends and talking, maybe everyone can get together tomorrow night? Dinner here or at Whiskey Joe's?"

Camden nods. "Here sounds good. I think Em and Blaire have the evening off, but I'll check with them."

She goes over and hugs her brother. "Thank you," Trazia whispers, her voice muffled by his shoulder. Camden squeezes her tight before letting go.

Having Camden back home and talking to us gives me hope that everything will go right from now on. The biggest struggle I've been avoiding is telling my parents about their upcoming title change to grandparents.

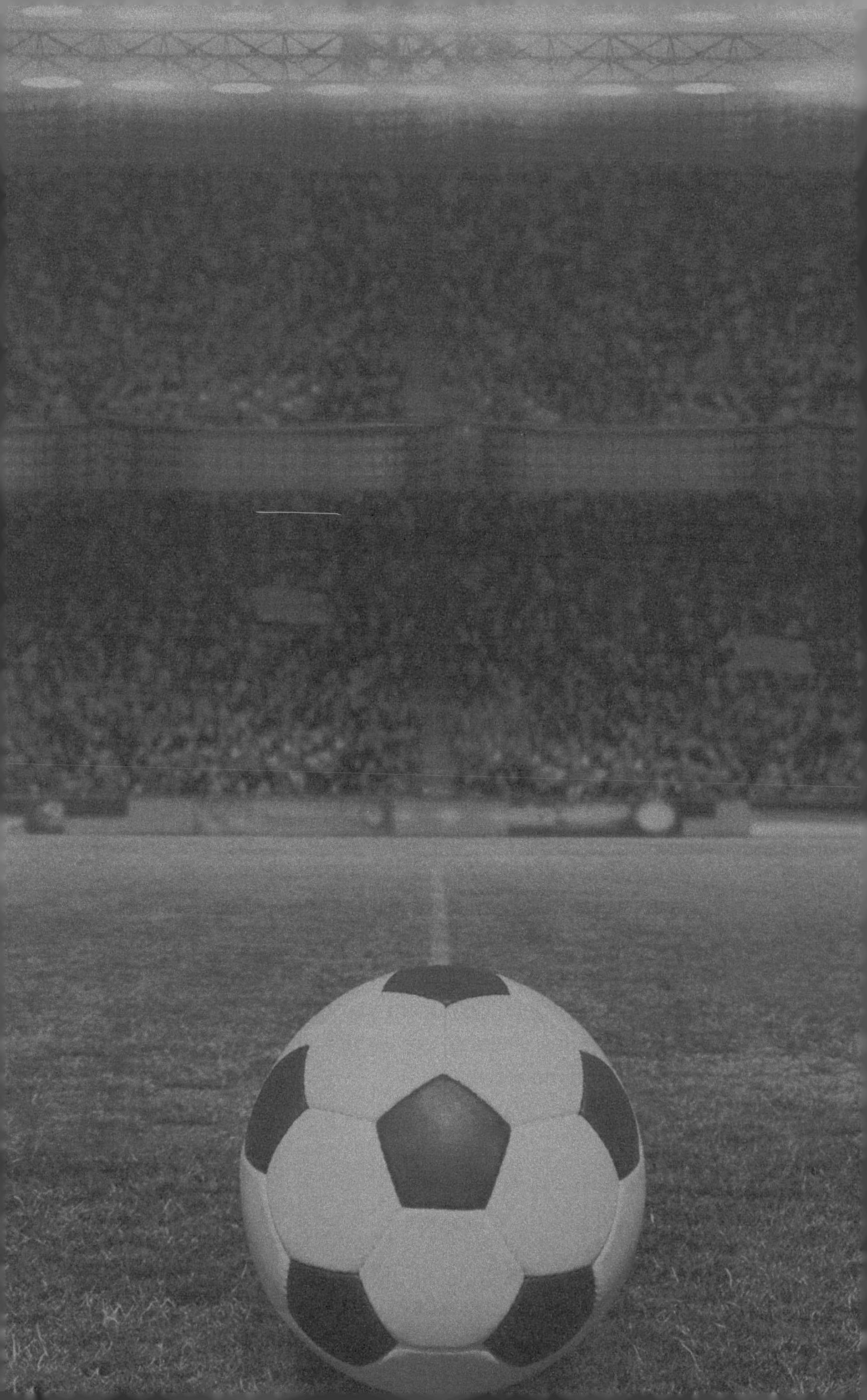

CHAPTER THIRTY-TWO

TRAZIA

The sun is shining, my brother and Maddox are friends again, and Bean is causing me only a little discomfort. Last night, he or she allowed me a restful sleep and I woke up feeling better than I have in weeks. Waking up in Maddox's arms doesn't hurt either. I much prefer that over waking up alone.

Maddox, Camden, Conrad, and Jules are playing volleyball in the pool while Blaire and Emree are reading, and Mateo and Levi are finishing off the burgers we ate earlier. A day like today was much needed, and everything feels right now.

Last night, Maddox confessed to me that he was struggling with how to tell his parents about Bean. They don't have a close relationship because of them leaving him most of his childhood, and he feels uncomfortable calling them to give details about his life.

I sat with him while he told me all of this, but inside I couldn't imagine feeling that way about my mom. She's someone who I could talk to about anything, and I want to call and update her on my life whenever there's a slight change. While I kept my thoughts to myself and let Maddox get everything off his chest, I was worrying inside about Bean and the relationship they would have with their grandparents.

"Baby mama, you coming in or what?" Maddox shouts from the pool.

Lowering my sunglasses, I glare at him. "What did I say about that nickname?"

Maddox laughs, and the sound sends chills through me. "Don't remember. Why don't you come over here and tell me again?"

"You promise not to pull me into the pool?" I ask, knowing the answer already.

With his hand in the air, Maddox crosses his fingers. "Of course not. I am an honorable man, Peach."

Everyone erupts into comical laughter at the blatant lie.

Standing from the comfort of my lounge chair, I slowly make my way around the pool to where Maddox is leaning against the edge. His arms are crossed over his wet chest, and there is a squint in his eyes from the bright sun.

The entire time his eyes follow me. Our friends go back to talking and goofing around in the water, but Maddox's full attention is gifted to me.

When I make it in front of him, he nods his head down for me to sit on the edge. Luckily I'm in my bathing suit and don't need to worry about getting wet. Though I did wash my hair this morning and was trying to avoid that getting soaked.

With my butt planted on the ground and legs dangling in the water, Maddox comes to stand between my thighs and wraps his arms around my waist. "Missed you," he tells me, leaning in to plant a soft kiss against my lips.

I massage his shoulders, knowing they are sore from his workout last night with Levi. "I was right over there."

He lifts himself up higher, pressing his mouth to mine in a harder kiss. "Too far," he says against my lips.

Maddox moves his mouth against mine, his tongue coming

out to trace the seam of my lips. I open and am immediately invaded with the taste of him. Beer and the mint chews he had after dinner. My hands leave his shoulders and tangle into the long locks of his hair, gripping at the base. He moans into my mouth when I pull a little too hard but doesn't back away.

"Ah, fuck, man, what did I say yesterday?" My brother groans from somewhere, but I'm too lost in the feel of Maddox's hands on my body and his taste.

Pulling away, Maddox drags my bottom lip between his teeth and opens his eyes. They're darker than they usually are and filled with lust. "Really wishing we didn't have a house full of people right about now."

I know exactly how he feels, and while I wanted to take our relationship slow, sleeping in the same bed as Maddox every night has made it harder and harder to resist him.

Wrapping my arms around his neck, I pull him close enough to rest my forehead against his. "Emree mentioned something about them going to a party tonight."

He pulls back, raising a brow. "Are they now? You in for a snuggle session with some Chinese food in bed?"

My nose scrunches up thinking about spilling anything in bed. "How about dinner on the couch and then a snuggle session in bed? I just started *Ginny & Georgia*, so I can catch you up on the first couple episodes."

"I would like to argue with you about watching some chick show, but I weirdly enjoyed that Vander-something you made me watch."

Smiling, I kiss him on the lips. "Trust me when it comes to TV shows. They may sound lame, but they're addictive. Even though I don't follow the Kardashians, their show gets you hooked."

"Traz, you coming out with us tonight?" Emree shouts from the other side of the pool where Jules has now joined her and Blaire.

Turning to Maddox, I give him a questioning look. He shakes his head once.

"No. Mad and I are going to have a date night in," I answer her.

She waggles her eyebrows. "Oh, I'm sure you are." The other girls ooh and ahh. Camden groans and dunks his head under the water.

Butterflies flutter in my stomach, thinking about having the house to ourselves tonight and what that could mean for Maddox and me. We haven't been intimate other than some heated make-out sessions here and there, but our plans for tonight feels like there is more to come.

While there have been ample opportunities for us to go all the way—especially with Maddox sleeping in my bed each night—I've stopped it before we go too far. My mind replays the morning after the night we had sex and Maddox completely disregarding it. Him not remembering hurt more than I've let on and I'm scared that'll happen again, even though I know he is sober each night.

The guys head to the stairs and get out of the pool. Blaire collects a handful of towels from the bench we placed them on earlier, and they all begin drying off. Maddox makes no move to get out and instead moves one of his hands from my hip to my lower stomach, caressing our little bean.

Our friends chatter, but I'm too lost in our own bubble to pay attention. "I was thinking about names earlier today," I tell him.

Maddox looks up at me through his long, dark lashes. "Yeah? What do you have in mind? Other than Maddox Junior, of course."

"Oh yeah, of course," I laugh. "For a girl, the name Myla kept sticking with me."

"Myla..." Maddox tests the name. "And what would her last name be?" His tone is cautious.

Cupping his cheek, I rub my thumb through his stubble. "Stone or Collins-Stone. You're their dad, Maddox. I would never take that away from you."

Lifting out of the water, he places a kiss on my stomach. His lips feel scorching against my skin. Any simple touch from Maddox sends tingles through me. I try not to let him see the effect he has on me, but when he glides his lips across my stomach, a shiver runs through me.

Hand in hand, we follow our friends into the house. While I love being around everyone and am glad the tension has faded away, I can't wait to have the house to ourselves tonight.

"Oh, this woman is a professional black widow. She totally has a trail of dead men behind her." Maddox is relaxed on the couch, with his feet resting on the coffee table. We're a few episodes into *Ginny & Georgia*, and he's just as addicted as I was when I started.

"She's amazing, though. Georgia is a badass mama, and I just love her southern accent." I snuggle up against Maddox's side.

His arm comes around me, holding me close. We finished off our Chinese food at least two episodes ago and haven't been able to take our eyes off the TV since.

"Yeah, but she's going to do something bad to my boy Paul Randolph. He's innocent in all of this, and she's going to drag him into some shit."

Reaching my hand up, I caress Maddox's cheek and pull him closer for a kiss. "I know, sweetie. Maybe she won't kill him."

He turns and plants a kiss on my lips before nipping my fingers. "Don't patronize me, Peach. I'm a Mayor Paul Randolph stan. He needs to be protected at all costs."

Laughing, I pull him back in for a deeper kiss, and that shuts him up. Maddox tangles his hand in my hair and moves his lips over mine, opening them and deepening the kiss. I moan the moment his tongue touches mine.

Maddox adjusts his hands to grip my waist and pull me onto his lap, his lips never leaving mine. With the thin material of my sleep shorts, I feel him hard and ready under me. Needing a breath, I pull back while Maddox's mouth moves down my neck.

My hips move of their own accord against him, searching for the friction my body so desperately needs. Maddox tightens his hands on me, halting my movements.

"As much as I would love to continue this right here, I do have this fear of your brother walking in and seeing us naked together. He's cool right now, but I don't really want to get my face bruised up with my ass out and all."

Leaning back, I smirk. "My room or yours?"

Without another word, Maddox scoops me up in his arms. I hold on tight as he cups my butt, taking us up the stairs to my room on the left. Shutting the door with his foot, Maddox gently drops me on the edge of the bed before tugging his T-shirt off.

"Whoa, buddy, slow down a second," I tell him while laughing.

Placing both hands on the bed, Maddox leans in close. "I've been sleeping next to you every night for weeks now, Peach. A guy can only take blue balls for so long."

Running my fingers through his hair, I tug him closer and crush my mouth to his. "Just don't forget this time," I whisper against his mouth.

"Hey." He pulls back, looking me in the eyes. "That will never happen again."

I nod. "I know."

Maddox places a knee on the bed, forcing me to scoot back as he comes down on top of me. My hands leave his hair and slide down his hard chest, tracing the smooth ridges across his stomach. He settles partly on top of me with one leg between mine.

"I don't want to hurt Bean," he whispers against my neck as he moves his mouth down to my collarbone.

"You won't," I breathe out. "Dr. Wilson said sex is perfectly safe as long as we aren't too…rough."

He throws his head back and laughs. "So no tying you up or throwing you around?" he jokes.

Trying to hide my smirk, I bite my lip. "Not for a few months, at least."

A growl comes from deep in his throat as he dives in, crushing his mouth to mine. With a feather-like touch, Maddox lifts my tank top higher up until my swollen stomach is exposed. He drops down and places a kiss on the smooth skin, sending goosebumps down by body.

"Seems you have me at a disadvantage here," he tells me. His breath tingling the skin above my sleep shorts.

"And why is that?" My words come out breathy.

Dragging his lips up my stomach, Maddox comes face-to-face with me. "Your shirt is still on." He stares down at the thin cloth barely covering my boobs.

Smirking, I look from my shirt to him before lifting my arms above my head. "And what're you going to do about it?"

Maddox makes quick work of getting my shirt off and tossing it somewhere in the room. One of his hands goes to cup my breast, and I moan from how sensitive they are now. His mouth finds mine once again as his body settles into me.

Not wanting to go slow anymore, I reach for the waistband of Maddox's sweats and begin pushing them down. He helps me by lifting his hips. Once I get them as far as I can with my hands, I use my feet to tug them the rest of the way. Maddox kicks them off, and they land somewhere with the rest of our discarded clothing.

"Commando?" I question when I feel the smooth skin of his behind.

Pulling back, he smirks. "Easy access for you."

Laughing, I pull him down to me and run my hands up his back. Maddox kisses the breath out of me while moving my shorts down my legs until I'm as naked as he is. A thin layer of sweat coats my skin as his mouth explores my neck, collarbone, and chest. My body feels on fire and I try to get closer to him, but no matter how hard I tug, he won't budge.

"Please," I beg as Maddox licks and sucks from one breast to the other.

I feel him smile against me. "Please what, Peach?"

Groaning, I throw my head back and squeeze my eyes shut. "Oh my god. Maddox, if you try and make me beg you to fuck me, I am going to knee you in your blue balls."

He settles between my open legs, nudging my entrance. "Well, we wouldn't want that, now would we?"

I gasp as Maddox pushes himself in. My nails dig into his shoulders as I breathe through adjusting to the fullness.

"Fucking hell," he groans into my neck as he pulls out and pushes in again.

With every stroke, he grunts into my ear and the sound is more erotic than anything I've heard before.

We move together like our bodies are in tune. I meet him thrust for thrust, and in no time, my body starts to feel inflamed.

Back arching, I finally let go. "Oh god…"

I grip the sheets while having an out-of-body experience, and as I come down from the high of my orgasm, Maddox's thrusts quicken as he searches for his own release. After one hard push, he crushes his mouth to mine, stifling a groan.

He collapses beside me, his arm lazily slung across my exhausted body.

We both lay there as we try catching our breaths. My body feels loose and satisfied, but I know I'm going to be sore tomorrow from using muscles that are rarely needed. I wouldn't trade anything for this moment, though.

"Feeling like shit, Peach," Maddox mumbles against my ribs.

His arm bobs with my chuckle. "Why is that?"

He lifts up to look me in the eyes. "Because how could I forget this the first time?"

The sadness on his face breaks my heart. "Mad, we need to leave the past behind us. What happened over spring break doesn't matter anymore. All that we should focus on is the now and our future."

"I'm just...I'm sorry, Trazia. If tomorrow morning you didn't remember this moment, I don't know how I would feel. Angry at you, but that doesn't seem fair. Honestly, I don't know how you didn't smack me or something the next morning."

I laugh and turn on my side, forcing us to come face-to-face. "I could never hate you, Mad. I love you too much."

His body goes stiff, and I can see his Adam's apple move with the silent gulp he takes. "Traz, I—"

"Don't," I interrupt. "I didn't tell you that wanting to hear it back. This is how I feel and I felt like it was important to tell you, but I don't ever want you to say it back out of obligation. Save it for when you truly mean it."

He nods. "It's just hard. I've never told a girl I love her before, and I want to make sure I'm not just telling you because I feel like I have to."

"Completely understandable." Standing, I grab my shirt off the floor and stare at Maddox on full display on my bed. He's unashamed in his nakedness, just like the guys told me when I moved in. "I'm going to use the bathroom, and then I want to sleep for the next ten hours. How about you get our show back up?"

With a smile, Maddox reaches for the remote. "Do what you need to, but the moment you come back to bed, that shirt is coming off. We're having naked sleepovers from now on."

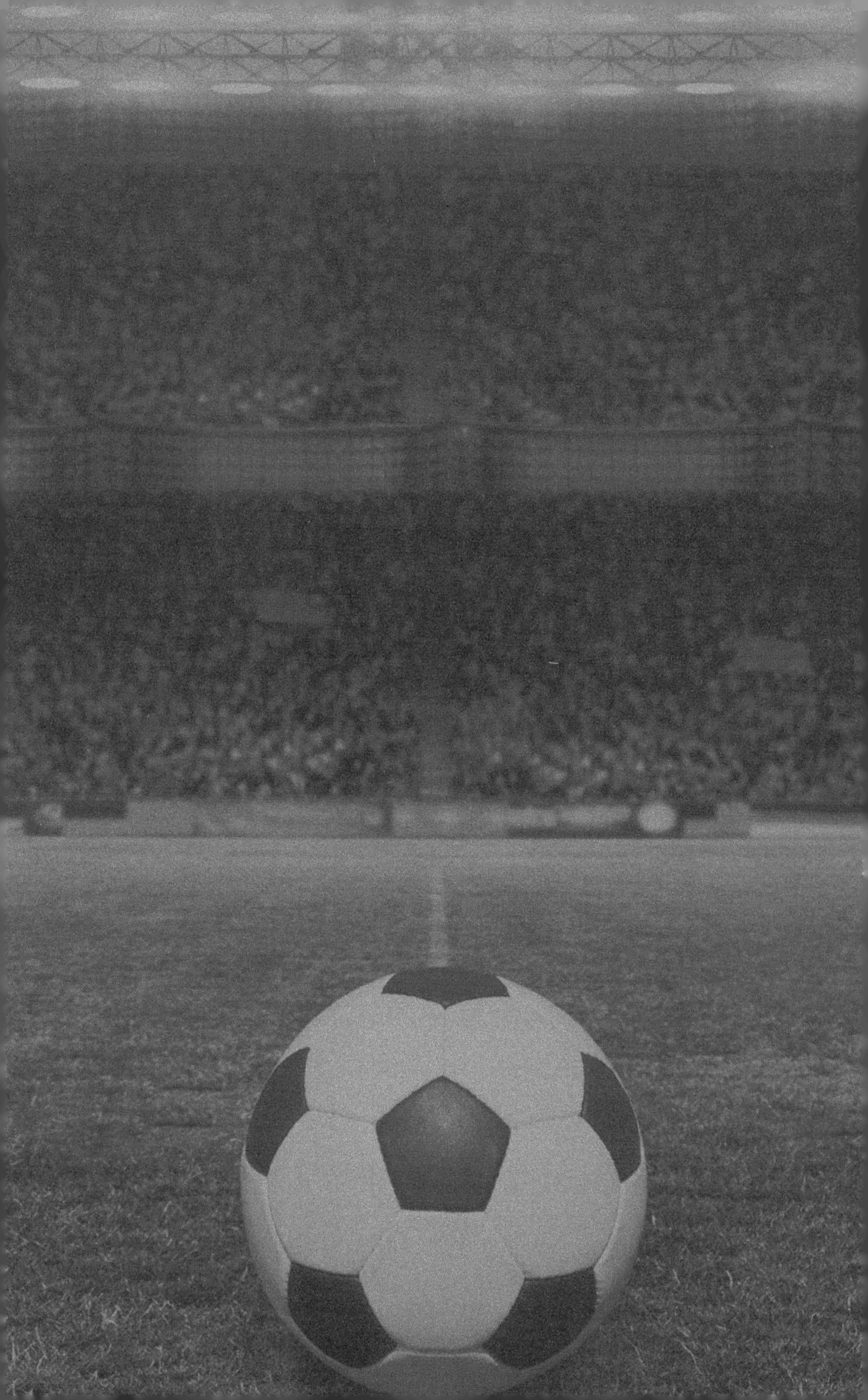

CHAPTER THIRTY-THREE

MADDOX

Taking a deep breath, I click the green button on my phone, and it begins to ring. I've put off calling my parents and sharing the baby news with them for too long, and I know I need to bite the bullet and get it done.

My parents and I have never had a close relationship. Truthfully, I don't think Jack and Veronica Stone ever wanted to be parents. Even after having me, they never left their honeymoon and travel phase. When they weren't spending weeks or months in another country, Dad would spend more time at the office than at home, while Mom developed a newfound interest in solo travel.

Dad made his money through investing and discovered he was so good at it that he started his own company at thirty-five. It was ranked in the *Fortune* 500 companies a few years ago.

The line continues to ring, and just before I hang up, my mom answers. "Hey, Maddy."

Even with our estranged relationship, something inside me warms hearing my mom use my childhood nickname. "Hi, Mom. You and Dad home?"

"We are. Just got back from Indonesia yesterday. Your dad had to fire Lewis and is not happy about it. The man was leaking information to their top competitors and your dad feels betrayed. Lewis has been with him for fifteen years."

Lewis started with my dad's company as a temp right out of college and went on to become his personal assistant. Earning my father's trust in this business was difficult, and Lewis had achieved that. Stabbing him in the back was not something I thought would ever happen.

"That's some shit, Mom. Sorry to hear that."

She laughs on the other end. "You didn't call to hear about your father's work drama. What's going on? Was everything okay with your last semester?" I rarely call either of my parents unless it's to update them on how school and soccer are going.

"Yeah, yeah. Last semester of school was good. Not making the dean's list or anything, but grades are good, and we ended the soccer year with another championship."

"That's wonderful, Maddox."

Scratching my head, I sit on the edge of the bed and take a deep breath. "Well, the thing I was calling about is kind of important. You see...I'm having a baby."

The line goes dead silent on the other end, and for a moment I think she hung up.

"Oh wow," she finally says. "I-I'm not sure what to say. Are you positive it's yours?"

While I don't particularly like this question, I was prepared for it. "Yes, it's my baby."

More silence.

Mom lets out a breath. "Is it safe to assume since you're telling me that the girl is keeping it?"

"Yes. We both plan on keeping it. We're dating, and it's pretty serious. She's great, Mom. I think you'll like her." Thinking about Trazia has me smiling in the middle of a difficult conversation. I've never been serious enough with someone to get to the *meet your parents* part.

"I can hear how much you care about this girl in your tone. While I won't lie and say I'm thrilled about this, if you're happy, then all is right." She doesn't sound angry like most parents would be, but my parents have both been void of certain emotions for as long as I can remember.

"Trust me, we both know we're insane for taking this on. Trazia just started college, but we both have great support systems here. Her mom is close by, and her brother lives with us. It's Camden, my roommate since freshman year." My parents haven't visited me once, so they haven't gotten the chance to meet him or any of the other guys.

"Mmm, I remember you talking about him a few times. I'm sure he's taking it well that you and his sister are having a baby," she tells me with a laugh.

We talk for a few more minutes, and Mom tells me she'll give the news about their new titles to my dad when he gets home. Once I hang up the phone, I feel better, like a weight has lifted off me. Telling my parents about the baby was something I've been putting off, and now that it is done, I can focus more on classes starting next month and what Traz and I plan to do once the baby is born.

Trazia and I have discussed a little about our living situation once the baby is here. Conrad is more than happy living with Emree and Blaire, but I feel bad for taking his room and now practically living in Trazia's. We could live with the baby in that large room until I graduate and then figure out our next plan.

The guys have assured me that they have no issues with her and the baby being here for our last semester of school. Part of me wonders if that will change if there's a crying baby waking everyone up in the middle of the night. None of us have much experience with newborns, so I don't think they know what they're saying yes to.

The bedroom door swings open, and Trazia comes in with an armful of Target bags. "Oh, hey. What are you doing up here?" She drops the bags on the bed and comes to stand between my legs.

"Just got off the phone with my mom," I tell her as I grip her waist.

Trazia's face drains of color, and her eyes grow wide. "How did that go?"

"Not bad. Clearly she wasn't jumping for joy at me having a kid while in college, but she's not going to disown me or anything. I'm sure she'll visit once the baby is born." I don't have high expectations when it comes to my parents.

"I'm glad she's not angry. We kind of got lucky in the parent department then because I'm sure most would flip at their almost nineteen and twenty-one-year-old kids having a baby."

Smirking, I run my hands up Traz's back under her shirt. "That's right. Someone has a birthday next week. What are we thinking of doing? Weekend getaway? Beach trip? Are you working that day, because I think it should be against the law to work on your birthday?"

She throws her head back and lets out the sweetest laugh. "No, not working. Jannette likes to give all the employees the day off on their birthday, so I get to enjoy a three-day weekend."

"How do you feel like celebrating? It's your weekend, so anything you say goes."

She taps her pointer finger against her chin. "Hmm, I do have the sudden urge to begin nesting, which I read in the baby books is normal during the second trimester. What if we do a little baby shopping? Maybe get a crib and some other necessities."

Her smile shows me this has been something she has been excited about. "I think that sounds like the perfect day."

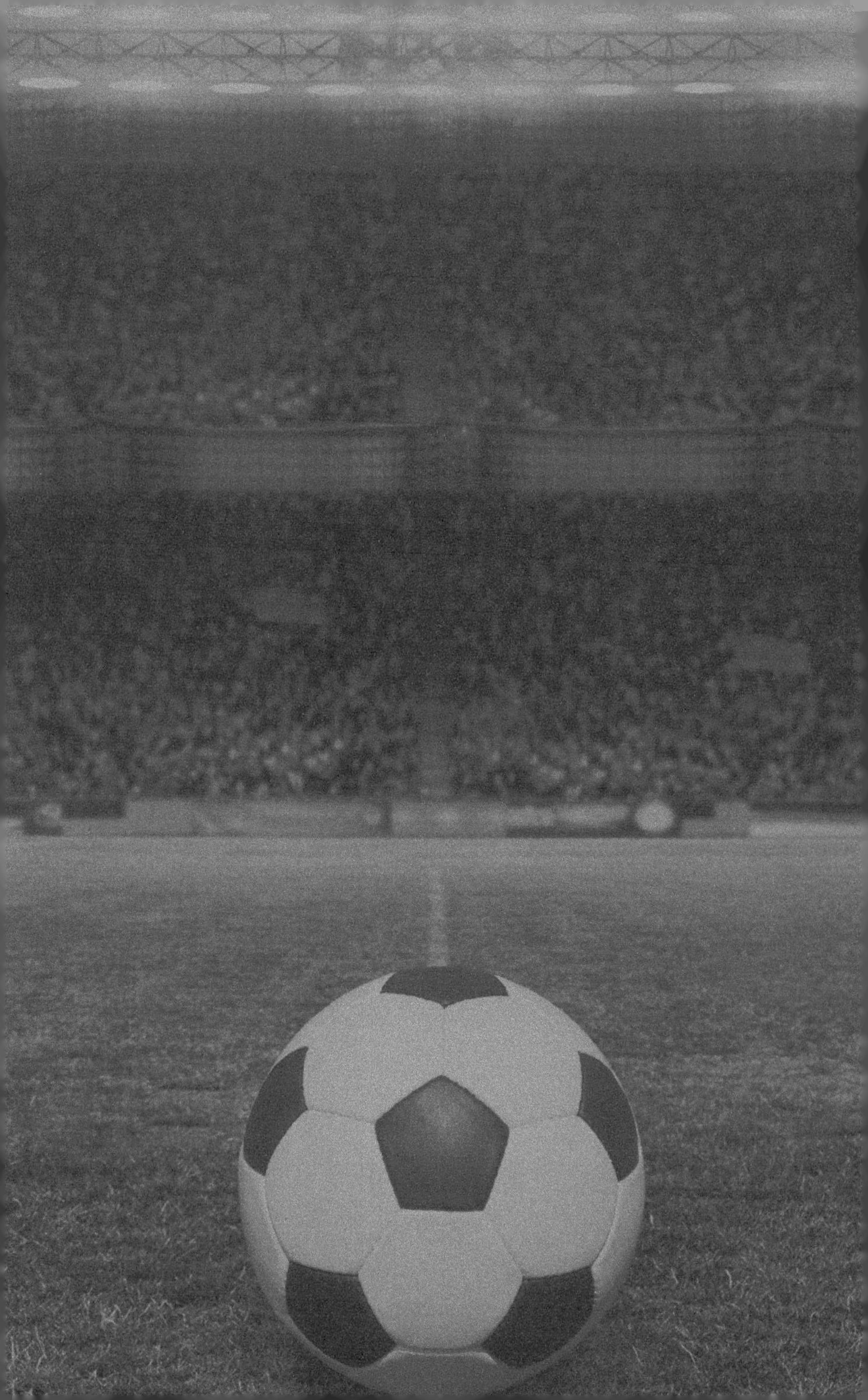

CHAPTER THIRTY-FOUR

TRAZIA

"Fuck this shit," Camden grumbles as he tries to attach two pieces of the crib together.

After an eventful day shopping for our little bean, Maddox said my birthday present from the guys was them helping put together the crib and gliding chair. So far Mateo has stormed off, angry that he lost a screw, and Levi has complained nonstop about being hungry and how he can't work under these conditions. Conrad has been hiding downstairs, claiming he is on the phone with his sister, but Maddox thinks he's avoiding the manual labor.

Maddox has been humming off and on as he tests the glider to make sure it moves properly, effectively avoiding working on the crib that has angered most of our roommates.

"You sure you don't want me to take a look at those instructions? I don't think putting this crib together should be giving you high blood pressure." I've offered multiple times and have been met with refusal.

"Absolutely not," Maddox tells me from his spot on the chair. "What you can do is come get cozy in your new chair. It glides perfectly."

He stands and motions for me to take a seat. Once I'm in the chair, it moves just a little until I glide back and forth using my foot. "Oh, this is nice. Will definitely help with those late-night feedings."

Maddox leans down and kisses me on the lips. "You look sexy with all this baby stuff around," he whispers in my ear while covering my belly with his large hand.

"Ah yes, feeling bloated is the new sexy."

With a gentle caress, he feels our baby through me. "Nah, Peach. No bloating going on. Just a sexy-as-hell woman carrying my baby."

"Dude, don't lie. Even she said her feet have gotten weirdly swollen," Levi grumbles from his spot under our bed where he thinks the lost screw may have gone.

"Shut the fuck up, Lumberjack," Maddox growls out and kicks Levi's leg sticking out from under the bed.

I laugh as I get out of the glider. "Don't be mean to him. We all know I've been sporting cankles for a week now."

"Aha!" Levi cheers as he stands. "Found the little fucker." He holds up the lost crib screw.

Camden snatches it from his hand. "Finally. Now we can be done with this and move on to food."

While we all stand around and watch, Camden puts the screw in place and tightens it. The crib took a while to get together, but seeing it makes this feel more real. This is where our son or daughter is going to be sleeping at night. Right beside us.

As my body changes, Bean's existence feels less like a dream. I've been reading as many mommy blogs and books as I can to prepare for the next few months and the birth. I know being young is going to come with opinions from all kinds of people, and I want to become as knowledgeable as I can for what is to come.

I'm still only showing a little, yet I feel more connected to

Bean than I thought I would. The mama bear in me is already protective of them, yet I don't even know who they are. The baby books and mom blogs mentioned this would happen, but I hadn't felt it yet until recently. My little baby has my entire heart, and I don't even know their name.

I look down at the pile of tiny clothes we got today. Since Maddox and I decided not to find out the gender, we stuck with neutral colors. The greens and yellows are becoming my favorite, though. The crib is white with dark tan sheets, and the glider is a cream color that makes it almost match with the décor in this room.

Maddox is staring at me with a serious look on his face from across the room. "What are you doing thinking so hard over there?"

He shakes his head and plasters on a smile that is not his usual easygoing one. "Nothing at all. You want to go out for dinner or call something in?"

I tap my finger against my chin. "Hm, I like the idea of getting cozy in some pajamas and hanging out here. Pizza sounds good, too. Maybe some wings."

Smiling, he walks over and kisses me on the nose. "I'll order it."

Before he can pull his phone out, Emree, Blaire, and Jules walk in. "Don't bother. We were already planning an ice cream run, so we can pick the food up on the way. Want to tag along, Traz?"

I jump up, leaving the small articles of clothing behind. "Oh yes. Ice cream sounds amazing right now. Ice Dreamland has some new flavors, and I would love to check them out." My stomach grumbles at the thought.

Emree swirls her keys around her pointer finger. "Let's get this show on the road. Boys, text us what kind of pizza and wings you want." She blows kisses at them before walking out of the room.

Maddox grabs my hands, pulling me to his chest. "Be safe and wear your seat belt."

I smile and wrap our linked hands behind my back. "Of course. Love you," I whisper against his mouth.

Those two words come out so effortlessly now that I've confessed my feelings to him. The torn look on his face is evident, and I know that he is struggling with his feelings about this. I don't want to make it harder on him, but I also am not someone who hides how I feel about someone.

"Don't," I whisper low enough just for him to hear. He nods, understanding my meaning behind the single word. He doesn't need to profess his love because I feel it through his actions and the way he cares for me.

I give him a small smile and kiss on the lips before following the girls out of the room.

"That was painful to watch," Levi says loud enough for me to hear outside the door. If only he knew how hard it is for me to see Maddox struggle with something that comes so easily to most people. It makes me wonder if he will ever be able to tell me those three words.

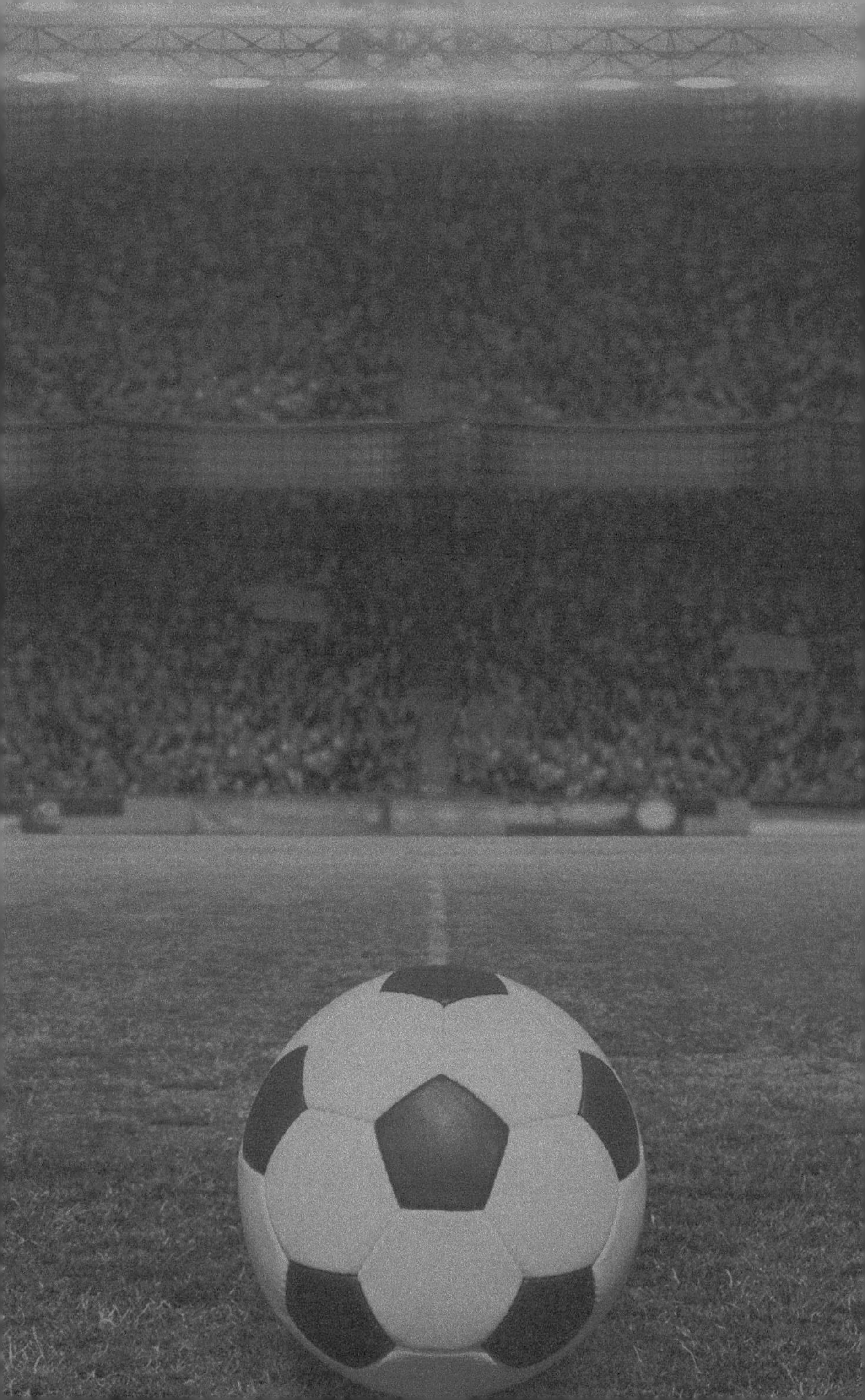

CHAPTER THIRTY-FIVE

MADDOX

"That was painful to watch," Levi announces to the entire room.

I shoot him an annoyed look. "How about we not eavesdrop on people's conversations?"

Camden laughs. "Lumberjack has a point. Why did you leave my sister hanging there?"

"Oh, so now you're all cool with us and want me to confess my feelings to her?"

He raises a brow, taken aback by my forwardness. "Being cool with you and her together is one thing, and not wanting my sister to be in a one-sided relationship is another."

"It's just that I've never done the whole relationship thing before. Trazia fell so easily into these new roles, and I don't know when or if I'll get there."

"How about we ask the resident commitment-phobe?" Levi tells us as he walks toward the bedroom door. "Conny, get your ass up here."

A moment later, Conrad and Mateo come through the doorway. "What's up?"

"How did you know you loved Emree?" Levi asks.

Conrad looks confused. "Are we talking about our feelings or something? That's a random question."

"Trazia told Maddox she loves him, and he isn't able to confess his feelings to my sister."

Understanding flashes across Conrad's face. "Ah, I see. I'd say the moment I knew I truly loved Em was when I was about to lose her. That thought alone did me in. My life is complete with her in it, and she makes me a better man."

"That was deep." Mateo laughs. "You guys are fucking whipped."

"Just wait your turn, man. We never thought it would happen to Conny, yet he's practically living with Emree at this point," Camden states.

"Practically? Blaire has me paying part of the electric and water bills because she says I shower too much and don't know how to turn the lights off."

We all laugh, with the exception of Conrad. "My girl has a point. You grew up in a privileged life. She's just trying to humble you."

Conrad scoffs at Camden's comment.

"Back to the subject at hand. Maddox, how do you feel about Trazia?" Levi asks.

Camden glares. "And be mindful of who's in the room."

Taking a deep breath, I sit down and sink into the mattress. "I don't know, man. She's great. Amazing. I feel happy when I'm around Trazia and enjoy spending time with her." Leaning forward, I rest my arms on my knees. "She goes to work, and I look forward to hearing how her day was. It's such a mundane thing for us to do, yet sometimes it's the highlight of my day."

Levi nods. "And what about partying? Do you miss that?"

"Fuck no. The last party I went to was boring, and when I left with Izzy, it felt empty. But just kissing Traz excites me."

"Watch it," Camden warns.

A MEMORY THAT ONCE WAS

I roll my eyes. "Your sister and I are dating and having a baby. Grow up."

Conrad steps toward me and puts his hand on my shoulder. "Listen, friend, I'm here to inform you that you're in love with Trazia Collins. Everything you feel means love."

"This is why you guys have been letting Em and Blaire drag you by the balls?"

They laugh. "Basically," Conrad agrees. "Love is fucked up and will have you doing weird shit."

"You won't regret a thing, though," Camden adds.

Someone's phone rings, and Mateo reaches into his back pocket and smiles. "Hey, you all got the pizza already because I'm dying here?"

The corners of his mouth turn down. "What? Where?" He listens to whoever is on the other line and looks to me and Camden. "Okay, we're on our way."

I jump up, not liking the worry in his voice. "Who was that?"

Mateo looks scared as his eyes bounce between Camden and me. "Jules. She...she said they were in an accident." My stomach drops. "They're rushing Trazia to the hospital. She wasn't conscious."

THE DRIVE to the hospital is a blur. All I remember is racing down the stairs and all of us piling into Levi's car and getting here in record time. I'm sure he broke a few traffic laws, but none of us are in the mindset to care.

Jogging, I slow as the automatic doors to the emergency department open. Huddled together in the waiting room are Jules and Blaire. Jules turns to see who entered the door and reveals Emree sitting in one of the chairs. Her arm is in a sling, and gauze is wrapped around her head.

My eyes scan the room, looking for Trazia, and come up empty. Realizing she's not here with them has my stomach sinking.

I take long strides over to where the girls are. "Where is she?"

Blaire's eyes are watery and red. Her eyebrows pinch together as she looks at Jules. "We don't know. Sh-she wasn't conscious when the ambulance got to us, and they took her away immediately. We've been trying to find out more, but since we're not family, they will only give us limited answers."

Camden, Mateo, Levi, and Conrad run in, and Camden and Conrad immediately go to their girls' sides. "What happened? Are you hurt?" Camden asks his girlfriend.

The floodgates release, and Blaire breaks down against Camden's chest. "We...were hit. By a drunk driver. Tr-Trazia was in the front, and...and he hit her side." Her words come out between sobs, muffled by Camden's shirt.

Not wanting to wait around for more details, I head to the front desk where an older woman is sitting in a desk chair while clicking something on the computer. "Trazia Collins. Where is she?"

She looks up, startled. "Excuse me, sir, but you're going to need to lower your voice." I didn't realize I was practically shouting at her. "Are you family?"

I've seen enough hospital shows to know you aren't getting answers unless there's a close connection to the patient. "She—she's my fiancée. Trazia Collins."

The woman types away on her keyboard, and what is more like a few seconds feels like hours. "Ms. Collins is with the doctors right now. She has a fractured collarbone, a broken humerus, and a severe concussion. When the ambulance brought her and another woman in, Trazia was unconscious and has been sent off for a CT scan."

"And...the baby? What about the baby?" My breathing is erratic as I try to remain calm.

The sides of her mouth turn down before she looks back to the screen and begins scrolling. "All of her injuries are on the right side of her body. The paramedics were notified about her pregnancy right away and did an ultrasound in the ambulance after stabilizing her. The doctors here also did one before sending her for the CT scan. Both detected a heartbeat." She looks up at me with sympathy in her eyes. "The baby is strong and appears to not have been injured. I'll go back and check on the status of your fiancée right now."

"Thank you," I manage to whisper out.

A hand comes down on my shoulder as the receptionist leaves her station. "Traz is going to be okay. She has to be," Camden whispers.

His words don't comfort me in the way I'm sure he hoped they would, but him trying to ease me when it's his sister who was hurt means a lot. I should be the one reassuring him that she is going to be fine and will be back home with just a small cast for her broken arm, but I don't have it in me to respond.

The only thing going through my head right now is how the last words I said to Trazia weren't "I love you" and the regret I have for not telling her about my feelings sooner.

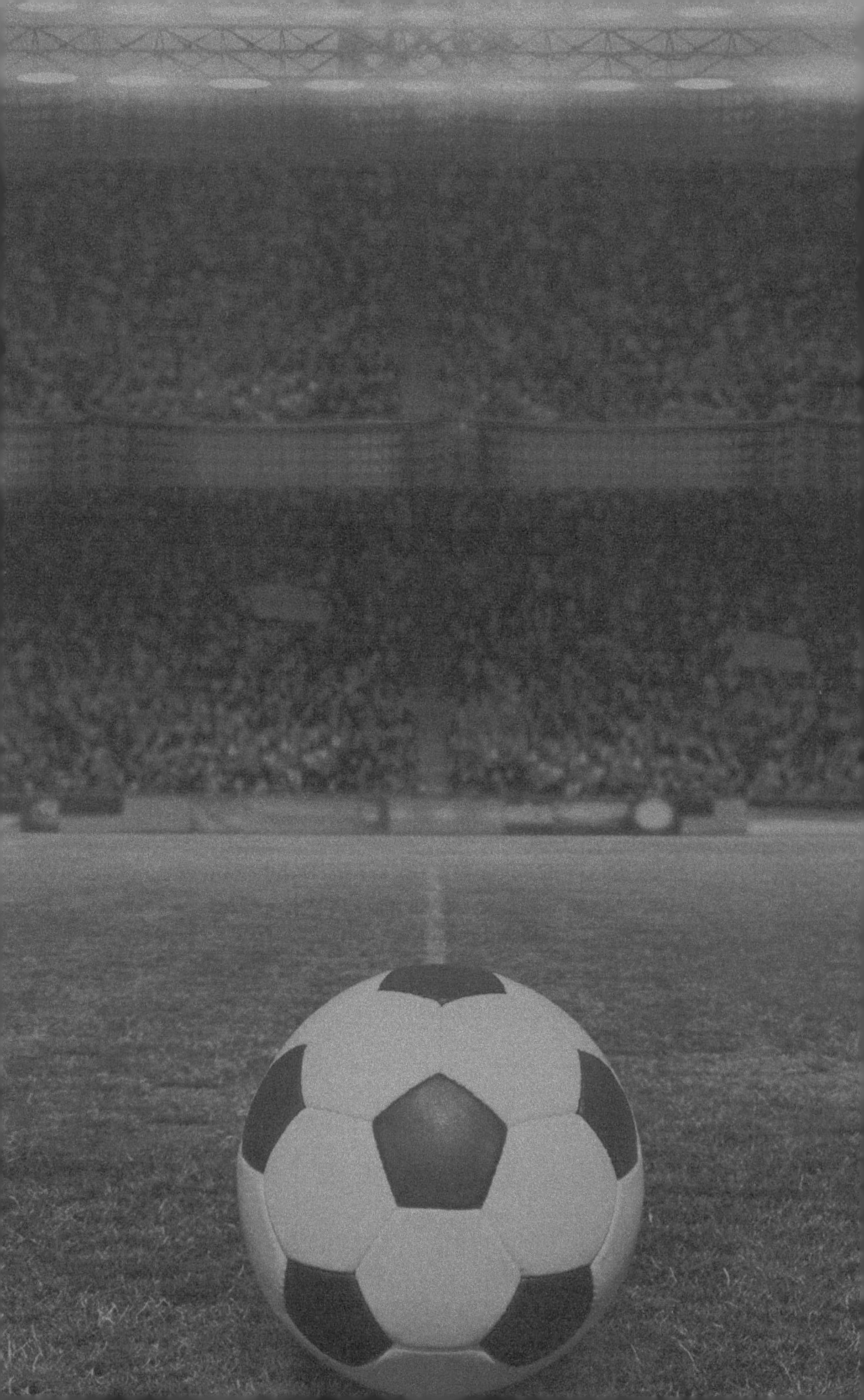

CHAPTER THIRTY-SIX

MADDOX

I've worn down the floor of the waiting room while we sit around waiting for answers about Trazia. The break in her humerus was worse than they thought, and she needed screws and plates to attach the outer part of her bone to help her heal faster and easier.

That was the most information I got about her. The receptionist—who I learned is named Trisha—said that the doctors were worried about nerve damage at first, but the break turned out to be clean and should heal fine.

My biggest worry has been that Trazia still hasn't woken up. She was taken for her CT scan and we don't have answers about those results yet. The impact was significant, most likely leaving Emree's car totaled. Trazia was in the passenger seat, and the collision was on the front end of her side of the car, which explains why she has the most injuries. She could have also easily hit her head during the accident, and I'm hoping it was minor and that's why she hasn't woken up yet.

"Collins family?" someone asks. I turn and see a woman in light blue scrubs and a white coat with a clipboard in hand, looking around the waiting room.

Camden and I practically race over to her with the rest of our friends behind us. The doctor steps back, startled by our group.

"Yes," we both reply.

She looks between the two of us. "Are you Trazia Collins's family?"

"I'm her brother, and this is her fiancé," Camden answers, keeping up with the charade.

The doctor looks to our friends behind us. "I'm Dr. Taylor. Are you okay with information being talked about in front of everyone or would you rather discuss this in a private room?" she asks me.

"This is her family." Aside from her mom, who is on the way, everyone here loves and cares about Trazia like family.

"She's in a room on the neuro ICU floor. The surgery to repair her humerus fracture was successful and she will be in a cast for a few months, but after that, she should be as good as new." A look of concern crosses her face. "The more serious injury is the one she suffered when she hit her head. The impact was hard enough to cause her brain to swell. We have to keep her in a medically induced coma while we wait for the swelling to go down."

"How…" My throat cracks, and I cough to clear it. "How long will that last? And what about the baby?"

"The baby is doing perfectly fine. We've been in touch with her OB-GYN about what is going on and also have our on-staff labor and delivery department nurses and doctor checking on her. As for the medically induced coma, there really is no definite answer I can give you. Brain injuries are hard for even the most trained doctors to pinpoint. What we do know is that she has a very mild swell which will most likely not cause any damage to her brain, but again, I can't confidently comment on that until she is awake and we can run more tests."

My chest tightens as she gives us the update on Trazia. She

looks to me, waiting for a response, but I don't have it in me to give her one. Partly because I don't want to believe what she told us, and the other part because I don't have it in me to put on a fake smile and talk right now.

Camden answers her, and she walks off through the restricted doors she came out of.

The automatic doors open, and a frantic Claire runs through them, looking around the waiting room until her gaze hits us. She rushes to us. Her eyes are red and swollen, and her hair is up in a messy bun. The clothes she has on don't match, and I can imagine she left the house with no thought of what she was wearing or how she looked, much like the rest of us.

"Where is my baby?" Claire looks at Camden, her voice filled with terror.

Camden grabs his mom by the shoulders, and she clutches onto him in a hug unlike any I've ever seen. It's as if she is hanging onto him for strength. Seeing someone who has held herself so strong after all she's been through look this defeated is hard to watch.

They pull back after a couple minutes, and Claire has a face full of fresh tear stains. "Her doctor just came out and gave us an update. She had to have surgery on her broken humerus, which they did. The concern now is she has some swelling on her brain, probably from hitting her head during the crash. They have her in a medically induced coma right now to help her heal."

Claire closes her eyes and takes a deep breath. "And the baby?" She looks at me when she asks this.

"They're fine. Healthy." I choke on the words.

The doctor comes back out with a nurse in dark blue scrubs. "Hello again. Trazia is ready to have visitors. Since she's in the ICU, we do limit how many people can be in her room. We can take you to see her," she addresses me when she says the last sentence.

I look to Claire, and she gives me an encouraging nod. "Okay. Thank you."

Camden pats my back as Claire gives me a kiss on the cheek before I follow the two professionals through the restricted doors.

We make our way down the long, bright hallway. Each room on the side is closed as they lead me to the elevator.

"Trazia is a little banged up, so don't be alarmed by her appearance. Her arm is wrapped for now until we get the cast on." Dr. Taylor looks at me with sympathy in her eyes.

The elevator stops on the fifth floor, and I follow them out. Dr. Taylor swipes her ID card, and the two doors blocking off the ICU area swing open.

This floor feels colder. As if there is less movement and life going on around here. With how quiet it is, I guess that would make sense. The only noise is the hushed voices coming from the nurses' station and the various beeps from open rooms.

We stop at a room at the end of the hallway and Dr. Taylor opens the door. I'm greeted by the sound of a steady beep as well as the news playing low on the television. In the center of the room is Trazia, with her arms hooked up to various machines surrounding her. If I didn't know any better, I would think she is sleeping peacefully by the way she's positioned and the relaxed look on her face.

The nurse pulls a recliner closer to Trazia's side and offers me the seat. I take it, but I don't touch her right away. Everything about this feels wrong. It feels like she's just asleep beside me, but it also feels like more. Traz is usually a light sleeper, and a room full of people would definitely wake her up. Her not making a sound or movement right now is the reminder I didn't need that she is in a coma.

Dr. Taylor comes to my side and places her hand on my shoulder. "Talk to her. Hold her hand. While there are conflicting opinions on this, I am someone who believes patients can hear their loved ones when they are in a coma. When we taper the medication keeping her in the coma after her brain swelling goes down, talking to and being near Trazia could help her come out of the coma easier."

Taking a deep breath, I grab Trazia's hand that isn't broken and am mindful of the IV. It's warm, but lifeless. She's not gripping me back like she usually would, and I fight off the stinging happening in my eyes. The lively, beautiful girl I've been falling for isn't the one in front of me.

"We'll give you two some alone time. She's allowed two visitors in here at a time as we don't want it to get overwhelming. You can bring in any of her other family members when you're ready." Dr. Taylor and the nurse excuse themselves, leaving me alone with Trazia.

I squeeze Trazia's cold hand with my large ones and lean forward, resting my arms on her mattress. "Hey, Peach," I whisper to her. "They said to talk to you, but I have to be honest, it's a little weird not knowing if you can hear me. I hope you can because I need you to know how important it is for you to heal so we can wake you up."

She lays there, not moving, and the sting in my eyes is back, but this time I don't fight the tears as they build up.

"I was so scared when we got the call about the accident. It felt like my body went on autopilot." I watch as her chest rises with each breath. Her baby bump is hidden under a couple layers of blankets and I reach forward with my free hand, resting it there and comforting our baby in the only way I know.

"You need to wake up, Peach. I fucked up, and I'm so sorry. You shouldn't have left today without hearing me tell you how much I love you. Because I do. Trazia, I love you more than I knew was possible and that...that scares me."

She lays there, not making a sound, and I bring her hand closer, kissing the top of it. "Please come back to me."

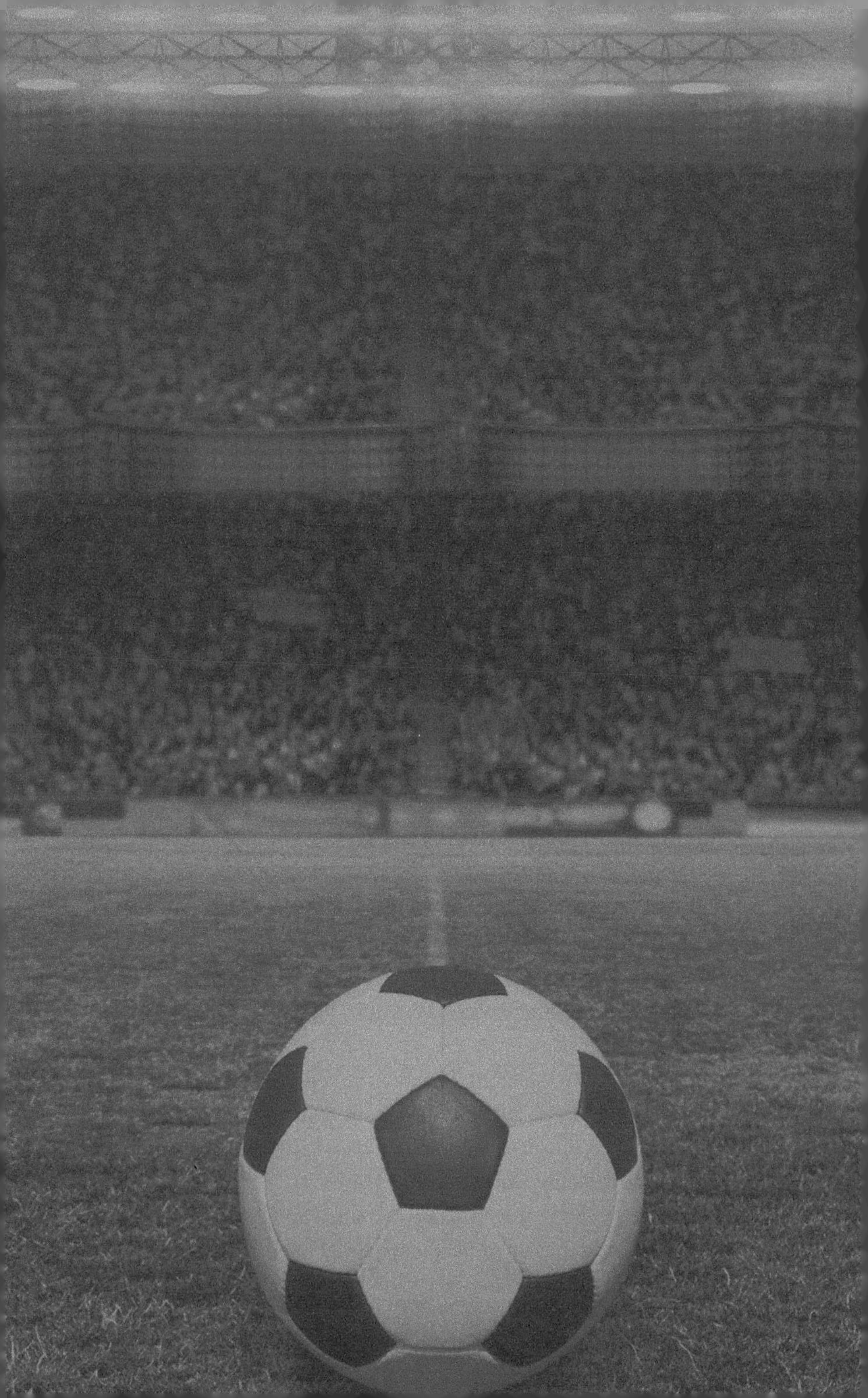

CHAPTER THIRTY-SEVEN

MADDOX

"Did Dr. Taylor tell you if they were going to bring her out of the coma today?" Claire asks as she puts her purse and jacket on the sofa before coming over to Trazia's side.

I rub the sleep out of my eyes and try to stretch the muscles that have been aching for the last two days. "They're going to do another CT scan this afternoon to see how much the swelling has gone down."

Claire hands me a hot coffee before taking her seat. "Thanks," I tell her as I bring the cup to my lips.

She moves Trazia's hair behind her ear and looks lovingly at her daughter. "She looks more like herself after the sponge bath yesterday. The dried blood in her hair was getting to be a lot."

I laugh as best I can with how exhausted I am. "Yeah, I'm glad they did that because I just know Traz would be mad at me if more and more people saw her like that."

We've been here for yet another day with little change to Trazia. The scan yesterday showed a little less swelling, but even the smallest bit of change is good news. I don't want them to bring her out of the coma too soon, but I also need her to wake up so we can go home and live our lives.

"You need to get a good night of sleep. And a shower. I know you want to be here with her at all times, but you have to take care of yourself too. What happens when she wakes up and sees you a complete mess? And how will you take care of her if you're dead on your feet?" Claire has a point. I've been sleeping in the uncomfortable recliner since we got here and haven't had a real shower. The best I've done is clean the important areas with a washcloth the nurses gave me and soap from the bathrooms outside of the ICU.

"You're probably right," I agree. "If I'm getting a bit grossed out by my own smell, I wonder what everyone else thinks."

"We think you need a deep, clean shower and some deodorant."

After collecting my things and grabbing Claire's keys after she insists I take her car, I kiss Traz on the forehead and reluctantly leave.

The bright morning light hurts my eyes after being under the fluorescents for so long. Fresh air was needed, though. Along with some vitamin D. Being holed up for just a couple days in a cold and stuffy hospital can take a toll on your body.

When I pull up to the house, I notice a couple extra cars in the driveway. Guessing everyone decided to crash here rather than stay at their apartments. Jules's and Blaire's cars are lining the side of the road outside of our house while my roommates' fill the driveway.

Once inside the house, I drop my wallet and keys by the front door and breathe a sigh of relief at being in the comfort of my own home. Without Trazia here, it feels different, though.

"Hey, man, any update?" Levi asks as he comes down the stairs in a pair of sweats and no shirt.

He follows me into the living room, and I collapse onto the

couch. "Not yet. They're taking her for another CT scan this afternoon and that will show if her swelling has gone down any more."

"Everything is going to be good. She's strong and healthy." I nod in agreement because saying it out loud feels like I will jinx it. "What do you need? Have you eaten a real meal since the accident?"

My stomach grumbles at the mention of food. "Not really. What they sell in the cafeteria is shit."

He slaps me on the shoulder. "The girls were on breakfast duty this morning. I'll see how it's going and snag you a plate."

"Thanks. I'm going to grab a shower before seeing everyone and will be right down."

Once upstairs, I pause, looking at the crib and glider in the corner of the room. Our bed is littered with small baby clothes that Trazia was going through before the accident. I walk toward the pile she was working through and grab a newborn onesie and clutch it in my hands.

We could have lost Bean two days ago, and it just hit me seeing their things scattered around like this. There could have been a completely different outcome than the one we got lucky with. Trazia is breathing, and the baby is healthy. All I need is for my girl to get better and come back home.

Someone clears their throat, and I wipe at my eyes where unshed tears were collecting. Camden comes in and he looks about as good as I feel, like he hasn't slept since he left the hospital.

"Glad you decided to come home and take a breather. My mom texted me when you left and wanted me to make sure you ate."

"Levi is already ahead of you there. He said the girls are making breakfast. I'll be sure to grab a plate before heading back to the hospital."

He nods and looks like he wants to say something. "Listen, I know the timing of this is wrong, but I need to say it. I'm sorry for how I reacted when I found out about you and Traz. After seeing you with my sister these last few weeks, and especially the past two days, I'm happy she's found someone like you in her life."

"Camden, I get it, man. How I feel about Trazia isn't the same as all the girls before her. She's so much more to me, and not just because of the baby. I've felt this pull toward her for years, but with her being younger and your sister, I kept the feelings I had to myself."

Hearing Camden admit that he can see how much I care for his sister means more than anything. I was worried how our friendship would change after the bombshell was dropped, and I feel like a weight has been lifted off my chest knowing I still have my best friend.

He comes closer and slaps his hand on the back of my neck, pulling me toward him. "She's gonna be okay," he whispers harshly. "She has to be."

I don't know if it's because I've been holding in my emotions for so long or what, but the hug from my best friend helps me release all the pain I've been holding in for two days. Tears freely fall from my eyes as Camden pulls me in for a tight hug.

I cry for Trazia. For our baby. For the fact that I wasn't there for them and how helpless I feel. There is nothing I can do to help her get better but sit around and wait, and I have never felt so useless in my life.

Camden comforts me while I let it all out. He doesn't tell me to "man up" or that men don't cry. Rather, he does what the best of friends do and becomes a shoulder to cry on. There are no words needed.

Once I've shed every tear in me, I pull back from Camden and wipe at my face. "Thanks for letting me dump all of that on you."

He smiles. "We all need someone to be our support during these hard times. Blaire is mine, and yours isn't available right now. We're all here for you."

"I don't know what I would do without you all."

He leaves me in the room to shower and get myself together again before joining everyone downstairs for breakfast. The hot water pounding down on me feels incredible on my sore muscles, and it helps relieve some of the tension I've been holding.

As I'm getting dressed, my cell phone rings from where I left it on the nightstand, charging. My dad's name appears on the screen.

"Hey," I answer.

"Glad I caught you. The lease is up on your truck this year. Do you want me to purchase it or would you want to look around for something else? Maybe something more kid-friendly?"

The casual question catches me off guard with everything that is going on in my life. "Um, Dad. Now really isn't a good time."

"Everything okay? You don't sound good, son." It's not common for my dad to initiate conversations about how others are doing because he's usually jumping on another call or going into a meeting.

"No. It's Trazia. She was..." The words are difficult to get out. "She was in an accident."

My dad goes silent on the other end. "What happened, son?"

I spend the next five minutes explaining to him what happened. He stays quiet other than a few snaps of his fingers directed at whom I assume is his assistant coming into his office. This is the longest I've had his undivided attention in a while.

"Stacy!" he shouts. I hear his new assistant on the other line. "Get the jet ready for me and Veronica to fly to Tampa as soon as possible. I'll call my wife and have her gather our things."

"Dad, no—"

"Maddox," he interrupts me. "My son calls and says that the mother of his child is in a coma after a car accident, and you think I won't be there to help any way I can? We'll be there soon, and I'll call around to some connections I have. She needs the best neurologist, and I'll make sure she gets it."

He quickly says goodbye and that he will let me know when they are on their way. This side of my dad is new for me, and I'm not sure how to adjust. This is the first time my parents are even coming to Braxton.

Pocketing my phone and wallet, I head downstairs and am greeted with a kitchen full of friends. The atmosphere is different than usual, and the absence of Trazia is noticeable. While it may not be ideal, I know being here with these people is good for me and will help get me back in better shape for Trazia.

Camden comes over with a plate full of food. "Emree even cooked the bacon to your liking. Burned to a crisp."

"Thanks," I tell him as I take the plate. "Um, so my parents are coming down."

The room falls silent, and a few forks clink against plates. All eyes are on me as they wait for any other information other than what I told them. Truth is, I feel about as lost as they look right now.

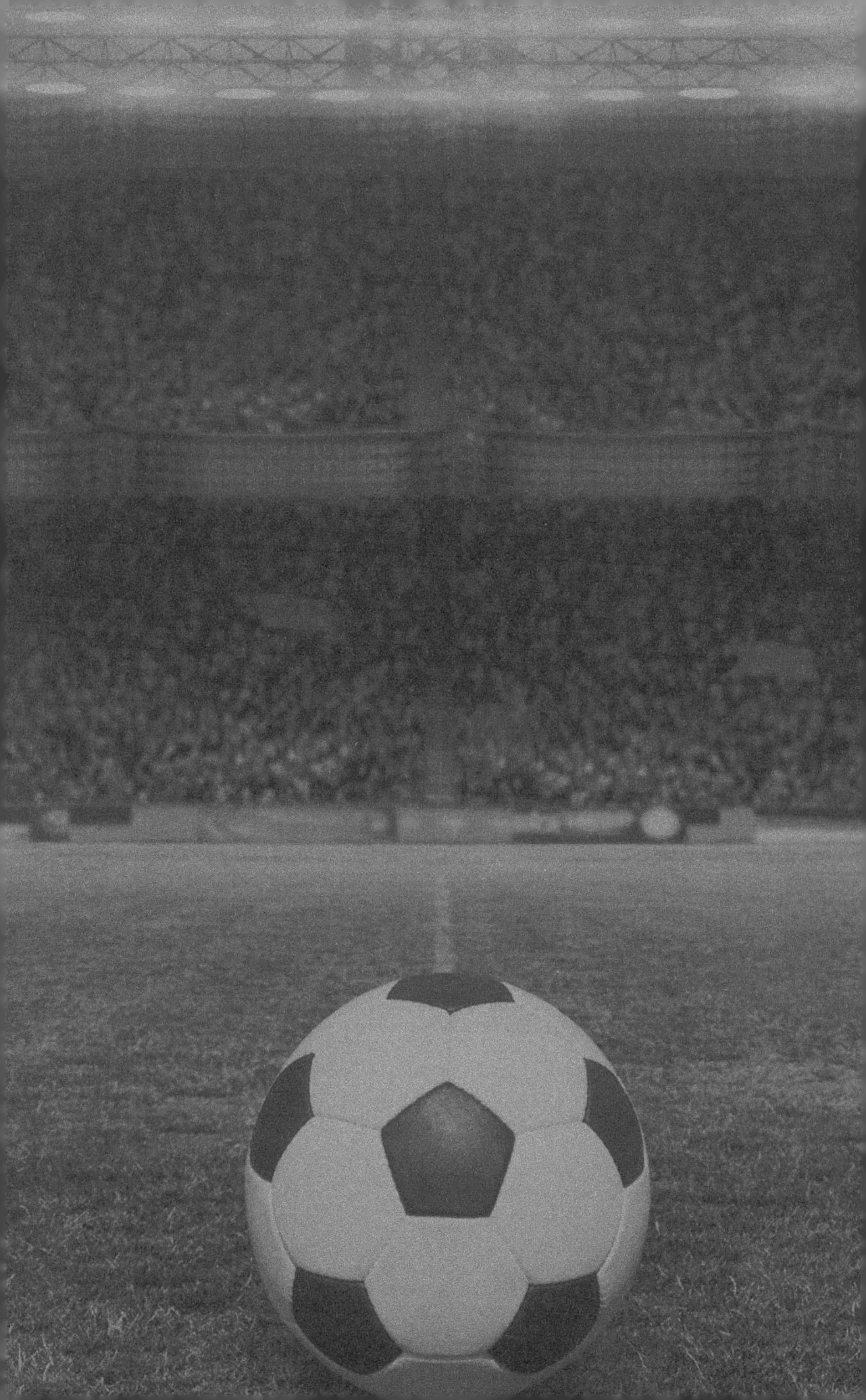

CHAPTER THIRTY-EIGHT

MADDOX

Claire is in the same spot that I left her when I left this morning. Only difference is, Trazia's bed is no longer in the middle of the room.

"Where is she?"

Muting the TV, she looks over at me. "They took her for a CT scan about ten minutes ago. Said they are hopeful this will be the one to determine if it's time to wean her off the medicine."

"That's good they're hopeful." Claire nods in agreement. "Um, so my parents are on their way here. I'm not sure how much Trazia has told you about them, but we aren't exactly close. Honestly, I'm kind of shocked they're coming here at all."

Claire gets up from her chair and comes face-to-face with me, grabbing my hands. "It doesn't matter about the relationship you have with your parents. Clearly they sensed this was the moment to step up, and all we can do is accept any kind of help they are here to offer. Lean on those around you, Maddox, including them. When Trazia is back home, she's going to need you, but you're also going to need help too."

We go out to the waiting room together where Blaire and

Camden decided to stay. Our friends said they would be in the café rather than take up more spots for other families here. Blaire has Camden's hand in her lap, and she's rubbing up and down his arm as she rests her head on his shoulder. I think back to what Camden told me back at the house and what his mom just said about needing help, and I realize we all have someone keeping us up during this time. While Trazia's accident has hit everyone hard, no one is going through this alone.

Claire updates her son and Blaire on what is going on with Trazia. Camden is visibly relieved when she tells him that the doctor is hopeful for good results.

For the next half hour, we sit around, waiting for someone to come out and give us answers. Conrad and Emree bring up some coffees and ask for an update, though we don't have any to give.

I start to doze off when I hear footsteps approaching. Dr. Taylor stops in front of us with a small smile on her face.

"Hello, all. I come with good news," she greets. "The scan showed that the swelling has gone down enough for us to begin lowering the dosage of medicine for Trazia to wake naturally."

A weight lifts off my shoulders. "How long will that take?"

"There's no telling. We don't want to cause more stress on her body, so it will need to be done slowly. Could be forty-eight hours or longer."

Two days. I can keep it together for the next two days. Trazia is young and strong. She'll come out of this in no time.

"Thank you, Doctor. For everything. You've been incredibly helpful." Claire holds her hand out to shake Dr. Taylor's.

Trazia is back in her room, and I give Camden and Blaire time to see her while Claire makes some phone calls to work and family friends.

"Heard the good news." Conrad takes the seat beside me.

I take the coffee he holds out, and while the caffeine is

much needed, I'm beginning to wonder when I'll hit the "too much" limit. "I'm so grateful they're seeing progress. While I was sitting in her room last night, I was reading about medically induced comas. Sometimes the longer they're in them, the harder it can be for the patient to come out of them."

"You know reading that shit isn't good for you. Especially sitting in this depressing place. Her doctor sounds hopeful, and we all need to hold on to that."

"You won't want to go through my search history then, because it looks like I'm studying for medical school."

He laughs. "I'm sure everyone has similar search histories the last couple days. I had to take Emree's phone away from her when she fell down a *Moms with Kids in Comas* blog."

"Jesus. Hopefully no one told Claire about that."

"I'm sure she's too busy with the amount of people that are calling and texting her. I've never seen someone's phone blow up like that."

"It's good to know she has that many people caring about her and Traz, though. We all need someone at times like these."

Everyone keeps talking about having that person to lean on in hard times. The only problem is, my person is lying in a hospital bed, and I don't know when she'll wake up.

SOMEONE SHAKES MY SHOULDER, and I jump up. I must have fallen asleep in the waiting room and now I have my father towering over me. He's dressed in his usual suit, but with a casual twist as he's forgoing a tie.

"Dad. Hey." I get up from my slouched-over position on the chair. "When did you guys get in? What time is it?"

He holds his hand out and helps me out of the seat. If I

thought my body was hurt from sleeping in the recliner beside Trazia the last two days, nothing compares to what this chair did to me.

"We arrived at the hospital about twenty minutes ago. Your mom is with Claire—who she adores already."

I stare at my father because I'm unsure who this man is in front of me right now. "Why are you two here?"

"What do you mean?" he asks, genuinely confused.

"You and Mom haven't exactly been the most comforting parents. I mean, this is the first time you've been to Braxton, and I've been going to school here for three years. Why are you here now?" I take a much-needed breath. "If there is some other reason you're here other than to support your son and the girl he loves, then just leave. I'm not in the mood for bullshit right now."

"Maddox...I-I'm sorry." His brows pinch together. "Your mother and I have done a lot of talking and self-evaluation the last few weeks since you told us about the baby. She's been beside herself that we aren't as involved in your life as we should be and has been wanting to be there for you more."

"You were barely around when I was growing up. Do you really think I'm going to let you two come in and out of our baby's life as you please? If you're serious right now, you need to step up."

Laying it all out there for my dad feels like a weight has been lifted off my chest. I've kept most of this to myself because my parents are who they are, and I've accepted that. After all the years of having a distant relationship with them, I never saw that changing.

"We're serious." The way he holds eye contact shows me he's telling the truth. "I'm sorry, son. After talking with your mother, it made me realize I turned into my own father and barely know my only son. I'm not sure when it happened, but work and travel consumed our lives and you were pushed to the back burner. It was wrong, but I promise if you let us, we'll be there. We want to not only be in your life but our grandchild's."

While I'm skeptical about how this could go, I do believe in giving people more chances after they realize how royally they fucked up. Trazia did so with me, and I've been grateful for that ever since. She was hurt and still gave me a second chance. Maybe my parents really have opened their eyes and will try to be in our lives.

"I'm glad you both have come to this realization." He smiles at me, and I swear I see a bit of liquid pooling in his eyes before he pulls me in for the first hug he's initiated with me in a long time.

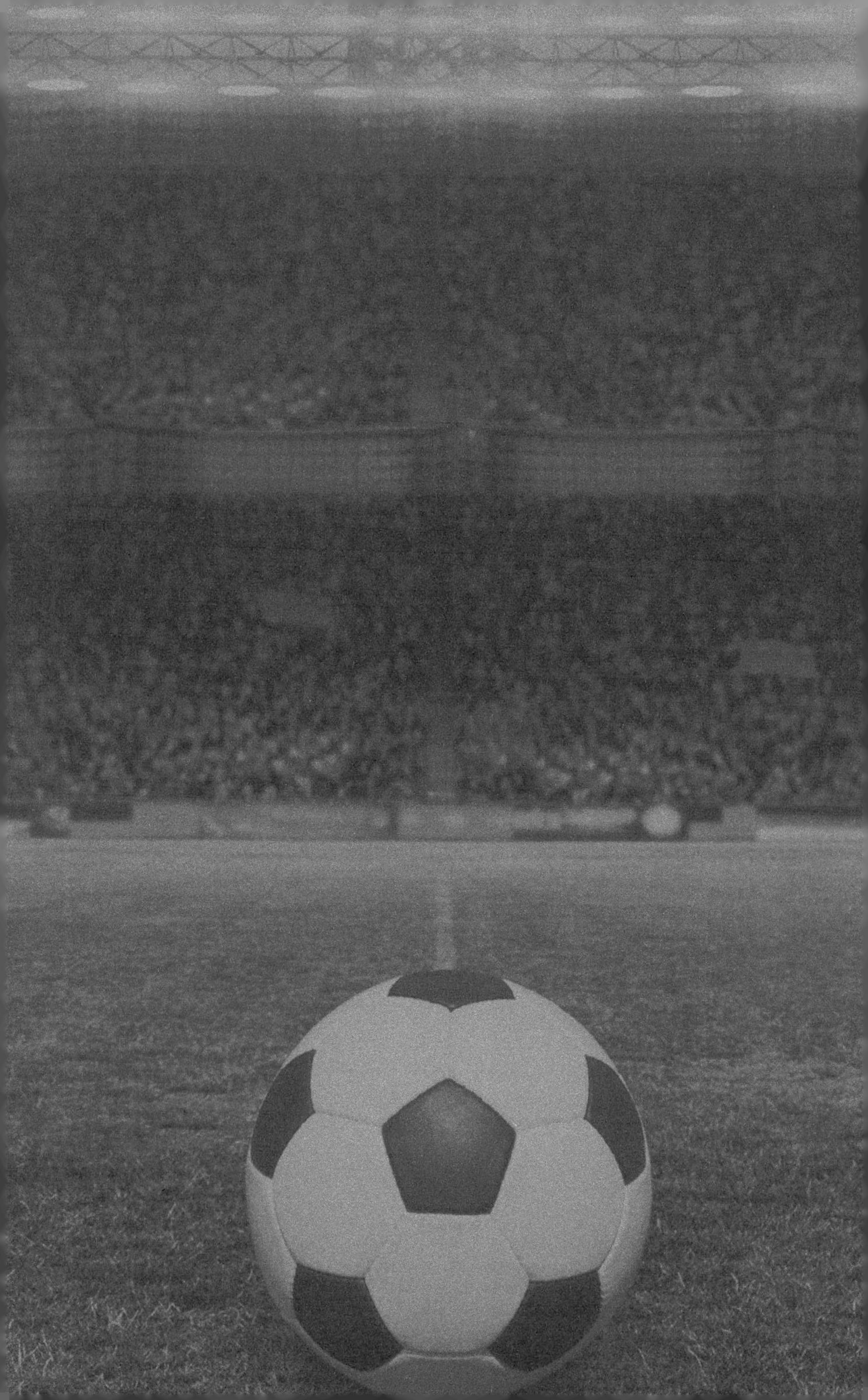

CHAPTER THIRTY-NINE

MADDOX

The steady beeping from the heart monitor has become a comfort to me for the last three days. At first it was hard to sleep with the noise and the lack of good spots to get comfortable in, but knowing it's the sound of Trazia's healthy heartbeat brings me ease now.

Last night, I had dinner with my parents in the hospital cafeteria. We talked more about their intentions, and my mom cried when I told her I spent more holidays with our housekeeper and my nanny than I did with them. I didn't mean for it to come out as harsh as it did, but sometimes the truth hurts, and this is one they are going to have to understand hurt me for years.

Claire and my mom seem to get along well. Mom has found some nurturing side of herself since being here, and she's made it her mission to make sure that Claire is taken care of. I haven't told her, but that simple gesture has helped me to worry less about Trazia's mom.

It's the dead of night and while I should be sleeping, I can't take my eyes off Trazia. From the moment the doctor started weaning her off the medicine, I've been unable to look away in case I miss her waking up or moving. The nurses told us to alert them of even the smallest of movements, like if she lifts her finger. That's one of the signs that she's coming back to us.

Her evening nurse comes in with a bright smile on her face for the nightly routine checkup. "You should get some sleep," she tells me as she checks Trazia's chart and vitals.

"Hard to sleep when she could wake up any minute."

After typing something into the computer attached to Traz's monitors, she looks at me with pursed lips. "It's only been a few hours. I've been in this department a long time. Get your rest now so she has you at your best when the time comes." She leaves the room with a soft smile on her face.

I try taking her advice, but sleep never comes. My mind is racing, and I'm scared of what could happen when she wakes. What if she doesn't wake up? What if she doesn't remember me? What if she has brain damage and they failed to detect it from the many tests they took?

When leaving the house earlier, I grabbed my laptop in the hope of finding ways to pass the time during the long night. Rather than playing games, I open a blank Word document and stare at the white page trying to think of what to tell Trazia.

Since her accident, I've had this urge to get all my thoughts and feelings out. Her doctor and nurses say they believe people in comas can hear their loved ones, but talking to her while she lays there looking as if she is sleeping is difficult, and I wonder if it would be easier if I first got the words written.

As I think back to the confessions I've wanted to tell her and what I hope our future holds, tears begin to well up. Thinking about how our future could be up in the air depending on what happens when she wakes scares me, and that's the first time I've admitted it to myself.

When our friends and family are here during the day, it's easier not to think about the what-ifs, but the nights when it's just Trazia and me, I have to force my brain not to think anything bad. Like how we could have lost our baby, or I could have lost them both.

The words are flowing as I let it all out on the keyboard. I've never been great when it came to English classes and coughing up essays for my professors, but if they could see me now, they'd be proud of how well this letter is coming out.

Times flies as I pound my fingertips on the keys. Trazia's monitor helps me keep a steady rhythm. I not only confess that I love her, but also the future I see with her. Our baby. Getting a house. Each of us graduating college. Moving away from the college district and closer to the beach because I know how much she loves the ocean, and I think she'll want to share that with our kids. And yes, more kids. How I can see her and Blaire opening a small school rather than working through the structured system.

As my fingers begin to cramp and the sky starts to lighten, my eyes grow heavy with exhaustion. I click save on the document, check on Trazia, and kiss her forehead, then lounge back in my recliner and hope when I wake up, my girl will be ready to come back to me.

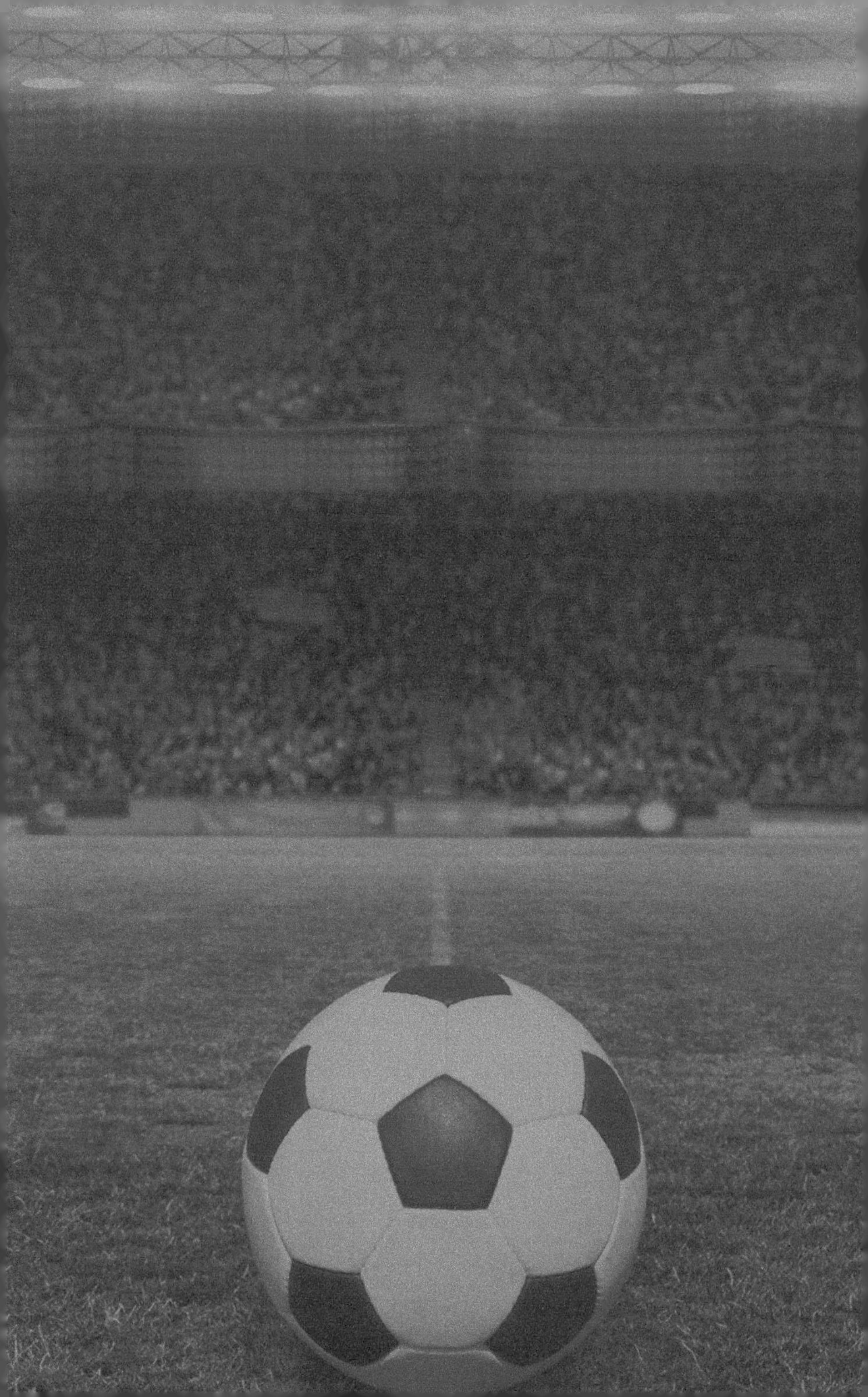

CHAPTER FORTY

MADDOX

"You're not really going to eat that, are you?" my mother asks for the second time as we get breakfast in the hospital cafeteria. So far, she has made a face at the breakfast sandwich I picked out and is now questioning the brownie and pudding cup I selected.

Picking up a second cup just to annoy her, I move along to the cashier near the exit. "When you've gotten as little sleep as I have, you get to eat whatever you want."

Mom whips out her credit card before I have a chance to hand my cash over. "While I understand the lack of sleep, I don't think that means you can fill your body with processed junk. Do you even know what is in sausage, Maddox? Add in the bacon in your sandwich and you'll have a heart attack before you're thirty."

Growing up with an almond mom was never fun. Even when she wasn't around, Veronica Stone had strict instructions on foods that were forbidden in the house. Anything with high-fructose corn syrup and dyes was never allowed. Neither were foods with too much sugar or grease. Basically, all the fun shit kids like to eat wasn't to cross the Stone home threshold.

But she did allow a variety of fruits, nuts, and veggies. Every kid's dream.

"Mom, enjoy your parfait and let me eat what I want." We take a seat at the table where my dad has been sipping his black coffee.

"Have you been getting on him about saturated fats again, darling?" Dad is notorious for having a liquid breakfast and sneaks in red meat during his lunches at work. Mom thinks he supports her limited diet, and that's part of how they keep their marriage afloat.

"Don't think there's a time I've had a meal with Mom without that being part of it. But I will tell you, I have to maintain a pretty healthy lifestyle during the soccer season. Helps that I learned from the eating habits I had growing up."

Her face brightens. "You have no idea how happy that makes me."

My parents were able to tear me away from Trazia's side long enough for breakfast, and it gave Camden and Claire some time alone with her. While I want nothing more than to be by her side every minute, I know it's selfish to take that away from her family.

I eat faster than I probably should, and based on the look my parents give me, it doesn't go unnoticed. My mom decides to keep her comments to herself this time around, though.

A frantic Mateo comes running into the cafeteria as I down my water bottle. He searches the room and moves quickly toward us, dodging people in the process.

"Hey, man. Trazia started moving her hand. Claire wanted me to come down and get you. Maybe your voice will help her come out sooner." I'm out of the seat and leaving my trash behind before he finishes his sentence.

She's only a few floors up, so I take the stairs two at a time. By the time I get through the ICU door, my heart is racing.

Whether it's from the cardio or the anticipation of Trazia waking up, I don't know.

Her door is open, and I walk right into the room. Claire is in the same chair she's occupied each day, and Camden is in the recliner I've been sleeping in. Her day nurse, Maribel, is at Trazia's side taking her blood pressure and putting numbers into her bedside monitor.

"Mateo said she moved?" I ask as I approach Camden's side and rest my hand on Trazia's blanket-covered leg.

Claire smiles up at me with misty eyes. "Yes. She gripped my hand too."

"Does that mean she'll wake up soon?" I ask Maribel.

She gives me the same pitiful smile everyone else has each time I ask that question. "You know I can't give you an answer, Maddox. It could be any minute or days from now. It's up to Trazia at this point."

Claire's and Camden's hopeful smiles help me to stay positive, because right now I'm close to doing something crazy like setting off the smoke alarm to get Trazia out of this deep sleep.

THREE HOURS LATER, and the most we've gotten from my girl is a hand squeeze and some more finger wiggles. While I was holding her hand in mine, watching TV, hers flexed and gripped mine, sending me into a panic mode thinking she was coming to. Since then, I've been lightly putting pressure on her to try and get that reaction again.

"You should talk to her," my mom suggests from her spot on the window bench. Camden convinced Claire to get some fresh air on a walk, and my mom came back to check on me.

I look down at Trazia and push the stray piece of hair behind her ear. "What would I even say?"

My mom stands and puts her magazine into her large purse. "Anything. Just the sound of your voice will be enough. I'll leave you two alone and go check on your father." She comes up and kisses my cheek before closing the door behind her.

The room feels empty with only the two of us. I take up my seat again and bring it as close to her bedside as I can and grab her hand.

"Hey, Peach," I start. "This is kind of weird and I'm not sure what to talk about." I squeeze her hand, looking for strength.

"We miss you, baby. I miss you, and it's only been a few days. Sleeping next to you in a hospital room is nothing compared to having you wrapped in my arms at night. If you wake up, we can get back to that. I know you'd much rather get out of this stiff bed and be home in our own bed." I laugh, knowing she would much prefer the Tempur-Pedic mattress I bought two years ago.

I watch her face, looking for any movement. Her fingers twitch again in my hand.

Raising her hand, I rest my forehead against her soft skin. "There's something I need to tell you and I hate myself for not saying it sooner. You're the most important person to me, Trazia Collins. I need you in my life. Our baby needs you. The kids to come are going to need you. We have so much ahead of us, but you have to wake up for it."

I sit there clutching to her when I hear the faintest sound. "Okay."

Shooting up, I smile when I see Trazia's heavy eyes are slightly open. The sides of her mouth are lifted up ever so slightly, as if she is trying to smile but isn't strong enough.

"Peach, are you really here?" I ask as I cup her face with both my hands.

She slowly lifts hers and holds on to my forearm. "I think so." Her voice is husky and low, but I'm able to hear the most beautiful sound after going without it for days.

Not wanting to waste another second, I lean forward and place a soft kiss on her lips. Trazia sighs the moment I touch her, and I all but sink onto the bed with the relief that washes over me.

Pulling back, I look into her bright green eyes. "I should go get your nurse. And some water for you. Are you thirsty?" She nods. "Okay, nurse and water. Fuck, your mom too. She went on a walk with your brother, but she's been here the whole time, Peach. We all have."

After I leave a lingering kiss on her forehead, I turn to tell her nurse that she's awake, but Trazia calls my name to stop me. "Our baby?" she asks with worry in her eyes and tears building up.

"Perfectly healthy. You're growing a strong one, Peach." The smile on her face as she rubs her bump helps to assure me everything is going to be all right.

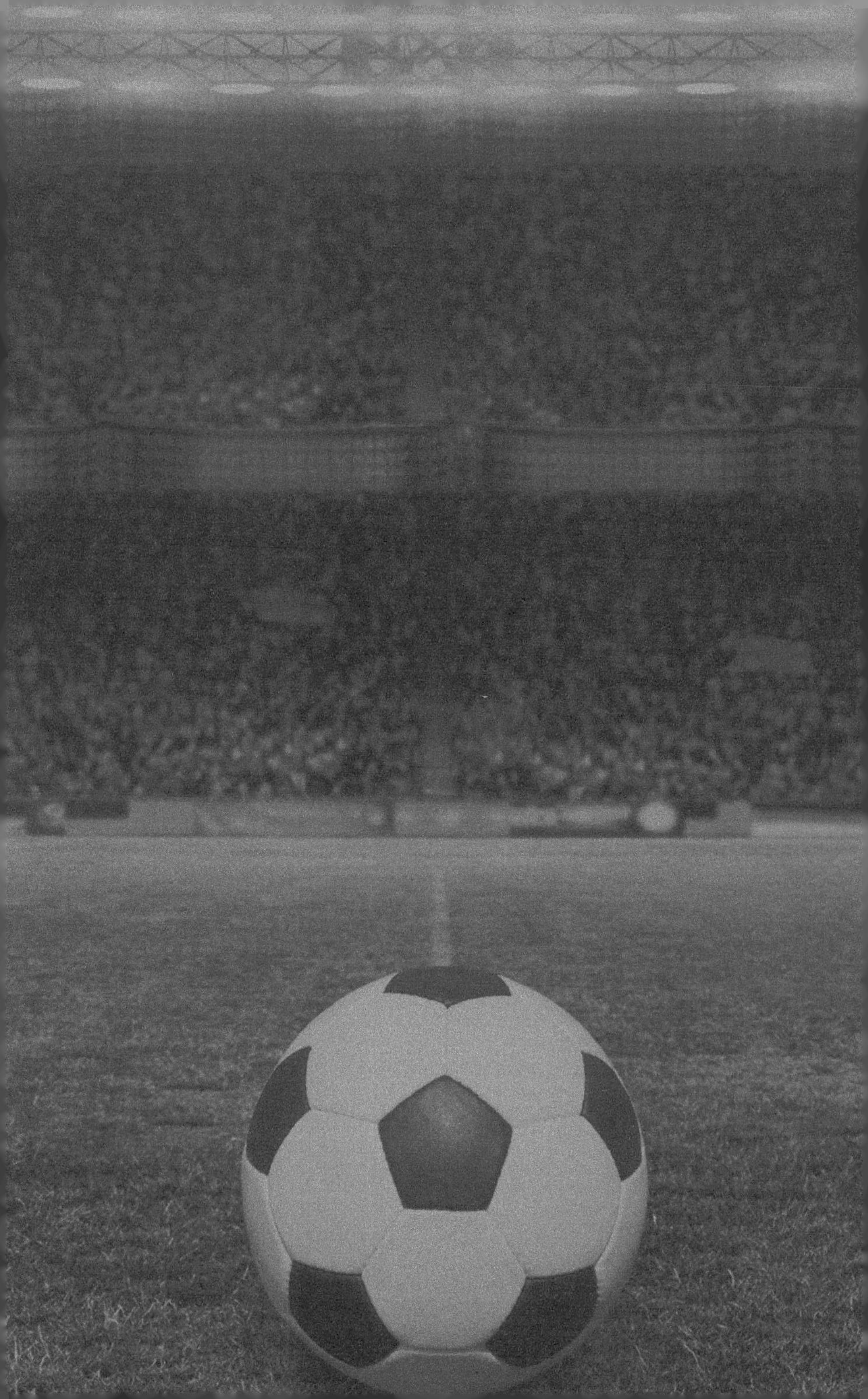

CHAPTER FORTY-ONE

TRAZIA

My head feels as if someone opened my skull, jumbled up my brain, and closed it up. The headache has been slowly relieving itself, and I've had brain fog since the moment I woke up. I've been told this is normal and will eventually go away.

After Maddox alerted the nurse that I was awake, she paged my doctors before putting me through a few memory tests, which I passed, much to Maddox's relief. My mom and brother both came back, breaking the two-visitors-allowed rule. The room has been filled with people for the last hour and all I want is for them all to leave, which isn't fair seeing as how they've been by my side for the last few days. But even though I've been asleep, I feel exhausted and like I could use a good, long nap right now.

"You've passed every one of my tests, Miss Collins. With how significant the accident was, I'm happy the worst you will be leaving us with is a humerus fracture." She smiles at my family and then me. "We are going to keep you longer to monitor any brain swelling, but once you're in the clear, we will get you home and in your own bed."

Thinking of my bed and getting back to my normal life is all I need right now.

"Are you sure it's not too soon? What about her head?" Maddox asks as he holds my hand.

"Her doctor will do another CT scan, but if the swelling shows no signs of coming back, she will be in the clear. We will have you monitor her at home. Any ongoing headaches or lightheadedness, you'll need to give us a call."

Maddox's relief is visible as he nods in response to her answer.

We're left alone for the first time since I've woken up as we wait for the neurologist and my OB-GYN. "Let's hope they release me from here soon because these pillows are not for comfort."

Everyone laughs as I adjust the flattened pillows yet again.

"You want me to try and get some more?" Camden asks.

I sink back into the bed. "No, it's fine. I'm just spoiled with the fancy bedding Maddox has back at home. I could use a ginger ale, if you don't mind getting one for me?"

He nods. "You got it."

Once my brother is gone, my mom starts going into planning mode. "Sweetheart, I can set your old room up for you to come stay there until you're healed. There is a lot of PTO I've saved up over the years, and I could always take a leave of absence if needed."

"Stay with you?"

She gives me a smile that is warm and loving, and I know it is going to be hard for me to tell her I don't want to go back home and recover. I want to be in my bed at Braxton and especially with Maddox.

"Of course. You're going to need help for the next few weeks, and it is best for someone to watch over you after a head injury like this," she explains.

Maddox clears his throat. "I mean no disrespect, Claire, but I'm more than ready to take care of Trazia at our house."

My mom looks hesitant as her eyes bounce between the two of us. "Are you sure about that? She will need someone checking on her throughout the night, and what about the stairs in your house? She may be too weak to go up and down them."

I rub my belly, waiting for his response. "I'm confident. She won't be lifting a finger, and I'll carry her up and down the stairs when needed. She can rest and focus on ordering everything we need to get ready for the baby. Plus, I've already talked to her professors, and she's able to complete the rest of the semester online, which Blaire and I can help with since we've taken these classes."

"Is that what you want?" she asks me.

"It is. I'll be much more comfortable in my bed."

Maddox squeezes my hand. "We do have the extra bedroom if it will make you feel better being there when she gets home." This man. I swear, he doesn't even realize how big his heart is.

"You two are adults. It's time for me to pass off the nurturing duties to the man who holds her heart." My mom smiles as she looks at Maddox and me. "But that won't stop me from making some homemade meals to make it easier."

"I'd appreciate that because no one can survive on Maddox's cooking."

He rolls his eyes, but there is an amused smile on his face. "I'll accept that help anytime you want to offer it."

I watch as my mom and Maddox go over the meals she plans on making, thinking about how lucky I am to be surrounded by the most loving people.

Since waking up from the accident, I have tried not to think about how bad the outcome could have been. Maddox told me Emree's car is totaled, with most of the damage being on my side. The fact that I'm able to walk away with minimal broken bones and a minor head injury has me more grateful than I could ever be. Especially with Bean being unharmed.

I owe my life to the medical team here and my friends and family. I have a feeling that without their love and care, recovering would be much more difficult.

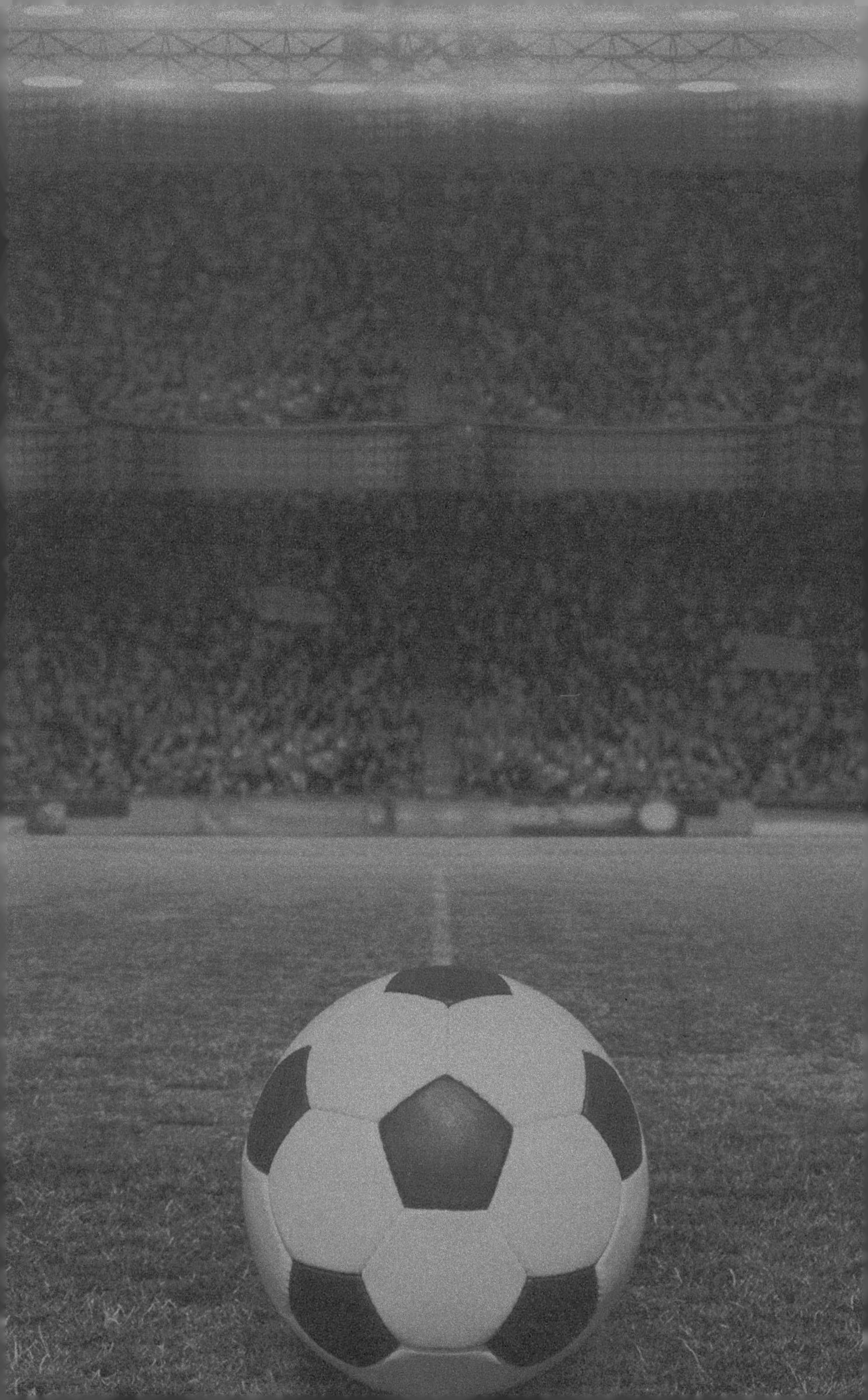

CHAPTER FORTY-TWO

MADDOX

After a week in the hospital, Trazia has officially been cleared to go home. Which is good because the sweet, loving girl we have all grown to know has become irritable and restless. Since they moved her from the ICU to the general hospital floor, she hasn't gotten a single full night of sleep. The nurse comes in constantly to wake her up and take her temperature and vitals.

"This is such bullshit. I can walk out of here perfectly fine," Trazia grumbles, again, as the nurse pushes her through the hospital.

Her ever-so-patient nurse lets out a laugh. "Once again, Miss Collins, it's hospital protocol. The moment you're outside, you are free to run around as much as you would like."

Trazia huffs. "Fine. But don't think I won't."

I roll my eyes because this is how the last few days have been. She's persistent to do everything on her own, even against her nurses' orders. Even though she isn't considered a fall risk, they want to assist her to the toilet and shower in case she gets lightheaded. She was able to convince them that I was enough to help her and that I was going to need to do it when we're back home. After they showed me what to look out for and how to support her, they were assured I could handle it.

The sliding doors open, and Claire is waiting beside her SUV with a bright smile on her face. "Thank God. Get in the front seat, Mom. We have to escape this place." Trazia tries to put her feet on the ground and get up, but her nurse halts her with a firm hand on her shoulder.

"Could you at least wait until I stop and lock the wheelchair?"

"Fine. Park it, woman." Her nurse stops and comes to Trazia's side with both her eyebrows raised. "Please?" Trazia adds.

The moment the wheels stop in front of the car and it is safely put in park, my girl is up and out of her seat. "Free at last. Listen, Jackie, no hard feelings. You've been great, but it's time for us to part."

She looks between the two of us and laughs. "With you both as parents, that child is going to be born with sarcasm oozing from them. Good luck to you, and don't hesitate to come back here if anything feels off." With a wave, she disappears into the hospital.

Trazia one-arm hugs her mom before getting into the front seat. "Let's roll, family. I'm ready to snuggle up in my bed with my Kindle and some Netflix."

While Claire gets settled in the driver's seat, I load mine and Trazia's stuff in the trunk. "We're all set," I tell them.

"Thank you, sweetie." Trazia smiles back at me. "Ma, do you mind if we swing by Taco Bell? I could use a few dozen soft tacos and maybe a Mexican pizza."

Her mom laughs and turns onto the main road from the hospital. "Of course. Maddox, do you want to text your friends if anyone wants some food?"

I shoot a message to our roommates' group chat and everyone puts their order in. Claire is ever so patient as I read off what they all want. I try handing her my credit card, but she swats it away.

Trazia starts in on her tacos while Claire drives us to the house. She devours two of them during the drive and goes on about how bad the hospital food is the whole time.

Pulling into the driveway, I smile when I see the giant *Welcome Home, Trazia!* sign hung up above the garage and balloons tied to the lights on each side. Emree, Jules, and Blaire have been texting nonstop to find out when she was being released because they wanted to set up something for her but were keeping it a secret.

"Oh my gosh," my girl gasps from the front seat as she leans forward to get a better look. "You guys didn't need to do this."

"It was all the girls. They didn't tell me what they were doing."

I'm out of the car and helping Trazia to her feet just as Claire puts it in park. Even though the doctors cleared her, I'm still worried about dizziness and falling over.

The front door opens, and a smiling Camden and Blaire come out. "Yay, you're home!" Blaire cheers.

Camden told the rest of our friends it may be too overwhelming to have everyone here when Trazia got home, so it was better for her to get settled in before seeing more people. Even the guys living here made sure to give her enough time to unwind.

"You didn't have to do this," Trazia tells Blaire as she walks away from me and into her friend's arms for a tight hug.

Blaire clutches onto Trazia as she buries her face in her neck. The two have a silent moment and we stand around, giving them their time.

After a couple minutes, they pull back, and both have tears

running down their faces. "I'm so happy you're out of that place. We have everything set up for you."

Trazia looks at her with confusion as Blaire links their arms together and directs everyone into the front door. "What do you mean set up?"

I listen in, also curious what she means.

The house smells like fall candles, and there are a few lit up around the living room. Everything is cleaned, and there isn't any clutter to be seen. The couch cushions even look fluffier than they normally do.

"You guys didn't have to clean up just for me," Trazia tells her brother and Blaire as she takes in the downstairs area.

"That was all Jules and Levi. You know how big of clean freaks they are. Upstairs is the fun stuff Emree and Blaire put together," Camden explains with a smile directed to his girlfriend.

They have my curiosity piqued because I wasn't aware of anything special going on. "If it's a new flat-screen TV, we thank you very much."

Blaire rolls her eyes. "No. The surprise is not that, but it is for both of you. Want to head up and see?"

Dropping the bags, I rush to Trazia's side and lift her into my arms, being mindful of her broken arm. "Your chariot awaits."

She laughs as she holds on to my neck, and we all follow Blaire up the stairs. Our bedroom door is closed, and Blaire grabs the handle, swinging the door open with a creak. Inside, our room is freshly cleaned. The bed is made, and there is a basket full of Trazia's favorite snacks, a pair of fuzzy socks, and hot chocolate packets. There's a new fluffy blanket draped over the end of the bed.

I release Trazia before stepping fully into the room. When she walks in, she gasps at something on the other side of the bed near the window.

A MEMORY THAT ONCE WAS

Over there is a complete setup for the baby. The crib is put together, and there are a variety of stuffed animals in there. The glider has a new blanket and pillow on it, and in the corner is the white dresser we picked out to store all of the little one's clothes.

"We also washed and put away the baby clothes you had bought so far. Plus, Emree found a few other cute outfits while we were shopping for the other stuff." Blaire smiles proudly as she walks Trazia to that side of the room.

"It's perfect," my girl confesses softly. "It's all beautiful."

Above the dresser is a gold circle mirror that matches the room. Some baby books are stacked in the corner, with tiny baby shoes lined up in a row.

I come up behind Trazia, resting my hands on her stomach. "It's perfect for our little bean."

Blaire smiles proudly. "Your bathroom is set up with new bath soaps and candles to help you relax. I also made sure to charge your Kindle and even downloaded a few new releases from while you were in the hospital."

"What did I ever do to deserve you?"

"You just focus on healing. Emree already made dinner for you tonight, so that's covered. She made chicken pot pie—your favorite."

Trazia goes up to Blaire and Camden, hugging them both with her good arm. "Thank you. You guys are the best."

After saying goodbye to her mom, who promised to be over tomorrow with a variety of meals, Camden and Blaire give us some space to get Trazia settled in. She wants to shower the hospital smell off her, but with the cast, it is easier said than done. Luckily, Blaire thought ahead and stashed some Saran Wrap in the bathroom.

With some careful maneuvering, I'm able to get Trazia's arm wrapped perfectly and assist in washing her hair. Once she's finished putting on her skincare products and wrapping her hair in a towel, she's exhausted and ready to get into her own bed.

When she's comfortable, I make sure she has a water bottle beside her and set an alarm for when she needs to wake up, like her doctor instructed.

I get in on my side of the bed, and Trazia scoots over to wrap her arm around one of mine while laying on her side. "Are we going to talk about your parents being here, or should that be a conversation for another time?"

A couple days ago, I told Trazia about my parents being here and the conversations we've been having. She was proud of me for standing up for myself and is glad they seem to have opened their eyes to the neglect I went through as a kid. She wanted to meet them, as did they, but I felt more comfortable not having that happen while she was recovering in the hospital.

"I want to do everything on your time. The moment you're up for meeting new people, I'll invite them over for dinner. My mom and yours are apparently already friends, so we'll have to have Claire there as well."

She laughs and tightens her hold on me. "Let's do it tomorrow night. I'm excited to meet them and would feel bad if they had to hold off coming over for another day."

"I'll call them in the morning," I tell her as I kiss the top of her head. "Now get some sleep. You're going to have a lot of people wanting to see you when you're up."

She sighs as she closes her eyes, and I sit there watching her. I try not to think too hard about how the outcome of this accident could have been different, but those thoughts creep in sometimes during quiet moments like this. Watching her at ease like this are some of my favorite moments.

"I love you," I whisper.

Trazia's eyes pop open. "What did you just say?"

"I love you, Trazia Collins."

Her eyes get misty, and she pushes herself up to plant a bruising kiss on my lips. I wrap my arm around her waist and gently pull her closer to me.

"I love you too. So much," she whispers against my lips.

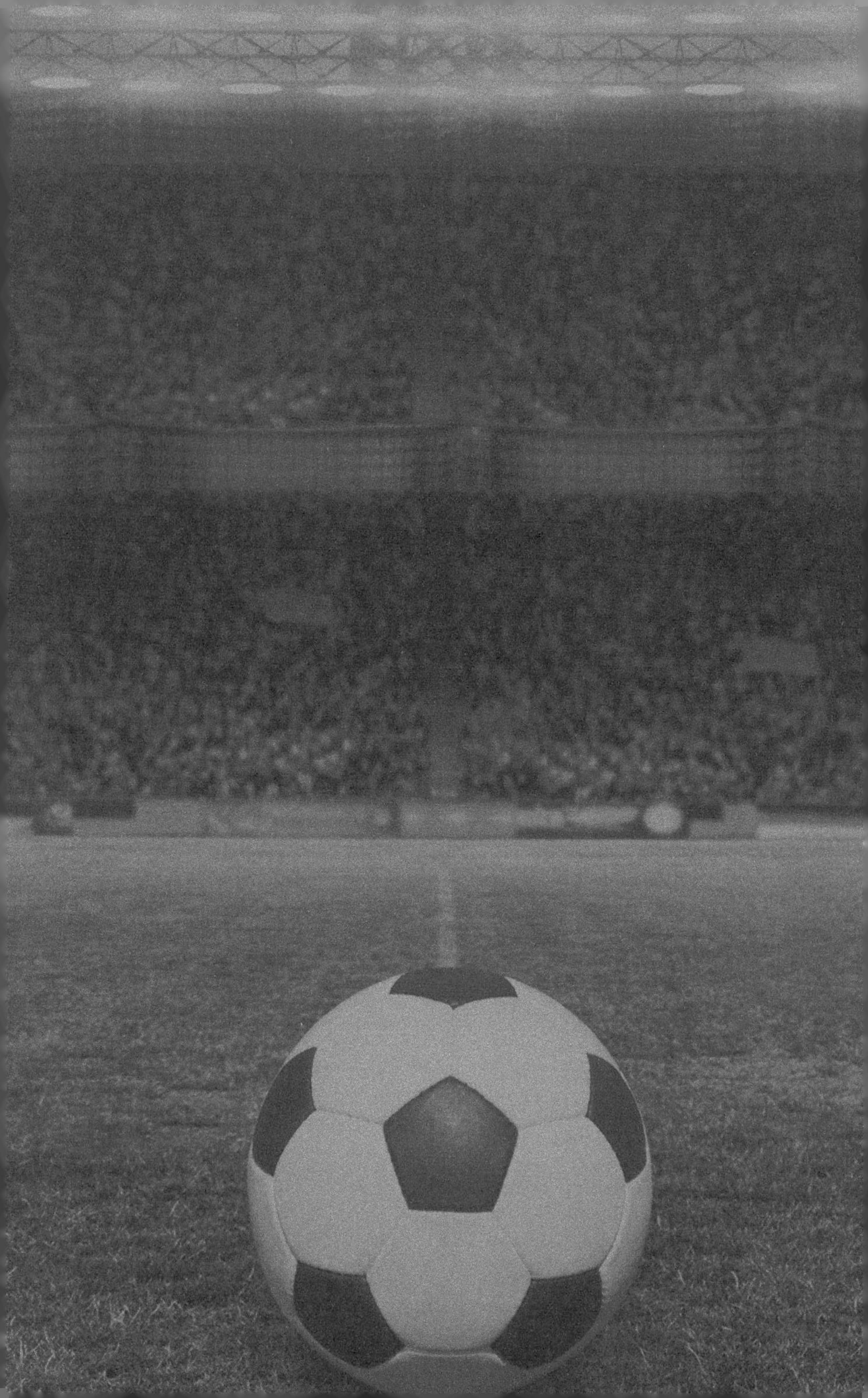

CHAPTER FORTY-THREE

TRAZIA

"What color does the mom even wear to a baby shower when she doesn't know the gender?" I ask Maddox while looking through my closet.

He's sitting on the bed, fully dressed, and ready to go. "Don't know. Black?"

Turning, I narrow my eyes at him. "That's for funerals."

"Peach, anything you wear is going to look beautiful. The thing is, we have to actually get dressed and go for everyone to see your gorgeous self."

I'm six and a half months pregnant and tired of it already. My feet are swollen, my back hurts nonstop, and the constant heartburn is becoming an issue. With how large Bean is, finding clothes that look cute and are comfortable is a struggle.

"What about green? That's cute, right?" I ask Maddox as I pull out a flowy hunter-green dress that hits above the knee with lace at the top.

"I think it's perfect."

Undoing my robe, I pull the dress over my head, and it falls perfectly over my body. I bought the dress last month and it was too big. Glad to see it won't go to waste with my growing belly. With my hair braided up and the light makeup I did earlier, I feel like this is the perfect baby shower look.

After slipping on some sandals, I stand in front of Maddox with my arms open. "Okay, I'm ready."

He smiles up at me and reaches for my stomach, caressing it. "The hottest baby mama there is."

After he kisses Bean, he stands and plants a soft kiss against my red lips. Ever since the accident, Maddox has been constantly by my side. When I felt up to going back to work, he insisted on driving me to and from each shift when he didn't have class or practice, which started back up last month. If I was there for a long day, he would stop in and bring everyone lunch. My coworkers and Janette love him and try to get him to come in when he drops me off.

"Get your hands off me before you smudge my lipstick," I tell him as I push his shoulder.

Maddox laughs and grabs my hand. "Let's get going. I'm sure they're all waiting downstairs for us."

We all agreed to have the shower at the house and to keep it small. I only wanted our friend group and parents here. Maddox's parents decided to rent a condo in the city so that they could come and stay here more often rather than checking into a hotel each time. His mom wants to be more involved, especially when the baby is born. Plus, she and my mom have become friends. They do regular lunch and shopping dates with my mom's friend Carrie when Veronica is in town.

Downstairs the house smells like fresh baked goods and sweetness. The girls kept the shower a complete surprise from me, so I have no idea what I'm walking into.

The living room has a pile of various shaped gifts beside the TV, and there is a *Mommy to Be* sash laying over the sofa chair. Maddox grabs it while I take in the plethora of presents from our friends and family.

A MEMORY THAT ONCE WAS

"They did too much. It's one baby. How much could they need?"

"You'd be surprised by that, sweetie," someone says from behind me. My mom is standing under the archway connecting the living room and kitchen. "Those little buggers will spit up or poop through several outfits a day. You can never have enough clothes and burp cloths."

"Well, that's good to know. We may have to get a second dresser for this one's wardrobe," I say while pointing to my stomach.

I walk over to my mom and wrap her in a hug as best I can with the boulder between us. "Thanks for being here, Mama."

"I wouldn't miss it for the world," she whispers in my ear. "I'm so proud and happy for you, baby girl."

Having my mom in my corner has been a blessing. She is always available whenever I call to ask questions about what my body is going through and has helped guide me with what the baby will need versus what would be nice to have for them. Her support means the world to me, and I try to make sure she knows that.

Past the kitchen, which is littered with a variety of party snacks, is a setup outside that screams we are throwing a baby shower. "Oh my gosh, they did not."

I walk through the sliding glass door. Outside they have large blocks that spell out B-A-B-Y. There are green and orange blown-up balloons all over, hanging from chairs, light fixtures, and the loungers. The whole backyard looks beautiful and straight out of a baby shower Pinterest board. There's even a backdrop against the house that says *Welcome, Baby Collins-Stone*, with clusters of various-sized balloons framing it.

"Happy baby shower!" everyone shouts when we're outside.

Emree is the first to come up and hug me. "We weren't really sure what to say, so 'happy baby shower' seemed to work the best."

Maddox and I laugh. "It's perfect. Everything is. You are all blowing me away. Thank you so much."

"We have to spoil our newest edition to the group," Jules tells us as she comes in for her hug.

Mateo stands off to the side by the guys with a beer in hand. "Full disclosure, we were told what to buy you, so the shopping is all Blaire, Emree, and Jules."

"What the fuck, man? You too good to buy something for my baby?" Maddox argues.

Mateo holds his hands up. "Not at all. But they wouldn't let me get the clothes I picked out and said they were ugly."

"Because they were," Emree states matter-of-factly. "None of those were gender-neutral outfits, and most didn't even match."

"He was manifesting you having a boy," Jules defends.

Mateo sticks his tongue out at Emree. "Yeah. What Jules said."

Veronica and Jack come up, both giving us soft hugs. While their relationship with their son is still a work in progress, I know Maddox enjoys them being around. He and his dad spend some time off on their own golfing when they're in town, and my heart is happy watching that relationship heal.

"What even goes on at a baby shower?" Levi asks, gaining everyone's attention.

I stay quiet and wait for someone else to answer. When everyone looks around waiting for someone to speak up, Maddox steps forward with a fresh beer in hand. "Hell if I know, but let the baby showering begin."

A MEMORY THAT ONCE WAS

TWO HOURS LATER, and I am baby showered out. We played games the girls found online that included feeding a partner baby food while blindfolded, smelling smeared foods in diapers to guess what they are, and a guessing game to see who got my belly size right. That last one was a wee bit insulting with some of the guesses.

Our parents left just a little bit ago after we opened presents. Thanks to our friends and family, we are more than ready for Bean to be here. There are several outfits, ranging in size from newborn to eighteen months. We have all the necessities, like a diaper bag, tub, stroller, car seat, and pacifiers. There is even more fun stuff like toys and books as well.

"Babies need a lot of shit," Maddox announces to the room as we go through the presents. "I mean, what the fuck even is this thing?"

Blaire takes it from his hand and reads the front. "It's to suck the boogers from their nose."

He looks at the box and then back to her. "Excuse me?"

"Yeah. You know, like when they have a stuffy nose and you need to clear it."

"You're telling me I have to suck the boogers from their nose with this tube thing?"

Blaire nods. "How else would you get their nose cleared?"

Maddox blinks, completely stunned by this new revelation, while I try to hide my laughter. "Why don't you just have them blow their nose like a regular person?"

I break and end up letting out a loud laugh that I quickly try to cover.

"They're babies, Maddox. Blowing their nose isn't a skill they have yet."

I pat him on the shoulder. "Don't worry, honey. I'll handle the boogie sucking." He shakes his head, seemingly okay with our compromise.

Holding up one of the baby's many outfits, I smile thinking

about them wearing it. "You all really outdid any expectation I had for a baby shower. This was such an amazing day, and I can't thank you enough. Bean is going to be the best-dressed baby thanks to their aunties."

"Just know there will be more shopping trips going on once we find out who this little baby is. Especially if it's a girl, because the clothing options for them is so much better." Emree smiles as she helps me fold the clothes.

When everything is packed in a large box to move upstairs, I have Maddox help me up and look at our group of friends in the living room. "I'm truly grateful to have each of you not only in my life, but in Bean's as well. They already have so many aunts and uncles that are going to be there to teach, protect, and comfort them. You're the best group of friends anyone could have, and I'm so happy to have been included."

"We're lucky to have such a sweet and loving person like you," Blaire tells me.

"Hell yeah. Even if Maddox hadn't knocked you up, we'd still want you around." Levi leans over and punches Mateo for his comment.

"Mateo, you are ever so sweet," I tell him with a laugh. "But really, thank you, guys. You didn't have to take in the homeless freshman who ended up being pregnant, but you did, and without hesitation."

"Wouldn't have had it any other way," Levi states.

Maddox wraps his arm around my waist. "Thanks, everyone. Truly don't think there is a better friend group out there."

"Enough with the feel-good moment. Let's get this crap upstairs and head over to Whiskey Joe's for some cornhole or something." Camden grabs a box and begins bringing it upstairs as the rest of the guys go to help.

When I started college, never did I think this would be how I would experience my first year. I've gained more in these last few months that I will cherish for life. A group of friends that is strong and cares for one another. A boyfriend who loves me. And a baby who I already love more than anything in this world.

Life may not always go the way you think, but sometimes the bumps along the way may lead you to a better destination.

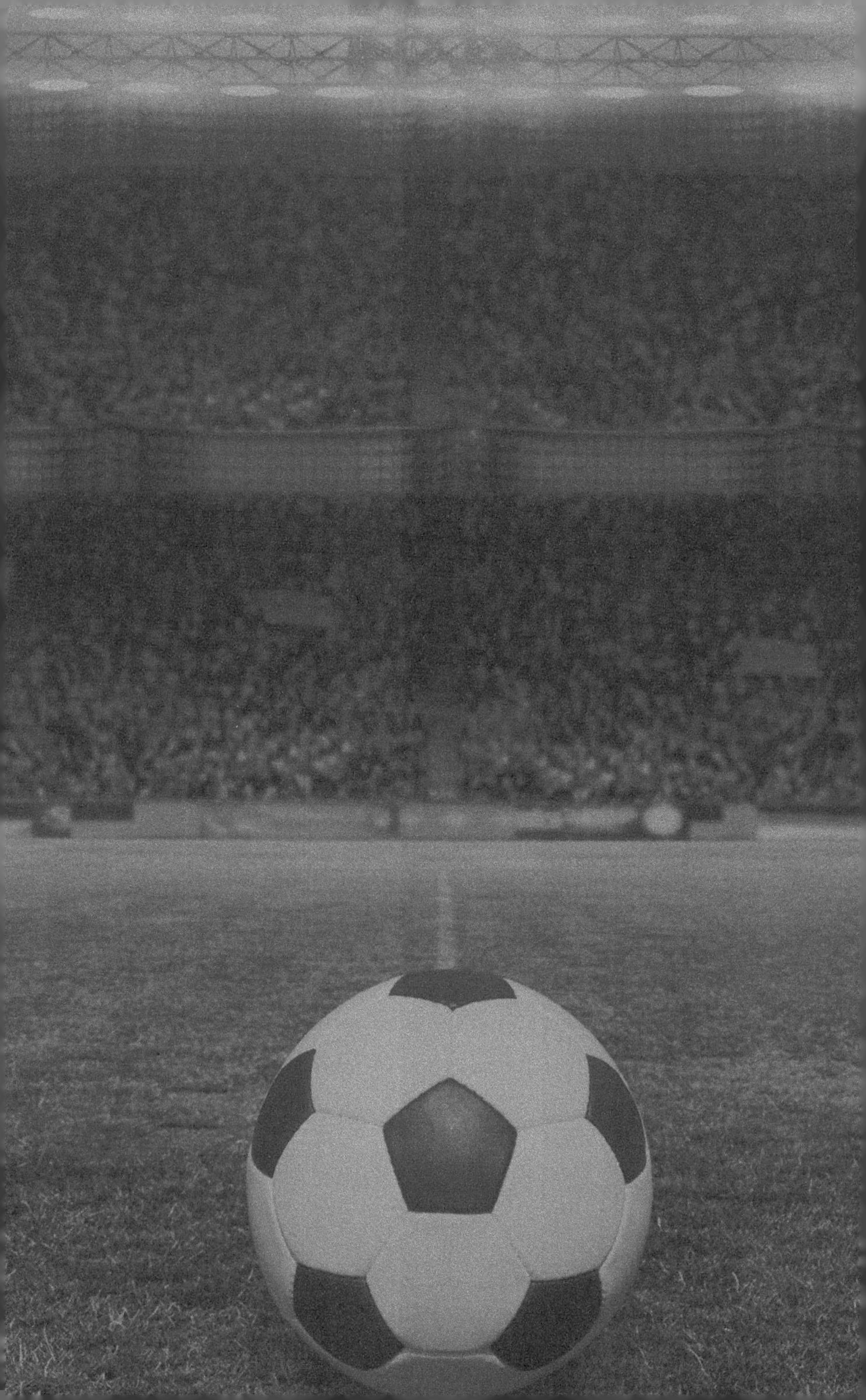

EPILOGUE

TRAZIA

"I'm going to kill you!" I shout, alerting all the nurses around me. "I swear to God, Maddox Stone, you are going to be dead. Do you hear me? Dead. As in not breathing." A pain shoots through my abdomen. "Six…feet…under," I breathe out.

Beside my hospital bed, Maddox is standing there not knowing what to do. We've been at the hospital for ten hours now, and I am only four centimeters dilated. The doctor has come in too many times and stuck her hand up me to check how far along I am, and if someone else puts their hands on me one more time, I am going to explode.

"You can't kill him, Traz. Last thing you want is no help and a newborn baby." My brother laughs from where he and Blaire are sitting on the couch in my room.

I roll my eyes. "Fine, then I'm at least cutting off his dick. Never again will he be touching me with that thing. It leads to this." I point to my stomach.

Maddox winces as Camden groans and Blaire laughs. "Please stop talking about you and my best friend's junk in the same sentence. It was hard enough living with you two for months."

"Peach, what can I do? Please, I can't stand to see you in pain," Maddox pleads.

I glare at him. "*You* can't stand to see *me* in pain? Oh, how convenient since *you* did this to *me*."

My mom comes out of the bathroom and walks up to the other side of my bed, laying a cold, wet washcloth on my head. "Honey, it takes two to make a baby. You can't keep blaming him."

Lifting my hand, I swat her arm away. "I am about to push out his giant child. He gets all the blame right now. Look at how big he is, Mom. This baby is going to rip me in half."

Maddox chuckles. "You've never complained about how big I am before." Camden groans again and covers his face with his hands.

"Do you want to live?" I ask him through clenched teeth.

Before he can respond, Dr. Wilson and the nurse come into the room with a new person in a white coat behind them. "Hello again. How are we doing?"

"Doc, I'm going to be honest with you. I need this thing out of me."

She laughs, and it makes me want to punch her. "If I had a dollar for every time a patient of mine said that to me." She shakes her head with a smile on her face. "I do come with good news. This is Dr. Brown. She is our anesthesiologist. Since you're far enough dilated, we can get that epidural inserted and help with the pain you've been experiencing."

Hope blossoms inside of me. "Hell yes. Do whatever you need to do, Doc. Give me the drugs, any drugs."

"Trazia," my mother lectures.

The two doctors and nurse laugh. "No worries. We'll get those drugs in you right away." The anesthesiologist looks at everyone in the room. "The process is a little...invasive. Anyone who won't be here during the birth should step outside of the room."

Blaire, my mom, and Camden get up to leave. My brother glares at Maddox when my boyfriend makes no move to follow them. Even though I'm pregnant with his child and we've officially been a couple for months, Camden still has his moments of wanting to kick Maddox's ass. I think the thought of his best friend seeing his little sister naked will forever haunt him.

Even though I have been a complete bitch to him for hours, Maddox holds my hand the entire time the doctors insert a giant-ass needle into my spine. While they walked me through this process at several of my appointments, nothing could have prepared me for how painful it is to have the epidural needle inserted. Even with the numbing injection, which was also painful, I wouldn't want to do any of that again.

For the next four hours, I lay in the hospital bed much more relaxed. I still feel pressure, but no pain like I did before. It's put me in a better mood. Levi, Mateo, Sage, Jules, Conrad, and Emree stop by to check on us. Emree brought me some gossip magazines since I've been here for so long, and she couldn't imagine how bored I've grown. I laughed and happily accepted them.

The sun has gone down, and, after much arguing, Camden, Blaire, and my mother agreed to go back to the house to get some rest. Maddox has been sleeping in the recliner or on the couch, never leaving my side.

The doctor comes in, whispering that she is checking me once again to see how far along I am. She makes sure not to wake Maddox, but after removing her glove, she smiles at me. "You ready, Mama? It's time."

My heart stops. This is it. I'm about to meet our baby.

Leaning over, I slap Maddox awake. "What, what?" he asks, startled.

"I'm about to push your giant baby out of my vagina, that's what."

In a blur, the nurses set everything up. They gather all the equipment needed, hook me up to the necessary monitors, and dress Maddox in his protective robe. Before I know it, Dr. Wilson is seated with a direct view of my most intimate area and is telling me to push. Maddox holds one of my legs open while the nurse holds the other, and I begin the process of getting this baby out of me.

After several pushes, multiple curses, squeezing Maddox's hand so hard he almost drops to his knees, and screaming so loud I am sure everyone on our floor heard me, our baby's cry fills my ears, and the floodgates break as I sob.

A boy. We have a baby boy.

Milo Maddox Stone. Born December fifteenth at three thirteen in the morning. Weighing seven pounds and four ounces. Nineteen inches long.

They clean him off and then lay him on my naked chest. He has a full head of dark blond hair, matching his daddy's. The moment he touches my skin, the crying stops. His eyes slowly begin to blink open as he takes in the world around him. His big, beautiful eyes are a light green. He is the spitting image of Maddox, and I couldn't be happier.

Beside me, someone sobs, and when I look over, tears are filled in Maddox's eyes and streaming down his face. Leaning forward, he kisses the top of our son's head and then my lips. "Thank you. Thank you so much, Peach. I love you more than anything in the world, and now we have the most perfect son."

Closing my eyes, I take in this moment. The man I love beside me. Our son on my chest. Nothing could compare to the love in my heart right now.

My family is perfect and complete.

While the doctor stitches me up, the nurses take Milo to the side to perform different tests and procedures on him. Maddox reluctantly leaves my side and watches over our son. He cries, and my heart breaks hearing my sweet baby boy in pain.

A shirtless Maddox comes over with our son resting on his

A MEMORY THAT ONCE WAS

chest. They put a tiny diaper on him, but other than that, he is naked against his daddy. I take in the view of him with our baby. Nothing could have prepared me for the image of seeing Maddox hold him. My heart feels complete.

We're left alone with Milo after a while, and we come down from the high of bringing him into this world. A lactation specialist comes in and Milo latches on like a pro, surprising her. Maddox watches in awe as I feed our son.

Once Milo is fed and burped, my family shows up. My mom is sad she missed the birth, but part of me is happy it was only Maddox and me. It feels more special that way. She cradles her first grandbaby in her arms, cooing at him in a baby voice. Camden and Blaire give Maddox and me hugs, and my brother hands me a bag of tacos. He said he knew I would be hungry, and Taco Bell is the perfect post-birth food.

After everyone has gotten their turn holding and loving on baby Milo, they leave to give Maddox and me some time alone to rest and take in being new parents. I must have drifted off to sleep for a while because when I woke, the sun was high. Maddox is sitting in the recliner with Milo on his chest.

"You know, sweet boy, I never expected to be this happy to be a dad. Didn't even think it would be something I would want, but I can't imagine not having you or your mom in my life. Crazy how that happens, huh?"

Closing my eyes, I pretend to be asleep while I continue to eavesdrop on their private moment.

"I love you so much, Milo. It hurts how much love I have for you. Sweet boy, I don't know how to do this dad thing, but I'm going to give it my best try. Your mommy is going to be the best mom in the world, though. She's loved you for so long and took amazing care of you while you were preparing to come into this world. Thank you for not being too hard on her in there. I wouldn't have been able to handle her being sick or in any more pain than she was."

I smile at his sweet words. Even before he knew the baby in me was his, he cared so much for me.

"While it may be unconventional, I'm happy I knocked up your mommy that night. I wouldn't change a thing about what happened between us. Well, maybe I'd have made it more romantic. A drunken quickie on vacation that I somehow forgot about isn't ideal for making a baby, but here we are."

My eyes shoot open. "Hey now, don't go telling our son about that night."

Maddox gifts me with that beautiful smile of his that lights up his face. "Need to be honest with him, Peach. He will need to learn from our mistakes because he's my son, so we know he is bound to have a few fuckups in his future."

Rolling my eyes, I huff at him. "He will learn from his father's past actions. He isn't even a day old and we're already talking about him possibly knocking up some girl in the future? I'm doomed."

Milo cries, and Maddox gently passes him to me. I lower the hospital gown and begin feeding him. He smiles around my breast, satisfied with having food.

Maddox watches us in amazement. "Ready for another?"

Lifting my head, I stare at him, trying to gauge if he is serious or not. "I am going to have to clean myself after peeing using a spray bottle for at least the next week, probably longer. Do not even think about getting me pregnant again for a while."

He smiles. "But we can do this again, right?"

Staring down at our son, I can't help but grin. He's more than perfect with his chubby cheeks, fair skin, and softness. "Yeah, we can do this again."

Maddox leans forward, and with his hand under my chin, he brings my face to look at him. "I love you and our family more than anything in this world. I can't wait to make you

Trazia Stone and have more babies. Thank you for giving me this life, Peach."

The tears come falling down my face as I smile against his lips. "I love you so much, Maddox. Thank you for this. For him. He's more than perfect, and I can't imagine my life without you or our baby boy."

"You have both of us. Forever."

Together, we get to take on this crazy life. Side by side, Maddox and I. To think this all started from a drunken night he thought was a dream and not a memory. I wouldn't change anything about how we began, because it led to this moment. Him, me, and our perfect baby boy. My family.

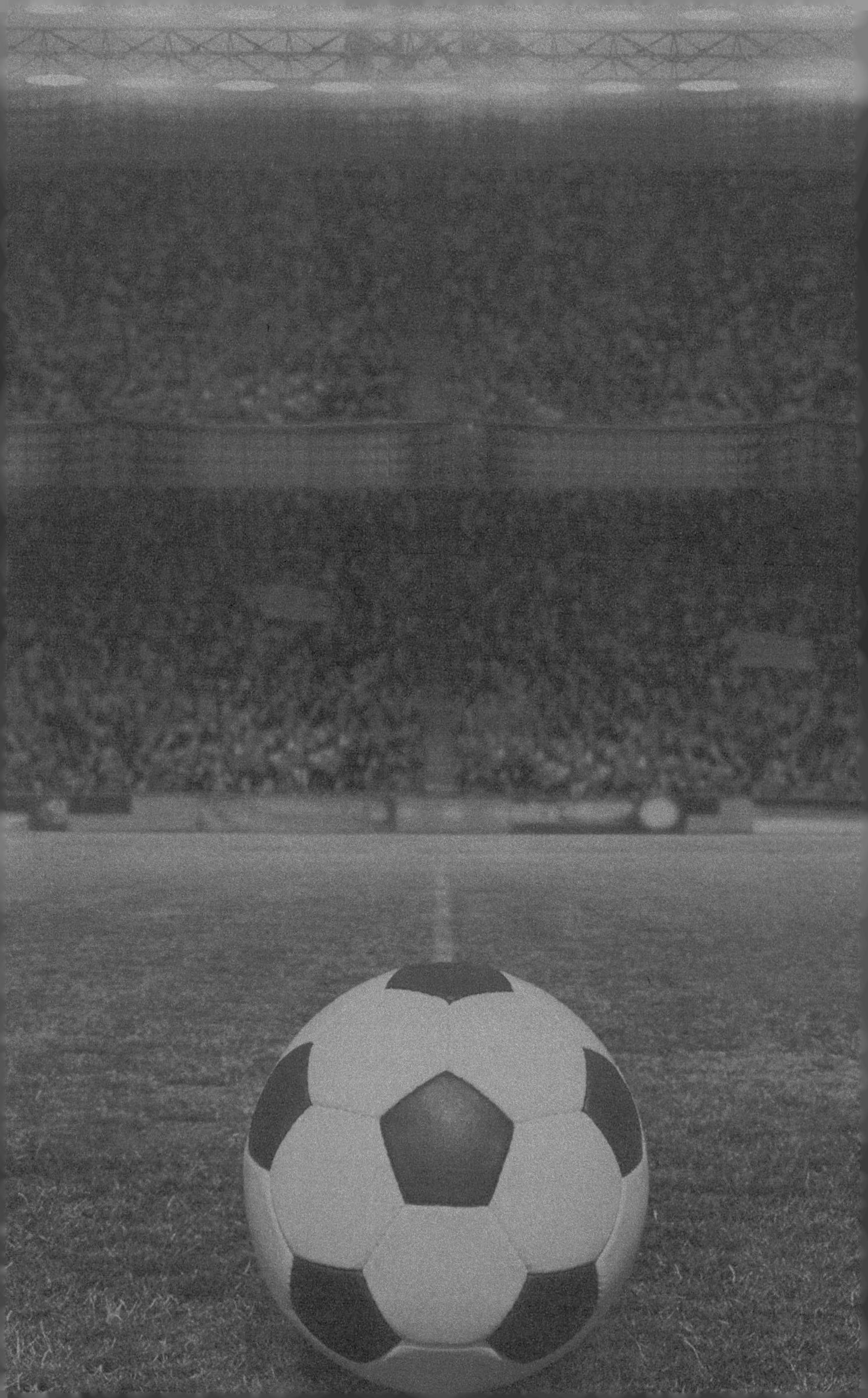

EPILOGUE 2

MADDOX

FIVE YEARS LATER

My arms begin to burn as I hold myself up, thrusting my hips faster and faster. "Fuck, baby, you feel so good."

My wife moans from under me. Her eyes squeeze closed as her head falls back, nails digging into my back. She comes, and it's the most beautiful sight. With a few more hard thrusts, I find my release and drop my head into the nook of her neck, biting her shoulder.

My weight has to be crushing her, but Trazia never complains. She holds me close to her, rubbing her hands up and down my back as we both catch our breaths.

"I think you did it that time," she tells me, and I can hear the smile in her voice.

It's been a year since we got married and Trazia promised me we could begin trying for another baby the moment we said, "I do." What she didn't expect was a quickie in the bathroom before the reception where I took her hard and fast from behind while she was in her wedding dress. She also didn't expect to spend our entire wedding night and the next two days locked in a hotel room before our flight to Costa Rica. My hope was to get her knocked up during that time before we enjoyed exploring and hiking the rainforest, but it turned out all my efforts came up empty.

We've tried to not let it discourage us that every pregnancy test she's taken came out negative, but I'd be lying if I said they didn't. Milo is five now, and with how many kids I want to fill this house with, we need to get knocked up soon.

I kiss her cheek and pull her hips closer to me, putting more of my weight on her. "That better have been it because that was some of my best work so far."

Trazia laughs, and I enjoy her naked body moving against mine. "You were on top of your game tonight. That little pillow move was nice."

Even though I know every negative test has made her question if there is something wrong with her, I'm glad my girl can enjoy lighter moments like this. The stress of trying to get pregnant can be too much sometimes, and I don't want her to think of this as a chore.

Rolling to the side, I take her with me and wrap my arms around her back. Holding her in my arms is heaven, and I will never get tired of these moments. Just the two of us in our bedroom, away from the world. The sun hasn't fully come up, but there are birds chirping outside.

"I love you, Peach." I cup her cheek and bring my mouth down to hers. She eagerly kisses me back.

Our bedroom door opens ever so quietly, and I pull the sheets up to cover our naked bodies. "Mommy? Daddy?" Milo's sweet voice fills the room, and I smile against Trazia's lips.

Peach holds the sheets to her chest as she sits up. "Good morning, sweet boy. What are you doing up so early?" It's barely six.

He climbs onto the bed, gripping the sheets to help him up. "I heard you scream and got scared."

I choke on a laugh, and Trazia slaps me. "Oh, honey, I was just having a bad dream. Daddy and I watched a scary movie last night."

Our son snuggles into her lap, and she begins playing with his curls. We haven't had the heart to cut his hair and it's now long enough to pull back into a ponytail, but he has big curls that would make anyone jealous.

"You shouldn't watch scary movies, Mommy."

"You're right, Bean. No more scary movies for me from now on." She pinches me when I start to laugh again. "How about we make some blueberry pancakes this morning since we're all up so early? Do you want to go downstairs and pick out your favorite blueberries while Mommy and Daddy get dressed?"

Milo jumps on the bed with excitement. "Yay. Pancakes." His slight lisp makes the word come out more like *pwancakes*, but we don't correct him.

With our son gone, Trazia hops out of bed in all her naked glory. I lean against the headboard with my hands behind my head and watch as she moves around the room, gathering clothes.

She must feel me staring because she looks over and glares at me. "Are you going to get up or just sit there?"

I pretend like I'm thinking about it. "I think I'll wait until my hot-as-fuck wife covers her naked body before I make a move. I'm quite enjoying you with no clothes on right now."

She rolls her eyes as she goes into the bathroom, but I see the color on her cheeks change. My girl loves how obsessed I am with her, and that will never change.

I didn't think my love for Trazia Stone could grow more, but it continues to. Every morning waking up to her and then seeing her each day with our son has been the most amazing five years of my life. I didn't think I would ever get this lucky in life, but I hit the jackpot with her.

TRAZIA

Keeping secrets from my husband is not easy, especially when they're as big as this. He kept questioning where I was going today, and I had to lie and tell him I was having lunch with Blaire and Grace, her nine-month-old. The truth is, Blaire is watching Milo for me today while I have a doctor's appointment.

This morning after Maddox woke me up with his head between my legs, I had to hide my excitement and lie because I didn't want to get his hopes up that the pregnancy test I randomly took at work last week was positive. As were the other three I ran out to buy that same day.

Maddox has been a positive light during this last year, and I don't want to get his hopes up if these end up being false positives. While I'm sure it's rare to get that many, I want to have my doctor confirm it before celebrating with my husband.

The doctor's office is cold, and all I'm wearing is the paper robe they provided and a pair of socks because I was too busy to get a pedicure this week. They were able to fit me in due to a canceled appointment, and I've been a nervous wreck the last few days waiting for this moment.

A knock comes from the door before it opens, and Dr. Wilson comes in with a wide smile on her face. I've been open with her about our struggles in the last twelve months and not getting pregnant, but she has assured me I am in perfect health and that sometimes these things take time. I'm sure I was just too hopeful it would be as easy as when we got pregnant with Milo.

"Congratulation, Trazia. You are definitely pregnant."

A sob escapes me as tears freely fall. I try to hold them back, but it's useless. I'm happy. Being a mom has been the best thing in my life, and I can't wait to add to our family.

Dr. Wilson hands me some tissues as I get myself under control. "I'm sorry. It's just that I'm over the moon and can't wait to tell Maddox."

She goes over to the ultrasound machine and begins pushing buttons and prepping. "Don't apologize. I know how hard this last year has been for you and Maddox. I'm glad this is the news I could give you today." She grabs the large wand used for a transvaginal ultrasound. "Now, let's go ahead and take a look at the newest Stone member."

After my appointment, the drive home is a blur. The photos are burning a hole in my pocket, and I need to get home to Maddox and tell him the news. I had these plans to surprise him in a cute way, but with the bomb Dr. Wilson dropped on me, I can't hold it in.

Blaire pestered me with questions when I picked Milo up, but I told her I couldn't say a word until Maddox knew. She was sad but understood.

The house smells like an Italian restaurant and I smile, knowing the cooking classes I gifted Maddox for Christmas two years ago are coming in handy. He's gaining all our trust, one meal at a time.

Milo runs over to his play area and begins gathering the blocks Uncle Conrad sent him last week. I drop off mine and Milo's bags before heading to the kitchen and greeting my husband.

He's wearing a *Kiss the Chef* apron as well as his usual fitted suit he wears to the office. After Milo was born, Jack decided to open a Tampa office for his business, and Maddox has been running it the last two years. Jack was here for a few years getting it together, but he has officially handed the reins over to Maddox, and now when he and Veronica stay at their Tampa apartment, they get to enjoy family time rather than work.

"Well, there's my sexy wife." He comes over and kisses me. With both hands on my hips, Maddox pulls me close so every inch of my body is against his. "Hmm, I missed you."

I laugh. "You just saw me a few hours ago."

He keeps kissing me. Pecking my lips, jaw, cheek, and neck. "Yes, but even minutes away from you is too long." I giggle when his scruff tickles my neck. "Just a few more hours until Milo is off to bed and we can get back to the baby-making sessions. I think if I put your legs in the air this time around, it'll help my boys get to where they need to go."

My body heats, but I try not to get distracted by his plans for tonight. "Actually, about that. I have some news."

Maddox keeps his hands on my waist but pulls back to look into my eyes. "Please tell me what I think it is."

The hopefulness in his eyes makes me smile. I nod. "Yes. We're pregnant."

With a scream, he wraps me in his arms and lifts me in the air, spinning me around. "Oh shit, Peach. We're having a baby."

Once he's set me back on my feet, I grab the pictures from my pocket. "About that. We're actually having two."

Maddox stares at the photos of our babies in awe, much like I did when Dr. Wilson told me there were two babies inside me. "There's really two of them?"

"Yeah. The doctor said I was about twelve weeks."

When Maddox looks up at me, his eyes are red and misty. "I love you. So much. Thank you, Peach. I didn't think our family could get any better than the three of us, but we're going to be a family of five now. Wow." He hugs me, holding on tight.

My life has never felt more complete than it does right now. I have the most perfect husband, a son I love more than life itself, my dream job running my own charter school with my sister-in-law, and two perfect babies on the way.

Want to read more of the Braxton U crew? Blaire and Camden's story is now available. Check out The Act of Trusting.

THE ACT OF TRUSTING

There was a sadness in her clear, gray eyes that I could see she tried to hide. A fight with her inner demons she didn't want to show anyone...

CAMDEN COLLINS

Life was going well for me. I was on the right track: captain of the soccer team, grades were passing, and I had the respect of my team. Girls threw themselves at me. It was every twenty-year-old's dream.

Then I saw her...

One look at her, and it all changed. Something about her drew me in. A sense of protectiveness to guard this small, sad girl. In her eyes, I could see the fight she had within herself...and I wanted to be there for her. To protect her and be someone to lean on while she fought whatever it was. Nothing else seemed to matter but the dark-haired, beautiful girl I couldn't stay away from.

BLAIRE WENTWORTH

I wasn't the same girl I was four years ago. My life was stolen from me one night and I'd never have the chance to get old me back. Now I was just existing, not living. I went through the motions of my everyday routine, staying quiet and keeping to myself. Trusting and letting people in was a constant struggle.

Until he showed up...

I'd never seen someone like him before. Not once had I described a guy as beautiful, but that's what he was. He struck something in me, and I didn't know how to handle that. I was chasing nightmares no one knew about. Ones I kept to myself for a reason. Could I let this new person into my life that I had kept closed off from many for far too long? What if I let my guard down and he ended up destroying me?

And that became my greatest fear...

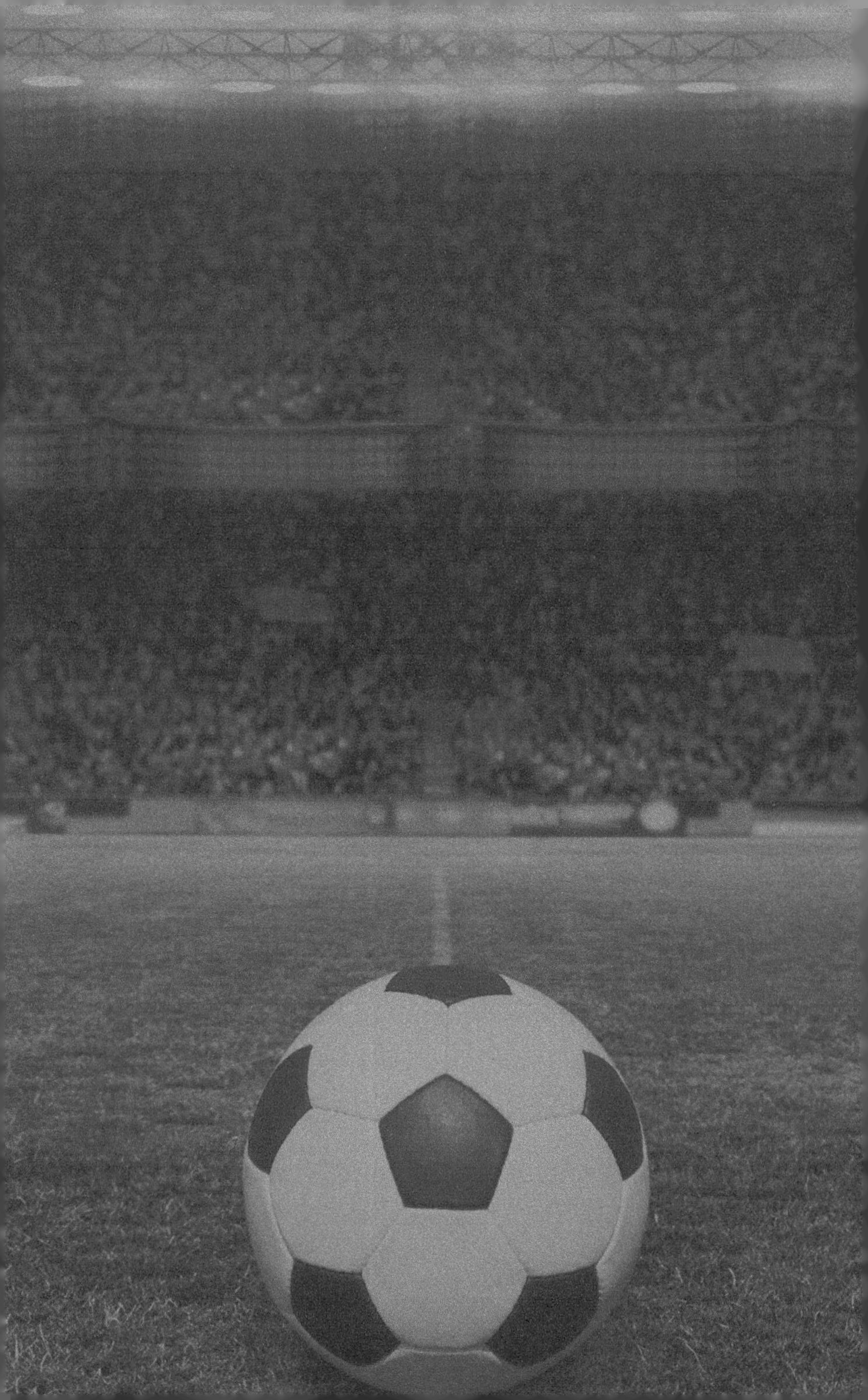

CHAPTER ONE

CAMDEN

Boobs. Boobs *everywhere*. Small boobs, large boobs, perky boobs, saggy boobs—hell, there are even a few fake boobs thrown into the mix. Although, I'm not a huge fan of hard tits. Oh well, still makes for a great sight.

It's the first party of the year and since the weather here in sunny Braxton, Florida, is perfect, what better way to kick off the new semester than a pool party? And of course, it has *nothing* to do with getting dozens of fine-as-hell coeds in as little amount of clothing as possible. That would be downright shameful of us, and we here at Braxton University are nothing but gentlemen.

The party is at the house I share with four of my teammates: Levi, Mateo, Conrad, and Maddox. We all play for the Braxton U soccer team and, if I do say so myself, we totally kick ass. Our team went undefeated last year, but we barely came out winners with only one damn goal ahead at the championship. With us being upperclassmen this year and losing some of our best players after graduation, we have to keep our heads on straight and focus.

"Heads-up," someone yells, right before a beach ball comes

flying toward me, almost knocking the beer out of my hand. They're lucky I have fast reflexes, or I would have been pissed that a perfectly good beer was wasted.

A familiar-looking blonde chick with an obvious fake tan comes strutting up. She bends down, a little too slow if you ask me, and retrieves the ball at my feet. When she stretches back to her full length, I notice a barely-there, bright pink bikini covers her inflated tits. *Hmm, inflated tit girl coming to collect the inflated ball. Seems ironic to me.*

After staring at her boobs for far too long, she must get the impression that I'm impressed by them. I wish I had the heart to tell her I'm an all-natural type of guy. Real boobs, even if they're smaller, are much more fun to play with than hard, fake ones. It just doesn't...feel right to me. Someone should really tell these girls before they spend thousands of dollars on something most guys aren't a fan of.

Someone yells out "Chloe" again and over the chick's shoulder, there is a group of guys in the pool staring at her, including a few of my teammates. She rolls her eyes and turns around to launch the ball in their direction. I'm about to make a quick run for it when a hand latches onto my forearm. Fake boobs, or as I've just learned is Chloe, runs her nails up my arm and starts rubbing my bicep. Most of the time, when a girl shows interest like Chloe obviously is, I'd take them up on their offer. You won't see me turning down no-strings-attached sex. I'm just not feeling it with this one. First, the attraction isn't there on my part. Once again, natural is my type. The fake tits, unnatural spray tan, unnatural blonde hair with purple highlights, and fake nails are actually having the opposite effect on me than I'm sure she thinks. It may be possible that my dick just went into hiding at the thought of going near one of Willy Wonka's employees. Second, I'm not looking to catch any kind of disease that'll have my junk out of commission for an unseen amount of time, and by the looks of this girl, she's a predator on the hunt for her next victim. *Good try, honey, but I'm smarter than you'd think.*

She leans in close, making sure to press her barely-covered boobs up against my arm, and begins rubbing my bare chest. It's a struggle to hold back the eye roll at her obvious moves. Do girls have this shit scripted now? I'm sure this is what Chloe does to every guy she wants to bed. The slight arm touch, then the hand roaming, and I'm sure what comes next is the lip biting while looking up at me through her eyelashes. Then she'll probably say something like, 'What do you say we head somewhere and *talk* for a bit?' and we all know she has no intentions of actually talking.

Chloe licks her lips, then gazes up at me through her long eyelashes. Running her long fingernail down the center of my chest to the waistband of my shorts, she says, "Camden Collins, what a nice surprise it is to run into you. I've never been with a forward before. I'm sure you know all about scoring. How about you show me that big old house of yours and we can have some alone time in your room?"

My body runs cold, despite the ninety-degree weather, when I realize who this is. While I haven't met her in person, every guy on the team knows who Chloe Stevens is. She's a well-known ball chaser and has been making her way through Braxton U soccer players since her freshman year. She usually goes for upperclassmen, although I remember her and Maddox having something going on last semester. Rumor has it she is trying to land a player who will make it past college ball and play pro or for a club team. All she wants is the money and status that come with it.

Ball chasers are what we call girls who go after guys on the team just because of our status as soccer players. Since we're one of the best college teams in the nation, a lot of us go on to play for overseas pro or club teams, and women see that as instant dollar signs. I can tell Chloe sees me like that by the sparkle and excitement in her eyes. No doubt she has plans of trapping a player and making him her sugar daddy. Really, she should have bigger dreams than becoming a gold digger.

Plucking her hand off the string of my board shorts, I take a step back, separating myself from the pro ball chaser. "Sorry, doll, I'm not feeling it tonight." By the look of shock on her face, I'd go ahead and say Chloe isn't used to rejection. I'm sure most guys here, including my roommates, would jump at the easy lay, but I'm getting tired of easy. I'm starting to wonder if there is a girl out there who doesn't throw herself at a guy just because of his status. Sure, I was all for it my first two years here, but it's starting to get old. I would rather a girl want me for me, Camden Collins the guy, and not Camden Collins the soccer player and team captain.

"I'm sorry, but are you saying you don't want any of this?" Chloe says, motioning to her body, making sure she points out the parts that are hidden behind the tiny fabric of her bathing suit.

I shrug my shoulders, seemingly unimpressed. "I'm sure you can find another guy for the evening." And with that, I walk away before I have to deal with the aftereffects of this chick's rejection. For some reason, I don't think she'll take it too well.

Heading toward the back door, I pass by an intense game of flip cup where a young girl is being shouted at by one of the football players because she can't get the red Solo cup to land right. Poor thing, she should have known better than to join a game with the big dogs. Those guys take anything with a winner at the end very seriously. I think it's them trying to make up for being one of the shittiest college football teams. Winning games like flip cup and beer pong make them feel a little better about themselves.

I'm too lost in the game going on in front of me that I don't notice my teammate and best friend, Maddox, come up in front of me and almost walk right into him. "Hey, man, I need you for the next game of beer pong. Levi is a lightweight and's about ready to pass out and you know Mateo's gone for the weekend," he says, shoving me in the direction of the beer pong setup.

There are five white tables set up with different levels of difficulty on each of them. When you have guys as good as Maddox and me playing, the standard ten-cup game isn't enough of a challenge for us. We like to make it interesting, so at one end there's six-cup beer pong, which is usually for the freshman girls who haven't played before, and then two tables of ten-cup games in the middle, and leading up to twenty-one-cup beer pong. The last table is much more of a challenge that most people avoid because with that amount of beer, you start to feel the effects of the alcohol before you're even halfway in. Fifty-five cups filled to the middle with beer will make any man weak. That is, except for Maddox and me. We're the only ones on campus who have won the fifty-five-cup beer pong challenge. Did we pass out after and spend most of the night puking cheap beer into a toilet? Of course. We drank a shit-ton. But it was totally worth it to have that title under our belts.

Two of my other teammates, Rodrick and Aaron, are filling the fifty-five cups with beer from the nearby keg. Maddox is beside me, bouncing on the balls of his feet, trying to get pumped up like he does before a game.

Maddox has always been an energetic guy. While not as competitive as some of the guys on our team, Maddox plays for the love of the sport, like me. We're both forwards, and since we've played together for so long, the two of us are in sync when we are on the field. That bond works when we're off the field also, which is the reason why we're undefeated in basically any drinking game we have at parties. Flip cup? No one can touch us. Quarters? Not a fucking chance. And beer pong? I think being the only ones at any party to win at fifty-five-cup speaks for itself.

Usually, Maddox isn't this excited about a game of beer pong, so to see him bouncing around and rolling his shoulders is unusual. When I turn to see who we're playing against, I know exactly why he's acting this way. Ben and Luis Moore. Seniors and twin brothers who are safeties for the Braxton football team and grade-A assholes. While most guys on the football team are chill, these two are hated by pretty much everyone. They're self-centered jerks who don't give a shit about anything or anyone. We've tried to distance ourselves from the twins after I caught them trying to bring a passed-out freshman to one of our bedrooms last year, but it's difficult to keep people out of an open party.

I grab Maddox's arm and pull him aside, ignoring the yellow-toothed smirk on Ben's face. "What the fuck are you thinking doing anything that involves them? Actually, why the hell are they even here? You know what pieces of shit they are."

"Don't worry, man," Maddox reassures me. "I was sending the douchebags packing, but then fuckface over there"—he points to Luis, the uglier of the two—"started spewing shit and talking about how great he is at life. I had to bring him down a few notches and remind him of the football team's losing streak. One thing led to another, and they challenged me to a game. I couldn't turn it down. It's you and me against the sleazy Moore brothers. We got this in the bag, bro." He holds up his fist, waiting for me to give him a knuckle punch, but I just roll my eyes and turn to face the table.

A small crowd has started to circle around us, waiting for the game to start. I'm sure seeing who the teams are, people are expecting some drama. While I'd love to do nothing more than knock these jerks on their asses and make them look like fools in front of everyone, I'm too frustrated by the fact that they're even here. I won't be taking my eyes off them until they're driving away from my house.

"Are we going to start this or what? Or are you pansies

afraid to lose your precious beer pong champ title?" Luis smirks, showing his crooked, yellowing teeth. Just the sight of this guy has a chill running up my spine.

Grabbing both ping-pong balls, I throw one of them in their direction and get ready for the toss-up to see who throws first.

Ben and I go head-to-head, making sure we don't break eye contact when we try to make a shot. With little effort, I come out the winner.

The game starts off pretty evenly. With this many cups, it is easy to make the first few shots. Once you start taking away the ones you've made, though, the challenge really begins with how many holes there are. I can see the struggle on Luis's face as he focuses on making one of the island shots. I just sit back with a cocky smirk on my face, already having made three of these this game.

He tosses the ball up into the air, letting it sail across the table and...completely misses the target and hits Maddox in the thigh.

The crowd laughs at the lame-ass shot and Luis shoots me a dirty glare, like it's my damn fault he has no hand-eye coordination.

Maddox and I throw next, both making the shot effortlessly, like we always do.

The crowd goes crazy with drunken cheers. Something cold and wet hits my bare back, and I'm sure there are others behind me soaked from someone's tossed beer.

When I glance at the twins, they're both scowling at Maddox and me. I mean, I would be too if I were losing and the other team were six cups away from winning. Judging from the number of cups they have left, the only way they stand a chance of winning is by a miracle. They're not even halfway there and I only feel the slightest of buzzes.

Ten more minutes go by and I'm really hoping we can be done with this game soon. I'm getting tired of having to drink this warm beer and I've had to take a piss for the last half hour.

Maddox and I have one cup left and surprisingly, the Moore brothers only have eighteen to make. They did a lot better than I thought they would, but by the sway in their stances and glossy look in their eyes, I'm guessing someone is going to be calling an Uber after Maddox and I sink this last one.

Maddox makes it into the cup on his shot. Now all I need to do is make it into the same cup and we can have two fifty-five-cup beer pong game wins under our belts.

Channeling out the crowd and everything around me, I focus on the ball in my hand and the cup sitting in the middle of the table on the other side. It's the same way I am when I'm playing in a soccer game. Everyone around us disappears and it's just me, the ball, and the cup. I think that's why Maddox and I work so well in these types of games. We've been trained to tune out screaming fans in stadiums, so a few drunken college kids is nothing to us.

I lift my hand and let the light ball glide through the air, straight for the cup. From this angle, I can't tell whether or not it will actually make it. I'm holding my breath, waiting for the ball to disappear behind that rim and call it a game. One, so I can get the douchebag brothers out of my house, and two, so I can relieve the pressure off my bladder.

The crowd around us is quiet, waiting to see what will happen. Maddox has his hands in his hair, clutching it tightly.

The ball is going...going...and going, until finally the musical sound of splashing beer rings in my ears.

"Holy shit, motherfuckers, we won!" Maddox yells and slings his arm around my shoulders.

Everyone around us is going crazy, splashing beer and hoisting bikini-clad chicks up into the air. You would have thought we won the damn World Cup by how excited these people are, not some college drinking game.

A MEMORY THAT ONCE WAS

When I look over at the Moore brothers, both have their jaws hanging open, stunned. I walk away from Maddox, who now has his tongue down some chick's throat, and make my way over to the losers.

Crossing my arms over my chest, I make sure to keep my balance now that I'm starting to feel the effect of the alcohol. "We let you guys have your fun, now get the fuck out of my house. I don't want to see either of you at one of our parties again."

Luis goes to say something, but Ben grabs his forearm, dragging him out of the house. *At least one of them was smart this time*, I think to myself.

After I watch them grab one of their football buddies and leave, I make a beeline for the back door, hurrying to get inside and take a piss.

When I reach the downstairs bathroom, I stop at the line of girls starting at the door and leading to the hallway. No way would I be able to hold it for that long.

There are only two other bathrooms in the house, one upstairs that Levi, Mateo, Conrad, and I share. Then there's the primary, which is in Maddox's room. The lucky bastard gets the biggest damn room in the house all because he drew the highest card when we got the place.

The crowd by the stairs is too congested and if I don't find somewhere to go now, my pants are the only option.

An idea comes to mind, and I decide, fuck it, no one will notice. Running out the back door, I make my way to the side of the house and, yes, the coast is clear. Quickly undoing the tie of my bathing suit, I lower it enough to pull myself out and let it all flow.

My head falls back, and I let out a loud moan at the relief. Nothing feels better than this moment.

Ten seconds go by, and I still have a steady flow going. When I feel it come to an end, a loud gasp comes from beside me. Turning to see who it is, I'm jerked to a stop at a hot-as-fuck girl standing there. She has long, dark brown hair that looks soft as silk as it hangs loose down her shoulders. Her skin is pale, as if she has not been spending the summer in the sun like the majority of everyone here. She's not dressed like the rest of the other girls either. Her black, basic T-shirt is flattering, hugging her perky, full rack, but flows down over her stomach and her shorts are surprising since I think the only bottoms girls are wearing tonight are the string kind. Nonetheless, her shorts make those long legs look hot as hell. How is it that this girl is turning me on more than the half-naked ones at the party?

When I make my way back up to her face, her eyes are wide and she's staring at me too. I mean, she's really staring at me... with my dick out...in my hand. Well, this isn't awkward or anything.

I go to make an introduction, but she quickly turns and runs in the other direction. Damn, nothing like having your junk out to ruin the moment.

ACKNOWLEDGMENTS

First and foremost, thank you to all the readers. Without you all, none of this would be possible. I've had the best time writing these stories and having you all enjoy them. I can't thank you enough and hoped you enjoyed Maddox and Trazia's story.

Rumi – Please don't ever leave me. You always know exactly where I'm going when editing these books and I'm beyond grateful to have you.

Cass – You are the best human out there. Not only are you an extremely talented designer, but a great friend and person.

Ellie – Thank you for once again perfecting the story.

Katie C. – Thank you for capturing the perfect image for Maddox and Trazia.

Katie M. – You are the best agent and I'm so happy to be part of the SBR Media family!

Kiki and The Next Step PR team – Thank you for being organized and put together where I am not! You helped me stay sane during this release.

To my friends and family – The constant support is always amazing. Thank you for believing in me.

ABOUT THE AUTHOR

Lexi Bissen is a new adult and young adult romance author who aspires to write in all genres, including paranormal—which started her obsession with words and fictional characters she cares about more than real people. She's also a coffee snob, reader, far too sarcastic, and dog rescue advocate.

Born and raised in Tampa, Florida, Lexi enjoys spending time with her family, taking in the sunshine with a good book, and giving the voices in her head a story. Writing has always been an escape for Lexi, where she can check out of her life and discover new, exciting places she makes up—but not in a crazy way.

When Lexi isn't writing, you can find her binging the latest Netflix show, laughing at her own jokes, or sipping iced coffee while spending way too much money at the bookstore.

Check out Lexi's website for updates on upcoming releases, current books, and where to follow on social media: https://www.lexibissen.com/.

Milton Keynes UK
Ingram Content Group UK Ltd.
UKHW042125211024
450028UK00010B/102

9 798218 527938